Praise for Michael Connelly

'Connelly is one of the great crime writers, a novelist who creates a fictional world so succinctly, and inhabits it so purposefully, that you are convinced it must be real. His mastery of place and character, his ease with dialogue, his control of plot gives his books a subtlety that is irresistible' *Daily Mail*

'A clever plot, full of twists, to make a first-rate legal thriller' *Sunday Telegraph*

'Connelly's fifth novel to feature roguish defence lawyer Mickey Haller is even better than last year's *The Black Box*' *Mail on Sunday*

'Expect surprises and plenty of dark moments in this punchy legal drama from an ever-reliable writer' *Financial Times*

'Connelly is superb at building suspense' *Wall Street Journal*

'In the crime fiction stakes Connelly is comfortably in the upper bracket' *Daily Express*

'A clever thriller with a brilliant double twist but also a heartfelt examination of the difference between natural justice and the law' *Evening Standard*

'Connelly masterfully manages to marry an absorbing courtroom drama with a tense and exciting thriller of detection' *The Times*

'While the themes of Connelly's LA crime novels are familiar (power, envy, corruption), his plotting is anything but' *Esquire*

'A story that's as old as the genre itself but Connelly's skill is such that it all feels entirely fresh and vibrant, but heartbreakingly poignant too' *Irish Sunday Independent*

By Michael Connelly

A former police reporter for the *Los Angeles Times*, Michael Connelly is the author of the Harry Bosch thriller series as well as several other bestsellers, including the highly acclaimed legal thriller, *The Lincoln Lawyer*, selected for the Richard and Judy Book Club. Michael Connelly has been President of the Mystery Writers of America. His books have been translated into 31 languages and have won awards all over the world, including the Edgar and Anthony Awards. He lives in Tampa, Florida, with his family. Visit his website at www.michaelconnelly.com

MICHAEL CONNELLY
THE BURNING ROOM

An Orion paperback

First published in Great Britain in 2014
by Orion Books
This paperback edition published in 2015
by Orion Books
an imprint of The Orion Publishing Group Ltd,
Carmelite House, 50 Victoria Embankment,
London EC4Y 0DZ

An Hachette UK company

7 9 10 8

A CIP catalogue record for this book
is available from the British Library.

ISBN 978-1-4091-5647-5

Typeset by Input Data Services Ltd, Bridgwater, Somerset

Printed and bound in Great Britain by Clays Ltd, St Ives plc

The Orion Publishing Group's policy is to use papers that
are natural, renewable and recyclable products and
made from wood grown in sustainable forests. The logging
and manufacturing processes are expected to conform to
the environmental regulations of the country of origin.

www.orionbooks.co.uk

For Detective Rick Jackson,
With thanks for your service to the City of Angels,
And hope that the second retirement sticks.
Hit 'em straight!

Teresa

Corrijans - Pathologist ♀

Soto — new partner

OCP — office chief police

CPT Crowder — head of open cases

CAPs — crimes against person

R HD — Robbery Homicide division

1

It seemed to Bosch to be a form of torture heaped upon torture. Corazon was hunched over the steel table, her bloody and gloved hands deep inside the gutted torso, working with forceps and a long-bladed instrument she called the "butter knife." Corazon was not tall and she stood on her tiptoes to be able to reach down and in with her tools. She braced her hip against the side of the autopsy table to gain leverage.

What bothered Bosch about the grisly tableau was that the body had already been so violated for so long. Both legs gone, one arm taken at the shoulder, the surgical scars old but somehow raw and red. The man's mouth was open in a silent scream. His eyes were directed upward as if beseeching his God for mercy. Deep down Bosch knew that the dead were the dead and they no longer suffered the cruelties of life, but even so he felt like saying, Enough is enough. Asking, When does it stop? Shouldn't death be the relief from the tortures of life?

But he didn't say anything. He stood mute and just watched as he had hundreds of times before. More important than his outrage and the desire to speak out against the continuing atrocity inflicted on Orlando Merced was Bosch's need for the bullet Corazon was trying to pry loose from the dead man's spine.

Corazon dropped back on her heels to rest. She blew out her breath and temporarily fogged her spatter shield. She glanced at Bosch through the steamed plastic.

"Almost there," she said. "And I'll tell you what, they were right not to try to take it out back then. They would have had to saw entirely through T-twelve."

Bosch just nodded, knowing she was referring to one of the vertebrae.

She turned to the table, where her instruments were spread out.

"I need something else . . ." she said.

She put the butter knife in a stainless-steel sink, where a running faucet kept the water level to the overflow drain. She then moved her hand to the left of the sink and across the display of sterilized tools until she chose a long, slender pick. She went back to work with her hands in the hollow of the victim's torso. All the organs and intestines had been removed, weighed, and bagged, leaving just the husk formed by the upturned ribs. She went up on her toes again and used her upper-body strength and the steel pick to finally pop the bullet loose from the spinal column. Bosch heard it rattle inside the rib cage.

"Got it!"

She pulled her arms out of the hollow, put down the pick, and sprayed the forceps with the hose attached to the table. She then held the instrument up to examine her find. She tapped the floor button for the recorder with her foot and went on the record.

"A projectile was removed from the anterior T-twelve vertebra. It is in damaged condition with severe flattening. I will photograph it and mark it with my initials

2

before turning it over to Detective Hieronymus Bosch with the Open-Unsolved Unit of the Los Angeles Police Department."

She tapped the recorder button with her foot again and they were off the record. She smiled at him through her plastic screen.

"Sorry, Harry, you know me, a stickler for formalities."

"I didn't think you'd even remember."

He and Corazon had once had a brief romance but that was a long time ago and very few people knew his real full name.

"Of course I would," she said in mock protest.

There was almost an aura of humility about Teresa Corazon that had not been there in the past. She had been a climber and had eventually gotten what she wanted—the chief medical examiner's post and all of its trappings, including a reality television show. But when one reaches the top of a public agency, one becomes a politician, and politicians fall out of favor. Teresa eventually fell hard and now she was back where she started, a deputy coroner with a caseload like anyone else's in the office. At least they had let her keep her private autopsy suite. For now.

She took the bullet over to the counter, where she photographed it and then marked it with an indelible black pen. Bosch was ready with a small plastic evidence bag and she dropped it in. He then marked the bag with both of their initials, a chain-of-custody routine. He studied the misshaped projectile through the plastic. Despite the damage, he believed it was a .308-caliber bullet, which would mean it had been fired by a rifle. If so, that would be a significant new piece of information in the case.

"Will you stay for the rest, or was that all you wanted?"

She asked it as if there were something else going on between them. He held up the evidence bag.

"I think I should probably get this going. We've got a lot of eyes on this case."

"Right. Well, then, I'll just finish up by myself. What happened to your partner anyway? Wasn't she here with you in the hall?"

"She had to make a call."

"Oh, I thought maybe she wanted us to have some alone time. Did you tell her about us?"

She smiled and batted her eyelashes and Bosch looked away awkwardly.

"No, Teresa. You know I don't talk about stuff like that."

She nodded.

"You never did. You're a man who keeps his secrets."

He looked back at her.

"I try," he said. "Besides, that was a long time ago."

"And the flame's gone out, hasn't it?"

He pushed things back on subject.

"On the cause. You're not seeing anything different from what the hospital is reporting, right?"

Corazon shook her head, able to move back as well.

"No, nothing different here. Sepsis. Blood poisoning, to use the more common phrase. Put that in your press release."

"And you have no trouble linking this back to the shooting? You could testify to that?"

She was nodding before Bosch was finished speaking.

"Mr. Merced died because of blood poisoning, but I

4

am listing cause of death as homicide. This was a ten-year murder, Harry, and I will gladly testify to that. I hope that bullet helps you find the killer."

Bosch nodded and closed his hand around the plastic bag containing the bullet.

"I hope so too," he said.

2

Bosch took the elevator up to the ground floor. In the past few years the county had spent thirty million dollars renovating the coroner's office but the elevators moved just as slowly as ever. He found Lucia Soto on the back loading dock, leaning against an empty gurney and looking at her phone. She was short, well-proportioned, and 110 pounds at the most. She wore the kind of stylish suit that was in vogue with female detectives. It let her keep a gun on her hip instead of in a purse. It said power and authority in a way a dress could never say it. This one was dark brown, and she wore it with a cream blouse. It went well with her smooth brown skin.

She glanced up as Bosch approached and then stood up hurriedly like a kid who'd been caught doing something wrong.

"Got it," Bosch said.

He held up the evidence bag containing the bullet. Soto took it and studied the bullet through the plastic for a moment. A couple of body movers came up behind her and pulled the empty gurney toward the door of what was known as the Big Crypt. It was a new addition to the complex, a refrigerated space the size of a Mayfair Market where all of the bodies that came in were staged before being scheduled for autopsy.

"It's big," Soto said.

Bosch nodded.

"And long," Bosch said. "I'm thinking we're looking for a rifle."

"It looks like it's in pretty bad shape," Soto said. "Mushroomed."

She handed the bag back and Bosch put it in his coat pocket.

"There's enough there for a comparison, I think," he said. "Enough for us to get lucky."

The men behind Soto opened the door of the Big Crypt to wheel the gurney in. Cold air carrying a disagreeable chemical scent blasted across the loading dock. Soto turned in time to see a glimpse of the giant refrigerated room. Row after row of bodies stacked four high on a stainless-steel scaffolding system. The dead were wrapped in opaque plastic sheeting, their feet exposed, toe tags flapping in the breeze from the refrigeration vents.

Soto quickly turned away, her face turning white.

"You okay?" Bosch asked.

"Yes, fine," she said. "That just grosses me out."

"It's actually a big improvement. The bodies used to be lined up in the hallways. Sometimes stacked on top of one another after a busy weekend. It got pretty ripe around here."

She held a hand up to stop him from further description.

"Please, are we done?"

"We're done."

He started moving and Soto followed, falling in a step behind him. She tended to walk behind Bosch and he didn't know if it was some sort of deferential thing to his age and rank or something else, like a confidence issue. He headed to the steps at the end of the dock. It was a shortcut to the visitor parking lot.

"Where do we go?" she asked.

"We get the slug over to firearms," Bosch said. "Speaking of getting lucky—it's walk-in Wednesday. Then we go pick up the file and evidence at Hollenbeck. We take it from there."

"Okay."

They went down the steps and started crossing the employee parking lot. The visitor lot was on the side of the building.

"Did you make your call?" Bosch asked.

"What?" Soto asked, confused.

"You said you had to make a call."

"Oh, yes, I did. Sorry about that."

"No problem. You get what you need?"

"Yes, thanks."

Bosch was guessing that there had been no call. He suspected that Soto wanted to skip out on the autopsy because she had never seen a human body hollowed out before. Soto was new not only to the Open-Unsolved Unit but to homicide work as well. This was the third case she had worked with Bosch and the only one with a death fresh enough for an autopsy. Soto probably hadn't been counting on live autopsies when she signed up to work cold cases. The visuals and the odors were usually the most difficult things to get used to in homicide work. Cold cases usually eliminated both.

In recent years the crime rate in Los Angeles had decreased markedly across the board, including and most dramatically the number of homicides. This had spurred a shift within the LAPD's investigative priority and practice. With fewer active murder cases, the Department increased its emphasis on clearing cold cases. With more than ten thousand unsolved murders on the books in the past fifty years, there was plenty of work to go around. The Open-Unsolved Unit had nearly tripled in size over the course of the previous year and now had its own command staff, including a captain and two lieutenants. Many seasoned detectives were brought in from Homicide Special and other elite units within the Robbery-Homicide Division. Also, a class of young detectives with little if any investigative experience was brought in. The philosophy handed down from the tenth-floor OCP—Office of the Chief of Police—was that it was a new world out there, with new technologies and new ways to look at things. While nothing beats investigative know-how, there is nothing wrong with combining it with new viewpoints and different life experiences.

These new detectives—the "Mod Squad," as they were derisively called by some—got the choice assignment to the Open-Unsolved Unit for a variety of reasons ranging from political connections to particular acumen and skills to rewards for heroism in the line of duty. One of the new detectives had worked in IT for a hospital chain before becoming a cop and was instrumental in solving the murder of a patient through a computerized prescription delivery system. Another had studied chemistry as a Rhodes Scholar. There was even a detective who was formerly an investigator with the Haitian National Police.

Soto was only twenty-eight years old and had been

on the force fewer than five years. She was a "slick sleeve"—not a stripe of rank on her uniform—and made the jump to detective by being a twofer. She was Mexican-American and spoke both English and Spanish fluently. She also punched a more traditional ticket to the detective ranks when she became an overnight media sensation after a deadly shoot-out with armed robbers at a liquor store in Pico-Union. She and her partner engaged four gunmen. Her partner was fatally shot but Soto took down two of the robbers and held the second pair pinned in an alley until SWAT arrived and finished the capture. The gunmen were members of 13th Street, one of the most violent gangs operating in the city, and Soto's heroics were splashed across newspapers, websites, and television screens. Police chief Gregory Malins later awarded her the Department's Medal of Valor. Her partner received the award as well, posthumously.

Captain George Crowder, the new commander of the Open-Unsolved Unit, decided the best way to handle the influx of new blood into the unit was to split up all the existing partnerships and pair every detective who had OU experience with a new detective who had none. Bosch was the oldest man in the unit and had the most years on the job. As such he was paired with the youngest—Soto.

"Harry, you're the old pro," Crowder had explained. "I want you watching over the rookie."

While Bosch didn't particularly care to be reminded of his age and standing, he was nonetheless happy with the assignment. He was entering what would be his last year with the Department, as the clock was ticking on his DROP contract. To him, every day he had left on the job was golden. The hours were like diamonds—as valuable as anything on earth. He thought that it might be a good way to finish things, training an inexperienced detective and passing on whatever it was he had to pass on. When Crowder told him his new partner would be Lucia Soto, Bosch was pleased. Like everybody else in the Department, he had heard of Soto's exploits in the shoot-out. Bosch knew what it was like to kill someone in the line of duty, as well as to lose a partner. He understood the mixture of grief and guilt that would afflict Soto. He thought that he and Soto could work well together and that he might train her to be a solid investigator.

There was also a nice bonus for Bosch in being teamed with Soto. Because she was a female, he would not have to share a hotel room when on the road on a case. They would get their own rooms. This was a big thing. The travel component to a job on the cold case squad was high. Oftentimes those who think they have gotten away with murder leave town, hoping that by putting physical distance between themselves and their crimes, they are also outdistancing the reach of the police. Now Bosch looked forward to finishing his time in the Department without having to share a bathroom or put up with the snoring or other emissions from a partner in a cramped double at a Holiday Inn.

Soto might not have been hesitant when pulling her gun while outnumbered in a barrio alley, but watching a live autopsy was something different. She had seemed reluctant that morning when Bosch told her they had caught a live one and had to go to the coroner's office for an autopsy. Soto's first question was whether it was required that both partners in an investigative team attend the dissection of the body. With most cold cases, the body was long in the ground and the only dissection involved was the analysis of old records and evidence. Open-Unsolved allowed Soto to work the most important cases—murders—without having to view a live autopsy or, for that matter, a homicide scene.

Or so it seemed until that morning, when Bosch got the call at home from Crowder.

The captain asked Bosch if he had read the *Los Angeles Times* that morning and Bosch said he didn't get the paper. This was in keeping with the long-standing tradition of disdain that existed between the two institutions of law enforcement and the media.

The captain then proceeded to tell him about a story on the front page that morning that was the origin of a new assignment for Bosch and Soto. As Bosch listened, he opened his laptop and went to the newspaper's website, where the story was similarly receiving a lot of play.

The newspaper was reporting that Orlando Merced had died. Ten years earlier, Merced became famous in Los Angeles as a victim—the unintended target of a shooting at Mariachi Plaza in Boyle Heights. The bullet that struck Merced in the abdomen had traveled across the plaza from the vicinity of Boyle Avenue and was thought to have been a stray shot from a gang confrontation.

The shooting occurred at 4 p.m. on a Saturday. Merced was thirty-one years old at the time and a member of a mariachi band for which he played the *vihuela*, the five-string guitarlike instrument that is the mainstay of the traditional Mexican folk sound. He and his three bandmates were among several mariachis waiting in the plaza for jobs—a restaurant gig or a *quinceañera* party or maybe a last-minute wedding. Merced was a large man, thick in the middle, and the bullet that seemingly came from nowhere splintered the 'mahogany facing of his instrument and then tore through his gut before lodging in his anterior spine.

Merced would have become just another victim in a city where the media hits and runs—a thirty-second story on the English news channels, a four-paragraph report in the *Times*, a little more longevity in the Spanish media.

But a simple twist of fate changed that. Merced and his band, Los Reyes Jalisco, had performed three months earlier at the wedding of city councilman Armando Zeyas, and Zeyas was now ramping up a campaign for the mayor's office.

Merced lived. The bullet damaged his spine and rendered him both a paraplegic and a cause. As the mayoral campaign took shape, Zeyas rolled him out in his wheelchair at all of his political rallies and speeches. He used Merced as a symbol of the neglect suffered by the communities of East Los Angeles. Crime was high, and police attention low—they had yet to catch Merced's shooter. Gang violence was unchecked, basic city services and long-planned projects like the extension of the Metro Gold Line were long delayed. Zeyas promised to be the mayor who would change that, and he used Merced and East L.A. to forge a base and strategy that separated him from a crowded pack of contenders. He made it to the runoff and then easily took the election. All the way, Merced was by his side, sitting in the wheelchair, clad in his *charro* suit and sometimes even wearing the bloodstained blouse he wore on the day of the shooting.

Zeyas served two terms. East L.A. got new attention from the city and the police. Crime went down. The Gold Line went through—even including an underground stop at Mariachi Plaza—and the mayor basked in the glow of his successes. But the person who shot Orlando Merced was never caught, and over time the bullet took a steady toll on his body. Infections led to numerous hospitalizations and surgeries. First he lost one leg, then the other. Adding insult to injury, the arm that once strummed the instrument that produced the rhythms of Mexican folk music was taken.

And, finally, Orlando Merced had died.

"The ball's in our court now," Crowder had said to Bosch. "I don't care what the goddamn newspaper says, *we* have to decide if this is a homicide. If his death can be attributed medically to that shooting ten years ago, then we make a case and you and Lucky Lucy go back into it."

"Got it."

"The autopsy's gotta say homicide or this whole thing dies with Merced."

"Got it."

Bosch never turned down a case, because he knew he was running out of cases. But he had to wonder why Crowder was giving the Merced investigation to him and Soto. He knew from the start that it was suspected that the bullet that had struck Merced had come from a gang gun. This meant the new investigation would almost wholly center on White Fence and the other prominent East L.A. gangs that traversed Boyle Heights. It was essentially going to be a Spanish-language case, and while Soto was obviously fluent, Bosch had limited skills in the language. He could order off a taco truck and tell a suspect to drop to his knees and put his hands behind his head. But conducting careful interviews and even interrogations in Spanish was not in his skill set. That would fall to Soto, and she, in his estimation, didn't have the chops for it yet. There were at least two other teams in the unit that had Spanish speakers with more investigative experience. Crowder should have gone with one of them.

The fact that Crowder had not gone with the obvious and correct choice made Bosch suspicious. On one hand, the directive to put the Bosch-Soto team on the case could have come from the OCP. It would be a media-sensitive investigation, and having Soto, the hero cop, on the case might help mold a positive media response. A darker alternative was that perhaps Crowder wanted the Bosch-Soto team to fail and very publicly undercut the police chief's edict to break with tradition and experience when he formed the new Open-Unsolved Unit. The chief's jumping of several young and inexperienced officers over veteran detectives waiting for slots in RHD squads did not go over well with the rank and file. Maybe Crowder was out to embarrass the chief for doing it.

Bosch tried to push speculation about motives aside as they rounded the corner and entered the visitor parking lot. He thought about the plan for the day and realized that they were probably less than a mile from Hollenbeck Station and even closer to Mariachi Plaza. They could take Mission down to 1st and then go under the 101. Ten minutes tops. He decided to reverse the order of stops that he had told Soto they would make.

They were halfway through the lot to the car when Bosch heard Soto's name called from behind them. He turned to see a woman crossing the employee lot, holding a wireless microphone. Behind her a cameraman struggled to keep his camera up while he negotiated his way between cars.

"Shit," Bosch said.

Bosch looked around to see if there were others. Someone—maybe Corazon—had tipped the media.

Bosch recognized the woman but he could not remember from which news show or press conference. But he didn't know her and she didn't know him. She went right to Soto with the microphone. Soto was the better-known quantity when it came to the media. At least in recent history.

"Detective Soto, Katie Ashton, Channel Five, do you remember me?"

"Uh, I think . . ."

"Has Orlando Merced's death officially been ruled a homicide?"

"Not yet," Bosch said quickly, even though he was not on camera.

Both the camera and the reporter turned to him. This was not what he wanted, to be on the news. But he did want to get a few steps ahead of the media on the case.

"The Coroner's Office is evaluating Mr. Merced's medical records and will make a decision on that. We hope to know something very soon."

"Will this restart the investigation of Mr. Merced's shooting?"

"The case is still open and that's all we have to say at this time."

Without further word Ashton turned 90 degrees to her right and brought the microphone under Soto's chin.

"Detective Soto, you were awarded the LAPD's Medal of Valor for the Pico-Union shoot-out. Are you now gunning for whoever shot Orlando Merced?"

Soto seemed momentarily nonplussed, then replied.

"I am not gunning for anyone."

Bosch pushed past the videographer, who had swung around to film over Ashton's left shoulder. He got to Soto and turned her toward their car.

"That's it," he said. "No further comment. Call media relations if you want anything else."

They left the reporter and videographer there and walked quickly to the car. Bosch got into the driver's seat.

"Good answer," he said as he turned the ignition.

"What do you mean?" Soto responded.

"Your answer to her about gunning for the Merced shooter."

"Oh."

They drove out onto Mission and headed south. When they were a few blocks clear of the coroner's office, Bosch pulled to the curb and stopped. He held out his hand to Soto.

"Let me see your phone for a second," he said.

"What do you mean?" Soto asked.

"Let me see your phone. You said you had to make a call when I went into the autopsy. I want to see if you called that reporter. I can't have a partner who's feeding the media."

"No, Harry, I didn't call her."

"Good, then let me see your phone."

Soto indignantly handed him her cell phone. It was an iPhone, same as Harry had. He opened up the call record. Soto had not made a call since the previous evening. And the last call she had received had been from Bosch that morning, telling her about the case they had just caught.

"Did you text her?"

He opened the text app and saw the most recent text was to someone named Adriana. It was in Spanish. He held the phone up to his partner.

"Who's this? What's it say?"

"It's to my friend. Look, I didn't want to go into that room, okay?"

Bosch looked at her.

"What room? What are you—"

"The autopsy. I didn't want to have to watch that."

"So you lied to me?"

"I'm sorry, Harry. It's embarrassing. I don't think I can take that."

Bosch handed the phone back.

"Just don't lie to me, Lucia."

He checked the side mirror and pulled away from the curb. They were silent until they got down to 1st Street and Bosch moved into the left-turn lane. Soto realized they were not heading to the Regional Crime Lab with the bullet.

"Where are we going?"

"We're in the neighborhood. I thought we'd check out Mariachi Plaza for a few minutes, then go to Hollenbeck for the murder book."

"I see. What about firearms?"

"We'll do it after. Is this related to the shoot-out—your not wanting to go to the autopsy?"

18

"No. I mean, I don't know. I just didn't want to see that, that's all."

Bosch let it go for the time being. Two minutes later they were approaching Mariachi Plaza and Bosch saw two TV trucks parked at the curb with their transmitters cranked up for live reports.

"They're really jumping all over this," he said. "We'll come back."

He drove on by. A half mile later they came to the Hollenbeck Station. Brand-new and modern, with angled glass panels creating a facade that reflected the sun in multiple angles, it looked more like some sort of corporate office than a police station. Bosch pulled into the visitor lot and killed the engine.

"This is going to be pleasant," he said.

"What do you mean?" Soto asked.

"You'll see."

3

Bosch never liked being on either end of a takeaway case. When he worked Hollywood Homicide, the big cases were often grabbed by the elite Robbery-Homicide Division. Then when he worked RHD himself, he was on the other end of it, often taking cases away from the smaller regional squads. In Open-Unsolved that rarely happened because the cases were old and dusty. But the Merced case, though ten years old, was not housed in the Department's archives. It still belonged to the original two investigators who caught it on the day of the shooting. Until now.

Bosch and Soto entered the station through the work door, as the entrance off the black-and-white lot was called. They followed a rear hallway into the detective bureau and Bosch knocked on the open door of the lieutenant's office.

"Lieutenant Garcia?"

"That's me."

Bosch stepped into the tiny office and Soto followed.

"I'm Bosch and this is Soto. We're from Open-Unsolved, here to pick up the stuff on Merced. We're looking for Rodriguez and Rojas."

Garcia nodded. He looked like a classic LAPD administrator. White shirt, bland tie, jacket hooked over the back of his seat. He had on cuff links that were tiny little police badges. No cop would wear cuff links out on the street. Too gaudy, too easy to lose in a scuffle.

"Yes, we were alerted by command. They're ready for you. CAPs is back around the corner past the milking room."

"Thanks, Lieutenant."

Bosch turned to go and almost banged into Soto, who didn't realize they were finished with the lieutenant. She awkwardly stepped back and turned to leave.

"Uh, Detectives?" Garcia said.

Bosch turned back to him.

"Do me one favor. If you clear it, don't forget about my guys."

He was talking about the credit that would go along with solving a high-profile case. The trouble with a take-away was that often the divisional detectives did a lot of the groundwork and then the big shots from down-town came in and scooped the case and with it all the glory that followed an arrest. Having been on both sides of takeaway cases, Bosch understood what Garcia was asking.

"We won't," he said. "In fact, if you can spare them, we'll use them when the time is right."

Bosch was talking about making an arrest. If they reached the point that they had a suspect and Bosch was putting together a warrant or an arrest team he would circle back for Rodriguez and Rojas.

"Good deal," Garcia said.

They left the office and found the CAPs table in an alcove past the station's lactation room. The city had re-cently mandated that all public facilities have a "family" room where employees or citizen visitors could have privacy while breast-feeding their babies. None of the nineteen police stations in the city were designed to include a lactation room, so the edict went out that one of the interview rooms in each detective bureau be transformed into a space that met city requirements. The rooms were repainted in soothing pastel tones, and cartoon stickers were added as well. Sometimes in overcrowded situations, the rooms were used during investigations, the unwitting suspects being interrogated in front of the likes of SpongeBob SquarePants and Kermit the Frog.

The Hollenbeck CAPs squad consisted of five desks pushed together in such a way that two pairs of detectives faced each other, and the squad leader's desk was located at one end of the desks. There were only two men sitting at this configuration under the "Crimes Against Persons" sign, and Bosch assumed they were Oscar Rodriguez and Benito Rojas.

There was a stack of three blue binders on the desk in front of one of the men. Bosch could read the name MERCED on the spine of two of them. The third just said TIPS. Also on the desk was a cardboard box sealed with red evidence tape. Leaning next to the desk was a black carrying case for what Bosch assumed was Orlando Merced's instrument. There were bumper stickers festooning the case, announcing its travel to many towns and regions through the Southwest and Mexico.

"Hey, guys," Bosch said. "We're from Open-Unsolved."

"Of course you are," said one of the men. "The big shots have arrived."

Bosch nodded. He had been the same way in the past

when a case was taken away from him. He held his hand out to the angry detective.

"Harry Bosch. And this is Lucia Soto. Are you Oscar or Benito?"

The man reluctantly shook Bosch's hand.

"Ben."

"Good to meet you. And I'm sorry about this. We both are. Nobody really likes this from either side. A takeaway. I know you've done a lot of work, and it's not really fair. But it is what it is. We all do what the geniuses in command tell us to do."

The speech seemed to placate Rojas. Rodriguez looked impassive.

"Just take the stuff," Rodriguez said. "Good luck, guy."

"Actually, I don't just want to take the stuff," Bosch said. "We'd like your help. I'd like to ask you about the case. Now, and later as we get into it. You two are the brain trust. Since day one. I'd be shooting myself in the foot if I didn't ask for your help."

"Did they get the bullet out?" Rodriguez asked.

"They did," Bosch said. "We just came from the autopsy."

Bosch reached into his pocket and pulled out the bullet. He handed the bag to Rodriguez and then watched his reaction. He turned and handed it to his partner.

"Holy shit," Rojas said. "This looks like a .308."

Bosch nodded as he took the bag back.

"Think so. Our next stop is the bullet lab at Regional. You guys never had it as a rifle, did you?"

"Why would we?" Rodriguez said. "We never had the goddamn bullet."

23

"Did you look at X-rays from the hospital?" Soto asked.

The two Hollenbeck detectives looked at her like she was out of line questioning their work. Bosch could ask because he had the experience. But not her.

"Yeah, we looked at X-rays," Rodriguez said, an annoyed tone in his voice. "The angle was bad. All we got was the mushroom. Couldn't tell dick from that."

Soto nodded. Bosch tried to get the focus off of her.

"Hey, if you guys aren't too busy right now, we'd like to buy you a cup of coffee and talk about what's in those books."

Bosch could tell by the reaction on Rodriguez's face that he had made a misstep.

"Ten years on a case and we get a cup of coffee," he said. "Fuck you very much but I don't need any coffee."

Rodriguez pointed his chin at Soto.

"Besides, you've got *heroina con la pistola* on your team, man. Lucky Lucy. You don't need us."

Bosch realized that it wasn't just the losing of the case that bothered Rodriguez. He was incensed that he was still working in a divisional detective squad while Soto had been elevated with zero experience to Open-Unsolved. Harry saw that the situation could not be helped at the moment and decided to get out of the station before things went further south. He noted that Rojas had not joined his partner in deriding Soto or the reassignment of the case. He would be the one Bosch would come back to when they were ready.

"Okay, we'll just take the stuff, then."

Bosch moved forward and put the three binders on top of the evidence box and picked it all up.

"Lucia, get the guitar case," he said.

"It's a *vihuela*, bro," Rodriguez said. "Better get it right for the press conference."

"Right," Bosch said. "Thanks."

He straightened up with his burden and checked the desks to see if there was anything he'd missed.

"Okay, guys, thanks for the cooperation. We'll be in touch."

He headed out of the alcove with Soto following.

"You do that," Rodriguez said to their backs. "Bring coffee."

They were out in the parking lot before either of them spoke.

"I'm sorry, Harry," Soto said. "I really shouldn't be on this case. Or even in this unit."

"Don't listen to them, Lucia. You'll do fine and I'm going to need you like crazy on this case. You'll be very important."

"What, as a translator? That's not detective work. I feel like I've been given something I don't deserve. I've felt this way since they gave me my choice of detective assignments. I should've taken Burglary."

Bosch put the box and the binders down on the hood of the car so he could get out the keys. He popped the trunk, and going to the back of the car, they barely fit the instrument case and the box and binders into the trunk. Once it was all in place Bosch flipped the latches on the case and opened it. He looked at the *vihuela* without removing it. A single bullet hole splintered the polished facing of the instrument. He closed and latched the case. He then turned and finally responded to his partner.

"Listen to me, Lucia. You would've been wasting your

time in Burglary. I've only worked with you a few weeks but I know you're a good cop and you're going to be a very good detective. Stop undercutting yourself. As you just experienced, there will always be people out there to do it for you. You just have to block them out. They want what you have and you can't help that."

Soto nodded.

"Thank you. Please call me Lucy. When you call me Lucia I feel like we'll never be real partners."

"Lucy, then. You've got to remember something here. This kind of case is a takeaway. A swoop and scoop. Nobody likes it when the RHD comes in and Bigfoots a case. People say things but they get past it. Those guys? Before this is over they'll be very helpful to us. You watch."

She looked unconvinced.

"I don't know about Rodriguez. He's got a major board up his ass," she said.

"But at the end of the day he's a detective and he'll do what's right. Let's go."

"Okay."

They got back in the car and drove out 1st, past the Chinese Cemetery and over to the 10 freeway. From there it was a two-minute cruise up to the exit for Cal State, where the Regional Crime Laboratory was located.

The crime lab was a five-story structure that stood in the middle of campus. It had been built as a partnership between the LAPD and the L.A. County Sheriff's Department, a logical decision since both agencies together handled more than a third of the crimes that occurred in the state of California and many of those crimes overlapped their jurisdictions.

However, inside the lab, the departments maintained many separate facilities. One of these was the LAPD's Firearms Analysis Unit, which included the so-called bullet lab where technicians worked in a low-light room using lasers and computers to attempt to match bullets from one case to another.

This was where the hope of the Merced case lay. The investigation conducted by Rodriguez and Rojas may have been thorough ten years before but they never found a bullet shell from the shooting and the slug had remained inside Merced's body until now. The chances were slim but if the bullet removed from the victim's spine during the autopsy could be matched to any other crime, then a whole new avenue of investigation would open for Bosch and Soto.

The normal protocol at the lab was to submit a bullet or shell casing for analysis and wait in the backlog, sometimes for weeks, before getting an answer and a report. But on walk-in Wednesday, bullet cases could be walked in and handled on a first-come first-served basis.

Bosch checked in with the bullet lab supervisor and was assigned to a technician appropriately named Gun Chung. Bosch had worked with him before and knew that Gun was the name on his birth certificate and not a nickname.

"Gun, how's it going?"

"Very well, Harry. What have you brought me today?"

"First of all, this is my new partner, Lucy Soto. And second, I've brought you a tough one for today."

Chung shook hands with Soto and Bosch handed him the evidence bag with the bullet slug in it. Chung used a pair of scissors to open the bag and removed the slug.

He hefted it in his hand and then held it under a lighted magnifier that he pulled over by its mechanical arm.

"It's a Remington .308. Soft-nose—gives you maximum mushrooming. A round like this is primarily used for long-range shooting."

"You mean like a sniper rifle?"

"More likely a hunting rifle."

Bosch nodded.

"So can you do anything with it?"

Bosch was asking whether the condition of the slug would preclude it from comparative analysis. The slug had gone through the front and back wood panels of Orlando Merced's *vihuela* and then penetrated his body mass before lodging against the twelfth thoracic vertebra of his spine. The bullet had mushroomed during these impacts, leaving very little of its shaft intact. The shaft was where striations from the barrel of the gun the bullet had been fired from would create a unique pattern, allowing it to be compared to other projectiles in the BulletTrax database.

With the bullet Bosch had just handed to Chung, there was no more than a quarter inch of undamaged form. Chung looked closely at it through the magnifier and seemed to be taking his time deciding if the slug was a candidate for ballistic profiling. Bosch did his best to lobby him while he looked.

"Ten-year-old case," he said. "The coroner just took that out of the victim's spine. I think this might be our only chance to move things along."

Chung nodded.

"It's a two-step process, Harry," he said. "First, I have to see if there is enough to work with here. And second, even if we put it in the data bank, there is no guarantee of a match. The database on rifle projectiles is limited. Most of our bullet crimes involve handguns."

"Understood," Bosch said. "So what do you think? Enough there?"

Chung pulled back from the magnifier and looked up at Bosch and Soto.

"I think we can try," he said.

"Perfect," Bosch said. "What kind of time are we looking at?"

"It's a slow day. I'll work it up right now and we'll see what happens."

"Thanks, Gun. Should we leave you alone or hang out?"

"Either way. There's a cafeteria on the first floor if you want to go get coffee."

"Sounds like a plan."

Bosch and Soto had no sooner sat down in the cafeteria, Bosch with black coffee and Soto with a Diet Coke, than Harry's phone buzzed. It was Crowder back at the PAB.

"Harry, where are you?"

"At Regional with the bullet."

"Anything good?"

"Not yet. We're waiting to run it through the database."

"All right. Well, I need you to get back here right away."

"Why, what is it?"

"We got the Merced family here and the media and the press conference is in twenty-five minutes."

"What press conference? We don't have—"

"Doesn't matter, Harry. The number of reporters here hit critical mass and the chief called a press conference. The ME already put out that they're ruling it a homicide."

Bosch almost cursed Corazon's name out loud.

"The chief wants you and Soto standing with him," Crowder said. "So get back over here. Now."

Bosch didn't answer for a moment.

"Harry, did you hear me?" Crowder said.

"I heard," Bosch said. "We're on our way."

4

There was a large media room used for press conferences on the second floor down the hall from media relations. Bosch and Soto were being held in a small staging room next door, where a lieutenant from media relations named DeSimone told them how the press conference would be choreographed. The plan was for Chief Malins to speak first and then introduce Orlando Merced's family. The microphone would then be turned over to Bosch and Soto. Since most reporters in attendance would be representing Spanish-language media, Soto would be made available for interviews in Spanish after the main press conference. Bosch cut DeSimone off in mid-explanation to ask him what exactly was being announced at the press conference.

"We're going to talk about the case and how Mr. Merced's death yesterday has rebooted the investigation," DeSimone said.

Bosch hated words like *rebooted*.

"Well, that takes about five seconds," he responded. "Do we really need a press confer—"

"Detective," DeSimone cut in, "by ten o'clock this morning my office had already received eighteen requests for a briefing on this case. Call it a slow news day if you want, but this has caught the media beast's attention. It's reached a point that we believe a press conference is the best way to go. You summarize the case, tell them the results of the autopsy—they already know it's been ruled a homicide—and go from there. You say the bullet that has been in the victim's body for ten years is now being compared to thousands of others in the national data banks. Then you answer a few questions. Fifteen minutes in and out and you're back on the case."

"I don't like press conferences," Bosch said. "You ask me, they never add anything. They only complicate things."

DeSimone looked at him and smiled.

"Guess what? I'm not asking you. I'm telling you, we're doing a press conference."

Bosch glanced at Soto. He hoped she was learning something.

"So when do we do this?"

"The media's already in the room and waiting. We go in with the chief. So as soon as he comes down, we go."

Bosch felt his phone vibrating in his pocket. He stepped away from DeSimone and answered the call. It was Gun Chung.

"Make my day, Gun," he said. "Please."

"Sorry, Harry, no can do. There's no match on BulletTrax."

Bosch caught Soto's eye again and shook his head.

"You there, Harry?"

"Yeah, Gun, I'm here. Anything else?"

"Yes, I think I've identified your weapon."

That eased some of Bosch's disappointment.

"What've you got?" he asked.

"Six grooves, right twist at twelve-one—I think what

you have here is a Kimber Model 84. It was called the Montana in the catalog—a hunting rifle."

The grooves and twist were aspects of the interior rifling of the gun barrel. They allowed Chung to identify the model if not match the bullet to a unique weapon. It was better than nothing and Bosch was pleased that new information had come from the autopsy.

"Does it help?" Chung asked.

"Every piece of information helps," Bosch said. "Is it an expensive gun?"

"Not cheap. But you can get them used."

Bosch nodded.

"Thanks, Gun."

"Anytime. You want to pick this up or want me to hold it here?"

"I need to pick it up and take it to property."

"You got it. And remember, Harry, you get me a shell casing and we've got a whole different story. There are more casings in the database than slugs. You get me a casing and then we might be in business."

Bosch knew that wasn't going to happen. It was not like you could find a shell casing from a shooting ten years old.

"Okay, Gun, thanks."

Bosch put the phone away and walked back to DeSimone.

"That was the bullet lab," he said. "The slug we took out of Merced has no match on the computer. We're back to square one. Cancel the press conference—there's nothing to say."

DeSimone shook his head.

"No, we don't cancel. You just don't mention the

bullet. Make it a request for public help on the case. There was a tremendous outpouring of support ten years ago and you need it again now. You can do this, Bosch. Besides, you don't want to announce the bullet is a dead end. You want the shooter to think you might have something."

Bosch didn't like the Department's media guy telling him his own business—it was the reason he had not mentioned that Gun Chung had tentatively identified the model of the rifle that had been used in the shooting. He thought about simply turning and walking away rather than staying for the charade of the press conference. But that would leave Soto alone and forced into something she probably didn't understand. It would probably also result in Bosch's being pulled off the case.

Just then DeSimone's radio squawked and he was told the chief was on the elevator coming down.

"Okay, let's do this."

They stepped into the hallway and waited for the elevator to arrive from ten. When the doors opened, the chief stepped out, followed by a man Bosch immediately recognized as Armando Zeyas, the former mayor who had championed Orlando Merced's cause ten years before. The chief had brought him back in for the press conference. Or perhaps Zeyas had pushed his way back in. It was said that he was readying a run for governor now. Using Merced's case had helped him politically once before. Why not again?

For Bosch such cynical thoughts came easily. He had been around the block a few times. But he noticed Soto's eyes light up when she saw Zeyas. He was a true hero in the Latin community. He was a trailblazer.

Zeyas and the chief were followed by a man Bosch also recognized. He was Connor Spivak, chief political strategist for the former mayor. It looked like he was along for the ride with Zeyas in the not-so-secret plan to win the governor's mansion in the next election.

DeSimone stepped up to the chief and whispered in his ear. Malins nodded once and came over to Bosch. They had known each other for decades. Roughly the same age, they had taken a similar trajectory through the Department: patrol, Hollywood Station detectives, Robbery-Homicide Division. While Bosch had found his home at RHD, Malins had ambitions beyond solving murders. He went into administration and quickly moved up the ranks of the command staff, finally being appointed to the top slot by the Police Commission. He was nearing the end of his first five-year term and would soon come up for reappointment. It was believed that a second term was a foregone conclusion.

"Harry Bosch," he said cordially. "I hear you are having trouble with the notion of a press conference."

Bosch nodded, a bit embarrassed. The space was tight and the others could hear the conversation. Still, he didn't back down from his apprehension about discussing the case in front of the media.

"The one lead we had—the bullet slug—isn't panning out, Chief," he said. "I don't know what there is to say."

Malins nodded but disagreed with Bosch's assessment.

"There's plenty to say. We need to reassure the people of this city that Orlando Merced will not be forgotten. That we are still looking for whoever did this and that we will find them. That message is more important than anything else, including a piece of lead."

Bosch held back on what he really thought.

"If you say so," he said.

The chief nodded.

"I do. Everybody counts or nobody counts—isn't that what you told me once?"

Bosch nodded.

"I like that!" Zeyas said. "Everybody counts or nobody counts. That's good."

Bosch couldn't hide his look of horror. In Zeyas's mouth it sounded like a campaign slogan.

The chief looked past Bosch at Soto, who was standing her usual two steps behind. He reached around Bosch to offer his hand.

"Detective Soto, how are they treating you at Robbery-Homicide?"

Soto shook the chief's hand.

"Very well, sir. I'm learning from the best."

She nodded toward Bosch. The chief smiled. She had given him an opening.

"This guy?" he said. "He's a silverback, Soto. Learn all you can from him while he's still here."

"Yes, sir," Soto said eagerly. "I'm learning every day."

She beamed. The chief beamed. Everybody was happy. And Bosch realized that it had been the chief's plan to put him with Soto. Crowder had only been following orders.

"Okay," DeSimone said. "Let's go. The Merced family is already in the conference room, sitting in the first row. Chief Malins will take the podium first and introduce them. Then the former mayor will say a few words, and then Detective Bosch will discuss—"

"Why don't we go with Detective Soto," the chief said.

"She knows everything Detective Bosch knows on the case, correct? Yes, let's do that. You don't mind, do you, Harry?"

The chief looked at Bosch. Harry shook his head.

"I don't mind," he said. "It's your show."

The group moved down the hallway. One of De-Simone's underlings was standing outside the open door to the media room. He stepped inside to give the get-ready signal to those waiting. Lights, cameras, and recorders were switched on.

Soto came up close to Bosch and whispered.

"Harry, I've never done this. What do I say?"

"You heard DeSimone. Just keep it short, say we're reviewing the case and could use the help of the community. Anybody who remembers something or knows something about the case, call the tip line or call Open-Unsolved directly. Don't mention the rifle. We want to keep that for ourselves."

"Okay."

"Just remember, keep it short. The politicians will talk long. Don't be like them."

"Got it."

The group moved into the room. There was a stage with a podium at its center, and three rows of tables for reporters were arranged in front of it. Behind the tables was another stage, where video cameras were set up to shoot over the heads of the reporters. Bosch and Soto followed the chief and the former mayor onto the stage and stood at the back. Bosch glanced at the first row in front of the reporters. There were four people, three women and a man, but Bosch didn't know how they were related to Orlando Merced. He was so new to the case that he had not met any family members yet. That was another thing that bothered him about the whole setup.

"Thank you for being here," DeSimone said into the podium's microphone. "I will now introduce the chief of police, Gregory Malins, and he will speak, followed by former mayor Armando Zeyas, and then Detective Lucia Soto. Chief?"

The chief took the position in front of the microphone and spoke without the use of notes. He was fully accustomed to being in front of reporters and cameras.

"Ten years ago Orlando Merced was hit by a stray bullet in Mariachi Plaza. Mr. Merced was paralyzed by the injury and struggled mightily to recover and to lead a productive life. Yesterday morning he lost the fight, and we are here today to say he will not be forgotten. My department's Open-Unsolved Unit has taken over the case as of today and will be vigorously pursuing the investigation until we determine who shot Orlando Merced. As you know, his death has been ruled a homicide, and we will not end this investigation until we arrest the person responsible on a charge of murder."

He paused there for a moment, perhaps to let the print reporters feverishly taking notes catch up.

"With us here today are members of Orlando's family. His father, Hector, and mother, Irma. His sister, Adelita, and his wife, Candelaria. We pledge to them that we will not forget about Orlando and that our investigation will be vigorous and complete. Now former mayor Armando Zeyas, a personal friend of Mr. Merced's and his family, will say a few words."

The chief stepped back and Zeyas took his place.

"It was through Orlando Merced that I learned the pain of crime and violence when it is visited on our community," he began. "I also learned much more from this man, who became a friend. I learned perseverance. I learned compassion. I learned what it is to make do with the cards you are dealt. I saw firsthand the resilience of the human spirit. Orlando never asked, 'Why me?' He just asked, 'What's next?' He was a hero to me because he took what life gave him and made the best of it. In many ways that was more beautiful than the music he once made with his instrument. I pledge to offer my help with this investigation in any way I can. I may no longer be mayor, but I love this community and its people. It is times like this that we pull ourselves together and truly become the City of Angels. It is times like this that we understand that in our city and in our society, everybody counts or nobody counts. Thank you."

DeSimone returned to the mike and told the audience that the case was now in the hands of Bosch and Soto. He said Soto would provide the update and would be available to repeat it in Spanish. Lucy tentatively stepped to the mike and lowered it so it was at the level of her mouth.

"Uh, we are now pursuing all avenues of investigation and ask for the community's help. Ten years ago, there was an outpouring of help from the public. Many people called and offered help and tips. We ask that anybody with information about this shooting please make contact with us. You can call anonymously to the Department's tip line or call the Open-Unsolved Unit directly. Even if you have information that you think we already know, please call us."

Soto turned and glanced back at Bosch as if to ask whether there was anything else to say. Zeyas took the moment to move back to the podium. He gently put one hand on Soto's back and used the other to pull the microphone over to his mouth.

"I just want to say that ten years ago I stood before the media and personally pledged twenty-five thousand dollars to anyone who provided information that solved this crime. No one ever collected that reward and the pledge remains in place, except that now I double it to fifty thousand dollars. Additionally, I will work with my former colleagues on the city council and seek a matching amount from the city. Thank you."

Bosch almost groaned out loud. Putting a financial bounty on the case would change the complexion of the calls that came in. The reward pretty much guaranteed that he and Soto would be sifting through dozens of worthless calls, people taking wild shots in the dark in hopes of getting some money in return. The former mayor's reward offer just changed everything.

DeSimone moved up next to Soto and asked the reporters if there were any questions. Many of them called out at once and DeSimone had to handle choosing. The first reporter, a guy Bosch recognized from the *Times*, asked what the exact cause of death was and how Merced's death ten years after the shooting could be classified as a homicide. Soto glanced back at Bosch, unsure how to answer. Bosch stepped up and pulled the microphone over.

"The autopsy was conducted just this morning, so nothing is yet officially recorded. But the Coroner's Office believes that Mr. Merced's death will be directly traced to the shooting that occurred ten years ago. The unofficial cause of death is blood poisoning, which is directly linked to the wounds Mr. Merced suffered in the shooting. We are therefore handling the investigation as a homicide."

In a quick follow-up, the reporter asked if the bullet had been recovered from the body and whether it would be useful in the investigation. Bosch kept the microphone. He was aware that the reporter was speaking clinically about the body of a man much loved by the four people in the room's front row.

"Yes, the bullet was recovered and taken to the Regional Crime Lab for analysis and matching. We believe the bullet will be very useful in our investigation."

"Has any match been made to the bullet?" another reporter called out.

DeSimone quickly moved in on the podium from the other side of Soto and pulled the microphone away from Bosch.

"We're not going to get into that right now," he said. "The investigation is active and ongoing and we are going to leave it at that for now."

"Why is a very inexperienced investigator assigned to the case?" the *Times* guy called out.

There was a pause, as it was unclear who should answer or if anyone should answer at all, since DeSimone had just closed the press conference. DeSimone finally started to speak.

"As I said, we're going to leave it—"

The chief moved up behind him and tapped him on the shoulder. DeSimone stepped back and the chief took over.

"Detective Soto may be short on chronological experience but she is long on street experience and knowing what it means to be a police officer in this city. We have teamed her with one of the most experienced detectives currently serving in the Department. No one has investigated more homicides in this city than Detective Bosch. I have no worries about who is conducting this investigation. We will get the job done."

The chief then stepped back and DeSimone once again said there would be no more questions. This time the edict stuck. Reporters started getting up and the cameramen started breaking down their equipment. Bosch stepped off the stage and went to the front row, where he shook hands and introduced himself to the four members of the Merced family. He quickly realized that they understood very little of what he was saying. He signaled Soto over and asked her to set up an appointment with them for as soon as it would be convenient. Bosch wanted to talk to them but not under the focus of the media.

Bosch stepped back and watched Soto go to work. DeSimone came up to him then and said the chief wanted to speak to him in his office. Bosch left the media room and walked down to the elevators, hoping to catch up with the chief and his entourage. He was too late. He took the next elevator up to the tenth floor and entered the OCP, where he was quickly ushered into the inner sanctum. Malins was behind his desk waiting. There was no sign of Zeyas or his front man.

"Sorry, Harry, for putting you out there. I know you never liked dog and pony shows."

"It's okay. I guess it had to be done."

"We really need this one. Do your best."

"Every time."

"That's why I told Crowder to call you."

Bosch nodded, unsure if he was supposed to say thank you for being paired with a homicide rookie on a case fraught with political implications and the potential of failure.

"Anything else I should know, Chief?"

The chief looked away for a moment and studied his blotter. He picked up a business card and held it out to Harry across the desk. Bosch took it and read it. It had Connor Spivak's name and number on it.

"That's the mayor's man. Keep them in the loop as your investigation progresses."

"You mean the former mayor, don't you?"

Malins gave him an *I don't have time for this* look.

"Just keep them in the loop," he said.

Bosch put the card in his shirt pocket. He knew he would tell Spivak as little as possible about the investigation. The chief probably knew this as well.

"So," he said. "You think I'm an old gorilla . . ."

The chief smiled.

"Don't take offense, Harry. It's a compliment. The silverback is the one that knows the most in the troop. Has all the experience. I saw a show on National Geographic—that's how I know that you call a group of gorillas a troop."

Bosch nodded.

"Good to know."

5

They convened in Captain Crowder's office after the press conference. Bosch, Soto, Crowder, and Lieutenant Winslow Samuels, the second in command of the Open-Unsolved Unit. Bosch updated them on the findings from the bullet lab, notably that Merced had been shot with a rifle—a fact heretofore unknown during ten years of investigation. Bosch explained that for the time being he wanted to keep this piece of information out of the media and Crowder and Samuels agreed.

"So where do you go with it from here?" Crowder asked.

"A rifle changes things," Bosch said. "A drive-by with a rifle? Come on. Unlikely. A stray bullet from the neighborhood? Maybe. But the rifle still gives us something new."

"Well, it's definitely outside our unit's protocol," Samuels said. "No magic bullet, no case. This should be flipped over to Homicide Special, let them deal with it."

The Open-Unsolved Unit followed a protocol when it came to investigating cold cases. It relied upon new evidence as the criteria for reengagement. That new evidence usually came from the application of recent advances in forensic sciences to old cases and the establishment of national databases to track criminals through DNA, ballistics, and fingerprints. These were

44

the big three. The magic bullets. Without a hit on one of these databases, a case would be considered not viable and routinely returned to the archives.

Following this protocol, the Merced case would normally be returned to the archives. The bullet recovered from the victim's body found no match in the national ballistics database. While a type and model of weapon had been identified, it normally would not be enough to pursue. But because of the media attention and politics surrounding this case, not to mention the interest from the OCP, there was no doubt that the case would be pursued. What Samuels was saying was that it should be done by someone other than Bosch and Soto and the Open-Unsolved Unit. The lieutenant was the squad whip, responsible for the unit's statistics and justifying its cost in terms of cases cleared. He didn't want to see one of his teams get bogged down in a shoe-leather case.

"I want to keep it," Bosch said, looking at Crowder. "The chief gave it to us, we keep it."

"You've got sixteen open files last time I counted, Bosch," Samuels interjected.

"All of them waiting on lab results. We've got something going on this case. The rifle is the first new lead in ten years. Let us run with it. If something comes back from the lab on one of the other cases, we'll handle it."

"Besides, we just did the press conference," Soto quickly added. "How's it going to look if we're on the case today and off tomorrow?"

Crowder nodded thoughtfully. Bosch liked Soto's add to the argument, though she probably didn't realize that she was crossing the tube—walking in front of a shotgun held by Samuels. She might pay for that later.

45

"For now we leave things as they are," Crowder said. "You two work this thing and let's meet again in forty-eight hours. I'll update the OCP from there and decide whether we keep it."

"It's not a cold case," Samuels said. "The guy died yesterday."

"We'll talk in forty-eight," Crowder said, ending the discussion.

Bosch nodded. That was the first thing he had wanted to hear—that he and Soto were keeping the case, at least for another two days. But it wasn't the only thing he wanted.

"What about when the phone starts ringing with calls for the reward the former mayor's putting up?" Bosch asked. "Can we get any help with that?"

"That was just a publicity stunt," Crowder said. "He's running for governor."

"Doesn't matter," Bosch said. "We're still going to get calls and we can't be stuck on the phone all day."

Crowder looked at Samuels, who shook his head.

"Everybody's got active cases," Samuels said, referring to the other teams in the squad. "And now you two are dropping out of the mix. I can't see dedicating another body to it."

Losing Bosch and Soto for an unknown amount of time was only barely palatable to Samuels. Giving up additional detectives to answer tip calls was not something he was even remotely willing to entertain.

Bosch had expected the request to be rejected, but the turndown might be useful to mention later if he and Soto asked for something else. Crowder had a give-and-take management style and a reminder that he had turned

46

down their last request could tip the scales toward approval.

"And another thing," Samuels said. "Was this guy Merced even a citizen?"

Bosch looked at him for a moment before answering. Soto jumped in ahead of him.

"Why?" she asked. "Does it matter?"

She got to the point. If Samuels was suggesting that extra hands not be put on the case because the victim was not a citizen, then she wanted that out in the open. Bosch liked that she had asked the question. But before Samuels answered, Crowder cut off the issue.

"Let me see what I can do," Crowder said. "Maybe one of those ladies in the OCP can come down here and answer calls for a few days. I've been thinking about asking the chief for help with all the call-ins we get on a daily basis anyway. I'll let you know. I gotta say, after the fucking Zeyas gave this Department, I really wouldn't mind seeing him stroke out a check for fifty grand."

"Roger that," Bosch said.

It was true. Zeyas had been no friend to the Department while he was in the mayor's office. He had the allegiance of a council majority that adhered to his policies and granted his requests. Over the eight years they had control of city government, they had repeatedly slashed the Department's overtime budget and taken a hard line on even minimal pay increases for the city's nine thousand sworn officers.

Bosch knew the meeting was over. He stood up and Soto followed suit. Samuels stayed seated. He was going to discuss things with the captain after they left.

"Forty-eight hours and let's talk, Harry," Crowder said.

"You got it."

Bosch and Soto returned to their cubicle, where their desks were pushed to the right and left half-walls and they worked with their backs to each other. This was a holdover from the way the pod had been set up with his previous partner, Dave Chu. It had worked well because Chu was a veteran investigator and didn't need Bosch watching over him from across the desk. But Soto was not even close to veteran status and Bosch had requested that City Services come out and reconfigure the space so that the two desks faced each other. He had made that request the week Soto started in the unit and was still waiting.

On Bosch's desk was the instrument case along with the evidence box and the binders they had dropped off before heading to the press conference. Bosch had been waiting since they left Hollenbeck to open the box and get his hands into the case. He remained standing and used a penknife to cut the red tape on the box. There was no chain-of-evidence sticker on the box, so he had no idea how long ago Rojas and Rodriguez had sealed it.

"I liked what you said in there," Bosch said. "About us keeping the case."

"It was a no-brainer," Soto said. "Why do you think Samuels asked if Merced was a citizen?"

"Because he's a pencil pusher. He cares about statistics and keeping the most people working the most cases, because that leads to better statistics. He'd like us to forget about Merced and move on to an easy one."

"Meaning that if Merced wasn't a citizen he wouldn't count, and we could move on to the next one?"

Bosch looked up from the box at her.

"Politics," he said. "Welcome to Homicide."

He opened the box and was surprised to find it contained very little. He took out two stacks of DVD cases held together with rubber bands. He put them aside and then lifted out individually bagged pieces of bloody clothing. It was the mariachi outfit Merced had been wearing when he was shot.

"Son of a bitch," Bosch said.

"What?" Soto asked.

He held up the brown paper bag containing a white blouse with dried blood on it.

"This is Merced's shirt," he said. "He was wearing it when he got shot."

He handed the bag to her and she held it with both hands as she looked into it.

"Okay," Soto said. "And?"

"Well, I don't know a lot about the case yet because we haven't looked at the books, but I do remember that when Zeyas was running for mayor back then, he kept rolling Merced out in a wheelchair at all his rallies. And sometimes he was supposedly wearing the bloody shirt he'd had on that day at the plaza."

Soto's face revealed shock that Zeyas, her hero, would stoop so low as to stage a fraud before the public to gather sympathy and votes.

"That's so *sad* that he would do this."

Bosch had long been cynical about all politicians. But he felt bad delivering the lesson to Soto.

"Hell, he probably didn't even know," he said. "You

49

know that guy Spivak who works for him and was there at the press conference? He's been around city politics for as long as I can remember. He's the kind of guy who could cook this up and not bother his candidate with the details. He's a pure mercenary."

Soto handed the bagged shirt back to Bosch without a word. He put it on his desk with the other articles of clothing and looked back into the box. There was a stack of 8 × 10 crime scene photos on the bottom and that was it. He was disappointed that the case had resulted in so little in the way of physical evidence.

"That's it," he said. "This is all they came up with."

"I'm sorry," Soto said.

"What are you sorry about? It's not your fault."

He picked up one of the DVD stacks and snapped off the rubber band. There were six different plastic cases and they were marked with names, dates, and events—all but one having occurred before the day of the shooting at Mariachi Plaza. Four were weddings and two were birthday celebrations.

"These must be videos of Merced's band performing at weddings and stuff," he said.

He took the band off the next stack and found different markings on each of the three cases.

1st STREET BRIDGE
MARIACHI SUPPLIES & MUSIC
POQUITO PEDRO'S

"'Poquito Pedro's,'" Bosch read out loud.

"Little Peter's," Soto said.

Bosch looked at her.

"Sorry," she said. "I guess you knew that."

"Stop saying you're sorry every five minutes. I think

these are camera views of the plaza. Poquito Pedro's is a restaurant a half block down the street from the plaza—I saw it today when we went by—and they put cameras on the First Street bridge back then to try to stop the suicides."

"What suicides?"

"About ten or twelve years ago a girl jumped off the bridge into the concrete riverbed. And then there were a bunch of copycats. Other kids. Weird, like suicide was contagious or something. So CalTrans put up cameras so they could monitor the bridge at the com center, where they have cameras on popular suicide sites. You know, so if it looks like somebody's getting their courage up to jump, they can send somebody out to try to stop them."

Soto nodded.

"We'll have to look at these," Bosch said.

"Now?" Soto asked.

"When we get to them. We have to read through the books. That's always the starting point."

"How do you want to split them up?"

"I don't. We both need to familiarize ourselves with all aspects of the case. We both read through everything— even the tip binder. But if we send them out to get a second copy, we'll lose a week waiting. So why don't you go first and I'll go back to the lab and pick up the slug and Chung's report. By the time I get back you'll probably be on the second book and I'll take the first."

"No, maybe you should start. I have my meeting at one today. I could go back to the lab now, then go grab lunch before hitting Chinatown. By the time I get back, you'll be on the second book."

Bosch nodded. He liked the idea of being able to dive

into the murder books right away. By "my meeting," Soto meant her weekly visit to a Department shrink at the Behavioral Sciences Center in Chinatown. Because she had been involved in a shooting involving fatalities —in this case her partner and two gunmen—it was required that she have continuing psychological evaluation and post-traumatic stress therapy for a year after the incident.

"Sounds good."

He put the two DVD stacks to the side of his desk and put the packaged clothing back into the evidence box. He then moved the box to the floor behind his chair and focused on the instrument case. Before opening it he studied all the stickers covering its front panel. It showed Merced had been a traveling musician with stops all across the Central Valley up to Sacramento and south through all parts of Mexico. There were stickers from U.S. border towns in Arizona, New Mexico, and Texas as well.

Bosch opened the case and studied the *vihuela*. The compartment it was set in was lined with purple velvet. He gingerly lifted the instrument out and held it up by its neck. He turned it so he could see the exit hole made by the bullet in the back. It was larger than the entry hole on the front because the bullet had mushroomed during the first impact.

He now held it to his body like a musician, checking where the bullet hole would line up with his own torso.

"'Stairway to Heaven,' Harry."

Bosch looked into the next module. The request had been called out by Tim Marcia, the squad jokester.

"Not my style," Bosch said.

According to the *Times* account he had read that morning, Merced had been sitting on a picnic table when struck by the bullet. Bosch sat down on his desk chair and propped the instrument on his thigh. He strummed its five strings once and checked the alignment of the bullet hole again.

"After you pick up the stuff from Chung, go over to ballistics and see if you can get someone to meet us at Mariachi Plaza tomorrow with a trajectory kit."

Soto nodded.

"I will. What's a trajectory kit?"

"Tubes and lasers."

Bosch strummed the *vihuela* again.

"We've got two holes in this and then we have where the bullet ended up in Merced. If we can make an approximation of his location and position, we may be able to get a line on where the bullet came from. Now that we know it was a rifle, I think we are looking for a perch."

"You don't think Rojas and Rodriguez already did this?"

"Not if they thought it was a handgun or a drive-by. Like I told the captain, the rifle changes everything. It means this probably wasn't random. It probably wasn't a drive-by and it might not even be gang related. We're starting from scratch and the first thing we have to do is figure out where the bullet came from."

"Got it."

"Good. See you after Chinatown."

6

Bosch could always tell a lot about detectives and how they worked their cases by the case files they kept. Full and complete summaries, legible notes, and a logical flow of reports were all hallmarks of a well-run investigation. Bosch also knew that most detective pairings had a division of labor. Often one investigator was charged with the paperwork because of his or her flair with the written word or because it simply suited his or her personality. It was as simple as dividing brains and brawn. In his own partnerships Bosch always preferred to avoid the paperwork. But it didn't always work out that way and he always paid attention to detail when he was the writer of record.

It appeared to Bosch that Rodriguez was the keeper of the record when it came to the partnership of Rojas and Rodriguez. His signature was on almost all of the documents and this gave insight into his resentment at having the case taken away. His summaries were concise and complete. No cop-speak or Joe Friday just-the-facts-ma'am shorthand. His witness summaries managed to capture the personalities of the individuals as well as their statements, and this was very helpful to Bosch. It also made him realize that he had sized up Rodriguez and Rojas wrong during the confrontation at Hollenbeck. Rodriguez was upset because he cared about the case, whereas his partner, Rojas, didn't share the same visceral connection to it. It meant Bosch needed to find a way to connect to Rodriguez and overcome his anger. He was the go-to guy.

The basics of the case were laid out in the first pages of a blue binder that only now would be called the murder book. The incident report from April 10, 2004, contained the who, what, when, and where and was the baseline document of the case.

Orlando Merced and his three bandmates had finished a gig early in the day, a girl's fifteenth-birthday party that was held by her parents on the island in the middle of the lake in Echo Park. It was a Saturday—the busiest day for work—so the band drove in their van back to Mariachi Plaza in hopes of picking up a second job for the evening. The plaza was crowded with other mariachis waiting and hoping for work. The four men who made up Los Reyes Jalisco found a place to sit at a picnic table on the east side of the plaza. The four men played their instruments and followed the tradition of dueling musically with other bands in the plaza. The clash of music was so loud that very few people in the plaza heard a shot. Those who did hear it reported that it came from the west side of the triangular plaza, where it is bordered by Boyle Avenue. According to a report written by Rodriguez after sifting through witness statements, Merced was sitting on top of the precast concrete table with his feet on the bench. His bandmates did not hear the shot and did not notice he was hit until he toppled from the picnic table to the ground. One of the musicians called 911 at 4:11 p.m.

Because the shot was heard by some and not by

others, the scene at the plaza was described in the reports as chaotic. Those who heard the shot or saw Merced fall over panicked and ran for cover. Those who did not know what was going on were confused. Some followed those running and some turned in circles, wondering what was going on. The investigation produced no witness who saw a gunman firing from a passing car or on foot. No one was seen by witnesses or discerned on surveillance videos as a suspect fleeing the scene, but many earwitnesses agreed that the shot had come from the Boyle Avenue side of the plaza.

North Boyle Avenue was the main drag in the Boyle Heights area and also traversed the heart of the turf controlled by a large and violent Latino street gang known as White Fence. The gang derived its name from the white picket fence that surrounded the La Purisima Church. The gang's origins reached back to a men's club at the church in the 1930s. The name White Fence evolved over the decades to become a symbol of the dividing line between the city's white Anglo power elite and the Latin populace of East Los Angeles. The line between those with money and those who cleaned their houses and cut their lawns. Ethnic pride and solidarity aside, the gang became one of the most violent and feared in the city, often preying upon that same Latin populace. WF graffiti marked almost all the walls and surfaces of Mariachi Plaza. The LAPD's Gang Intelligence Unit suspected that WF members regularly charged a "tax" on the musicians who waited for work there.

White Fence became the initial focus of Detectives Rodriguez and Rojas. Branching off from Boyle Avenue and creating the rear border of the plaza was Pleasant Avenue, where several hard-core members of White Fence were known to live. Though Orlando Merced's bandmates told the investigators they were not embroiled in a dispute with White Fence, nor had they been approached to pay a gang tax, Rojas and Rodriguez focused on the Pleasant Avenue gangsters in the initial stages of the case. Several of the gang members were detained and questioned through the days that followed the shooting. None provided anything that implicated the gang or led to another possible motive or source for the shooting.

No shell casing was found on Boyle or Pleasant Avenue and the exact origin of the shooting was never determined. It seemed baffling to Bosch that a shooting across a plaza where more than fifty people were gathered did not produce a single credible witness. Such was the power and threat of White Fence.

Rojas and Rodriguez also conducted a background investigation into the victim to attempt to determine if Orlando Merced had been a specific target in the shooting. There was nothing in their conclusions that suggested this was the case. It appeared to them and was subsequently announced to the public that he was a random and innocent victim.

The detectives were soon reduced to chasing down call-in tips from the public. None of these panned out. No suspect list was ever formulated, but it was clear from the number of reports in the casebooks that the detectives focused much of their attention on a second-generation White Fence shot caller known as C. B. Gallardo. The initials stood for Cerco Blanca. He had been named by his father after the gang he had pledged his allegiance to.

Rojas and Rodriguez followed a routine investigative strategy with Gallardo: bring him in on a smaller charge and sweat him on the bigger one. They were convinced Gallardo knew who had fired the shot into Mariachi Plaza even if he had not ordered it himself. They knew Gallardo ran an auto body shop that was a front for a chop shop where cars stolen by gang members were dissected and sold across the U.S. and in Mexico for parts and scrap metal. In this case, they worked with auto theft detectives to raid El Puente Auto on 1st Street ten days after the shooting. Gallardo was arrested for auto theft and possession of stolen property when ID numbers on a variety of parts in the shop were tracked to cars reported stolen from the Westside and the San Fernando Valley.

But the man named for the gang he was affiliated with did not crack. Despite several hours of interrogation regarding the Merced shooting, Gallardo refused to admit any involvement and eventually refused to talk to the detectives at all. In the end, he pleaded guilty to a single count of auto theft and spent six months in the Wayside Honor Rancho.

Rodriguez's casebook summation on C. B. Gallardo was that he remained a strong suspect in the Merced shooting. The report suggested that the motive behind the shooting was to instill fear in the musicians who sought work in Mariachi Plaza and make them more amenable to paying a protection tax to White Fence. According to this theory, Merced was a random victim, the unsuspecting receiver of a bullet fired without aim into the plaza. The last time the Hollenbeck detectives had spoken to Gallardo was two years before, when he was incarcerated at the penitentiary up in San Quentin for an attempted murder conviction. As before, Gallardo told them nothing.

Bosch finished his review of the two casebooks before Soto got back from her appointment in Chinatown. He moved on to the DVDs from the evidence box, playing them on his laptop. He started with the performance videos. He watched several minutes of the band playing at a variety of indoor and outdoor events. He primarily focused on Orlando Merced, watching the man play and how he held his instrument. In all but one of the videos he was standing while playing, but there was a single video of the band on a stage at a wedding and all four of the musicians were sitting on chairs. Bosch noted that Merced did not rest his instrument on his thigh as he played. He held it up higher, leaning it against the shelf of his burgeoning stomach. This would be important to consider when they attempted to re-create the trajectory of the bullet that struck Merced. How he sat when he played and how he held the instrument would be two of the key things to understand.

One of the performance videos was dated the same day as the shooting and it was a recording from the birthday party at Echo Park where Los Reyes Jalisco had played earlier in the day. While Bosch had fast-forwarded through most of the other videos, he watched this one in its entirety, hoping to pick up on something that would give a clue as to what happened later that day. He knew, of course, that Rojas and Rodriguez had certainly done the same thing, but he was undaunted. If nothing else,

Bosch was confident in himself as an investigator and believed he observed things others did not. He knew this was egotistical, but a healthy ego was a requirement of the job. You had to believe you were smarter, tougher, braver, and more resilient than the unknown person you were looking for. And working cold cases, you had to believe the same thing about the detectives who had worked the case before you. If you didn't, you were lost. It was this sense of the mission that he hoped he could impart to Soto in the final year of his career.

The Echo Park video showed a happy family celebrating their daughter's *quinceañera*. Many friends and family members were on hand, and picnic tables were covered with traditional foods and gifts. The girl at the center of attention wore a white dress and a tiara with the number fifteen on it. She had a court of honor that included six other girls. There was dancing and the band played songs that Bosch assumed were traditional to the celebration. At one point the girl's parents carried out two cultural traditions, the mother presenting her daughter with the "last doll," symbolizing the end of childhood, and the father changing her shoes from flat sandals to high heels, symbolizing the beginning of womanhood.

There was much love and poignancy captured on the video. It drew Bosch's thoughts away from the case to his own daughter. He carried a constant burden of guilt when it came to her. Bosch was a single parent but mostly an absentee parent because of the hours consumed by his work. His daughter was seventeen now and she'd had no sweet sixteen party. He had never staged any kind of birthday celebration for her other than to celebrate it by themselves. Watching the party in Echo Park, he was reminded of his many failings as a father and it put a catch in his throat.

Bosch turned the video off. He had seen nothing on it that had given him pause or any clue to the shooting that would happen just a few hours later. Merced and his bandmates were professional and did not mingle with the party guests. They were rarely the focus of the camera but were seen in backdrop during several moments of the video. Bosch ejected the disc and moved on to the second stack of DVDs.

These DVDs contained film from surveillance cameras near the plaza. As such, they were not specifically focused on the plaza and only captured segments of what happened that day. To Bosch's surprise the first video he viewed showed a grainy, long-distance image of Merced actually being shot. As far as he knew, this had never been made public. The video was taken from inside the mariachi supplies and music store located across 1st Street from the plaza. The camera was mounted in an upper corner of the store and its purpose was to document and discourage shoplifting. However, its reach was through the front plate-glass window of the store and across 1st to the plaza.

Bosch backed up and replayed the shooting portion of the video several times, watching Merced strumming his instrument until the impact of the bullet embedding in his spine knocked him backwards off the table to the ground. He then finally let the video continue and intently watched the action that followed the shooting. The images were murky because of the distance and the writing on the music shop's window. The focus of the camera was also obviously set on the interior of the store as opposed to the activities across the street.

At the moment of the bullet's impact, Merced was surrounded by his bandmates. He sat on the table with his feet on the bench seat. On his right side sat the accordion player, and standing to his left and a step back was the guitarist. Moving into position behind the table was the trumpet player, who was holding his instrument in two hands and bringing it up to his mouth to play.

Again, Harry watched the shot knock Merced backwards off the table. The trumpet player immediately ran to the right of the frame and out of the picture, while the guitar player started to duck under the side of the table, turning his guitar so it shielded his body. The accordion player seemed confused by what had just happened. It appeared by his body language that he did not realize at first that Merced had been shot. It was only when he saw the guitar player ducking under the table that he too slid down and moved under its shelter. After a long moment, both men moved from the table and over to Merced to help him. The trumpet player came back into the frame and also knelt down next to his fallen comrade.

Bosch continued to watch the video. Soon people came running up to the picnic table and gathered around the shooting victim. It became hard to see Merced in the middle of all the others and the activity.

Over the next thirty minutes Bosch watched as paramedics and police responded to the shooting call. Merced was initially treated while lying on the pavement and then hoisted onto a gurney and wheeled out of the frame. The picnic table and immediate area were cordoned off with yellow crime scene ribbon and officers started corralling witnesses for detectives. The video ended at that point and Bosch wondered if Rodriguez and Rojas had edited the video or if there was more that had come from the music store.

Bosch checked the two other videos but neither was as interesting or as useful to him. Both had time codes that allowed him to sync up the moment of the shooting but they provided little new information. One was from a parking lot camera at Poquito Pedro's at least a block away. It did not actually show much of Mariachi Plaza but rather showed the intersection of Boyle and 1st. Bosch saw no apparent drive-by vehicle pass on the tape, no gang hoopty speeding through the intersection in the seconds after the shooting went down.

The third surveillance video came from the suicide camera on the 1st Street bridge. It was several blocks from the plaza and its view of the shooting was blocked by the old hotel at the corner of Boyle and 1st. Bosch watched it once, dismissed its usefulness, and ejected it from the laptop.

He thought about things for a moment. He knew he should set up an appointment with Rodriguez and Rojas to sit down and go over many details of the case rather than do it piecemeal, but he picked up the phone anyway and called the detective bureau at Hollenbeck. He asked specifically for Rodriguez even though Rojas might be more forthcoming.

"This is Detective Rodriguez."

"This is Bosch. How are you doing?"

No answer. Bosch waited a moment and pressed on.

"I just finished a review of your case files on Merced."

He paused. Still nothing.

"I'm not going to blow smoke up your ass by telling you how thorough you guys were. You already know that. But I have a few questions. I could have asked for Rojas because he wasn't a prick today but I asked for you. This is your book, Rodriguez. I can tell. I figure you're the one I need to talk to. Can you help me out?"

No answer again but this time Bosch waited. Eventually Rodriguez responded.

"What do you want to know, Bosch?"

Harry nodded. His instinct was right. The good ones all had that hollow space inside. The empty place where the fire always burns. For something. Call it justice. Call it the need to know. Call it the need to believe that those who are evil will not remain hidden in darkness forever. At the end of the day Rodriguez was a good cop and he wanted what Bosch wanted. He could not remain angry and mute if it might cost Orlando Merced his due.

7

After the phone call Bosch went on the computer and started to type up his first report on the Merced case. It was primarily an update on the case, including a cause of death report and an evaluation of existing evidence and investigative leads. He was twenty minutes in when his desk phone rang. He picked it up without looking at the display, assuming it was Soto calling in after her psych session.

"Bosch."

"Yes, I want to register for the reward."

Bosch realized it was a call spawned by the ex-mayor's announcement. As he responded, he pulled up the Internet window on his computer and went to the *Los Angeles Times* website.

"What do you mean, 'register,' sir? It's not a lottery. Do you have information that can help us?"

Sure enough, there was a story already up on the front page of the news site, complete with a photo of Zeyas at the press conference, announcing the reward.

"Yeah, I got information," the caller said. "The shooter is named Jose. You can mark it down."

"Jose what?"

"I don't know that part. I just know it's Jose."

"How do you know this?"

"I just do."

65

"He was the shooter."

"That's right."

"Do you know this man? Do you know why he did it?"

"No, but I'm sure you will get all of that once you arrest him."

"Where do I arrest him?"

The man on the other end of the line seemed to scoff at the question.

"I don't know that. You're the detective."

"Okay, sir, so you are saying that I need to go out and find and arrest a man named Jose. No last name, no known whereabouts. Do you know what he looks like?"

"He looks Mexican."

"Okay, sir, thank you."

Bosch hung up the phone, banging it hard into the cradle.

"Douche bag," he said to himself.

The phone rang again while his hand was still on it. He answered it with an annoyed tone in his voice.

"Bosch."

"Yes, I have a question on the reward."

It was a different man's voice.

"What is the question?"

"If I turn myself in, do I get the reward?"

Bosch paused for a moment. His instinct was that this was as bogus as the first call.

"Good question," he said. "I don't see why not. The reward is for information leading to a conviction. I think a confession would qualify. Do you plan to confess?"

"Yes, I do."

"But we would have to be able to prove you did

it. Can't just take your word for it, you know what I mean?"

"I understand."

"So why'd you do it?"

"Because I hate that mariachi shit. This is America. You come here, you should play American music."

"I see. And what weapon did you use?"

"My Smith and Wesson. I'm a good shot."

Bosch nodded to himself, instinct confirmed.

"I'm sure you are. Thanks for the call."

He hung up, then stared at the phone for a long moment, expecting it to ring right away. Sure enough it did, but he could see on the display that it was an internal call. He picked it up.

"Bosch."

"Detective, this is Gwen in the PBX."

One of the in-house operators. Bosch wasn't exactly sure where she was located in the building. The PBX operators handled all calls that came in on the general lines—like the main Robbery-Homicide Division number that was included in the *Times* story—and distributed them as required.

"Yes, Gwen."

"I've got a Spanish speaker now for the Merced reward. Do you want to take it?"

Bosch shook his head. The onslaught he warned Crowder and Samuels about was beginning.

"I don't have a Spanish speaker right now. Get a name and number and someone will call them back."

"Will do."

Bosch hung the phone up a little more gently this time. He switched over to the *La Opinión* website, clicked on the *Locales* page, and, sure enough, saw another photo of Zeyas and a story on the Merced case and the accompanying reward offer. He was a bit stunned by how fast the media were moving on the story.

He went back to the report he was writing and picked up the pace. He wanted to get out of the office, whether Soto got back soon or not. He had a feeling that the phone would soon become an anchor wrapped around his neck. He would drown in these calls. Before he finished typing, the phone rang one more time, and it was the very first caller again.

"Hey, you didn't take my name for the reward."

"That's correct, sir. I don't want your name."

"Well, what about the reward?"

"There is no reward. Not for you."

"I'm telling you, it's a guy name Jose. He did it."

"If we arrest a guy named Jose, you call me back, okay?"

This time Bosch slammed the phone down so hard in its cradle, he drew the attention of detectives in the other cubicles. He didn't offer any explanation. While his hand was still on the phone, it rang again. He picked it up and gruffly said, "What?"

"It's Gwen from PBX?"

"Oh. Yes, Gwen, what is it?"

"I just wanted you to know that the Spanish speaker refused to give me her name or number."

"Okay, Gwen. I guess that's one call I don't need to worry about. Thank you."

After that, Bosch quickly wrapped up the report he was writing, printed it out on three-hole-punch paper, and clipped it into the murder book. He then picked up the phone, called the PBX number, and asked for Gwen.

"Gwen, it's Detective Bosch. I'm going to be out in the field and my partner is not available. Can you forward any calls that come in regarding the Merced case and the reward to Lieutenant Samuels?"

"Lieutenant Samuels. Yes, I can."

"Good. Thank you. Why don't you make a note there that all such calls should go to the lieutenant until further notice from me."

"Will do, Detective. Have a good day."

"You, too, Gwen."

Bosch stood up, checking the clock on the wall over the doorway to the squad. Soto's psych sessions generally lasted an hour, with a half-hour travel time on either side of it. Even if she went by the crime lab to pick up the slug from Gun Chung, she should have been back by now. This annoyed him because Soto had a tendency to disappear or lose track of time. He wanted to keep things moving but she was missing in action. He didn't want to call her cell in case she was still in session with Dr. Hinojos, the Department's head shrink. But he was frustrated because Soto hadn't bothered to shoot him a text saying she had been held up. He should not be the one sending out texts and making where-are-you calls, anyway.

He grabbed his keys and the video discs. At the sign-out board on the wall next to the door he wrote *Lab* next to his name and headed out.

Rodriguez had told him that he and Rojas had not taken the surveillance recordings to the lab to see if any enhancements could be made to the visuals. He'd explained that it didn't seem to be a worthwhile move considering that the videos did not capture the shooter. Additionally, ten years ago video forensics amounted to little more than a lab rat taking a second look at the footage the detective had already studied.

Today was different. There was a dedicated video-and-data-imaging unit with experts who could amplify sound and visuals, often bringing forward information that was not apparent during casual viewing. The last decade had seen an explosion in the use of videos as tools of investigations. L.A. was a city of cameras, public and private, and it was standard case protocol now to look for cameras at a crime scene in the same way it had always been standard to knock on doors and look for witnesses. This necessitated the formation of the VFU—the Video Forensics Unit. Not all cameras were created equal and it took some expertise to maximize the potential of images and sounds captured at or near crime scenes.

It took Bosch twenty minutes to get over to the lab. On the way, Soto called him and told him she had just finished her psych session.

"She was backed up with new shooters," she said. "But I'm on my way to the lab now to pick up the slug."

"Don't worry about it," Bosch said. "I'm on my way there now with the videos. I'll go see Gun and pick up the slug."

"I thought . . ."

She didn't finish but Bosch knew what she was going to ask.

"Right, yeah, I looked at them all and there wasn't a whole lot there," he said. "The camera in the music shop picked up Merced getting hit but it's all pretty murky. I'm hoping the video unit can do something with it."

"Okay."

She didn't sound mollified.

"If you want I can wait, let you take a look before running it over."

"No, no, go ahead. You might as well. Are you coming back to the squad after?"

"Actually I'm trying to stay away from the squad. The ex-mayor's reward has already hit the media sites and the calls are coming in. I want to work the case, not the phones."

Bosch pulled into the parking lot outside the crime lab building and started looking for an open slot.

"But what if we get the right call?"

"It's a million to one, you ask me. But if someone really can deliver the shooter, they'll get to us. Anyway, right now I have all the calls going to Samuels. Maybe that will light a fire and get him to put somebody on the calls so we can work the case."

"Okay, so what time do you want me to set up the ballistics trajectory for tomorrow?"

Bosch had forgotten about that. Now he thought it might be too soon.

"I want to hold off on that now. Let's see what they come up with in video. It might help set the trajectory."

"Okay. Where do you want me to go now?"

"Give me thirty minutes and meet me at Mariachi Plaza. Let's see if the media's left the place alone."

"That'll give me time to hit Starbucks. You want something?"

Bosch thought a moment about his caffeine level.

"No, I'm good. I'll just see you there."

Bosch parked and got out. While he was walking toward the glass doors of the lab building, his phone rang again. It was Lieutenant Samuels.

"Bosch, where the hell are you?"

"About to go into the lab—I wrote it on the board. What's up?"

"What's up is the phone is starting to go crazy with tip calls."

"What do you want me to do about it, L-T? I'm working the case. I've got two stops in the lab here and then I'm meeting my partner at the crime scene. I told you this was going to happen."

"Where's Lucky Lucy right now?"

"She has her psych session on Wednesday afternoons. Anything good coming in?"

"How the hell should I know? You set this up, Bosch!"

"I didn't set up anything. I didn't want any reward put out there in the first place. I knew—"

"Never mind. I'll put someone on the phones. Starting tomorrow morning."

Samuels hung up before Bosch could respond. But he was smiling when he pushed through the doors to the crime lab.

8

Lucia Soto was already at Mariachi Plaza when Bosch got there. There was no obvious sign that anybody from the media was still on the scene. Bosch crossed the plaza, taking it all in. It was beginning to get crowded with musicians hoping to pick up evening gigs. The sidewalk parking spaces running along Boyle Avenue were bumper to bumper with vans brightly painted with the names and phone numbers of bands. The benches and tables in the plaza were all occupied.

Soto was talking to three men squeezed onto a single bench, their instruments in cases at their feet. They were wearing matching black half coats with gold brocade and white blouses with string ties. Bosch nodded to them as he joined his partner. Soto was holding some kind of iced-coffee drink with whipped cream at the top.

"Harry, these men were here the day Merced was shot," Soto said excitedly.

"What do they remember?" he asked.

"They were sitting right here. They jumped up and went behind the statue when they heard the shot."

Bosch looked behind the bench at the bronze statue of a woman, hands on her hips, wearing a shawl over a patterned dress. The statue was on a large concrete-and-wooden pedestal. The plaque on the base of the statue identified the woman as Lucha Reyes, the queen of the mariachis, who lived and performed in L.A. in the 1920s. She was from Guadalajara.

"Were they interviewed at the time?"

Soto spoke to the men in Spanish and then translated their answers to Bosch even though he understood a lot of what was said.

"Yes, they gave statements."

Bosch nodded but he could not remember any of the statements from the murder book involving witnesses reporting that they had used the statue for cover. They had probably been left out as inconsequential.

"Ask them to show us where they hid by the statue."

Soto asked the men, and one got up and went to the statue. He crouched down, put his hands on the pedestal, and acted like he was looking around the legs of the statue to see who was shooting. He was looking toward Boyle Avenue.

Bosch nodded again as he tried to see it the way it was that day.

"What made them think the shot came from over there?" he asked, pointing.

Soto translated and the man shrugged at first, and then one of the men still on the bench answered in a cadence too fast for Bosch to understand.

"He said he heard the shot and ran for cover. The other two men followed but weren't sure they had heard anything. They just saw everybody running."

"What did he see?"

Two men shook their heads and the third said, "*Nada.*"

"Did they know Merced?"

Again Soto translated and listened.

"Not really," she finally told Bosch. "They knew him from the plaza, waiting for jobs."

Bosch stepped away and walked toward the escalators that led down to the underground Metro station. The glass structure that served as its roof had a distinct Aztec motif and was designed as a giant eagle's wing sheltering the entrance. The feathers of the wing were multicolored glass panels that threw the sun across the plaza in blends of color.

There was a wide tiled staircase between the up and down escalators. Bosch turned at the top of the stairs and looked back across the plaza. He then scanned to the left across 1st Street at the music store, where the camera had captured the Merced shooting. Bosch moved a small step to his right and figured that he was very close to where the picnic table that Merced had sat on had been located. He knew this assumption had no forensic validity. A ballistics team would deal with that later. But for now Bosch knew he was near the spot where Merced was sitting when he caught the bullet.

He looked back toward Boyle Avenue, in the direction the bullet had come from. Since Bosch had now discounted the idea that the bullet had been fired from a passing car or even from ground level, his eyes focused across the street on the structure that occupied the corner across from the plaza. In earlier years Bosch had known the Boyle Hotel well. Unofficially but better known as Hotel Mariachi, the three-story stone building of Queen Anne design was more than a hundred years old and one of the oldest standing structures in all of Los Angeles. But it had fallen into disrepair over the decades until it was little more than a cockroach-infested flophouse for traveling mariachis and transients. More than once Bosch had gone into Hotel Mariachi with a mug shot in hand, looking for a suspect he had traced from a crime scene.

But all was different now. The Boyle Hotel had gotten a multimillion-dollar makeover in concurrence with the Metro station project at Mariachi Plaza. It was no longer even a hotel. It was a mixed-use complex offering affordable apartments and commercial spaces. Its redbrick facade and signature rooftop cupola were preserved in the renovation process, but even at so-called affordable rates, the rents were too high for most of the mariachis who passed through East L.A. They had to rent elsewhere now.

Soto came over to Bosch and followed the line of his stare.

"You think the shot came from there?" she asked.

"Could have," Bosch said. "Let's go check it out."

They walked back across the plaza, Bosch seeing that more and more musicians were starting to crowd around the benches and tables. It was almost five and time to look for and hope for work. Bosch noticed a small shop behind one gathering of musicians. Libros Schmibros. The sign on the door said it was a bookstore and lending library. He pointed at it without breaking stride.

"Before this was all Latino, it was Jewish," he said. "In the twenties and thirties. By the fifties everybody was moving out to Fairfax."

"White flight," Soto said.

"Sort of. I think one of my grandparents lived here. Something about this place I remember. The old

Hollenbeck station, coming here with my mother in the fifties . . ."

There was some kind of hazy, vaguely uncomfortable memory Bosch couldn't get at. For the first eleven years of his life he lived with his mother, and at times they were as transient as the denizens of the old Hotel Mariachi. There were too many places to remember and it was all fifty years ago. He tried to change the subject.

"Where'd you grow up, Lucy?"

"All over. My mother's side was from Orange County down by El Toro and my father's family was from up here. His parents got pushed out of Chavez Ravine in the forties. They ended up in Westlake and I was born there. But I mostly grew up in the Valley. Pacoima."

Bosch nodded.

"I guess that means you're not a Dodgers fan, then," he said.

"Never gone to a single game and never will," she said. "My father would kill me if he ever heard I went."

It had been one of the biggest landgrabs in the city's history and Bosch knew the story well, having tried all his life to counter his love of baseball and the Dodgers with the ugly story buried beneath the diamond where, as a boy, he watched Sandy Koufax and Don Drysdale pitch. It seemed to him that every gleaming success in the city had a dark seam to it somewhere, usually just out of view.

For decades Chavez Ravine was a poor enclave of Mexican immigrants who were crowded in shacks packed among the hills and tried to make their way in a place where they were needed but not necessarily wanted. The end of World War II brought new prosperity to the city and federal money to provide housing for the poor. The plan was to move everyone out of Chavez Ravine, steamroll it, and then rebuild it, creating an orchard of low-income housing towers to which the former inhabitants of the little valley would be invited to return. The development would even be given a name that reflected the grand American dream of reaching for the brass ring: Elysian Park Heights.

Some left the ravine willingly and some had to be pushed out. Houses, churches, and schools were razed. But no towers were ever built. By then the world had changed. Building towers for the poor was labeled socialism. The new mayor called it un-American spending. Instead, the city of the future decided it needed a professional sports team to secure its image and standing as more than a movie colony and hazy outpost on the western edge of the country. The Brooklyn Dodgers came west and a gleaming baseball stadium was built where those towers for the poor were supposed to be. The residents of Chavez Ravine were permanently scattered, their heirs carrying a deep-seated grudge to this day, and Elysian Park Heights was a pretty name that never made it past the blueprints.

Bosch was silent until they crossed Boyle and came to the double doors of what once was Hotel Mariachi. The door was locked and there was a keypad next to it for contacting tenants and the management. Soto looked at Bosch.

"You want to go in?"

"Might as well."

She pushed the button next to a sticker that said "Oficina." The lock was buzzed open without any

78

inquiry over the intercom as to who they were. Bosch looked up to see a camera mounted overhead in the corner of the door's trim.

Soto opened the door and they entered a vestibule. There were a building directory and a map inside glass cases attached to the wall. Bosch looked at the map first and realized that the restoration project had also been a consolidation project. Three buildings had been joined into one complex. The front building—the original Boyle Hotel, also known on nineteenth-century plat maps as Cummings Block—was now repurposed as commercial space, and the two adjoining buildings were apartment buildings. Bosch moved on to the directory and saw a variety of small office listings, most of them for Attorney/*Abogado*.

Bosch saw a set of stairs to the right of the doorway and started up.

"The manager's office is down here, Harry," Soto said.

"I know," he said. "We can stop by after looking around."

On the second floor Bosch saw three separate glass-doored entrances to offices, two of which were for attorneys, the signs on both doors promising *Se Habla Español*. The third office—room 211—appeared to be unrented and empty.

Bosch stepped back and looked around the hallway. It was clean and bright, not what he remembered from previous visits to the building. He remembered tiny apartments and at the end of the hall a communal bathroom that smelled like a sewer. He was happy the building had been saved from such disrespect and disrepair.

Harry headed up the stairs to the next level and Soto trailed behind him. On the third floor, there were more offices, half of which appeared vacant. He tried a door marked "Roof" and it was unlocked. He took the next set of stairs up to the cupola and Soto followed him up.

The cupola had a 360-degree view, including an expansive reach across the bridge back to downtown. Bosch could see the concrete river and the train tracks that wrapped around downtown like a ribbon. Turning east he looked down on the plaza. He saw the members of one band putting their instruments into their minivan—they had gotten an evening gig.

"Do you think the shot came from up here?" Soto asked.

Bosch shook his head.

"I doubt it. Too open. And the angle is probably too steep."

He raised his arms as if sighting down the barrel of a rifle. He pointed the imaginary gun at the top of the Metro stairs. He nodded to himself. It was too steep for a bullet to go through Merced's instrument and torso at the apparent angle.

"I also think this is restored up here. I don't think there was anything up here ten years ago."

Bosch noticed a man sitting by himself on a bench in the plaza. He was looking up at Bosch. The door at the bottom of the stairs to the cupola opened and a woman quickly came up to them, speaking in rapid-fire Spanish. Soto moved toward her, pulling her badge to show her they were police. The woman spoke too fast for Bosch to understand, but he didn't really need to. He knew that she was upset that they were on the roof.

Eventually Soto translated.

"This is Mrs. Blanca. She said we can't be up here and we should have gone to the management office first. I told her we apologize."

"Ask if she worked here before the renovation."

Blanca shook her head and said no before the question was translated.

"You speak English?" Bosch asked.

"A little bit, yes," Blanca said.

"Well, you answer any way you would like. This building—it's protected, right? Historical Society?"

"Yes, it has landmark status. First built in 1889."

"What happened to the hotel records when they came in to renovate?"

The woman looked confused and Soto translated the question and the answer.

"She said all of the old hotel books and the front desk were saved by the Historical Society. They're in city storage now but they want to make a display here."

Bosch nodded. He had seen nothing in the investigative logs kept by Rodriguez and Rojas about knocking on doors or interviewing anyone in Hotel Mariachi about what they had seen or heard during the shooting in the plaza.

He thought that was a mistake.

9

Bosch stayed late at the office, rereading the reports and summaries in the murder book and writing down any new observations or questions that came to him. His daughter was always busy on Wednesday nights with the Police Explorer unit she had joined at Hollywood Station. It was a group open to high school kids who were considering careers in law enforcement. They got a firsthand look at police work and often took part in ride-alongs and other operations. It was usually a full evening of activities, so there was no reason for him to go home, even though the day had started before dawn with the phone call from Captain Crowder.

The football field-size squad room had cleared out for the day and Bosch enjoyed the complete silence of the space and the darkness beyond the windows. He intermittently got up from his cubicle and walked the length of the room, wandering among the other cubicles and looking at the way other detectives set up and decorated their desks. He noticed that in several of the pods the detectives had gotten rid of the Department-issued, government-grade desk chairs and replaced them with high-end models with adjustable arms and lumbar-support systems. Of course, this being the LAPD, the owners of these chairs had secured them to their desks with bicycle locks when they left for the day.

Bosch thought it was all pretty sad. Not because personal property wasn't safe in the Police Administration Building, but because the Department was more and more becoming a deskbound institution. Keyboards and cell phones were the main tools of the modern investigator. Detectives sat in twelve-hundred-dollar chairs and wore sleek designer shoes with tassels. Gone were the days of thick rubber soles and function over form, when a detective's motto was "Get off your ass and go knock on doors." Bosch's tour of the squad room left him feeling melancholy, like maybe it was the right time for him to be winding down his career.

He worked till eight and then packed everything into his briefcase, left the building, and walked down Main Street to the Nickel Diner. He sat at a table by himself and ordered the flat iron steak and a bottle of Newcastle. He was just getting used to eating alone again. His relationship with Hannah Stone had ended earlier in the year and that meant a lot of evenings by himself. He was about to pull some of his work materials out of his briefcase but then decided to give the work a rest while he ate. He passed the time talking with Monica, the owner, and she topped off his meal with a maple-glazed-bacon doughnut on the house. It put a new charge in his bloodstream and he decided it was too early to go home to his empty house.

On the way back to the PAB he stopped by the Blue Whale to see who was playing and who was coming later in the month, and he was pleasantly surprised to see Grace Kelly on the stage with a four-piece band. Grace was a young saxophonist with a powerful sound. She also sang. Bosch had some of her music on his phone and at times thought she was channeling the late, great Frank Morgan, one of his favorite sax men. But he had never seen her perform live, so he paid the cover, ordered another beer, and sat at the back of the room, his briefcase on the floor between his feet.

He enjoyed the set, particularly the interplay between Grace and her rhythm section. But she closed with a solo and it stabbed deeply into Bosch's heart. The song was "Somewhere Over the Rainbow," and she produced a sound from the horn that no human voice could ever touch. It was plaintive and sad but it came with an undeniable wave of underlying hope. It made Bosch think that there was still a chance for him, that he could still find whatever it was he was looking for, no matter how short his time was.

Bosch left after the first set to go back to the PAB. Along the two-block walk he texted his daughter to see if she was still out with the Explorers. She texted back right away saying she was already at home and about to go to sleep, tired from the day of school followed by the Explorers gig. Bosch checked his watch and realized time had moved swiftly. It was almost eleven. He then called Maddie to say good night and tell her he would work late since she was already going to bed.

"You'll be all right if I don't get home until later?"

"Of course, Dad. Are you working?"

"Yeah, I'm heading back to the PAB from eating. Just need to go over some stuff."

"Well, it sounds like you're drinking."

"I had a beer at dinner. I'm fine. I'll only be a couple more hours."

"Be safe."

"I will. What did they have you kids doing tonight?"

"We were at a DUI roadblock. Mostly just observing. There was one guy. He wasn't drunk but he was completely naked. It was gross."

"Yeah, well, welcome to Hollyweird Division. I hope you're not scarred for life by that."

"I'll get over it. They wrapped him in a blanket and booked him."

"Good. Now go to sleep and I'll see you in the morning before school."

Bosch disconnected and wondered once again if his daughter really wanted to be a cop or if she was going through the motions to please him in some way. He thought maybe he should talk to Dr. Hinojos about it. Maddie spent an hour with her every month, seeing the police psychologist in an unofficial capacity. Hinojos did it as a favor, having volunteered her time since Maddie had come to live with Bosch following her mother's death.

When he got back to the squad room, it was still deserted, but his eyes immediately stopped at his partner's desk. Soto's handbag was sitting on her chair. She usually dropped it there in the morning when she came in and went to get coffee. She'd take out just the money she needed and leave the purse on her chair. But it was now 11 p.m. and there was the purse. He wondered at first if she had forgotten it when she left earlier but that seemed impossible because she kept her keys and, when off duty, her weapon in the large leather bag.

He did a 360 and scanned the squad room. There was no sign of her. But now he thought he had picked up the slight whiff of coffee. Soto was there. Somewhere.

He pulled his phone and shot her a text asking where she was. Her answer made him even more confused.

Home. About to hit the hay. Why?

Now Bosch didn't know what to do. He texted back.

Nothing. Just wondering.

When he sent the second text, he thought he heard a slight bell tone from somewhere close by. Bosch always kept his text notification on vibration alert, since most of his messages came from his daughter and he didn't want a dinging text to interrupt something at work. But Soto was different. She had hers set to an audible tone, and Bosch was sure he had just heard it. He typed out another text.

See you tomorrow.

He hit send and this time stood perfectly still and listened. Almost immediately he heard the bell again. He tracked it to the open door of the case closet on the other side of the squad room.

The case closet was actually a huge storage room where all the murder books and evidence boxes from case files under consideration by the Open-Unsolved Unit were stored. The space was big but the cases were so many that the year before, the Department had installed a rolling shelving system like the one often found in college library stacks and big law firms in which the rows of shelves are on tracks and can be collapsed. It allowed for more storage in a confined space. When a detective needed to get to a specific murder book, he or she had to crank open the row where that book resided. Each pairing of detectives in the OU had both sides of an entire row for their cases.

Bosch quietly stepped to the open door of the case closet and looked in. The smell of coffee was stronger now. He saw that the row that Soto and he shared for their cases was cranked closed. But ten feet farther down the bank of floor-to-ceiling shelves, the row belonging to another pair of detectives had been cranked open.

Bosch went into the room and quietly moved down to the open row. He hesitated when he got to the opening, then edged forward and looked around the corner into the three-foot-wide aisle between shelves.

No one was there.

Confused, Bosch looked toward the end of the room. Around the last set of shelves was an open alcove. There was a copy machine there. He now moved toward the alcove and was a few feet away from the corner when he heard the copy machine go into motion.

The machine gave him good sound cover. He stepped forward quickly and looked into the alcove. Lucia Soto was standing at the copier, her back to Bosch. On the work counter to her right was an open murder book, its binder rings spread apart. Next to the binder was a stack of three more murder books. And next to them was a steaming cup of coffee from LA Café, the nearby twenty-four-hour place.

Bosch watched silently as Soto went about copying the records and reports from the murder book. The copy tray was filling with paper.

Bosch didn't know what to do. He had no idea why, but she was obviously copying the records of a murder case that was not assigned to them. He backed up and checked the opening in the shelves. Each team in the unit was assigned specific years for which they were responsible. Each detective team put their business cards in slots on either side of their row. He saw that the open row belonged to Whittaker and Dubose. Bosch couldn't remember offhand which years Whittaker and Dubose were assigned to but the four murder books Soto had with her at the copy machine looked old. The blue vinyl of the binders was cracked and faded, the pages inside yellowed.

Bosch looked toward the alcove and thought about leaving as quietly as he had come in, but a rush of thoughts came to him and gave him pause. First, he thought how foolish Soto was being by copying the files. Every detective in the squad had a copier code that had to be tapped into the machine's keyboard in order for it to function. This meant there would be a trail that would tell how much Soto copied and when. The second idea that pushed through to Bosch was the common knowledge that in recent years entrance standards for the Department had been lowered. People with minor drug busts and gang affiliations had gotten in. It was believed by some that organized crime and even terrorist organizations had infiltrated the force. Bosch wondered if Soto could be working for someone outside the Department, acting as a double agent: cold case detective by day and case intel gatherer by night.

He thought that he was probably letting his imagination get the best of him, but she had after all just lied to him in her texts. What was it she didn't want him to know about?

Bosch had never been one to quietly back away from a problem. All at once he decided what to do and went back to the alcove. Lucia was removing a thick stack of copies from the machine. She didn't notice him, because she was completely absorbed in her efforts.

"You get what you needed there?"

Soto nearly jumped out of her shoes. As it was, she had to stifle a scream when she whipped around to see Bosch. It took her a moment to compose herself and then respond.

"Harry! You almost scared me to death. What are you doing here?"

"I think that's the question *you* need to answer, Lucia."

She made some kind of motion with her hands, as if trying to catch her breath after the scare he put on her. It gave her time to come up with an answer.

"I'm just looking at some old cases, that's all."

"Really? Cases that don't belong to you? To us?"

"I'm trying to learn homicide work, Harry. I look at cases. Sometimes I copy them so I can take them home. I know that's against policy but . . . I didn't think it was a big deal. I couldn't sleep, so I came in to make some copies."

The story and her delivery of it were almost embarrassing in their phoniness. Bosch moved into the alcove and over to the work counter. He flipped over the contents of the binder from which she had been copying documents. He read the front page, which was always the initial report and summary of the case. He immediately recognized it.

"So you're just randomly pulling and looking at cases?"

"Yeah, something like that."

Bosch looked at the spines on the other binders and quickly realized that all four books were from the same case. It was the 1993 Bonnie Brae apartment fire case. Nine people—most of them children—perished in an apartment in the Westlake area. The victims had been in an unlicensed day-care center in the low-income complex's basement and had become trapped by flames and smoke. Half the children crammed into the small space died of smoke inhalation. The fire was labeled arson but no arrests were ever made, despite a task force composed of fire department arson experts and LAPD investigators.

Bosch shoved the loose pages she had been copying into a binder and then stacked all four of them before picking them up. He turned and walked past Soto.

"Bring your coffee," he said.

He carried the binders out to their cubicle and put them down on his desk. He pointed Soto to her desk and told her to sit down. She moved her purse off the chair and sat.

Bosch stayed standing, pacing a short track behind her and talking to her back. She sat with her head bowed, eyes down like a suspect who knows the charges are coming.

"I'm only going to have this discussion with you one time," he began. "If you lie to me and I find out, then we are finished as partners and I'll see to it you are finished as a cop—Medal of Valor or not."

He paused and looked at the back of her neck. He knew she could feel it. She nodded.

"The Bonnie Brae fire," he said. "I didn't work it, but I was here and I remember. Nine deaths, never cleared. The rumor at the time was that Pico-Union La Raza started the fire because the apartment manager wouldn't let them deal in the building. That's all I know. Like I said, it wasn't my case, but it was a big case and rumors and stories get around."

He stopped his pacing, grabbed the back of her chair, and turned her to face him.

"Now you come along after becoming a hero for taking down a couple of Thirteenth Street shooters, and it so happens that the Thirteenth and Pico-Union street gangs are sworn enemies for all of eternity."

Bosch pointed to his temple.

"So now I find you copying files on Bonnie Brae and I think to myself, Didn't this girl tell me she was born in Westlake before moving out to the Valley? And I gotta ask myself, Who is she pulling files for?"

"It's nothing like that, Harry. I—"

"Let me just finish here. You don't need to talk just yet."

He turned away from her and looked down at the binders stacked on his desk. He was full of steam now. He turned back.

"It's well known in this Department that they let their guard drop when they had to fatten the ranks, and in-filtrators got in. People who are something else first and cops second. But I'll tell you right now, this isn't how I'm going to go out. You think I'm some old fool you can pull shit on right under my nose and I won't know it? I've thought there was something off about you from the start. You don't want to be a cop. You want to be something else."

"No, you're wrong."

She started to stand up but Bosch put his hand on her shoulder and held her in her seat.

"No, I'm right. And you're going to sit there and tell me what you're doing and who you're doing it for, or we're going to be here till the sun comes up and people start coming in and asking what's going on."

She reached across her body with one hand and Bosch tensed. But her hand went to her left wrist. She unbuttoned her cuff and violently pulled the sleeve up her arm. She turned her arm to reveal the tattoo on the inside of her forearm. It was an RIP list with five names on a tombstone. *Jose, Elsa, Marlena, Juanito, Carlos.*

"I was in that basement when the fire started, okay?" she said. "These are my friends. They died."

Bosch slowly stepped over to his desk and pulled out the chair so he could sit down. He looked at the binders for a moment and then back at his partner.

"You're trying to solve this thing," he said. "On your own."

Soto nodded and pulled her sleeve back down.

10

In the morning Bosch and Soto met in the squad room, checked in on the board, and then went directly back to Bosch's car for the drive over to the regional lab. Bosch had already been summoned by the video analyst he had left the discs with the day before. Initially the analyst, Bailey Copeland, had told Bosch she would need a couple days to work with the three discs—and that schedule included bumping the case up to the front of the line because of the importance and media attention it was receiving. But that morning, she called Bosch while he was driving in on the 101 and told him she had come up with something he should look at sooner rather than later.

On the way over, Bosch and Soto said little about the night before and his discovery of her secret investigation. Bosch immediately understood her motivations. He had similarly been driven to solve a case from his own past. So he had told her that he would help her, but it had to be done right. With less than a year to go in his plan to retire and take his pension in a lump-sum payment, he could not be sure the Department wouldn't use any infraction to fire him to avoid the payout. He told Soto that if they could come up with a plan that would result in the official transfer of the Bonnie Brae case to them, then he would join her in working it. But he warned her that working a case that was not hers was a dangerous move in the Department—for her as well as him.

The video-and-data-imagery unit was on the third floor of the regional lab. Copeland was waiting for them in a video booth where there was a sound-and-video board set up on a lab table in front of a multiscreen wall display. The room was dimly lit and small, and Copeland had pulled in extra stools for Bosch and Soto.

"Thanks for coming in early," Copeland said. "I'm going to show you what I have here and then go home."

"You pulled an all-nighter on this?" Bosch asked.

"I did. I got excited and couldn't leave it."

"Thank you for that. Show us what you've got."

The lab table was elevated and Copeland was a short woman. She stood during the demonstration, and sitting behind her, Bosch and Soto could still easily see the screens.

"Okay, let's just run through it once and then we can go back. The first thing I did was create a triangulation program for our three videos. The time counters on at least one of them was off, so what I used to base time on was the one thing that is in each video."

She clicked a button on a keyboard and three of the screens in front of them came to life, each showing its angle on Mariachi Plaza or the streets in front of it. She then almost immediately hit another key and the images froze. Copeland pointed at the center screen, which showed the video from the music store.

"You see the Ford Taurus here, passing the music store. That car is on each video."

She pointed the car out on each of the screens. Bosch could already see that the clarity of each video had been greatly improved from when he had viewed them the day before. Copeland had fine-tuned them, made them crisper.

"By calibrating the three videos off the movement of that car, we can run all three simultaneously. Now let's watch."

She hit a key and the videos continued. The three screens were right next to each other and so it was not difficult for Bosch to watch all three at once. Copeland had found the triangulation point—the Ford—more than a minute before the shooting, so they watched and waited in anticipation before finally seeing Merced topple off the table to the ground and his bandmates start to scramble.

"Okay, so let's watch again in slow motion," Copeland said. "Tell me what you see."

She started the playback again. Bosch's eyes were primarily drawn to the center image, which showed Merced sitting on the table. It was the cleanest video and it was the only one showing the victim. It was eerie watching in slow motion, knowing what was to come. Soto, who had not seen the videos before that morning, leaned forward to watch more closely.

Bosch tried to pull his vision back to all three screens at the moment Merced was shot. But he didn't see anything that drew his attention when the shooting occurred.

Copeland stopped the playback.

"So did you see it?" she asked.

"See what?" Bosch asked.

Copeland smiled.

"Let's switch these around."

She typed in a command and the three camera angles

changed positions. Now front and center was the angle from the parking lot camera at Poquito Pedro's restaurant.

"Okay, watch again."

Copeland replayed the video in slow motion and Bosch kept his eyes on the center screen. Though clearer than when he viewed the video on his laptop the day before, it was still a grainy view of the street and a portion of Mariachi Plaza from a distance of two blocks.

"There," Soto said. "I saw it."

"Saw what?" Bosch asked.

"In the window."

She pointed to a second-story window of the Boyle Hotel. It was a darkened room.

"Good eye," Copeland said. "Let's watch again."

She replayed the sequence again, and this time Bosch watched only the window his partner had pointed out. He waited and at the moment of the shooting, he saw a small pixel of light flash in the darkness. Copeland stopped the playback.

"That?" Bosch asked.

"Yes, that," Copeland said. "You have to remember that most surveillance video, especially from ten years ago, is shot on slow speed because of storage capacities. The frame rate on this camera is ten."

"So you're saying that little dot of light is the muzzle flash?"

"Yes, exactly. It's all the camera caught but it's enough. The shot came from that window."

Bosch stared at the frozen image on the screen. He knew there was no longer any need for the trajectory study. The shot had come from a second-floor room in the Mariachi Hotel.

"Here's what I have," Copeland said.

She put in commands that blew up the center-screen image. She centered the window on the screen and they studied the white dot in the field of black.

"We have to get those hotel records, Harry," Soto said.

"That's room 211," he said.

"Search warrant?" she asked. "Keep everything clean?"

Bosch nodded again.

"I'm not finished," Copeland said.

She reconfigured the screens so the angle on Merced was at the center again. She then put an isolation circle on one of the band members. It wasn't Merced. It was one of the men standing. The trumpet player. She hit the playback and the circle stayed on him, keeping him in focus while the rest of the screen slightly blurred.

"Watch him," she said.

Bosch did as instructed and watched the shooting once again but this time seeing only the trumpet player as he reacted to Merced's being shot. He moved quickly away, running offscreen.

"Okay," Bosch said, apparently not seeing what Copeland wanted him to see. "What are we looking at?"

"Two things," Copeland said. "First his reaction. This has nothing to do with video enhancement. I'm just talking about his reaction. Watch the others."

She moved the isolation circle to one of the other men and replayed the video. It was the accordion player who sat right next to Merced on the table. The man saw Merced topple off the table and started smiling, presumably because he thought it was some kind of stunt. But then he saw the guitar player ducking under the table and dropped down too, pushing himself under as best he could.

"And now the guitar," Copeland said.

The circle moved to the man standing and playing the guitar at the rear corner of the table. He too was initially confused when Merced was hit, but then he understood and ducked down to use the table as well as his guitar as cover.

"Let's see the trumpet player again," Bosch said.

They watched in silence.

"Again," Bosch said.

They watched again.

"Okay," he said, "let's see the whole thing again without any isolation."

When the replay was over he just stared at the screen.

"You see what I mean?" Copeland asked. "I'm not talking about him running. That's understandable."

"You think he knew the shot was coming?" Soto asked.

"I don't know about that either," Copeland said. "But what I'm talking about is that he shows no confusion about it. Just the flight instinct. It's like he knew right away that Merced was shot, and the other guys tumbled to it late."

Bosch nodded. It was a good observation—one that had escaped him during the multiple times he had watched the video the day before. He had focused solely on Merced and not paid proper attention to the other band members.

"Which one is that?" he asked.

"The trumpet—I think that was Ojeda," Soto said. "Angel Ojeda. He's the one who said in his statement that he ran."

"Okay, let's talk about Mr. Ojeda's position now," Copeland said. "With the triangulation, I was able to make a digital model of the shooting. It's crude because I thought it was better to go with speed over quality."

She typed in commands and killed all but the center screen. She then opened up a crudely animated version of the shooting from the angle of the music shop. The band members were little more than stick figures with letters affixed to them. Merced was marked A and Ojeda was figure B.

"This program measures spacial gradations and accurately re-creates a multidimensional animation that we can manipulate."

With her keyboard and mouse she controlled the screen. The view moved out through the window of the music store and close up on the four men located on and around the table. She then clicked the command and the shooting took place in slow motion, the bullet's trajectory marked by a red line that crossed the screen and struck the figure sitting on the table—Merced.

"Okay, so let's start over but move over top," Copeland said.

The image shifted so that they were now looking down on the table. An overhead shot. Copeland ran the simulation, and the bullet again streaked into the picture as a red line hitting Merced. At the moment of impact the figure that was Ojeda, the trumpeter, was in motion behind the table. It was clear that if the bullet had not hit Merced, it was on course to strike Ojeda.

"Wow!" Soto said.

Copeland ran two more simulations. The first one was another overhead version but it was high in the sky and took in the entire plaza, adjoining streets, and the Boyle Hotel. This simulation showed the red line of the bullet streak across the screen from the hotel to the picnic table, again convincingly showing that Merced stopped the bullet before it could have hit Ojeda.

The last simulation was a ground angle of the entire shot from the hotel to the table. Copeland stopped the program at the point the bullet struck the figure that was Merced. She then ran it again and then a third time before letting the simulation go to the end.

"You'll have to talk to the guys in the gun shop about trajectory and target lead, all of that," she said. "But it is possible, when you look at this, to see that if figure B was being tracked with a scope, the shooter could have fired before realizing that figure A—your victim—was in the line of fire."

Bosch nodded.

"Tunnel vision. Some people call it 'scope blindness'— all you see is the target."

He stood up. He was too charged to remain sitting.

"The trumpet player," he said. "We need to find him."

Copeland took a disc in a plastic sleeve off the side of the worktable and handed it to Soto.

"I made a copy of the animation. I hope it helps. We would build a more detailed model if it was ever needed for court use."

Soto nodded and took the disc.

"Got it," she said. "Thanks."

"Bailey, get some sleep," Bosch said. "You earned it."

11

Bosch and Soto hurried back to the PAB and divided up the work. It was decided that Bosch would write up the search warrant for the Boyle Hotel records and take it to the CCB to be signed by a judge. Meanwhile, Soto would work on locating the surviving three members of Los Reyes Jalisco—her priority being Angel Ojeda, the trumpet player.

While Soto went for coffee before beginning her task, Bosch went to the captain's office and knocked on the door. He wanted to give Crowder a brief update on the case. It was unusual for Bosch to keep his supervisor so closely informed about a case but he wanted to make sure Crowder was not falling under the sway of his lieutenant in terms of moving the Merced investigation out of Open-Unsolved and over to Robbery-Homicide. If Crowder knew that progress was being made, he would be less likely to move the case. After all, if Bosch and Soto actually solved it, then Crowder as their supervisor would be in for all the kudos that came with an arrest.

To Bosch's dismay Crowder picked up his phone and called Samuels into the office so he could hear Bosch's report. Harry had hoped to keep Samuels out of this loop, since the lieutenant was pushing for the case to be transferred.

Bosch quickly updated both men on the key information from the video-and-data-imaging unit—that they now knew where the shot came from and were working toward finding out who had rented that room at the Hotel Mariachi on the day of the shooting. He didn't bother telling them about the animation Bailey Copeland had made that indicated the bullet that hit Merced might have been meant for Angel Ojeda, the trumpet player. Bosch wanted to pursue that aspect further before bringing it to Crowder and Samuels. He did tell the two supervisors that Soto was tracing the three other band members so they could be reinterviewed.

"Okay, Harry," Crowder said. "You're making good progress. Keep it going."

"Okay, Cap."

"We're putting Holcomb on the tip line," Samuels said. "Starting today. Quarles has court."

Sarah Holcomb and Eddie Quarles were one of the other teams in the unit. Quarles was the veteran and Holcomb was one of the new transfers. They had a case that was currently on trial, and as the senior partner, Quarles would have the lead and therefore be assisting and testifying in court. Holcomb could attend trial but would have little to do. Rather than leave her there as a spectator, Samuels pulled her back into the unit to handle the reward calls that came in on Merced. Normally Bosch would have wished for a more experienced detective vetting the calls, but in this case having one of the unit's rookies on the tip line would work better with a plan he was formulating.

When Bosch got back to his desk he found a cup of coffee from the vending machine on the first floor. A good cup of coffee never came out of that machine but it always did the job and he appreciated that Soto had gotten it for him.

"I'll get the next round," he said to his partner, who was already back at her computer.

"No worries," she said without looking away from her screen. "It all squares up in the end."

Bosch opened up his laptop and went to work on the warrant. He used a basic template for the first several pages, just filling in blanks about where he wanted to search and what he was looking for. The difficult part was narrowing down where the Boyle Hotel's old records were currently located. The renovation project had been carried out by one agency and the materials Bosch sought had been turned over to another. That agency, the Historical Society, had them in storage somewhere. But the location of the targeted materials aside, it was the probable cause summary that counted most in the document, and there was no template for that. He had to persuade a judge to grant him the authority to temporarily seize the records of the now-defunct hotel. He had to show cause for why the records were pertinent to his case.

It took him the rest of the morning to finish the search warrant. Shortly before lunch he printed it and asked Soto to read it over. It was a way of instilling "partnership" and teaching her the ropes. The search warrant was one of the investigator's most useful tools. After she was finished he told her he was going to walk it to the courthouse while she continued to run down locations on their interview subjects. She reported that she had already tracked two members of Los Reyes Jalisco and that they were both local, but Angel Ojeda—the one they most wanted to talk to—was proving difficult to find. He had split from the band and even apparently left Los Angeles very soon after the shooting. Nothing had come up on law enforcement databases, and the INS base showed his Permanent Resident Card had not been renewed three years ago.

"Maybe the other two know where he is," Bosch suggested.

"That's what I'm thinking. Or maybe they can give us a line on somebody who can give us a line. Are you free this afternoon to do this?"

"Yeah, we need to keep momentum. We can drop the search warrant at the Historical Society on the way."

"Cool."

The place Bosch was going was the Clara Shortridge Foltz Criminal Justice Center but nobody ever called it that. The name was too long and too difficult to collapse into the easy parlance cops liked to use. Most cops and lawyers called it the CCB for Criminal Courts Building or the 2-10 for its address on West Temple Street. It was a slightly uphill block from the PAB and Bosch walked it because it would take much longer to drive over and find a parking space.

Bosch was in luck. The on-call judge who handled administrative matters including search warrant applications was Sherma Barthlett, a jurist Bosch had known since she was a prosecutor. They had always had a professional but easy rapport and when Bosch sent word to her through her clerk that he was there with a warrant, he was immediately invited back to her chambers. More often than not the warrants went back to the chambers for the judge's consideration while the detectives cooled their heels in the empty courtroom.

"Harry, I can't believe you're still in the game," she said as he entered.

She got up and came around from behind her desk to formally shake his hand.

"Barely," he said. "I've got about a year left on my DROP contract but some days I'm not even sure I can make that."

"You? They'll probably have to drag you out. Sit down."

She gestured to a chair in front of her desk while she returned to her spot behind it. She was a very pleasant woman whose easygoing demeanor always belied her ferocity as a prosecutor and now as a judge. Back when she was a prosecutor her nickname was "The Accountant" because not only did she specialize in financial crimes but she had a marvelous memory for all things numerical—from penal code numbers to phone numbers to the sentences received by violators in her cases years before. Bosch had worked with her twice in the nineties on murder cases motivated by financial gain. She had been a taskmaster but he couldn't complain. They got first-degree verdicts both times. He handed the search warrant application across the desk to her.

"What have we got here?" Barthlett said as she began flipping through the pages to the summary. "This is a records search."

"Right," Bosch said. "Looking for a name on a hotel registry."

"The Historical Society . . ."

Bosch didn't respond. She was just reading out loud. He waited.

"I remember the Merced case. I was out of the D.A.'s Office but I do remember this one. So now he's died."

"Yes. It's been in the papers."

"Between what I do here and my husband and kids, I have so little time to read the paper . . . I'm always out of the loop."

Bosch just nodded, even though the judge's eyes were on the document he had brought.

The judge picked up a small gavel that was on her desk and Bosch realized that it was actually a pen. She signed the front signature page of the warrant and handed it back to him with a smile.

"I hope it helps, Detective."

"Me, too. Thanks, Judge."

He got up and turned to the door.

"When's your retirement date?" she said to his back.

He looked back at her.

"Supposed to be end of next year," he said.

"Supposed to be?" she asked.

Bosch shrugged.

"You never know."

"You'll make it, Harry," she said. "And I hope Jerry and I get invited to the party."

Bosch assumed Jerry was her husband. He smiled.

"You're on the list."

From the courthouse he walked through the Pueblo and over to Alameda. His first stop was Philippe's for a French Dip sandwich. Getting food at Philippe's had worked the same way for more than a hundred years.

Customers lined up at the deli counter in front of carvers and waited patiently to order their sandwiches. The trick was to pick the fastest-moving line. Carvers who were chatty with the customers were slow. Bosch chose a woman who looked like she was all business and he chose right. His line moved efficiently and soon he was sitting at one of the communal tables with his sandwich, a side of potato salad, and a Coke.

The food hit the mark as usual and Bosch was tempted to wait in line for another round but decided to stay hungry. The French Dip hadn't been the only reason he had chosen Philippe's. The restaurant was across the street from Union Station. When he was finished Bosch stepped out and crossed Alameda to enter the great hall of the train station. There was a bank of old-style phone booths near the entrance and he went into one to make a quick call, wrapping his tie around the mouthpiece to muffle his voice.

12

Soto was ready and waiting when Bosch got back to the PAB. The two members of Los Reyes Jalisco she had located were both in North Hollywood and just a few blocks apart, meaning they were most likely still associated as musicians and friends. They needed to be interviewed to see if they had any new thoughts or recollections about the case. Hopefully they also would have a line on Angel Ojeda, whose whereabouts remained unknown.

"I thought we'd drop off the warrant at the Historical Society and then head to the Valley," she said. "Get a head start before the traffic gets bad."

"The traffic's always bad," Bosch said.

The first man to be interviewed was named Esteban Hernandez, the band's guitar player. He lived in a large apartment complex on North Lankershim that had a center courtyard with a filled-in pool where tenants gathered during the day. As Bosch and Soto walked down the exterior walkway to apartment 3-K, the men who were gathered in one group on what was now the concrete surface of the pool looked up at them and talked openly. Bosch picked up the words *policia*, *heroina*, and *la tiradora* and knew they had recognized Soto.

When they got to 3-K, Bosch knocked loudly and they waited.

"Those guys down there, they made you," Bosch said. "I heard 'em."

"From TV," Soto said.

"That bother you? Didn't Thirteenth Street put out a bounty on you?"

"Supposedly. But then they got the message."

"What message?"

Before she could answer, the apartment door was opened by a heavyset man Bosch was able to recognize from the music store video of the Merced shooting. Wide shoulders and skinny hips with an ample belly and a thick push-broom mustache.

"Mr. Hernandez?" he said. "LAPD."

He flashed his badge and then introduced Soto. She spoke to Hernandez in Spanish and he responded in kind. They were invited into the small but neat efficiency apartment. Hernandez sat on a cot that had been made up to look like a couch with several pillows propped against the wall behind it. Bosch stayed standing near the door and let Soto move front and center, since this was going to be her interview. She remained standing as well, positioning herself directly in front of Hernandez.

Bosch could understand most of the interview from Soto's side of it. She started off explaining that the Merced shooting had now become a homicide and that she and Bosch were investigating the matter. She asked a few open questions getting at whether Hernandez remembered anything new about the shooting or if he had any thoughts ten years later. Hernandez was more difficult for Bosch to understand. His voice was raspy and he may have been drinking before they got to him. He seemed to be slurring some words and mumbling others. But it did become clear he had nothing new to add to what was already in his statement and in the murder book.

Soto then asked him if he knew where the other two surviving members of the band, Angel Ojeda and Alberto Cabral, could be located. Bosch liked that she had asked about Cabral even though they had an address for him. It was a move that a more experienced detective would employ to check a witness's veracity. He appreciated that he didn't have to tell Soto to handle it that way.

Hernandez shook his head about Ojeda but pointed his thumb over his shoulder and gave an address for Cabral. Soto asked him a few more general questions and then, when the interview seemed to be over, she asked him why he thought Ojeda had run that day. Hernandez appeared to feign confusion.

"¿Qué?"

She asked him again, telling him there was a tape of the shooting and that Ojeda took off the moment Merced was shot, as if he knew what was going on.

Hernandez said he hadn't noticed Ojeda's movements because he was too busy ducking for cover once he realized Merced had been shot. Soto seemed to accept that but then opened a line of questioning about Ojeda, asking if he had enemies or had gotten into any kind of trouble around the time of the shooting.

Hernandez wasn't helpful. He either didn't know much about Ojeda or was acting as though he didn't. He did say that Ojeda had been with the band only nine months before the shooting and had dropped out of it right afterward. Hernandez and Cabral joined with two other musicians and continued to perform as Los Reyes Jalisco.

Soto asked where Ojeda had come from to join the band and Hernandez shrugged. He knew he was originally from Chihuahua but he couldn't remember the exact circumstances of him joining the band. He said he believed that Cabral had met him at Mariachi Plaza and brought him into the group because he thought that the addition of a trumpet player would help them score more and better jobs. As he talked, Hernandez seemed to remember more. He added that Ojeda was very handsome and that was also a consideration in adding him to the band. He came with a small following in the mariachi circuit, and it was believed that his looks might help them get jobs at the plaza, where any competitive edge was good to have.

Soto thanked Hernandez, and Bosch nodded. The detectives then drove a few blocks farther up Lankershim to a very similarly designed apartment complex where Cabral lived. However, Cabral was not at his apartment or in the courtyard, where a group of men were sitting around a grill, preparing a meal. When asked by Soto about Cabral and his possible whereabouts, the men shook their heads. They were no help.

Bosch and Soto were so far north of downtown and the PAB that they decided to sit in the car for a while and wait to see if Cabral showed up. Bosch moved the car to a red no-parking curb near the gated entrance of the complex so they would be sure to see the musician if he entered.

"So what do you think?" Soto asked once they were parked and watching.

"I think you handled that interview really well," Bosch said.

"Thank you."

"And I think what I thought before. We have to find Ojeda. I hope he didn't go back to Chihuahua, because that'll be a needle-in-a-haystack job."

"I don't know. His green card lapsed. Makes me think he went back."

"The question will be why."

Soto nodded.

"Did you believe Hernandez, that he didn't keep track of him?" she asked.

Bosch thought for a few minutes and nodded.

"I think so. Musicians are an itinerant sort. They come and go, float around."

Soto nodded and they were silent for a while. Then he remembered Soto's unfinished story.

"What you said before about the bounty and Thirteenth Street, you didn't finish. You said they 'got the message'?"

She nodded.

"Yes, some guys from Gang Intelligence went to visit some of the OGs and told them that if anything happened to me, it would instigate an all-out war with the LAPD, and that Thirteenth Street would never get any business done. Big blue would be all over them."

"And what? They promised no harm would come your way?"

"That's what they said."

Bosch nodded and continued to think about Soto and

112

her journey. His next questions went back to the Bonnie Brae case.

"What do you remember from that day?" he asked. "About the fire. You were, what, six or seven?"

Soto composed her thoughts before answering.

"I was seven and the thing I remember most is the smoke coming under the door. We had tried to leave but we had to go back because the fire was in the stairwell and the stairs at the other end of the hallway were blocked. So we went back and closed the door and there was no other way out."

"Was there a teacher?"

"Yes, Mrs. Gonzalez . . . she died. We were in there and nobody came to help and pretty soon the smoke started to come in. We had these aprons that we used when we painted, and Mrs. Gonzalez and her helper, a lady named Adele, cut them with scissors so we could dip them in the fish tank to get them wet, and then we wrapped them around our faces and over our noses and mouths."

"That was smart."

"But the smoke kept coming in and we were coughing and gagging. So we all went into the supply closet and closed that door, except there wasn't room for Mrs. Gonzalez so she stayed out and she kept calling for help. Yelling for help."

"But nobody came?"

"Not for a long time. And pretty soon we didn't hear her anymore and the smoke was coming into the supply closet."

Bosch imagined how scared they all must have been. All those little kids and one adult left.

"Then the smoke was too much for us and we all went to sleep. Only some of us didn't wake up. A fireman saved me. Gave me mouth-to-mouth and then they put a breathing mask on me. I remember being in the truck and seeing them working on my best friend, Elsa. They couldn't save her. They saved me but not her. I didn't understand that."

Bosch wasn't sure what to say, so he said nothing for a long time. When he finally spoke it was to pick out one of the positive parts of the story.

"Did you ever know who that firefighter was?"

"No, I never did. I thought maybe his name would be in one of the reports but I haven't seen it so far."

Bosch nodded but his attention had been drawn to the side-view mirror. A car was coming up slowly along the line of cars parked at the curb. It was an old shit box with its windows down. It looked like a drive-by hoopty.

Bosch pulled his gun off his belt and held it down in his lap, the barrel pointed at his door.

"What is it?" Soto said.

"Hopefully nothing."

Soto shifted sideways in her seat so her back was to her door. She pulled her weapon as well and held it with two hands in her lap.

"Just don't shoot me," Bosch said.

He noticed that his voice was tight. Adrenaline was flowing into his bloodstream. The car was two spaces back now and Bosch could make out at least three figures in it. Two in the front, one in the middle in the backseat.

It slowly cruised by and Bosch made eye contact with the front passenger and then with the man in the backseat. Both men had full-neck tattoos. They stared back at Bosch but made no furtive moves and the car kept going. Once it passed, Bosch eased his grip on his weapon and checked the car's plate.

The microphone for the police radio was on a cord so old it had lost its coil and had to be draped over the rearview mirror. Bosch grabbed it and called the communication center to give the plate number and get a rundown on the car's ownership.

"Recognize them?" he asked Soto while he waited. "Are they Thirteenth?"

"No. They look like bangers, but who knows. Why would Thirteenth be all the way up here?"

"You. Those men in the courtyard where Hernandez lives, they made you as the shooter in the Pico-Union thing. If any of them had connections to Thirteenth . . . maybe they think if they take you out off their turf, there won't be a problem."

Soto didn't say anything. Bosch continued.

"And the *cholos* in that hoopty were young bucks. They don't always listen to the OGs who make deals with cops. They try to make a name for themselves."

The dispatcher came back with the report on the plate number. The car was registered to an owner with an address in the town of San Fernando, the tiny city in the middle of the Valley surrounded on all sides by Los Angeles.

"Not Thirteenth Street turf," Soto said as he hung the mike back over the mirror.

"Let's not take any chances."

The car in question had turned right a block up the street. This meant that they could be coming back around for another look-see or something worse.

Bosch started the car and pulled out from the curb. He went down the street and turned where the car had turned. He navigated around the block but never saw the car again. He came back to the same parking space and pulled in.

"Maybe it was nothing," Soto said.

There was a false hopefulness in her voice.

"Maybe," Bosch said.

They waited another half hour, with no sign of Cabral. Bosch said they'd give it another ten minutes, and five minutes later a city bus pulled to a stop at the corner and several people got off, including a man Bosch was pretty sure was the accordion player from the video.

"That him?"

Soto stared and eventually nodded.

"I think so."

They got out of the car in unison. Bosch was on the street side and he looked around, still wary of the car and the gangbangers who had scoped them out earlier. He saw no sign of them and came around to join his partner on the sidewalk.

The man they thought was Alberto Cabral was carrying two cloth shopping bags that appeared filled with groceries. The bags looked like they were heavy with cans and other staples. Bosch and Soto blocked his path and Soto badged him and confirmed his identity. She started out speaking English.

"We need to speak to you about the Orlando Merced shooting," she said.

Cabral attempted to shrug but the weight of the bags he carried in either hand impeded him.

"I don't know anything," he said in a thick accent.

"Did you hear that Mr. Merced has passed away?" Soto asked.

"Yeah, I heard about it," Cabral said.

"Do you know where Angel Ojeda is?" Bosch asked.

"Yeah, I know him."

"Do you know where he is? We need to talk to him."

Soto repeated the question in Spanish and Cabral answered in English.

"Yeah, he went to Tulsa."

"Tulsa, Oklahoma?" Soto asked.

Cabral nodded. He put the bags down on the sidewalk to rest his arms. Bosch realized that this was the wrong place to be doing the interview, especially since it looked like the interview was going to produce a line on Ojeda. He reached down and picked up the nearest bag.

"Let us help you. Let's take your groceries in and we'll talk inside."

Five minutes later they were in Cabral's threadbare apartment, where, like his bandmate Hernandez, he lived alone and sparely. All the night work and inconsistency of gigs had made for a lonely life. There was no sign of a wife or children. No framed photos, no school drawings on the refrigerator. Bosch thought of a bumper sticker he had once seen: "Play Accordion—Go to Jail." In many ways it appeared that Cabral's life as a mariachi musician had been its own form of incarceration.

"How do you know Angel Ojeda is in Tulsa?" Soto asked.

Without the bags weighing his arms down Cabral could now shrug, and he did so.

"I don't know," he said. "When he quit the band he

said he was going to Oklahoma to run his uncle's bar."

"So this is ten years ago?" she asked. "Right after Orlando got shot?"

He nodded.

"Pretty soon after, yes."

Cabral was standing in the tiny kitchen, putting away his groceries, while Bosch and Soto stood on the other side of the counter. He opened the refrigerator door to put away a small carton of milk. A fetid smell of food kept too long despite the cold storage wafted into the room.

"Have you heard anything about him since?"

"No."

"But you're sure it was Tulsa?" Bosch asked.

"Yes, Tulsa," Cabral insisted. "I know because I had to send him a money order with the last money he made with us."

Bosch moved into the kitchen, crowding Cabral. These next few questions were important.

"Do you remember where you sent the check?"

"I told you, Tulsa."

"The address. Where in Tulsa?"

"I don't remember. It was the bar where he worked."

"Do you remember the name of the bar?"

"Yes, because it was El Chihuahua."

"That was the name of the bar in Tulsa? El Chihuahua?"

"Yes, I remember that. Because it was where he was from. Chihuahua the place, not the dog."

Bosch nodded. The name of the bar was a good piece of information. He decided to change tacks with Cabral.

"Why did you bring him into the band?" he asked. "He wasn't from Jalisco."

Cabral responded with another shrug.

"We wanted a trumpet and he was always there at the plaza, available. He could play. I said, 'Why not?'"

"Was he in trouble with anybody?"

"I don't know. He didn't say this."

"Did he ever talk to you about the shooting? I mean after. Before he went to Tulsa."

Instead of shrugging, Cabral frowned and shook his head.

"Not really. He just said that we were lucky and Orlando wasn't."

"He never said that he knew what happened? He never said he knew who fired the shot and why?"

Cabral looked sharply at Bosch, surprised by the question. Bosch read it as a legit reaction.

"No, never," Cabral said.

Bosch believed him. He looked around the apartment, thinking about what else to ask. He saw a tiny desk in the corner that had a stack of ledgers and a Rolodex on it.

"So you're the band's manager, right?" he asked.

"Yes," Cabral said.

"You make the bookings?"

"I do. When there are bookings to be made. Not so much work anymore for the mariachis. Traditions don't mean much anymore."

Bosch nodded again. He agreed with that.

It had been a good interview. It gave them something to pursue. But rather than leave it, Bosch decided to throw Cabral a curve ball. Sometimes it worked to catch an interview subject off guard.

"What about the drugs?" he asked.

Cabral squinted his eyes.

"What drugs?" he asked.

"We were told Ojeda was a user."

Cabral shook his head.

"Not around me. We had a rule. No drugs."

"Okay," Bosch said. "No drugs."

It had been worth a shot.

After concluding the interview they returned to the car, and as Bosch was walking around the rear bumper, he noticed the gang car from before was now parked across the four-lane street and down about forty yards. With a nonchalant glance he discerned that there were still three figures in it.

He unlocked the Ford but opened the rear door. He slipped off his jacket so the gun and badge on his belt were readily visible. He took his time folding his jacket and then leaned into the car to put it on the backseat. Soto had already gotten into the front passenger seat. Bosch spoke calmly to her.

"Your friends are back."

"What friends?"

"From San Fernando."

"Where?"

"Right across the street."

She clocked the car and concern spread on her face.

"What do you want to do?"

"You call backup and sit tight. I'm going to go pay them a visit."

"Harry, you should wait until—"

He closed the door and went to the rear of the Ford. He popped the trunk, leaned down, and released the snaps on the shotgun rack. Using the trunk lid as a blind he glanced into the street and waited for a moment when the traffic was clear. He could hear Soto on the radio reporting an officer needing assistance—the non-emergency request for backup. The moment the street was clear he stepped away from the trunk with the Remington 870 and started to cross diagonally, directly toward the gang car. Almost immediately he heard its engine fire to life.

He racked the action on the shotgun, putting a round into the chamber. He made it to the center median before the car lurched away from the opposite curb into a screeching U-turn and took off.

"Hey, where're you going?" he called after the speeding car.

Soto came running across the street, her weapon out and at her side.

"Harry, what the hell were you doing?" she yelled.

He didn't answer at first. He watched the car until it turned right at the next block and disappeared.

"Sending a message," he finally said.

"What message?" she said. "We don't even know if they were Thirteenth."

"Doesn't matter who they were. Our gang is bigger than theirs. That's the message."

A patrol car came coasting down the street behind them, its blues on but no siren. Bosch leaned down, holding the shotgun across his thighs, to talk to the driver.

13

The only thing Bosch regretted about his decision to grab the shotgun and confront the gangbangers trying to intimidate them was that it cost them nearly an hour of explanation and waiting while patrol units flooded the zone and tried to find the vehicle. Once it was determined that the vehicle was GOA—patrol speak for gone on arrival—Bosch and Soto were cleared to proceed on their way. But neither the slow-moving afternoon traffic that hampered their drive back downtown nor the sideshow Bosch had created with the Remington could dampen the flow of momentum Bosch was feeling.

The video analysis coupled with now having a line on Ojeda in Tulsa—even if it was ten-year-old information—was giving the case undeniable speed. If the trumpet player went to Oklahoma after the shooting, Bosch felt confident they would be able to pick up his trail. The plan would be to confirm his location and then go there to interview him in person. While Ojeda wasn't a suspect in the shooting, it seemed obvious now that he knew more than he had ever revealed. He allowed the original investigation to go down the wrong road— random gang violence—when there may have been an entirely different motivation for the shooting. If Ojeda held that secret, then it couldn't be handled in a phone call or as a favor by the police in Oklahoma. He told

Soto that they were going to need to persuade Crowder to send them to Tulsa to handle it themselves.

"Have you ever been?" Soto asked.

"Tulsa? I've only flown in and out. I had a case about five years ago where we had science on a guy who lived up in a small town north of Tulsa. One of those places that later got wiped out by a tornado. It's a funny story. I mean now. I was pretty pissed off then and it changed how we deal with other departments."

"What happened?"

He told her the story. It began with a cold hit on DNA from a 1990 home invasion robbery, rape, and murder. The match was to a fifty-eight-year-old ex-convict named Frank Tomlinson, whose criminal history stretched all the way back to repeated stints in juvenile hall. Tomlinson had long been off the grid, his whereabouts unknown since he jumped a parole tail in 2006. But he still had family in L.A., so Bosch and his partner at the time, Dave Chu, put together a play. They first applied for and received a court order allowing them to eavesdrop on phone calls made by Tomlinson's elderly mother and his brother. Bosch then knocked on their doors and inquired about the suspect, dropping hints that he needed to talk to Tomlinson about a murder from 1990. Meantime, Chu was in the wire room, waiting to listen in on any calls that went out from their homes after Bosch's visit.

Sure enough, the brother placed a call to Tomlinson and warned him about the police visit. The call was traced to a cell tower located in the tiny town of Beacon, Oklahoma. Bosch made contact with the Beacon Police Department and spoke to a Sergeant Haden, who looked at an e-mailed photograph of Tomlinson and identified it as a photo of Tom Frazier, who worked as one of the town's two cab drivers. Bosch inquired as to whether the police department had the manpower to keep an eye on Frazier/Tomlinson until Bosch and Chu could get there the next day. The concern was that the call from the brother might spook the suspect and cause him to once again disappear. Haden said surveillance would not be a problem but offered to go ahead and arrest Tomlinson and hold him in the town jail. Bosch said no, that they wanted to casually interview the suspect before he was placed under arrest and could exercise his right to legal counsel.

Haden agreed not to approach the suspect and told Bosch to e-mail the details of their flight to Tulsa. Haden said he would pick Bosch and Chu up at the airport and take them directly to the suspect's home, where he would be, since he worked the night shift.

What Bosch didn't learn until he got there was that the town of Beacon was so small that its police department had only four officers, which amounted to one officer on duty at any given time. When Haden went to pick up the two L.A. detectives at the airport down in Tulsa, he left Tomlinson unwatched. The suspect made his move and left town. He was long gone by the time Bosch and Chu got to the ranch where he had lived—and where Haden had been watching until it was time to go to the airport.

"You have got to be kidding," Soto said.

"I wish," Bosch said.

"Did you ever get the guy—Tomlinson?"

"Eventually. He tried to do the same thing, start over in some Podunk town with a Podunk police department in Minnesota. Except that department had a chief who had retired out of L.A. and religiously checked the wanted posters that came across his desk. He recognized Tomlinson and made the arrest. That was last year."

"Well, at least they got him in the end."

"Yeah, but that little snafu in Oklahoma got him another four years of freedom. It's a funny story until you consider that."

Bosch's phone vibrated and he checked the screen. It was the Historical Society, so he took the call. The secretary to the director told Bosch that the material requested in the warrant had been retrieved from storage and was available for pickup. Bosch said he was on his way.

The squad room was almost deserted when they got back. Soto carried the hotel registration book they had just picked up at the Historical Society, because it had been decided in the car that she would work the names. She had already looked at the name registered to what was room 211 on the day of the Merced shooting, the room where the shot was believed to have come from. Rodolfo Martin was listed as the guest in that room. But she would run the names of all guests listed on the registry through various law enforcement data banks, checking for criminal records, aliases, and anything else that would draw attention to them.

She immediately went to work while Bosch tried to catch the captain before he left for the day. He was hoping to get travel approval so he could book a flight to Tulsa. Crowder was already standing and pulling on his suit coat when Bosch entered the office.

"Harry, make me happy," he said.

It was his normal greeting when a detective entered without being called in.

"We're working on it, Cap. It looks like we have a line on a key witness in Tulsa and—"

"What kind of witness?"

"He was one of the victim's bandmates. Some stuff has come up and we really need to talk to him. In person."

"What's wrong with a phone call?"

"He's not a forthcoming witness. We think he knew something he didn't say before. With the original team. That, plus he split town right after the shooting."

"Aren't these mariachi guys kind of itinerant? They go where the work is, right?"

"That's true, but you don't leave Los Angeles for Tulsa if you're a mariachi. The work's here."

Crowder adjusted his jacket and sat back down behind his desk to continue the conversation.

"Maybe he's the only mariachi in Tulsa."

Bosch stared at him blankly for a moment.

"Are you saying we can't go, Captain?"

"Is he considered dangerous?"

Bosch nodded, not because Ojeda was considered dangerous but because he now understood why Crowder was hedging on the trip to Tulsa. He was worried about the travel budget. He had sent a memo out a couple weeks earlier saying that travel in the last two months of the year would be considered and approved on a priority basis because the unit's travel budget—already the highest of any unit in the Department—had been depleted earlier than expected. It was memos like these—seemingly putting a changing value on catching killers—that frustrated Bosch to no end.

Crowder was asking if interviewing Ojeda would be a dangerous assignment because he knew if he sent only one detective, he could cut the cost of the trip in half.

"That's not going to work," Bosch said.

"What's not going to work?" Crowder responded.

"Sending just one of us. If you go with one, it will have to be Soto because we don't know if this guy speaks English. She's good—I can already tell that. But I don't know if you want to send her out by herself a month into the job."

"No, you're right . . . "

"She's got to go and I've got to go. We think this guy may have been the intended target."

Crowder didn't respond to that. He said nothing else, which Bosch took to mean that he was contemplating turning the whole trip down and telling Harry to handle it by phone.

"You heard what I said, right? We think the bullet may have been meant for this guy in Tulsa."

"Yes, I heard what you said. You left out that you only *think* he's in Tulsa. He could be in Timbuktu as far as you know for sure."

"True. But if he is, we'll pick up the trail in Tulsa."

That was greeted with another dose of silence.

"Look, Captain, there's gotta be some discretionary funds up there on the tenth floor," Bosch finally offered. "I mean, Malins is all over this. So let him put some money where his mouth is. . . . Or maybe we go to the ex-mayor, since he's the one throwing reward money around."

Crowder made a calming gesture with his hand.

"We don't want to go to the ex-mayor. He's already caused enough problems for us."

And then he made his decision, moving quickly from all out to all in.

"Okay, look, don't worry about the money. The money's my issue. When do you want to go?"

Bosch answered quickly, hoping to seal the deal and get out of the office before there was another change of mind.

"The sooner the better. We've got a line on him working in a bar. I'd like to get out there tomorrow. If he's going to be at the bar he'll probably be there then—Friday being paycheck day and the start of the weekend."

"All right, plan on that. I'll know where the money comes from by tomorrow morning."

"Thanks, Captain."

Bosch went back to the cubicle. When he got there he saw that his seat had been pulled over to Soto's desk and was occupied by Sarah Holcomb, the detective Samuels had put in charge of handling phone-in tips spawned by the reward announcement.

"We get anything good?" he asked as he entered the small cubicle.

Holcomb immediately started rising from the stolen desk chair. Bosch put his hand on her shoulder.

"Don't worry, it's okay. I'm going to go get a cup."

"You sure?"

"Sure. Either of you want coffee?"

Both women said no.

"Well, did you solve it for us, Holcomb? Get a confession?"

"Not quite."

Soto handed him a tip sheet.

"This one's interesting, though," she said.

Bosch took the page and read the summary Holcomb had written.

> Caller said Merced shooting connected to Bonnie Brae fire 1993. Caller said Merced knew who set the fire and was threat.

Bosch checked the back of the page to see if there was any more. It was blank. He handed it back to Soto, who had turned in her seat and was staring up at him, knowing the call had come from him.

"I take it this was anonymous?" he asked.

"Yes," Holcomb said. "It was from a pay phone at Union Station. I checked out the number."

Bosch looked over the top of the page at her. He was surprised she had taken the initiative to run the number. But that was also why he had taken the precaution of calling from a pay phone.

"I guess we should take a look at it," he said. "'Ninety-three—I think that year belongs to Whittaker and Dubose. We should talk to them, see if this rings a bell. Seems kind of thin but maybe we can take a look at the book on Bonnie Brae. Cross-reference it for names."

"Do you want me to do that?" Holcomb asked eagerly.

"No, we'll talk to them," Bosch said. "Just don't put too much stock in these call-ins. People have agendas, you know?"

"Oh, yeah," Holcomb said. "Some of them are so transparent about it, too."

"Anything else halfway legit?"

There was a whole stack of tip sheets on the desk.

"Not really," Holcomb said. "I was just giving Lucy the lowlights."

She referred to a clipboard on which she had condensed the calls to one-liners.

"Let's see," she said. "Caller said talk to 'Sleepy,' who is in the neighborhood over there and knows about all the White Fence shootings."

"'Sleepy,'" Bosch said. "Okay."

Holcomb moved down her list.

"Female caller says the mayor knows all about who did the shooting. I'm assuming she meant the ex-mayor but I didn't talk to her. That one came in on the overnight tape. Anonymous. Somebody with a heavy Spanish accent."

"Nice," Soto said. "Rat out the guy who put up the reward."

Bosch smiled.

"You have to admit, the motive's pretty creative," he said. "Zeyas had Merced shot *and* paralyzed so he could roll him out during the campaign to help win the election."

"Great plan," Soto said. "Worked perfectly."

"What else?" Bosch said.

"Well, we got several suggestions that we look into white supremacy groups," Holcomb said. "Several more that were sure the drug cartels were behind the shooting. And we had one caller who says the shooter was this guy named Felix who was angry because he had hired some mariachis from the plaza and they had performed badly. Oh, and there was also the guy who called in and said he was sure it was the Mexican Mafia, only he wasn't sure why."

"All in all, very helpful," Bosch said.

"You bet," Holcomb said. "And I haven't even mentioned all the calls from the racists who said Merced got exactly what he deserved simply because he was Mexican."

It was all part of what was expected when a reward was put out to the public. All the crazies came out. None of it surprised Bosch and none of it was worth a second thought—except for the follow-up on the Bonnie Brae tip. He thanked Holcomb for her perseverance and left to get a cup of coffee out of the machine on the first floor.

When he got back, Holcomb was gone. Bosch and Soto conferred and he told her to bring a packed bag to work the next day because it looked like they were going to go to Tulsa to find and question Ojeda.

"There might be a problem," she said.

"Tell me," he said.

"I was just on the computer and I did find a bar called El Chihuahua, but when I called and asked—"

"You called?"

"Yes, you said we needed to try to confirm he was there."

"Yeah, but not by calling him directly. That could spook him."

"Well, as it turns out, I didn't talk to him directly or even indirectly. I called and asked if he was in and the man who answered said no one worked there named Ojeda."

"Maybe he quit. It's been ten years."

"I asked. You know, did he ever work there, and this guy on the line said no, that he'd never heard of him. And he said he had been there ten years."

Bosch thought about that for a long moment, juxtaposing it with Cabral's information. Cabral had seemed honest and sure of what he had told them.

"We're still going," he finally said. "Tomorrow. I hope you didn't have plans."

She shook her head. Bosch already knew she didn't have a boyfriend and he now knew that much of her free time was probably spent on the Bonnie Brae case.

"Well, should I call the Tulsa police and see if Ojeda is known to them?"

"No, you never do something like that. Remember what I told you about Beacon? You don't tip the locals unless you have to."

Chastised, Soto changed the subject.

"How do you want to handle Whittaker and Dubose?" she asked.

"You handle it—if it's me, they might think something's up. Just keep them out of it. Tell them we got the tip and ask for a look at the books."

"What if they saw my name in the reports? On the witness list. I was interviewed back then."

Bosch shook his head.

"That's not how they work. They didn't read the reports. They only accessed the case for scientific evidence. They don't move their asses unless there's science."

Soto nodded but looked concerned.

"What?" Bosch asked.

"Did you make sure there were no cameras near the phone booth when you made that call?" she asked.

That froze Bosch for a moment. He had not been that careful.

"I didn't even check," he finally said. "But this tip isn't going to pan out, so there will be no reason for anybody to check for cameras."

"Well, we didn't expect Holcomb to be running the numbers either," Soto said. "But she did. I don't want you getting into trouble."

"Don't worry, I won't."

"Well, it's just that there's some rumors going around that the Department's so heavy with these DROP contracts that they're looking for ways to push people out before the end of the contract to save some money."

"Now, how did you hear something like that? You're at least twenty years away from even thinking about a DROP contract."

"The *Blue Line*. There were some letters from officers in last month's issue. That's what they were saying."

Bosch nodded. He had read the same letters. The Deferred Retirement Option Plan had started out as something with the best intentions all around. It was a plan to keep experienced officers and detectives working for the Department instead of taking those skills elsewhere when their pensions maxed. In effect, it allowed them to bank their pensions and start over at full pay with a second pension accruing and earning high interest. But politics and bureaucracy set in and the plan had to be offered to anyone who reached twenty-five years in, no matter their job or skill level. Now too many were on the DROP, and the interest was threatening to bankrupt the plan. The Department was looking for ways to stop the bleeding, including forcing officers out of their five-year contracts early.

"I'm not worried about it," Bosch said. "The only thing I have to worry about right now is you and making sure you're ready to carry the torch when I'm out of here."

Soto looked at him and tried to hide a smile.

"I'll be ready," she said.

"Good," he said.

Bosch's daughter had a rare night at home. With Explorer meetings and activities and even a part-time volunteer job delivering dinners to shut-ins, she seemed to use the house only for sleeping these days. This bothered Bosch because he knew his time with her was short, but he also knew she was pursuing things she wanted. And all the activities counted as public service at her school and would help round out her application package for college. She had her eye on Cal State, Los Angeles, where there were top criminal justice and forensics programs. Bosch was pleased with her choice because it was still in the city. Besides that, the school was located on the same site as the lab, which would afford him the opportunity to see her at school on occasion during his last few months on the job.

They spent the evening preparing a swordfish steak dinner and talking about the Explorer assignment for the following Tuesday. Maddie and others in her Explorer unit were going to be used in an undercover sting operation in which they would be wired and sent into convenience stores in Hollywood to see if employees would allow them to purchase alcohol. Maddie was excited about it, and as undercover operations go it was relatively safe. But Bosch wanted to make sure she understood that in any operation, there was always a possibility of things going sideways. She couldn't rely on the undercover officer who went into the store ahead of her or the patrol units waiting nearby. She had to keep her eyes open at all times.

"I will, Dad, I will," she said.

In recent months she had perfected the dismissive, I-know-this-already tone when speaking with him on almost any subject.

"It doesn't hurt to repeat it," Bosch said. "You want me to be there?"

"No, that would be embarrassing!"

She said it as though he had suggested tagging along on a prom date.

"Okay, okay, just checking."

They were on the back deck, where he was grilling the fish on a small gas grill. He flipped the steaks and changed the direction of the conversation.

"So I'm hoping to be back by Sunday afternoon," he said. "Maybe we can have dinner again that night."

He had already told her about the trip to Tulsa. She was used to his frequent work trips and was always fine by herself.

"Sunday I have M-O-W," she said. "Sorry."

Meals on Wheels. Her volunteer work for the organization had greatly cut into the time Bosch enjoyed most with her—sharing a meal and talking.

"Maybe I need to sign up for that. It might be the best way for me to see you at night."

"Dad, you know I need to do this. I want to get into

Cal State and get some scholarship money. This will all help."

"I know, baby, I know. Here I am complaining and I'm the one going to Tulsa."

He used a fork to push the steaks onto a plate. Dinner was ready.

"You have to go," she said. "You don't have many cases left."

Bosch nodded. She was right about that.

On the way inside to the table, she told him she was thinking about getting a nose ring over the weekend so she could really look the part for the sting operation.

Bosch managed not to drop the plate.

"You mean you are going to put a hole through your nose where there isn't supposed to be a hole?"

"Yeah, I think it will be kind of cool. I won't have to keep it. Less permanent than a tattoo."

The food smelled great but Bosch wasn't sure he was hungry anymore.

14

Bosch and Soto took an 11 a.m. flight to Tulsa with a stop in Dallas. They got lucky on the first flight and had an empty seat between them in economy class. This became the storage space for the murder books from both the Merced and Bonnie Brae cases. Bosch was determined to use any downtime during the trip to review the Bonnie Brae case for Soto and to continue to read and reread the reports on the original Merced investigation. He firmly believed and it had been his repeated experience that the answers to most cases are hidden in the details. Both cases offered volumes of details.

Bosch decided that on the first leg of the trip he would devote his time to the Bonnie Brae books. After Dallas he would be back on Merced.

The Bonnie Brae murder books were not divided chronologically, as was the case with Merced. Usually, lengthy or wide-ranging investigations that required multiple binders were still chronologically composed. Detectives filled one book after the other as they proceeded and this allowed a linear review of the case. The Bonnie Brae investigation had originally been carried out by the Department's Criminal Conspiracy Section, which was the investigative unit that handled arson cases and liaised with fire department investigators. With nine victims, the case from the outset was broken into specific avenues of investigation. The first murder book was a catchall for the case chronology and other reports generated during the investigation. Book 2 was dedicated solely to the identification and background of the victims. The next binder was dedicated to the investigation of the Pico-Union La Raza street gang. The fourth was fat with reports on the analysis of the origin of the fire and its spread through the Bonnie Brae Arms apartment building. This last binder was also the repository for all the media reports accumulated on the case. It was before the Internet, and the city's newspapers were the main source of reporting in the community. The plethora of news clips shoved into large envelopes made this last binder the thickest of them all.

While not entirely linear in presentation, murder book 1 was the binder most resembling a standard murder book and so it was the place Bosch started. As he worked his way through the book, Soto was on her laptop, writing the initial report on the investigative moves that led to their trip to Tulsa. It was required that work trips be fully documented in order to justify the hit to the unit's travel budget. In this case, Captain Crowder had gotten funding for the trip through a discretionary fund attached to the budget of the OCP, so documentation was imperative.

Most of the reports in the book that Bosch was reviewing had been composed by a detective 3 named Jack Harris. His rank was equal to that of a sergeant and he was the lead investigator of the five-person CCS task force pulled together to work the case. Bosch knew none of the detectives from past experience, though he had heard of Harris. He believed Harris was retired now, but during the eighties and nineties he seemed to frontline a number of CCS cases that either made news or were known within the Department. There was no reason to think of him as anything but competent, and that weighed in Bosch's thinking as he delved into a case that had been unsolved for twenty-one years. He knew the chances were slim that he and Soto would be able to change that outcome. Whittaker and Dubose had already told them as they handed over the binders that they had thoroughly reviewed the case the previous year, looking for a scientific foothold, but had come up dry. The mandate of the Open-Unsolved Unit was to search old cases for new attack angles—those most often being areas where new forensic sciences could be applied. DNA and fingerprint technologies were the mainstays of this effort. And there was no such evidence in the Bonnie Brae case.

Bosch had not expressed his pessimistic thoughts to his partner because of her emotional connection to the case. He promised Soto a full review of the lengthy files and he would conduct that review without taking anything away from his efforts on the Merced investigation. The plane ride was his chance to begin.

The Bonnie Brae fire did most of its damage with smoke. The fire itself was largely contained to a single hallway and a room in the basement where large trash Dumpsters were positioned beneath two trash chutes that served the five floors of apartments above. The fire gutted the trash room and spread only into the basement hallway. But smoke from the blaze spread rapidly through the building, up stairwells, hallways, and the trash chutes. The fire and attendant smoke cut off the escape route of the children and teachers in the makeshift and unlicensed day-care facility in one of the basement rooms.

A key reason the case had gone unsolved for so long was that a precious two weeks went by before the fire was determined to be arson. That kind of delay in a homicide investigation was usually too hard to overcome. Most cases not solved in forty-eight hours were never solved. A two-week delay in an investigation made the odds of success even longer.

The delay was caused by the case initially being called accidental by fire department arson experts. The origin was determined to be a Dumpster located beneath one of the trash chutes. It was believed that combustion occurred when flammable materials already in the waste bin came in contact with a burning cigarette butt tossed into the trash chute from one of the floors above. It was a day before the scheduled trash pickup, and the complex's maintenance man reported that the bins in the trash room were full. The fire quickly spread to the wooden ceiling joists and was carried throughout the room. The fire burned so intensely that there was nothing but wet ash left in the bin once the fire was extinguished.

Despite the fire department's declaration that the fire was accidental, patrol officers out of Rampart Division immediately started picking up street talk from snitches that the cause was intentional. The story repeated by many in the snitch world was that the Pico-Union La Raza gang had been having issues with the manager at Bonnie Brae over his refusal to let the gang openly sell drugs in the complex. The word was that the fire had been meant as a warning to the manager that there would be consequences if he continued to thwart the gang's drug enterprises. The deaths that resulted were unintentional.

It was nothing more than street talk until lab analysis of samples of the charred rubble from the burned-out trash bin came back from the state fire lab in Sacramento. Gas chromatography testing found at least two ILRs—ignitable liquid residues—in all batches of samples collected from the trash bin at the fire scene. The accelerants were listed in the report as petroleum and something called Varsol. The report concluded that there was no reasonable explanation for the presence of these chemicals in large quantities in the trash bin, and the case became an arson investigation.

Bosch looked over at Soto, who was typing something on her computer.

"You're online there, right?"

"Yes, what do you need?"

"Can you Google something? It lists Varsol here as one of the ILRs. What is—"

"It's a high-grade paint thinner. Expensive. It's used a lot in machine shops and auto-repair shops to clean engine parts."

Bosch just looked at her, impressed by her knowledge.

"I Googled it before when I first started reading the reports," she said. "Once they identified the accelerants, it helped set the path of the investigation. Because Varsol is expensive, they figured it was something handy to the arsonist rather than something he went out specifically to buy. So they figured it had to be someone who worked at a place where this stuff was on hand. The arsonist used the waste mix that came from cleaning oily machine parts—Varsol and grease. He probably put it in a container, lit it, and dropped it down the trash chute."

"Molotov cocktail."

"Right."

"Wouldn't that have made an explosion? A sound . . . people would have heard?"

He realized he was talking about her—as a child—being among those people.

"That's one of the things I remember most, being asked that. But the trash room was at basement level and down the hall from the children's room. And we were loud, you know? Ten kids in a confined space like that. I never heard anything. I wish I had."

Bosch nodded. He wondered if Soto somehow felt guilty over not having heard the firebomb explode when she was seven years old and playing with her friends. It wasn't her fault but he knew he could never convince someone who carried something like that inside for twenty years.

He went back to reading the reports.

"Let me know when you get to the tampon affidavit," Soto said.

Bosch looked up at her, thinking he had misheard her.

"What?"

"The tampon affidavit. It's a hoot."

He nodded and went back to reading the investigative chronology. After the ILRs were confirmed, the LAPD's Criminal Conspiracy Section was called in to investigate the case along with the fire department, but the investigation had lost momentum in the intervening weeks.

The investigators focused on the information coming in from the streets that pointed toward the fire being a gang scare tactic that went wildly beyond what it was planned to do. The apartment complex's manager was a key witness in this investigation and he provided information about the ongoing threats from the Pico-Union gang. The CCS sought and received a wide-ranging search warrant that was served on the homes and workplaces of twenty-nine members of the gang four weeks after the deadly fire. Before dawn a task force composed of CCS investigators and officers from the Gang Intelligence Unit hit the locations simultaneously, the search resulting in the seizure of drugs, weapons, and potential evidence in the arson case as well as the arrest of twenty-two of the targeted gang members on charges related to the seized drugs and weapons.

Reading a copy of the document returned to court after the search warrant was served, Bosch saw that very little had been seized that directly related to the arson. The only thing that came close was a gallon container of Varsol from an auto-repair shop where one of the gang members, an apprentice mechanic named Victor Chapa, was employed. Everything else listed on the warrant return was window dressing—drugs and guns that looked good spread out on a table for the media to photograph but that amounted to nothing in terms of evidence in the Bonnie Brae case.

Still, the seizures and arrests were enough to put the squeeze on Pico-Union La Raza. Most of the gang members had records and were facing prison or jail time if they were convicted on even the minimal charges. It gave Jack Harris and his team powerful leverage with which to squeeze out cooperation and turn gang brother against gang brother.

The man at the center of the squeeze play was Victor Chapa. Of everybody caught in the net, he was the one with direct access to the accelerant found in the ashes of the fire. Though the manager of the Bonnie Brae complex could not identify him as one of the gang members who threatened him, and Chapa provided an airtight alibi, he was still seen as the man who most likely obtained the fuel and probably built the firebomb. This latter assumption was based on the fact that though he did not live with a woman, a box of tampons was found in a bathroom cabinet in his apartment during the court-ordered search. The tampon was known to the CCS arson experts to be used often as the wick attached to a Molotov cocktail.

Chapa was arrested during the search of his apartment for possession of cocaine. This was based on residue in a pipe fashioned out of a piece of a car antenna found in a living-room ashtray in an apartment shared by four men. It was a bullshit case that would never go the distance but it was enough to hold and sweat him for forty-eight hours. He was questioned at length and then booked in a cell where an undercover officer was posing as another custody. Aside from providing the details of his alibi, Chapa spoke neither to his interrogators nor to his cellmate. He gave up nothing. He was twenty-eight years old at the time and a long-term member of Pico-Union. He had also been to state prison on a stolen property bust. He stood tall and was released on a bond after his arraignment—a hearing at which his attorney also produced an affidavit from a former girlfriend stating under oath that she had left the box of tampons found in Chapa's apartment.

"The old tampon defense," Bosch said.

"Works every time," Soto said.

Bosch looked over at her computer screen and saw a map.

"What's that?"

"I found El Chihuahua. Tulsa has an area called Little Mexico. It's there."

"Good. We'll check it out tonight."

"Doesn't look like the kind of place you're going to fit in, Harry."

"Yeah, we'll see."

He went back to reading. According to the investigative chronology, none of the gangbangers brought in during the dawn raid copped to any knowledge of the Bonnie Brae fire. All denied it, all claimed to be insulted that the gang would be suspected of having anything to do with the deaths of nine people, most of them children, and all of them from La Raza—the gang's home turf.

In that sense, the bust itself was a bust and that ratcheted up the pressure on Harris and his team. It was the case of the year and the press was all over it—the Department's Media Affairs Office was demanding daily updates on the investigation. The pressure pushed Harris into a play that backfired fatally. He chose to continue to squeeze Chapa by strategically putting the word out through the snitch network on the streets in Pico-Union that the police raid had produced a cooperating witness who would soon be taken before a grand jury.

The idea was that Chapa would feel the pressure and come in. He would have no choice but to grab the lifeline the police were throwing him and cooperate by admitting his part in procuring the firebomb and revealing the name of the man who dropped it down the trash chute.

Chapa was placed under surveillance as a protective measure and Harris waited for results as the pressure came down on the mechanic.

He didn't have to wait long. On the second day of the surveillance—once all of Pico-Union had been properly seeded with the story about a cooperating witness—Harris and company saw their squeeze play fall apart with what were most likely deadly consequences for Chapa.

The team was set up on the 6th Street auto-repair shop where Chapa worked as an apprentice mechanic. All customers and cars going in and out of the three-bay garage were watched from a rooftop vantage point. Ground teams stood by around the corner, ready to trail Chapa when he left work for the day.

But Chapa never left work. When the shop closed and the garage doors came down, Chapa was not among the employees leaving. Citing a potential threat to life, the police broke into the shop without a warrant and found no sign of Chapa. An internal investigation concluded that the CCS ploy and surveillance became known to Chapa and members of his gang. He was either forcibly or voluntarily spirited out of the shop in the trunk of a customer's car that was picked up after repair work had been completed that day. Chapa was never seen again, despite a standing warrant for his arrest for failure to show for a court hearing relating to his drug charge.

With Chapa gone and Harris and his team under internal investigation for the handling of the suspect, the momentum of the investigation lagged. The task force was disbanded and the case was moved through a series of CCS detectives over the years. Eventually it became reactive rather than proactive. Every time a member of Pico-Union La Raza was arrested for any reason, he was questioned about the Bonnie Brae fire by the current CCS detective handling the case. These efforts proved futile and the case eventually grew cold.

The back of the binder Bosch was reviewing contained a large folded chart that delineated the hierarchy of the Pico-Union La Raza circa 1993. Its edges cracked and tore in places as it was unfolded for the first time in years. Soto leaned over to look at it with Bosch.

"You look at this before?" Bosch asked.

"No, I never got to it," she said.

The diagram showed the names and photos of the gang's shot callers. Most of the photos were mug shots from prior arrests. The chart also noted whether each man was currently incarcerated in 1993 and what his area of responsibility to the gang was, whether it be in drug sales, transportation, production, weapons, muscle, and so on.

"This might be a place to start," Bosch said.

"How so?" Soto asked.

"We run these names. Some will be dead but some of them will be in prison, I'm betting. We could use that. Go see them, offer them daylight. Somebody might flip. If somebody in that gang did this, then somebody's still gotta know. We hit the right guy looking for a way out of the pen, we might get lucky."

"I wonder why Whittaker and Dubose didn't do that."

"Because they're lazy. If a case has no science, they move on to the next one. No need to leave the office."

Bosch started to carefully fold the chart back up without further damage.

"Don't be like that," he continued. "You want to be a good detective, go out and knock on doors."

"I will, Harry," Soto said. "I promise."

The pilot announced that they were beginning the descent into Dallas. Bosch decided he'd put the binders aside and rest his eyes. He still had much to look through, including the envelopes containing all the newspaper reporting on the case. All of that would have to wait until he next had time for the Bonnie Brae case.

"What about Chapa?" he asked. "You think dead or alive?"

"Definitely dead," Soto said. "Or else he would've turned up somewhere by now. He's probably buried somewhere in the desert."

Bosch just nodded. He thought she was probably right. Chapa didn't disappear from that garage of his own volition. There was no loyalty in a gang once the scent of informant blood was in the water.

The plane banked toward Dallas and Bosch changed the subject.

"You like barbecue?" he asked.

"I guess," Soto said. "Sometimes."

It wasn't an enthusiastic response. He just nodded.

"Why?" she asked.

"There's a place in the DFW terminal called Cousin's," he said. "It's good stuff. I think I'll hit it before the next flight."

"I think I'll just meet you at the gate. That okay?"

"Sure. Did you check the bible before we split? Anything on Tulsa?"

He was talking about a journal kept in the unit in which detectives contributed reports on cities they had visited on cases, noting good places to eat and stay that were within the Department's travel per diem. It also contained tips in regard to dealing with local law enforcement and judiciary. The unit had been operating for nearly ten years and there was no state in the union that had not been covered. The bible was thick with travel advice and there was even talk about trying to get it published as a fund-raiser. They were calling it *Blue Plate Special: A Cop's Guide to Digs, Dives, and Donuts.*

"I did," Soto said, as she flipped open a notebook. "Breakfast at a place called Jimmy's Egg, dinner at Mahogany—but that sounds to me like a strip bar. Another place called Brownie's has good pies."

Bosch smiled.

"Pies—that had to've been put in by Rick Jackson before he retired. He was always a pie man."

"You got that right. It was Jackson."

"Anything in there about the PD?"

"Yeah, Jackson listed a guy he worked with at Tulsa PD. Ricky Childers. He's a night-shift supe in the D bureau—at least he was two years ago. Jackson wrote *good people.*"

"Okay, then we go to him."

15

It was part of the Open-Unsolved Unit's travel protocol for detectives to check in with the locals and explain what they were in town for and where they planned to go. Usually it was just a simple courtesy and the Los Angeles detectives were allowed to go about their work. Often the locals preferred or required that one of their own tag along. And sometimes the visitors from L.A. needed local help finding someone or facilitating an arrest. As Bosch had explained to Soto, he had learned from experience that calling ahead about his impending arrival could lead to problems.

Sometimes locals would jump the gun and pre-scout the targets, which inadvertently tipped or spooked them. There'd also been cases where the locals had simply gone out and grabbed the suspect before Bosch got there, thereby robbing him of the ability to question the suspect before he was officially arrested and he lawyered up. There was also always the long-shot possibility that the target that Bosch was coming for was actually associated with the officer on the other end of the phone line. Bosch once called a detective in St. Louis in preparation for a trip there to make an arrest for murder. Little did he know that he was talking to a man who happened to be related by marriage to the person Bosch was coming to arrest. Bosch didn't learn of this connection until after he got there and found that the suspect had fled the night before.

"Never again after that," Bosch told Soto. "Now I always go in cold."

They got to the downtown headquarters of the Tulsa Police Department shortly before 8 p.m. They had first checked into a nearby hotel because it was unclear what the night ahead would bring and Bosch didn't want to lose the reservation should they not get to the hotel until after midnight.

A uniformed officer at the front desk seemed unimpressed by their LAPD badges but agreed to call upstairs to the detective bureau and ask if Detective Childers was available.

They were in luck. Childers was in and he told the officer to send Bosch and Soto up.

They took the elevator the one flight up, and on the second floor in front of the entrance to the detective bureau was another counter. Nobody was there and they waited a minute until a man came through the door behind the counter.

"How's Rick Jackson?" he said.

"Just retired," Bosch said. "And wherever he's at, he's probably golfing."

"I hope so."

The detective reached his hand across the counter.

"Ricky Childers. They put me in charge of this place at night."

They shook hands all around and Bosch handed Childers his badge rather than just flash it as he had done downstairs. Soto did the same. It was a show of respect.

"Did you guys call ahead?" Childers asked. "The captain didn't leave me anything on it."

"No, we just showed up," Bosch said. "This morning we caught a line on a guy we need to talk to and jumped on a plane. We didn't get the chance to call ahead."

Childers nodded but Bosch wasn't sure he believed the story. Childers looked like a capable and experienced man. He was mid-forties and in good shape. He had a drawl and a long mustache that drooped down the sides of his mouth. It all gave him the aura of a gunslinger from the Old West, which Bosch guessed he was well aware of and fostered. He wore no jacket and carried his weapon in a shoulder harness. That helped paint that picture, too.

"Who are we talking about here?" he asked.

"A witness on a case we're working," Bosch said. "A murder case. We need to talk to him again because we've come to believe he might not have told us everything he knew."

"Holding back on you, huh?" Childers said. "That ain't good. This fellow have a name?"

"Angel Ojeda," Soto said. "He's thirty-nine and we think he's been out here nine or ten years."

She handed Childers a sheet with a copy of Ojeda's last California driver's license.

"Nine or ten years?" Childers said. "Then you're working a cold case, huh?"

"Something like that," Bosch said. "The line we have on this guy is that he came out here to work at a bar called El Chihuahua. You know of the place?"

"Oh, sure, we know of it. On Garnet in East Tulsa. That's Little Mexico."

"What kind of place is it?"

"It's a dump with a pool table. Patrol goes in there a few times a week to break things up. You said this guy works there?"

"That info is almost ten years old. It's just a starting point."

"I'll take you out there if you want. But let's go on back to the squad first and see if we have anything on this Mr. Ojeda. Am I saying that right, Detective Soto? The J like an H?"

"You got it right," Soto said.

Childers pointed toward a half door at the end of the counter and waved them around. Working cold cases had brought Bosch into detective bureaus all over the country. There was a sameness to them all. The Tulsa squad room could have been in Seattle or Baltimore or Tampa. Cluttered desks, walls of file cabinets, wanted posters on every wall and door. The room was largely deserted because of the hour. Bosch saw a uniformed cop at one desk and a detective at another. Childers led them to his own cubicle.

"Grab a chair," he said.

Bosch and Soto pulled chairs away from empty desks and rolled them over. They all sat and Childers turned off a clock radio on his desk that was quietly playing country music. It sounded like Hank Williams Jr.

"Let's see what we got on this fellow," Childers said.

Looking at the sheet with the driver's license, he typed information into his desktop computer. Bosch assumed he was searching an internal data bank that would tell him if Ojeda had ever intersected in some way with the Tulsa police. Soto had already checked the national computers before they'd left L.A. and there were no hits.

Childers hit the enter button and held his hands up like he had just performed a magic trick. A few seconds later three words appeared at the top of the screen.

No Match Found

"Dammit," Childers said. "If he's been working at the Chihuahua, he would've come up as a witness, victim, reporting party, something. You sure your info is good?"

"It was good—about ten years ago," Bosch said. "Maybe he changed his name. What comes up if you just plug in El Chihuahua."

"You got all night?"

Childers typed the name of the bar in and this time the screen said there were 972 matches.

"And this thing only goes back seven years," he said. "We were on paper before that. You two want to sit here and look through all this? I'll let you have at it."

Bosch thought for a moment about what would be the best use of their time and how they could narrow the focus of the computer search. Soto beat him to it.

"I say we just go scope it," she said. "See if he's there. That's why we came."

"Sounds like a plan to me," Childers said.

Bosch nodded.

Childers drove. Little Mexico was a twenty-minute drive east from downtown. It was dark but the streets were well lighted and Bosch didn't see what he expected. The streets were wide with grassy medians. There were houses and churches and businesses with space around them. There were closed businesses, too. He saw a Tulsa patrol car parked at an out-of-business gas station. He had to look long and hard before he saw any graffiti.

"So," he said. "This is your barrio."

"This is it," Childers said.

Bosch was in the backseat, having given Soto the front. This would allow him to sit next to Ojeda should they find him and take him back to the PD for questioning.

Childers first made a slow pass by the El Chihuahua. It looked to Bosch like it had once been a Pizza Hut. It still had the red roof, but the windows were painted over, and there were a variety of hand-painted plywood signs affixed to the facade advertising *cervezas, chicharones,* and *desportes.* A lighted sign on a pole announced the name of the bar and depicted a cartoon of the dog breed named for the Mexican state of Chihuahua, its teeth bared for a fight and its front paws up and clad in boxing gloves.

It was near ten o'clock and the parking lot was full. Several men were milling about outside the doors on either side of the building, holding bottles and smoking.

"That's a violation right there," Childers said. "Open-container law—they can't be drinking outside."

"Good," Bosch said. "We can use that."

Childers pulled to the side of the road once they passed. He looked in the rearview at Bosch because he knew Harry called the shots in the partnership with Soto.

"What's the plan?" he asked.

Bosch thought for a moment.

"We passed a Shamu back there in the old gas station," he said. "Can we bring him in on this?"

"Shamu?" Childers asked.

"The black-and-white. Looked like the guy was writing reports."

"Shamu—like the whale. I like that. Yeah, I can get him over here."

"Okay, we get him. We all go in and look around. If we see our guy, we have the uniform ask him to step outside because we have a problem with the public drinking. If that works out, we get him in the car and Lucy and I take it from there. We don't mention L.A. and we use your badges."

Childers nodded.

"Sounds good."

He reached for the police radio between the seats and went through dispatch to instruct the nearby patrol car to respond to their location. He then signed off and put the radio mike down.

"How rough's the crowd going to be?" Bosch asked.

"We should be all right," Childers said. "But there ain't going to be a lot of women in there. Detective Soto might give them . . . pause, if you know what I mean."

"I can handle it," Soto said. "I didn't come out here to wait in the car."

Her tone invited no debate.

"Fine by me," Childers said.

They waited ten minutes for the patrol car to show. Childers flashed his lights as it was approaching on Garnet and the car crossed the oncoming traffic lane to pull up driver's-side window to driver's-side window. It was a one-man patrol, typical of cash-strapped municipalities. Childers knew the officer but didn't bother to introduce Bosch and Soto other than to explain they were from Los Angeles. He relayed Bosch's plan and the officer said he was good to go.

Childers turned the car around and they followed the patrol car to the bar. There were no parking spaces available in the lot. They drove down one side and around the back and then down the other side, stopping near the door where a group of men were standing, drinking and smoking. Most of them had probably been hassled before for drinking outside. Upon seeing the patrol car, they jostled to get back indoors.

Everybody got out of the cars and headed toward the door. Bosch heard the pulsing music coming from the bar. He moved to Soto's left side. It was a routine way for them to approach a door where it was unknown what would be behind it. He was left-handed and she was right-handed. It was the safest way to approach.

The uniformed officer was at least six-three and barrel-chested. His girth was accentuated by the bullet-proof vest under his uniform. He entered the bar first and started clearing a path through the crowd. Soto drew eyes, as expected, which worked to Bosch's advantage. He swiveled his focus and took in the faces, looking for one that approximated the ten-year-old photo of Angel Ojeda's driver's license from California.

He got lucky. Almost immediately he spotted a man behind the bar on the right side of the room who looked like Ojeda. He appeared to be one of three bartenders, but he wasn't taking orders or opening bottles of beer. He was leaning against a back counter next to the cash register and watching the crowded barroom. Soon his eyes came to Bosch and registered the white face in a sea of brown faces. Bosch knew in that instant that he had probably made Bosch as a cop. But he doubted Ojeda—if it was Ojeda—would have made him as a cop from L.A.

By now Bosch and Soto were not walking next to each other. The pathway through the crowd was too thin and they were moving in single file. Soto was much shorter than Bosch and her view was totally impeded by the crowd. Electronic dance music with a Latin beat blared from speakers. There were flat screens high on the walls and over the bar, showing soccer and boxing. The unmistakable stink of marijuana was in the air.

Bosch leaned forward and spoke loudly over Soto's shoulder and into her ear.

"He's here. Behind the bar. Tell Childers."

The message was sent up the line, and by the time the small troop made it up to the side of the bar, the patrol officer had his instructions. He signaled the man by the cash register over and told him he needed to step outside. The man hesitated, gesturing to the crowd as if to say he had to stay to take care of business. The big patrol cop leaned farther over the bar and said something that was convincing. The man raised the fold-over countertop and came out from behind the bar. He made some sort of hand signal to one of the bartenders he'd left behind and headed toward the nearest door. The patrol officer redirected him to the door that Bosch and company had come in through and they crossed the barroom again and exited.

Outside the bar, the man Bosch had zeroed in on immediately went on the offensive, directing his protest at the uniformed officer even though he should have known that the suits are always in charge.

"Why you hassling me, man? I have a business here."

"Sir, calm down," the uniform said. "We have a problem we need to—"

"What problem? There is no problem."

Bosch was sure it was Ojeda and was pleased that he obviously spoke English.

"Kevin, let me speak to the man," Childers said.

The officer stepped back and Childers moved in, getting right in the barman's face.

"What's your name, sir?"

"Why? Why do I give you my name?"

"Because we have a big problem here, sir, and if you don't start cooperating, it's going to get bigger. Now, what is your name?"

"Francisco Bernal. Okay?"

"You got an ID on you, Francisco Bernal? A driver's license?"

"I don't drive. I live behind the bar."

"Good for you. A green card, then? A passport?"

The man looked at Soto with an expression of disgust that she would be part of this shakedown. He pulled his wallet and from the billfold pulled a folded piece of paper. He handed it to Childers, who opened the paper and looked at it quickly before handing it to Bosch. He then stepped aside so Bosch could take things from there.

Bosch looked at the document and the patrol officer helped by holding his flashlight on it. It was a photocopy of a Permanent Resident Card identifying the man as Francisco Bernal. Technically, every bearer of a green card was required to carry it at all times. But the reality was that a Permanent Resident Card was precious and difficult to replace if lost or stolen. Most people carried photocopies and locked the originals away. These copies were usually accepted during casual police stops. But Bosch was also aware that it was easier to make a phony photocopy than a counterfeit green card.

As Bosch studied the document, a few bar patrons stepped outside to see what was going on. Childers aggressively moved toward them, pointing at the door and ordering them back inside. They complied quickly.

Bosch looked up from the document and eyed the man he still believed was Angel Ojeda.

"You know it's a misdemeanor to not carry the real thing, right?"

The man shook his head in frustration.

"This is bullshit," he said.

Bosch moved up close to him and held out a folded piece of paper that *he* had been carrying.

"Is this bullshit?" he asked.

The man grabbed the paper from Bosch's hand and unfolded it. It was the copy of the California driver's license with his old picture on it. Bosch saw a flash of recognition in the barman's eyes. It confirmed he was Ojeda.

"You just lied to a police officer," he said. "You have what I believe is a false identification and immigration document. Do you know what kind of trouble you're in?"

Bosch took a step back and nodded to the patrol officer.

"Hook him up, Kevin," he said.

The patrolman turned off his flashlight and went to work.

16

Just as every squad room looked the same to Bosch, so too did the interrogation rooms: Always stark, brightly lit cubes designed to instill hopelessness in those who waited to be questioned. From hopelessness comes compromise and cooperation. They had let Ojeda cook for close to an hour before Bosch entered the room. The plan was for Bosch to take the first shot, and if that didn't work, then Soto would replace him and work the witness from a different angle. She would be watching Bosch's effort on video in another room.

Ojeda was sitting at a small table. Seeing him in the cold light of the room, Bosch saw that he was a handsome man with a full head of jet-black hair, smooth skin, and a trim build. There was a weariness or sadness in his dark eyes. As Bosch pulled out the chair opposite him, he tossed Ojeda's photocopy of a supposed green card on the table.

"What do you want me to call you, Angel or Francisco?" he asked.

"I want you to call me a lawyer," Ojeda said. "I know my rights here."

Bosch nodded.

"You do have the right to a lawyer. But you know what happens once you bring in a lawyer? You get booked into the jail and we slap an immigration hold on you and there is no bail in the world for that."

A pained expression moved across Ojeda's face.

"That's right," Bosch said. "We checked with Immigration and we know your printout there is bullshit. You can wipe your ass with it because that's about all it's worth."

Most of this was a bluff. The chances of getting an Immigration confirmation on a Friday near midnight in Tulsa were next to nil. But Bosch was confident Ojeda didn't have a valid green card under the name Francisco Bernal. A legit card would have entailed a fingerprint check by Immigration, which would have produced his real name.

"So what happens is that after you've been in jail for about a month, you finally get a hearing before a judge," he continued. "But there's not really much you can do to help yourself when you have counterfeit papers. No defense for that, my friend. So you get shipped back to Chihuahua."

He let that sink in for a moment before continuing.

"So I gotta ask, is that really how you want to play this? If it is, just nod your head and I'll take you to the jail and I'll even give you a quarter to call that lawyer who can't help you."

Ojeda folded his arms. They had removed the handcuffs before placing him in the room. It was a little hint that they wanted something from him. That there might be a negotiation. But it had obviously been too subtle, since he had asked for a lawyer right off the top.

"Only I can help you," Bosch said.

Now Ojeda was beginning to see the play.

"What do you want?" he asked.

Bosch reached down and pulled his badge off his belt. He then put it down on the table so Ojeda could read it. Arms still folded, he leaned forward and did so.

"L.A.? Why are you here?"

"You know why, Angel."

"No, I don't. I haven't been in L.A. in—"

"Orlando Merced is dead."

Ojeda looked up at him. He didn't know, hadn't heard.

"He died three days ago and he died because of that bullet that was in his spine. The bullet that was meant for you."

Ojeda sat back up straight and stared at Bosch.

"Ten years ago you lied to us, Angel. You lied by omission. You know what that is? It's when you don't tell the whole truth, when you don't tell us everything you know."

"I didn't know anything."

"Yes, you did. You knew it all. You didn't tell us and—"

"No!"

"—that's obstruction of justice. But that was back then. Now it's a murder, and if you're not helping us, then you're helping the murderer, and that's a whole different thing. That's what they call *accessory after the fact*. Accessory to murder. And that means they don't send you back to Chihuahua until after you do your time in a California prison."

"No, this is crazy."

"Who took that shot at you, Angel? Who made you run to Oklahoma and change your name?"

Ojeda shook his head as if he were trying not to let Bosch's words get in his ears.

"Nobody made me do anything. You have this wrong. I changed my name because my uncle owned the bar and he wanted me to come out and act like his son. So I took his name and that's all."

Bosch reached across the table and took his badge back. He clipped it on his belt. It was a move that gave him time to think about what direction to go. He thought about the name from the registry from the Mariachi Hotel and knew he could buy a little time with it.

"Who is Rodolfo Martin?" he asked.

Ojeda shook his head again and looked confused.

"I don't know. I never heard this name."

"He was in the hotel across the plaza. He took the shot and you saw him. We've got it on video, Angel. That's why you ran. You saw the man with the gun and you saw he was aiming at you. Merced took that bullet for you!"

"No. I didn't see anybody. I—"

"*Who is Rodolfo Martin?*"

"*I don't know!*"

Bosch calmed himself and proceeded in an even tone.

"You need to start telling me the whole story or I can't help you. Tell me what happened."

For the first time, Ojeda nodded instead of shaking his head. Bosch knew then it was going to work. He was going to open up. He waited and finally Ojeda spoke with his eyes down on the table.

"When I was a musician I used to get women. Nice women. I get women now at the bar, but not the same kind."

It wasn't what Bosch expected to hear but he nodded.

He could see it. Ojeda was a strikingly handsome guy and a musician—back then at least. Bosch's daughter had recently told him about a study she had come across on the Internet that reported that in a blind street study, women were more likely to give their phone number to a man who approached them carrying a musical instrument case than to a man with a briefcase.

"Okay."

"And then I got with the wrong woman and all of this happened."

Bosch had been expecting it to be about drugs. Not a woman.

"Okay, tell me about the woman. Who was she? Where did you meet her?"

Ojeda scratched the back of his neck as he spoke.

"We had a gig. It was at a big house. It was like a castle on the mountain and there was a big dinner for someone special with many people. I met her there. At the end when we were packing our instruments, I went outside for a smoke, you know? She was there and we smoked. She gave me a phone number and told me I should call her."

"And you did?"

"She was beautiful. I called her."

"She was married?"

Ojeda nodded.

"She was married to the man who had the house. Very powerful man. Very rich. People said he was the concrete king. It was their house."

"She's married to this king with a castle but she wants you to call her."

Bosch didn't ask it as a question, but succinctly

summarizing Ojeda's story underlined the seeming absurdity of it.

"She told me—this was later—she said she was lonely but couldn't leave because he was dangerous. Very powerful and he had all the money. He made her sign a paper for it."

"A prenup. When exactly was this gig where you met her?"

"I don't know. I don't remember."

"How long before the shooting?"

"I'm not sure. But, yes, before. Obvious."

"Were you with the new band? Los Reyes Jalisco?"

"Yes, with them."

"Okay, so six months before the shooting? A month?"

"Like three months. In there."

"And you're saying you started an affair with this woman?"

Ojeda nodded.

"How long did it last?"

"Uh, many weeks."

"And the husband found out?"

Another nod.

"He came to me at my place and he threatened. He say he'd kill me if I didn't stop. You know, with his wife."

"Did you stop?"

Ojeda averted his eyes and then shook his head.

"No. I loved her very much."

The last bit sounded phony, as if part of an excuse system Ojeda had put together and kept fueled for ten years. It was about love, he told himself, not about a carnal need, not about every man's desire to take something off the top shelf. His desire ultimately destroyed a man's life. There had to be a valid reason.

"What about her? Did he tell her to stop with you?"

"He did but we did not stop."

Ojeda bowed his head as if acknowledging his decision had had fatal consequences.

"How long was it between when the husband warned you and when Merced was shot in the plaza?"

"Not long. A month?"

"Don't ask me. Tell me. How long?"

"A month."

Bosch leaned back and looked at Ojeda, trying to assess what he was hearing and the veracity of it all.

"What was her name?"

"Maria."

"Her whole name."

"Maria Broussard. But she was Mexican. Her name was Fuentes before she married her husband."

"And her husband's name?"

"Bruce."

"Bruce Broussard. You sure?"

"That's what she called him."

"Okay, and where was this big house where the party was? The castle."

"Up in the mountain. It was the whole side of the mountain."

"What was the address?"

"I don't know this. I was only there one time. And I was in the back of the van when we drove up."

"You met her the other times—when you got together—somewhere else?"

"She got hotels mostly. Once she came to my place."

"Which hotels?"

"Many hotels, all over the place. We met at Universal once. And that hotel downtown with the glass elevators on the outside of the building."

"Did you know from the start who she was? I mean, that she was married and that was her house?"

Ojeda hesitated.

"Don't lie," Bosch said. "You lie to me one time about any of this and we have a big problem."

"Yes, I knew," Ojeda said.

"Did the other men in the band know about you and her?"

"No, it was secret. Just her and me."

"How did her husband find out?"

"I don't know."

"She told him?"

"No. I think he followed her. Or he had someone follow her."

"Who is Rodolfo Martin?"

"I told you the truth. I don't know."

Bosch knew the name was most likely phony. You don't give your real name when you check into a hotel room to use it as a sniper's nest. He moved on.

"When was the last time you spoke to Maria Broussard?"

"Ten years. After the day Orlando got shot, I called her and told her I knew what happened. After that, I never saw her again."

"You told her that you knew the bullet that hit Merced was meant for you?"

"Yes."

"What did she say?"

"She said she didn't believe me. She said I was a liar. So that was it."

Bosch had taken no notes. He knew Soto was watching and writing, and that Childers had set up a camera.

He had one final question for the time being.

"You said the party where you met her was for a very special person. Who was that?"

"I don't remember his name. He was running for the mayor and at the dinner they charged people to raise the money."

Bosch sat still and looked at Ojeda. He now better understood the reasons he had disappeared and changed his name. Whether it was love or just a base human desire that he had followed, his choices had taken him into the dark waters where politics and murder swirl.

"Was it Armando Zeyas at the dinner? Was he the special man?"

Ojeda shook his head.

"No, not him."

"You sure? You remember what I said about lying?"

"I'm sure. It wasn't him. I know who he is. We played at his wedding. It was someone else who wanted to be mayor. He was a white guy."

One of Zeyas's opponents. The connection wasn't as direct but Bosch still felt dark waters rising.

Bosch found Soto sitting in the video room, where she had watched the Ojeda interview. She was alone. She had an open bag of potato chips from a machine. It reminded Bosch that he hadn't eaten since the brisket sandwich in Dallas.

"Where's Ricky?"

"He left about halfway through. Said he had his own stuff to do but would be around if we need him. Nice going in there."

Bosch picked up the bag and dug his hand into it for a potato chip. Soto didn't protest.

"Thanks."

"Ricky stayed until you got Ojeda to break. He said you were a 'true gator' and didn't need any help from him. What's that mean?"

Bosch shrugged.

"I don't know. He looks too young to have been in Vietnam."

"What did it mean in Vietnam? My grandfather was in Vietnam."

"Your grandfather? That makes me feel good."

She snatched the bag away from him, feigning annoyance that he had not given it back.

"Get your own—there are machines in the hallway. My grandfather was a lot older than you and a lifer in the Marines, believe it or not. What did it mean?"

"They had these CIA types they called 'gators'—short for interrogators. But they used what they called 'enhanced' methods and tools of interrogation."

"You mean like helicopters? Yeah, my grandfather told some stories."

Her memory threatened to trigger Bosch's own memories and he didn't need that now. He brought the discussion back on point.

"How much of that last part of the interview did you write down in your notes?"

"None of it yet."

"Good. Let's keep it off the record for now."

"Why?"

"Because it's a hot door and we have to be careful. You never open a door on a burning room. You approach cautiously and you—"

He stopped when he realized what he was saying.

"Sorry, that was not the right—"

"No, it's okay," she said. "I get it. We can keep it out of the report but what about the video? You don't want to erase it, do you?"

"No, we take the video but the captain won't look at the video. He'll just read our report and I don't want that last part to get to him yet."

"Got it."

"Good. What about that name? Bruce Broussard. You heard of him?"

She shook her head.

"It sort of rings a bell but I don't know from where," she said. "You?"

"No."

"Sounds like a big shot—the 'concrete king.' Do you believe Ojeda? About him and this woman with the rich husband falling in love."

Bosch thought for a moment and then nodded.

"So far I do. It could have been love from his side of it. The woman? I don't know yet. But we don't talk about this with anyone. Nothing in the reports, nothing to your friends, even if they have badges. We find out more about Maria Broussard first."

"What *will* you tell the captain? He'll want to know what he got for his money, sending us out here."

"I'll write the summaries and leave the name Broussard out for now. I know how to make it look like he got his money's worth. We need to try to get on a plane first thing in the morning."

"I'll check online. What about Ojeda?"

Bosch had to think about that for a moment. Letting Ojeda go could always result in his running again. It was a risk they'd have to take. Holding him on the phony ID and green card was a good way to turn a potential witness against the prosecution. He pointed to the equipment that lined one side of the room.

"We have the video of the interview. We take that and we write up a statement. One that includes the whole story. We get him to sign it and then we cut him loose. We keep it all out of the book for now. Just in case."

"Of what?"

"Of anything."

17

On Saturday morning Bosch and Soto caught the first flight to Dallas, where the airline had put them on standby lists for the next three flights to L.A. They had spent little more than twelve hours in Tulsa and less than a thousand dollars of city money in all. For what they had learned from Ojeda, Bosch thought that was a pretty good deal.

They got lucky in Dallas and made it onto the first flight. They then doubled down on the luck when the plane's captain, who had been routinely informed that two armed law enforcement officers would be on the flight, bumped them to the top of the upgrade list, and both snagged seats in first class—though in separate rows. Bosch felt embarrassed to have brought his to-go bag from Cousin's into such luxurious surroundings, where he was informed by the flight attendant that a complimentary lunch would be served. When he saw a soldier in camo coming down the aisle and making his way to the back, he handed the bag to him and told him it was the best chopped brisket sandwich he'd ever eat. The soldier took the bag.

"We'll see about that, sir," he said. "I'm from Memphis."

Bosch nodded. He had once spent a week in Memphis on a case, and a local detective took him to a different barbecue joint each day.

"Wet or dry?" he asked the soldier.

"Dry, sir."

"The Rendezvous?"

"You got it, sir."

Bosch nodded and the soldier moved on down the aisle. The woman behind him asked Bosch if he was giving anything else away and his face turned red.

Bosch was in the third row of the cabin and Soto the first. The pilot had made sure that they got aisle seats so they could act and move quickly in the event of a problem. This wasn't the first time Bosch had received such treatment. Most flight crews he had encountered welcomed an armed presence near the cockpit.

While waiting out a minor delay before departure, Bosch put in his earbuds and listened to music he had downloaded from a film about Frank Morgan, the saxophonist. It was a documentary and featured a tribute concert at San Quentin, where Morgan had been incarcerated for years before making his comeback in the jazz world. The tribute band was composed of players who had worked with or revered Morgan, and the dedication came out in the strong performance. He played the Dizzy Gillespie standard "The Champ" twice in a row, his favorite part being when Delfeayo Marsalis and Mark "the Preacher man" Gross traded fours on trombone and sax.

After the plane finally took off, Bosch stopped the music and got down to work. He and Soto had divided up the murder books and he still had the files from the Bonnie Brae fire investigation. Sitting next to a woman who looked like a young Hollywood executive, Bosch was concerned about opening the binders and possibly revealing photos of victims at the scene or after autopsy. So he slipped the thickest media envelope out of one of the binders and started reading through the newspaper coverage of the deadly fire.

The packet was filled with folded and yellowed clippings that were as fragile as the gang organizational chart he had opened the day before. The creases broke apart even as he carefully and slowly unfolded them. This happened often when he reviewed old case files, and his practice was to tape the separated pieces onto butcher paper—they kept a roll in the squad room—so that the disintegration could be curtailed and the stories refolded.

As would be expected, the Bonnie Brae fire drew a tremendous amount of coverage from the *Los Angeles Times*. The contents of the media packet were largely split in half, with the first half containing stories about the fire and immediate aftermath and the second being reports on the investigation that seemed to have been published at semiregular intervals—six months later, one year later, five years later, and ten years later. Apparently the editors at the newspaper either missed a chance at a twenty-years-later story or deemed it un-newsworthy. The last story in the packet was the tenth-anniversary story.

After determining what he had, Bosch started at the beginning. On day one, the *Times* was almost wholly dedicated to the fire. He unfolded an entire front page that had three photos and the start of three stories. The photo block contained two smaller photos depicting residents charging out of the smoky apartment building and two women embracing on the street, their faces streaked with soot and tears and wearing looks of utter anguish. The larger main image to the right of these and at center was of a firefighter emerging from the building and holding a young girl in his arms, her limbs hanging it seemed lifelessly. The firefighter had not waited to get out of the building before starting CPR measures. He was blowing air into her mouth as he was coming out of the building. Bosch read the caption below the photo block but it did not identify the firefighter or the girl and did not say whether she lived. He looked again closely at the photo and then two rows up the aisle, where he could barely see the top of Soto's head above the back of her seat. He wondered if she was the girl in the photo.

He had noticed that since he had started to work with her, there had been many small instances of luck turning his way. In the past forty-eight hours on this case alone he had felt lucky several times, from getting the cop-friendly Sherma Barthlett as the on-call judge for search warrants, to Ricky Childers's being there when they checked into the Tulsa PD, to getting first-class upgrades on the flight home. He felt in many ways that he was on a roll and it defied the law of averages, which held that you win some and you lose some. It had him contemplating the idea of luck and whether it was something random or possibly something that could follow certain people all their lives, including being the one to survive a deadly fire and a deadly firefight outside a liquor store. Perhaps Lucky Lucy was more than a nickname. And perhaps the luck she brought was contagious.

"Wow, that's what you call old news."

Bosch turned. The woman next to him was looking at

the yellowed and cracked front page he was holding. He smiled and nodded awkwardly.

"Yeah, I guess it is," he said.

"What are you doing?" she asked.

Bosch looked at her.

"Sorry," she said. "I'm just nosy. It looks interesting."

"I'm just checking out something that happened a long time ago."

"That fire."

She pointed to the photos on the newspaper front.

"Yeah," Bosch said. "But I can't really talk about it. It's a private matter."

"Can you tell me this?" the woman insisted. "Did that girl live?"

Bosch looked at the photo for a moment before answering.

"Yes, she did. She was lucky."

"I'll say."

Bosch nodded and the woman went back to reading a script. Bosch focused on the stories on the front page. There was the main story at the upper-right corner that contained the basics of what happened—at least as far as what was known on the day of the fire. There was a single-column sidebar below it with a headline:

Illegal
Day Care
Rampant

Bosch assumed that the purpose of the story was to show a causal relationship between the fire and the deaths in the building's basement day-care center.

Presumably a licensed facility would have had multiple exit routes in the event of a fire, and the children would have escaped, but the tone of the story seemed to imply that the children themselves had somehow brought on their own deaths by being involved in an illegal day-care center.

The third story was an investigation of the 210-unit apartment complex's health-and-safety inspection record, which was replete with violations over the past decade. The story also focused on the complex's owner-ship by a real-estate holding company that owned several other large complexes in the area, which also carried low rents and high incidences of health-and-safety-code violations. Written before the deadly fire was known to be arson, the story seemed intended to prepare the reader for an eventual conclusion that the blaze was started because some code was violated or ignored.

The stories jumped inside, where there were more sidebars and two pages of photographs from the scene. There was also a black-bordered box that listed the names of all the reporters who worked on the news-paper's coverage of the fire. Bosch counted twenty-two names and it made him miss the old *Los Angeles Times*. In 1993 it was big and strong, its editions fat with ads and stories produced by a staff of some of the best and brightest journalists in their field. Now the paper looked like somebody who had been through chemo—thin, un-steady, and knowing the inevitable could only be held off for so long.

It took Bosch almost an hour just to read the stories and study the photographs in the A section. Nothing he read gave him any ideas about proceeding any differently with the case. The only place where the *Times* coverage came close to what would eventually be the focus of the original investigation was an inside story that profiled the neighborhood and mentioned Pico-Union La Raza as the predominant gang. It quoted an unnamed police source calling Bonnie Brae Street a drive-through drug market where rock cocaine and black tar heroin from Mexico were plentiful.

Bosch noticed that Soto was getting up from her seat and holding her computer open. He quickly folded the newspaper and slipped it beneath the stack of other clips in case the photographs were something she didn't want to see.

Soto came back to his row, carrying her open laptop. She saw the stack of yellowed newspaper clippings.

"You're reading all of that stuff?" she asked.

"Yeah," he said. "You never know, sometimes you get an idea from it. You see a quote from somebody or something. I wrote down some names of people who were there that day—reporters and residents. Might be worth a phone call or something, see what they remember."

"Okay."

Bosch nodded to her computer.

"So what's up?"

She put her computer down on top of the news clippings so he could see the screen.

"I'm using the Wi-Fi and I think I found Broussard."

Bosch turned in his seat to block the possibly prying eyes of his seatmate and looked at the screen. He realized he was seeing a digital version of the *Los Angeles Times*. It was a story dated nine years before about the appointment of Charles "Brouss" Broussard to the

Parks and Recreation Commission by newly elected mayor Armando Zeyas. It was a short story because the commission that oversaw the city's parks was not a big news generator. The profile of Broussard described him as a local businessman who had been an important fund-raiser for local politicians for many years. The accompanying photo was a shot taken on the night of the mayor's election and it showed Zeyas with his arm around Broussard's shoulders. A smiling woman standing nearby was identified as Maria Broussard. She was much younger than her husband.

"Good work," Bosch said without looking up at Soto.

He tilted the computer screen back so he could see the photo better. He studied Broussard intently. He was a heavyset man in an expensive-looking suit. Maybe forty years old at the time of the photo. He had a full beard with an odd graying pattern that made it look as though bleach had leaked from the corners of his mouth and left a trail of white hair down to his jaw.

Soto leaned down so she did not have to talk loudly.

"But Ojeda said the fund-raiser where he met Maria was not for Zeyas," she said.

Bosch nodded. It was a discrepancy in the story.

"Either Ojeda lied or Broussard switched sides," he said. "We need to find out which one it is."

18

They had driven separately to LAX the day before because they didn't know the circumstances of their return and Soto lived south of the airport in Redondo Beach, while Bosch lived in the opposite direction, in the hills above the Cahuenga Pass.

They landed at 9:30, and as they walked toward the exit doors of Terminal 4, they discussed their schedule and agreed that they would meet at the office the next morning at eight and work half a day. This was perfect for Bosch because Sunday was his daughter's sacred day for catching up on sleep. If undisturbed, she would sleep till noon and then want breakfast. He would be able to get a solid four hours of work in on their cases before meeting up with Maddie.

They crossed the airport pickup lanes and entered the parking structure and then went their separate ways. Bosch felt excited. The short trip had been extremely profitable in terms of information gathered and case momentum. Even the plane ride home counted. Soto had identified their next investigative target, Charles Broussard.

As Bosch was driving down Century Boulevard after exiting the airport, he thought of something that he decided shouldn't wait—even until the next morning. He pulled his phone and called his daughter's line. She answered right away.

"What are you up to?" he asked.

"Just got up," she said.

"Have a plan for the day?"

"Homework."

"It's a beautiful day. You should be out having fun."

"You mean you're back already?"

"Just landed. But I might have to go in for a little bit. I'll be home before dinner."

"Dad, you said you'd be back on Sunday."

"I said I thought I would. What's wrong with getting home a day early?"

"I have a date tonight because I thought you wouldn't be here."

"You mean a date at the house?"

He failed to keep the concern out of his voice.

"No," she said quickly. "I meant, I said yes to this guy because I didn't think you'd be home. I'll call him up and say I changed my mind."

"No, look, don't do that. Go out. Have fun. Who is the guy? What's his name?"

"You don't know him. His name is Jonathan Pace and I know him from Explorers."

"He's not the sergeant in charge, is he?"

There had been a scandal once and he had warned her.

"No, Dad, gross! He's seventeen, just like me."

"But he knows your dad's a cop?"

It wasn't her first date but she had not had many. Bosch required her to inform all suitors that her father was a police detective who always carried a gun. It sent the proper message every time.

"Yes, he knows exactly who you are and what you do. He wants to be a detective, too."

"Really? Sounds like a keeper. When do you leave?"

"We're meeting at the Grove at seven to see a movie."

"By yourselves?"

"No, we're meeting other Explorers."

"Boys *and* girls?"

"Yes."

"Okay, I'll be home before you leave. And you know what?"

"What?"

"There's a bookstore in that place right next to the movie theaters. Why don't you kids check that out, too?"

"Dad."

They had reached a level where she could simply say *Dad* and Bosch would read it as synonymous with *Stop*. This was one of those times.

"Sorry, I thought books were fun."

"It's Saturday night. We're not going to sit in a bookstore, reading. We want to have some fun. We read books all week at school. I have to read for homework right now."

"Okay, got it. Is Jonathan Pace involved in the alcohol sting on Tuesday?"

"Yes, we all are."

"Okay. Maybe I'll meet him then."

"Dad, you already said you're not going to come! That would be so embarrassing that my father had to check on us like we're children."

"Okay, okay, message received. I won't be there if you don't want me there. Just be safe then and be safe tonight. I'll see you in a little while."

After hanging up, Bosch called directory assistance to get the number to the newsroom at the *Times*. The operator made the connection, and while he waited for the call to go through, he turned onto the circular entrance ramp to the 405 north. Depending on how this call went, he would either take the freeway up the Sepulveda Pass to Mulholland or jog east on the 10 toward downtown and the PAB.

The call was answered by someone who did not give a name but simply said, "Newsroom."

"Yes," Bosch said. "I'm looking for Virginia Skinner."

"She's off today. Can I take a message?"

"Can you *get* her a message? I don't have her number with me. I need to talk to her today and she'll want to talk to me."

There was a short pause and then an answer.

"I can try but I can't promise anything. What's the message?"

Bosch gave his first name only and his number, and the message was that Skinner needed to call him today or she would miss the story.

"That all?"

"That's it."

Bosch disconnected. Virginia Skinner was one of the few veteran reporters the *Times* had left in its downtown newsroom. Bosch knew her because twenty years earlier, when she had gotten the *Times* job after spending most of her twenties in journalism's minor leagues, she was placed on the police beat. She wanted nothing to do with covering cops and crime but it was the starter position and she was smart enough to know that the better she was at it, the faster she'd get promoted to the next slot.

She was right and she was good, and in two years she was on to the next beat, which was city hall. Covering local and state politics and government was what she wanted all along and where she had stayed to this day. And her name was perfect for the job, too. She specialized in political profiles that usually stripped candidates down to the bone and in many cases eviscerated their election chances.

But during those first two years, Bosch took a liking to her because of her accuracy and fairness. She had crossed his path on several stories and he spoke to her on and off the record, and never once did she burn him. In the following years, they had minimal contact, but there were always stories here and there where police and politics crossed. She would check in and he would give her what he knew and what he could say. Bosch certainly didn't like the idea of being any reporter's source, but at least he had never had cause to mistrust Virginia Skinner. He did have her phone number but it was hidden in his desk. He was not foolish enough to carry it in the contacts list on his phone. If his phone ever fell into the wrong hands and it was revealed that he had a direct connection to her, the ramifications in the Department could be career threatening. Command staff frowned upon media sympathizers—especially if the media was the *L.A. Times*.

As he drove, Bosch tried to recall the last time he had spoken to Skinner and what the story was. He couldn't remember. It had probably been two or three years before.

There was no callback by the time he got to the decision-making point on the freeway. He knew that because his daughter would be out during the evening, he could flip things around and go home now to spend some time with her, then go back down to the PAB to work at night. He struggled with this choice as he looked at the approaching eastbound lanes and then was saved by the phone. A call marked "private number" was coming in. He answered, putting the phone on speaker.

"Harry, it's Ginny Skinner. What's so important on a Saturday?"

"Thanks for calling. Let's start by saying all of this is off the record. You can't write anything about it."

"I don't know what it is, so it's hard for me to agree to that."

It was the typical catch-22 with all reporters. They wouldn't agree to hold something back until they knew what it was. But what if, upon knowing what the story was, they said they couldn't hold it back? Now Bosch had to carefully choose his words.

"Well, you know I work cold case homicides, right?"

"Right, and I also read my own newspaper. I know you are on the mariachi case."

Bosch frowned. He was hoping she would not know what case he was on.

"I have many cases working at once, Ginny. You know that."

"Well, cut to the chase, then, Harry. It's Saturday and a beautiful day outside. I'm turning fifty tomorrow and I want a last margarita before that happens. What do you want?"

"Really? You? Fifty?"

"Yes, really, and that's all I want to say about it. I shouldn't have even brought it up. What do you need?"

"Well, you guys write about campaign finance and all

of that, right? Do you keep all of those records from elections past?"

"Depends on how far back you want to go and which race. What are we talking about here?"

"I'd like to see donation lists for the mayoral elections going three back."

He thought that by spreading wide the net he was casting, it would be harder for her to figure out what his true target was.

"Ooh," she said. "That's a lot. We have all of this stuff computerized, but you're not asking to search for a needle in a haystack, you're asking for the whole haystack. You've got to tell me what you really want, Harry. Be specific."

Bosch considered ending the call and waiting until Monday to get the information he needed through proper channels. But his urgency to keep the case moving won out and he tried one more time to strike a deal.

"I can't be more specific without you agreeing it's off the record. For now. You'd obviously be first in if it comes to anything."

"And it is political? I cover politics, not crime."

Bosch ran into a slowdown across all eight lanes of the freeway as the traffic came to the 110 split. He thought maybe there was an event at the convention center. It was too early for a game or concert at Staples.

"It's both," he said.

"Politics and murder—that's always a good story," she said. "Okay, I give. We are off the record, on deep background. I do nothing with anything you give me until I get the high sign."

Deep background meant there would be no story until Bosch gave the okay. He was almost satisfied.

"You don't even tell your editor," he said. "You tell no one."

"I don't trust my editor," she said. "He'd tell everyone in the news meeting and act like it was his work. Agreed."

Bosch paused. It was the point of no return with a reporter. He felt he could trust Skinner, but the halls of the PAB were littered with the carcasses of cops who thought they could trust reporters.

He slowly merged onto the 110. His exit was less than a mile ahead but it might take him fifteen minutes to get there in the wall-to-wall traffic.

"Are you there, Harry?"

"Yes, I'm here. Okay, this is what I want. Do you know of a guy named Charles Broussard?"

"Of course. People call him Brouss, like the name Bruce. He's a money man. He owns a company that puts those concrete barriers on the freeways when there's construction, and there's always construction. What about him?"

"Do you personally know him?"

"No, but I may have talked to him once or twice for a quote or something. He was tight with Zeyas during that regime. I think he's on the outs at city hall now because he backed the wrong horse the last time around. So I get it now. Broussard was close to Zeyas, and Zeyas was close to this mariachi guy who got shot. I wrote about that guy during the first campaign. I was assigned to Zeyas, remember?"

"Look, don't jump to conclusions. Can you meet me

now? I want to know who Broussard gave money to in the past few campaigns. And I want to know about Broussard. Anything you might know."

"Meet you now? Can't we do this Monday?"

"If I wait till Monday, I don't need you, Ginny. I can get this stuff on my own then."

Now it was Skinner who paused.

"Come on," Bosch urged. "Do this and then I'll buy you a margarita for your last day as a forty-niner. They have to make a good margarita somewhere over there in the Pueblo."

"That's tempting," she finally said. "Okay, I'll meet you at the Spring Street entrance at one o'clock."

Bosch checked his watch. That was nearly two hours away.

"I'll be there," he said.

19

The *Times* was located directly across Spring Street from the PAB. The two buildings were so close that Harry once had a supervisor who closed the blinds on his office windows because he was certain there were *Times* reporters across the street watching him. Bosch parked in the underground garage at the PAB but didn't go up to the squad. Instead he decided to get in some exercise and walked down 1st Street toward Mariachi Plaza. He had no investigative intent in going there but it always felt good to him to return to crime scenes during an investigation. He called it listening to the scene. There were nuances and small details that could be picked up even years after the crime. Plus there was a sense of ghosts, some sort of presence of those who had been murdered. Bosch always felt it, whether anybody else did or didn't.

Downtown was perfectly warm compared to when he had stepped out of the terminal at LAX, which was located at the edge of the chilly Pacific. The walk down 1st Street and through Little Tokyo was pleasant as the sun warmed Bosch's shoulders. When he crossed the 1st Street bridge he noticed that someone had tied a clutch of flowers to one of the light poles at the center of the span. There was a cardboard heart that said "RIP Vanessa." For some reason Bosch pulled out his phone and took a photo of the sad little memorial for a woman, or more likely a girl, who had jumped to her death. The cameras that had been put up on the bridge obviously did not stop all jumpers.

He walked up to the rail and leaned over to look down. He wondered if Vanessa had regretted her decision during those last few seconds as she fell.

He checked his watch and moved on. A few blocks later he got to Mariachi Plaza. Because it was a Saturday, the small triangular public space was crowded with mariachis, locals, and food and flower vendors. He realized that the plaza would have been this active on the day Orlando Merced was shot. The shooter must have planned on that. There would be more camouflage, more panic, more people running in all directions on a Saturday. Had that been part of the plan?

He crossed 1st Street and started moving through the crowd. At least two of the bands were playing but it did not seem like a competition. It seemed as though the bands were warming up for the gigs that they hoped would follow in the afternoon and evening.

Bosch saw that the door of the bookstore was open and there was a crowd inside. He read the banner that hung next to the door.

LOS ANGELES IS LIKE YOUR BRAIN.
YOU ONLY EVER USE 20% OF IT.
BUT IMAGINE IF WE USED IT ALL.

Harry turned toward the Metro entrance because the walk over had taken longer than expected and he didn't want to be late for the meeting with Skinner. His plan was to take the Gold Line back across the bridge. He'd jump off at the Little Tokyo station and walk the rest of the way. It would save him fifteen minutes.

But as Bosch approached the escalator, a voice called to him from behind. He turned around and there was Lucy Soto.

"What are you doing here?" he asked.

"I was going to ask you the same thing," she said.

Bosch shrugged and made up a lie. He didn't want to tell Soto that he was going to talk to a reporter about Broussard. Not yet.

"I just wanted to see this place on a Saturday. You know, same day as the shooting. Wanted to get a feel for it. Listen to it."

"Same here."

Bosch nodded. He knew in that moment that she would be a good detective.

"Were you going down to the Metro?" she asked.

"Yes," he said. "I parked back at the PAB and walked over. The Metro will get me about halfway back."

"Don't tell me Harry Bosch carries a TAP card."

She was being sarcastic. It was a crack at him being old school and set in his ways. The Metro was new in the evolution of the city and it had been difficult for lifelong L.A. drivers to adapt to using it.

"Actually, I do," he said. "You never know when it will come in handy."

"How about I just give you a ride? I'm parked over there."

She pointed toward the line of vans belonging to the bands. Each one had the band's name and a phone number painted across the side panels. At the end of the line was a red two-seater with the top down.

"Sounds good. I think."

Her car was small and low to the ground. Bosch had to turn and slowly lower himself into the cockpit.

"I feel like I'm in a kayak or something," he said.

"Oh, relax," Soto said. "It's fun. I bet your daughter would like one of these."

"I wouldn't let her. You need a roll bar for it."

"Just sit tight and we'll be there in five minutes."

"No other way to sit in this thing."

She pulled away from the curb, slamming Bosch back into his seat and headrest. She made the light at Boyle and flew over the rise of the 1st Street bridge. Bosch felt himself about to smile but was able to contain it.

"So you never really said anything about Bonnie Brae," she yelled.

Bosch looked over at her. Her eyes were hidden behind sunglasses that had wind guards on the sides.

"That's because I'm not finished reviewing it," he called back. "I started with the clips on the plane today but have a lot more to read."

She nodded.

"Okay. Whenever you're ready."

They hit the light at Alameda and Bosch didn't have to yell once the car came to a stop.

"There's no guarantee that there will be anything there to work," he said. "I mentioned visiting some of these guys in prison to see if that's softened them up. But that's a long shot. They know that if even a whiff of them cooperating gets out, they could end up dead in the yard. It will be hard finding somebody willing to risk that."

"I know," she said, a hint of defeat in her voice.

"We'll see," he said.

They drove the rest of the way in silence and in two minutes she turned left on Spring and then over to the curb next to the PAB. She didn't realize she was dropping him closer to his intended destination—the *Times*—than she had thought. He gingerly pulled himself up and out of the car.

"Thanks for the ride. You going home now?"

She nodded and smiled.

"I'm going home."

"See you tomorrow, then."

"Yep. See you."

She took off and Bosch watched her until she made a turn a couple blocks down the street. He then crossed Spring to the sidewalk that ran alongside the Times Building.

There was an entrance at the corner of Spring and 2nd. Bosch walked in and saw an anteroom where Virginia Skinner was standing, typing on her phone. She looked different than Bosch remembered from the last time he'd encountered her in person at least two years before. It was the hair and the glasses. Both different, but both suited her better.

"Ginny."

She looked up and smiled.

"Harry."

"Sorry if I kept you waiting."

"No, not at all. You're right on time. I got so intrigued by your call that I drove in early to pull up some stuff and then came down here as soon as I was ready. You want to come up?"

"Sure."

But Bosch was a little nervous. In all his years of dealing with reporters from the *Times,* he had never been up to the newsroom. There was a deal in place allowing employees from the PAB, simply by showing their ID cards, to enter the Times Building and use the first-floor cafeteria. Bosch was a frequent user of that courtesy, since there were only snack machines in the PAB, but the newsroom was new and forbidding territory. Bosch was glad it was a Saturday and both the PAB and the newspaper building were understaffed. The fewer people to see him cross the gray line, the better.

The newsroom on the third floor was almost as vast as the squad room across the street. And just as empty. Skinner led Bosch to her cubicle, which was much like his. He looked around and saw the same sort of decorations on desks, the names written on seat backs, and the unkempt piles of paperwork and files.

"What?" Skinner asked.

"Nothing," Bosch said. "Just never been up here before."

"It's just a newsroom. And most of it's a ghost town. Pull that chair from that desk over here. No one works there anymore."

Her comments alluded to the state of the newspaper business as a whole and the *Times* specifically. Bosch had heard that nearly half of the newsroom was empty these days as the newspaper tried to adjust to falling circulation and the migration of readers to the Internet.

He brought the chair over and sat next to Skinner, who was already pulling up numbers on her computer screen.

"You said you were interested in the past three elections. Where do you want to start?"

"Let's go three back."

"That's what I thought and that's what I have up here. You are specifically interested in Charles Broussard, and you can see here that personally, corporately, and with in-kind donations, he was hedging his bets."

Bosch leaned toward the computer screen but what he was looking at didn't really make a lot of sense to him.

"How so?" he asked.

"He maxed out on two candidates," Skinner said. "Zeyas, who eventually won, and Robert Inglin, who was eliminated before the runoff."

Bosch knew the name Robert Inglin. He was a former city councilman and perennial candidate for local offices. He was from Woodland Hills and carried the vast backing of the Valley when he entered a race.

"What in-kind donations are we talking about?" he asked.

"To get that we would have to pull records on Monday," Skinner said. "But normally what that means is they sponsored an event that raised money for the candidate."

"Like a dinner."

"Exactly. Broussard provides the place, the staff, and the food, and all of that has to be reported as a donation. You can sort of see this in the numbers. Broussard made an in-kind donation here to Inglin on January twelfth in '04. You then look at other donors and you have scads of donations for two hundred fifty dollars each on the same date. It obviously was a dinner for Inglin, and it cost anybody who went two hundred fifty bucks a plate."

Bosch pulled out his notebook and wrote the date down. He believed it was the date that Los Reyes Jalisco played at a fund-raiser at the Broussard house and Angel Ojeda met Maria Broussard. If this could be confirmed, it would go a long way toward supporting Ojeda's veracity. This would be important if Bosch and Soto ever reached the point of going to the District Attorney's Office with the case to seek charges against someone.

"Okay," he said. "So when did Broussard give money to Zeyas?"

Skinner scrolled down the screen.

"He put his money on Zeyas after," she said. "First donation in May, right before the runoff."

She moved her finger across a line on the screen. Bosch leaned in to see and then wrote the date and the amount down in the notebook.

"That was the max?" he asked.

"Up until that point, yes," Skinner said. "The most he could do."

Bosch leaned back and looked at his notes. Between Broussard's going all in with Inglin in January and then all in with Zeyas in May, Orlando Merced was shot on April tenth. It made Bosch wonder about things. Was Broussard really hedging his bets and supporting two candidates equally, or had he changed allegiances from Inglin to Zeyas? And if so, why?

"What else, Harry?" Skinner asked.

"What happened in the next election?" he responded.

Skinner went to work on the computer and pulled up financial figures from the 2008 election. She typed in a search for Broussard's donations and then studied the results for a moment before speaking.

"He was with Zeyas again," she said. "Maxed out again."

"Did he hedge his bets?" Bosch asked.

"You mean donate to other candidates?"

Bosch nodded. She looked at the charts for a moment before drawing a conclusion.

"He contributed in many other races," she said. "Sometimes to two competing candidates. But when it came to Zeyas he never doubled down after that first run for mayor. He was exclusive to him."

"Okay," Bosch said. "Zeyas is now going for the governor's job. Has he started taking donations? Can you see if Broussard is still supporting him?"

"That would be under the state, so that will take a little more . . ."

She pulled up another screen of numbers and studied them.

"Yes," she finally said. "He's still a major funder—contributed to the Zeyas exploratory campaign for governor."

Bosch nodded and wrote a few notes down.

"Anything else?" Skinner asked.

"I think that's good," Bosch said. "Thanks for this."

"You owe me a margarita. But I'd trade it for your telling me what's going on."

Bosch was quiet a moment as he thought about how to answer. He had to give her something, because if he didn't, she might very well go off on her own, and that could be disastrous if she drew the notice of Charles Broussard.

"Tell you what," he finally said. "Let me have a day with what you've given me and then I'll come back to you. I don't want you going off and doing anything on your own. It could be dangerous."

Skinner held back a smile.

"Now you're really hooking me. You've got to tell me something, Harry. Pretty please?"

"Look, I really can't. You've been very helpful here and I owe you for that, but I need to check a few things out first. What are you doing tomorrow? I can—oh, never mind, it's your birthday. I forgot."

"Tomorrow I'm not doing anything. You think I want people to know I'm fifty? In this business it's an invitation to a pink slip. I shouldn't even have told you."

Bosch now held back a smile. He realized he was attracted to her. She was all business. He liked that about her.

"Tell you what," he said. "Let's have dinner tomorrow and we won't even mention it's your birthday. By then I think I can continue this conversation—as long as we're still off the record."

She looked at him suspiciously.

"The dinner, the birthday, everything off the record?"

"Yes, everything. But it's gotta be early. I have a daughter and she works till about eight-thirty. So let's say we get together at six-thirty or seven. Deal?"

She didn't hesitate.

"Deal."

20

Bosch took all the binders from the Bonnie Brae murder case home with him Saturday night. He decided that the strides being made on the Merced case required his full attention. No more jumping back and forth from case to case. He would finish the review of the deadly arson investigation and in the morning tell Lucy Soto his final thoughts on it before they moved on to Merced and the focus on Charles Broussard. With a clear direction now apparent, the Merced case demanded it.

Before getting down to work, he saw his daughter off on her date, telling her that he would have preferred to meet the young man she was rendezvousing with at the Grove shopping center. She countered that this was the way things were done these days and reminded him that it was not a one-on-one date but that several of the Explorers from the Hollywood Division were getting together for dinner and a movie. This mollified Bosch but he did not let her out the door without a hug and a promise of regular text updates—except during the movie, a science-fiction story starring Matthew McConaughey.

After she left, Bosch got down to business. He made a peanut-butter-and-jelly sandwich, stacked the Bonnie Brae murder books on the dining-room table, and put on a Ron Carter disc he hadn't listened to in a while. It was called *Dear Miles* and Bosch assumed that the 2007 recording was inspired by the bassist's time in the Miles Davis band of the 1960s. Bosch hadn't chosen it for the origin or the Davis standards it contained. He was looking for rhythm, and Carter's vibrant bass line leading the quartet would certainly bring it. He needed to get through the Bonnie Brae material on this night and then move on and back to the Merced case with an undeniable momentum. Ron Carter would help with that.

He picked up where he had left off. He pulled out the stack of newspaper articles, but this time, unfettered by the tight confines of an airline seat, he spread the stories he had read across the large rectangular tabletop in hope that the display of all the photos and headlines might shake something loose. An idea or maybe a detail of a photo he had missed or a word from a headline that would inspire an unseen connection.

He was still on the first day of coverage, reading the stories from inside the A section of the *Times*. The track "Seven Steps to Heaven" helped him pick up the pace and soon half his sandwich was gone and he had moved on to the first day's stories in the B section. These stories focused on the human element of the tragedy. There were short descriptions of the young victims who perished and a larger profile of Esther "Esi" Gonzalez, the day-care center teacher who died trying to protect the children from the smoke and flames. One photo dated a year before the fire showed the woman hugging a child in the day-care center. The accompanying story seemed to counter the front-page article that castigated the proliferation of unlicensed day-care centers in the city by describing this woman as a trusted caretaker of children who sacrificed herself in an attempt to save them. It was Bosch's thought that the reporters who had written the stories had not compared notes. One wrote about a tragic flaw in the system and one wrote about a hero who emerged from that system. He thought that maybe this was the newspaper's attempt to provide balanced coverage.

The story jumped to the next page, but Bosch could not find the clip in the remaining stack of crumbling newsprint. Then he flipped over the front page of the B section he had been reading and found the continuation on the back of it. It fit perfectly within the cutting.

He finished the story and felt a new urgency about solving the case. The loss of the children was the awful tragedy, to be sure. But it was Esi Gonzalez's full profile that brought home to Bosch the horror of the crime.

He flipped the clip over to study the photo of the woman again and then reread the story. When he turned it to read the continuation, another story caught his eye. It was unrelated to the Bonnie Brae fire. It was a column containing police briefs. The first one drew his attention.

Armed Robbers Hit Mid-City Check Casher

Two heavily armed and masked men stormed into a Wilshire Boulevard check-cashing company Friday and brutalized employees before escaping with the business's cash reserves, Los Angeles Police said.

The daring morning robbery occurred at EZBank, at the corner of the busy intersection of Wilshire and Burlington Boulevards. LAPD detective Augustus Braley said the robbers arrived at 10:30 a.m. in a dark sedan. Both gunmen left the car with its doors open and entered the premises of the check-cashing company.

Braley, of the Major Crimes Unit, said the robbers wore ski masks but fired their weapons at cameras inside the business, disabling them. It was believed based on witness descriptions that they were carrying AR-15 assault rifles. The robbers moved so quickly they surprised a security guard who was in the lobby of the business. One suspect struck the security guard repeatedly with the butt end of his weapon until he was knocked to the floor. One of the armed men then pointed a gun at the guard's head and threatened to kill him if other employees did not open a locked steel door and allow them behind the bulletproof, glass-enclosed counter. Once behind the counter, the gunmen forced two employees to empty a safe and three cash drawers of an undisclosed amount of money. The robbers then ran from the premises and fled in the getaway car.

Braley said that employees of the business had engaged a silent alarm when the robbers first entered the premises but the robbery occurred so quickly that the suspects were gone by the time police responded.

Investigators were looking into the possibility that the robbery was linked to others in Los Angeles in recent months. Two men brandishing similar weapons and wearing ski masks robbed a check-cashing store in Paramount six weeks ago. Braley would not say whether that robbery was suspected of being linked to Friday's crime.

The security guard, who was not identified by police, was treated by paramedics at the scene.

—Joel Bremmer, *Times* Staff Writer

Bosch read the story again. He realized that the fire call and the robbery occurred within fifteen minutes of each other on Friday, October 1, 1993.

"Mother's Day," Bosch said to himself.

He got up and went to a wall of shelves in the living room. These mostly held his records, CDs, and some of the DVDs his daughter had collected over the years. But there was an old Thomas Brothers map book of Los Angeles that had probably logged a couple hundred thousand miles in Bosch's cars over the years. He now had an updated map book in his car but also relied on his partners for GPS-generated directions whenever he needed them.

He took the map book over to the table and flipped through the pages until he found the one that included the Pico-Union area of the city and the start of the Wilshire corridor that led all the way to the Pacific. With a pencil he marked the location of the Bonnie Brae fire, between 7th and 8th Streets, and then the location of the EZBank robbery at Wilshire and Burlington. As he suspected, the two locations were close. The robbery occurred two and a half blocks north and one block west of the Bonnie Brae Arms. The distance could have been driven in less than two minutes.

Bosch sat back and studied the map and thought about the possibilities. "Mother's Day" was street slang for the day that government subsistence checks landed in mailboxes, usually the first of every month. The nickname came about because street hoods often came home to visit mother on the day she got her government check.

Street slang aside, Bosch knew that businesses like EZBank would fill their safes and cash drawers to be ready to handle the regular increase of check cashing that occurred on or near Mother's Day. The *Times* story did not say how much money was stolen in the robbery but Bosch knew that for the Major Crimes Unit to have taken on the case, it would have to have been six figures.

He knew of Gus Braley back in the nineties but had never worked with him. Major Crimes as it was then didn't even exist anymore and he was pretty sure Braley had retired before the turn of the century.

Bosch muted the music, then pulled his phone out and scrolled through his contact list. There was only one guy he knew who was in Major Crimes back then, the recently retired Rick Jackson. He had Jackson's cell number and hoped he hadn't changed it—he knew many cops did when they pulled the pin. He called the number and Jackson answered after two rings.

"This is Rick."

"This is Harry Bosch. You still remember me?"

Jackson laughed.

"Whassup, my brother?" he asked.

Now Bosch laughed.

"How long ago did you retire? The nineties? If I said something like that in front of my partner, she'd think I just came out of a time machine."

"Gotta love the nineties, Harry. What are you doing?"

"What am I doing? I'm working on a Saturday night and I'm sitting here wondering if you knew Gus Braley back in the day."

"Sure did. Old Gus—he was a son of a bitch. Tough guy."

"Still alive?"

"Oh, yeah. I joined this retired detectives group and we meet once a month for lunch. I don't go every time but I've seen him there. I think he comes in from Palm Springs. What's going on with him?"

"I'm looking at one of his old cases and want to ask him about it. You got a number that's good for him?"

"Yeah, hold on. I gotta look at my contacts on my phone to get it. I'll read it out loud then bring the phone back up, okay?"

"Okay. Whatever happened to the Rolodex?"

"Really."

Bosch waited while Jackson looked through his contacts list and then called the number out loudly. Bosch wrote it down on the edge of the Pico-Union map page.

"Got it?" Jackson asked with the phone back to his mouth.

"Got it," Bosch said. "Thanks. So how are you hitting 'em?"

Bosch knew very little about golf but knew that was a question often asked.

"Pretty good," Jackson said. "Playing a lot and practice makes . . . well, almost perfect. I'm down to single digits."

Bosch had no idea what that meant so he didn't know what to say.

"You miss us?" he asked, going in a new direction. "You miss the work?"

"Not yet. And I don't think I will. How long you got left, Harry?"

"I don't know. A little over a year, I think. I try not to think about it."

"You ought to take up golf, man. I'll take you out someday."

"Yeah, golf. I'll let you know."

Bosch couldn't picture it, especially the shorts he'd seen golfers wearing. He didn't own any shorts.

"So," he said, changing the subject. "We hooked up with your guy Ricky Childers in Tulsa. Good guy and he sent his regards."

"The book!" Jackson exclaimed. "The book comes through. You guys get a slice of pie while you were in town?"

"No, no time for pie."

"Anyway, I'm telling you, they should sell that book to a publisher. Just don't forget about me with the royalties."

"Don't worry, you'll get a piece of the pie."

Both men laughed. Bosch then thanked Jackson and promised to stay in touch. After disconnecting, Bosch immediately called the number Jackson had given him.

Braley didn't answer and the call went to a message. Bosch left his name and number and said he needed to talk to him about a case Braley had handled in 1993. He then gave his number again and disconnected.

He picked up the pencil and drummed it on the table. This review was not going the way he thought it would. He had something here. The case had a loose tooth and he couldn't leave it alone. He hoped he would hear from Braley soon.

He turned the music back up in time to hear "Stella by Starlight" and returned to the work in front of him.

He quickly finished reading through the newspaper stories. After the first ten days of multiple stories daily, the coverage waned and became little more than perfunctory updates on an investigation going nowhere. He then started through the other murder books, quickly reviewing the autopsies and photos of the dead children and the two adults. The photos were as hideous as they were sadly repetitive, but Bosch knew he couldn't look away. He thought of the names tattooed on Lucy Soto's arm and affixed them to children in the photographs. He would not need a tattoo to remember them.

An hour further into the review, Bosch tried calling Braley again, knowing full well that he had left a message and the retired detective would call when he received it. But he was surprised that the call was answered.

"Yes?"

Bosch muted the music with his remote again.

"Gus? Gus Braley?"

"Yes, who's this?"

"It's Harry Bosch. At Robbery-Homicide? I left you a message a little while ago today."

"I got it, yeah."

Bosch paused.

"Well, were you going to call me back?"

"Yeah, yeah, I was going to call. I was just sitting here thinking about '93 and wondering what case you were calling about. That was a busy year."

"The EZBank job over on Wilshire. You remember it?"

"EZBank . . . yeah, I remember it. Mother's Day. Two guys with AR-15s."

"That's it. I'm working from home tonight, no access

to the company computer and trying to catch up. Did you ever pop anybody for it?"

There was a pause.

"Bosch. I remember you. You're a murder cop, right? What do you care about a cash-box robbery from twenty-one years ago?"

"You're right, I'm a murder cop. I work cold cases now, and I'm looking at a case that I'm thinking maybe your guys could be good for. So did you ever make arrests, Gus? Name any suspects?"

There were a few seconds of silence while Braley was grinding it down.

"How'd you get this number, seeing that you're working from home on a Saturday night?"

"Rick Jackson. Call him if you want. He'll tell you I'm good people."

"I don't know, man. Saturday night, you gotta admit this is a little hinky. Who works Saturday nights in cold cases?"

Braley still used cop-speak from the nineties.

"Hinky or not, Rick will vouch for me. Can you help me, Gus?"

Bosch waited. He knew that the chances of his being able to pull either a digital or hard-copy file on a twenty-one-year-old robbery were not good. The statute of limitations would be long past on a robbery and it was unlikely the Department would have kept a physical file. Only cases with viable prosecutorial status were scanned and entered when the Department went through a massive shift-and-purge process as it moved toward digitized records. Bosch needed Braley to help him.

"That one we never cleared," Braley finally said.

"How much do you remember about it?" Bosch asked.

"I bet you remember the ones you never solved, right? Yeah, well, me, too. Fuckin' A, I do. I worked stickups and you work murders but the open cases still stay with you."

"They sure do. How much did they get in the robbery?"

"I remember that to the dime. Two-hundred sixty-six thousand, three hundred dollars."

Bosch whistled low.

"You're kidding me. In that neighborhood?"

"On Mother's Day they'd cash three, four hundred checks. That adds up."

"And these guys with the AR-15s knew that."

"Well, it wouldn't have taken a genius to figure it out, but we thought they probably had help from somebody inside. We just could never confirm it. Our pick for the inside man lawyered up faster than you can say, 'You have the right to remain silent.'"

"The security guard?"

"How'd you guess?"

"I don't know. Something about the way it read in the paper."

"I thought you didn't have the file."

"I don't. It's a long story, Gus, but all I have is a first-day newspaper clip, and after reading it I was thinking that if I was going to lean on anybody inside, it would be the security guard. Do you remember his name?"

"Nope. Rodney something or other—that's all I remember. He was white American and the two stickup guys were white and the one who did the talking had no accent. This Rodney character was also banging the girl behind the cage on the side. We found that out.

And she was the one who opened the door for them."

"Did you think she was in on it, too?"

"No, because she was the one who pulled the silent alarm before they made her open up. As soon as she saw guys in ski masks getting out of the car in front, she pulled the alarm. That put her in the clear in our book. But we grilled her pretty good anyway and dismissed her as being part of it. She just opened the gate because they had a gun to her boyfriend's head. So we zeroed in on him, thinking maybe he played her. He knew she'd open the door when she saw him all beat up and with the gun to his head. But nothing came of it. Maybe Rodney set it up, maybe he didn't."

"No other suspects came up?"

"Not right then. But when those two guys shot up North Hollywood on national TV a few years later, we took a look at them. They were white and worked as a pair, used ski masks, and carried AR-15s."

Braley was referencing the infamous 1997 shoot-out in the streets outside a Bank of America branch in North Hollywood. Two heavily armed and armored men engaged with police for nearly an hour in what was the most violent firefight with law enforcement ever seen on American soil. It was carried live on TV around the world. When it was over, three thousand rounds had been fired, eighteen cops and citizens were left shot and injured, and the two gunmen were finally dead. The bloody afternoon was analyzed in detail with every subsequent class of recruits that came through the Police Academy. And it was responsible for upgrades in the types and power of weapons LAPD officers were allowed to carry on their persons and in their work cars.

On that day, it seemed as though the entire police force had been outgunned by the two bank robbers.

Bosch had been there. The ongoing shooting drew hundreds of officers and detectives from all over the city. Bosch and his partner at the time, Jerry Edgar, had responded code three from Hollywood Station and arrived at the barricade on Laurel Canyon Boulevard just as the final shots were fired and the all-clear signal was given. They were then assigned to crime scene containment and the massive post-shooting investigation.

"What happened with that?" Bosch asked.

"We never made the connection," Braley said. "But not for lack of trying. Let me tell you a story about those two guys. Back in October '93—just a few weeks after the EZBank job—those two guys got arrested up in Glendale. They were pulled over on a simple traffic stop for suspicious activity around a bank, and the copper saw guns under a blanket on the backseat. They had a friggin' arsenal in the car—including two AR-15s—and they were about to hit the bank. They made an attempted robbery case against them and both went to prison for a couple years."

Bosch had an idea about where this story was going.

"You guys never heard about it at the time?" he asked.

"Not a word," Braley said. "Glendale kept it to themselves and we never heard about it until '97, when the shit hit the fan at Bank of America. So then we go back to that Glendale case and that's when we see they were using AR-15s within a month of our cash-box hit and think, *holy shit*, we've got something here. But you know what?"

"No AR-15s."

"Exactly right. Glendale had a confiscated weapons bonfire in '96 and those 15s went into the smelter. We never got a chance to see if they matched our case."

There was bitterness in Braley's voice and it was understandable. Bosch knew it wasn't the first time and by no means the last time that the lack of communication between law enforcement agencies let things slip through the cracks. In 1993, there was barely any digital tracking of weapons or cases. The computer revolution in law enforcement that would make for better and more immediate connections was just about to begin.

"So we never closed it," Braley said. "Then my partner, Jimmy Corbin, retired, and six months after him I pulled the pin, too. Nobody came in to carry the torch because Major Crimes was changing and nobody gave a shit anymore. You know how that went."

"Yeah, I do."

Major Crimes as an elite robbery squad was dissolved and the unit designation was later applied to the squad tasked with all terrorism-related investigations and intelligence gathering. The history aside, there was something that bothered Bosch about the mention of the North Hollywood bank robbers. Something he couldn't quite place or remember.

He let it go for the moment.

"Can I ask you a couple more questions, Gus?" he asked.

"Sure, might as well," Braley said. "I kind of like this, Bosch. You know, thinking about cases. I didn't miss it when I first retired and then I did. Now I sit out here and bake in the fucking sun all day."

Bosch made a mental note of this complaint for his own future reference and moved ahead.

"You remember the name of the girl who opened the door for these guys? You remember any other names?"

"No, sorry. I just remember Rodney. The girl was Mexican, from the neighborhood. They needed her in there to help translate. The other guy who was in there was Ukrainian. What was his name? It started with a B. Boiko, that's it. Max Boiko."

"So it was the security guard, the girl, and the Ukrainian guy. That's it?"

"Yeah. It was the morning and things didn't start cooking there until after the mail was delivered in that neighborhood about twelve. They had more help scheduled for the afternoon."

"Okay, what about the Ukrainian? Did you look at him?"

"We looked at everybody, Bosch. We were thorough. But the Ukrainian guy was a part owner with this group that owned two or three of those places around the city. We couldn't make it work. You know, why would he steal his own money? He was way over the insurance limit because of Mother's Day. He took a significant loss and it didn't make sense to us."

"Okay."

"But get this, he was also sleeping with the girl."

"You mean the translator?"

"Yeah, the Mexican. She was banging them both. I remember the Ukrainian was married and he was more worried about that than the money that got taken. He told me he'd lose more in the divorce if that got out."

Bosch registered all of this and wondered if any of it

had been a motivating part of the robbery. It was difficult to grasp the subtleties of the case twenty-one years later and without a file in front of him.

"Okay," he said. "Going back to the robbery, this newspaper story says they pulled up right in front of the door in the getaway vehicle."

"Yeah, so they could jump out and get in quick."

"I know these guys shot out the cameras but there must have been some video before that happened."

"Yeah, we had video. About five or ten seconds, so we got the make on the car but that was about it. We figured it was stolen anyway."

"Okay. But do you remember which way they pulled up from? The store was on the northwest corner of Burlington and Wilshire. Did they come from Wilshire or Burlington?"

Braley didn't answer right away. He had to carefully check the memory banks.

"Okay, don't hold me to this," he finally said. "But my memory is that they came down Burlington and then just pulled up in front of the door. That put the passenger side of the car four feet from the front door of the cash box. One guy got out that passenger side and went right in and took out the cameras. The driver jumped out and was following him in when everything went black."

"So they would've come down from Sixth on Burlington?"

"Right."

Bosch considered this. The route from the Bonnie Brae Arms to the EZBank location could have included coming south on Burlington from 6th.

"Okay, next thing," he said. "What do you remember

about how long the robbery took? First they take out the cameras, then they had the scuffle with the security guard, either real or not, then the paper said they made them open a safe and three cash drawers. How long did all of that take?"

"The longest part was the safe," Braley said. "They had to rough up the manager 'cause only he had the combo. They did the same thing again, only they put the gun on the girl this time and told him to open it or they'd put her blood on the walls. So he opened up the safe but it took him a few times because he's scared and fucks up the combo."

"And then the cash drawers. So how long in all?"

Again silence as Braley probed his memory.

"I'd say no more than six minutes—and that's actually long for this kind of thing."

"Right. And you said the girl hit the silent alarm right away."

"Yeah, she was good. As soon as she saw guys in masks in the car that pulled up, she hit it. That was verified on the video before it was taken out. She recognized the situation and hit the alarm. No hesitation, no delay. That's why we were pretty sure she wasn't in on it."

Bosch nodded. He could see the logic and conclusion Braley had made.

"How long after did officers arrive on scene?"

"That was long. Response time was something like eight or nine minutes. Everybody was tied up on a big fire down in Pico-Union. You remember the Bonnie—wait a minute, that's it, right? That's the case you're looking at."

"Did you ever look at it, Gus?"

"You mean like the fire was a diversion from the robbery? Yeah, me and Jimmy, we thought about it. But it didn't fit. Even after they said it was arson, we looked at it again, and it was neighborhood gang stuff. Drug stuff. We were looking for two white guys and it didn't fit."

"Did anybody from Criminal Conspiracy ever come to you to take a look at *your* case?"

"Not that I remember, no."

Now it was Bosch who was quiet. He thought about the two cases. The arson and armed robbery occurring almost simultaneously three and a half blocks apart. The advantage of time sometimes allowed Bosch to see things more clearly. No evidence in the Bonnie Brae case ever directly pointed to the motivation of the arson being gang or drug related. That was simply rumor turned to gospel by the media and the members of the community. But what was seemingly easily dismissed twenty-one years ago could not be dismissed now.

"I just remembered something about the guy we thought was the inside man," Braley said.

"Yeah, what's that?" Bosch asked.

"Like most of these rent-a-cops, he wanted to be a cop but wasn't good enough. He'd made applications to the sheriff's and then to us. He'd been accepted in the academy but then got washed out."

"Did you find out why?"

"Yeah, I remember we thought it was kinda strange, because he's banging the girl behind the counter and she was as brown as molasses. She was Mexican and he'd gotten washed out on a racial beef with somebody else in his class. Another Mexican."

"How long before the robbery was that?"

"Shit, you want me to do all your work for you? I can't remember. A couple years, at least."

Bosch thought about this last piece of information from Braley. He wondered if there might still be a record at the academy or the city personnel office regarding the security guard named Rodney. He would need the full name before he could find out. More food for thought was the seeming contradiction of Rodney having a racial problem at the academy and later being involved with a Latina.

"Thanks a lot, Gus," he finally said. "You've been a great help."

"Hey, call me back if you ever put something together, will ya?" Braley said. "I'd like to know."

"You got it, Gus."

21

Bosch got to the squad room at eight Sunday morning and found Soto already at her desk in the cubicle. Before he could tell her about the theory that had emerged the night before on the Bonnie Brae case, she swiveled around in her chair and started talking excitedly about her own findings on the Merced case.

"Yesterday, after I left Mariachi Plaza, I went up to the Valley to see Alberto Cabral. He let me look at the band's calendar from '04, and I found the Broussard booking. It was a fund-raiser—"

"—for Robert Inglin."

She looked stunned.

"You know?"

"Yes, I know."

Bosch didn't know whether to be mad at her for speaking to a potential witness without him or to admire her for her passion and drive on the case—to the point of putting in so much of her own time.

"You should have told me, Lucy. Talking to a witness like that, a lot of things can go wrong. Sometimes witnesses turn out to be suspects, and sometimes they're friends with the suspects and turn around and spill everything you just told them. You have to be careful and you should have at least told me where you were going so I could have decided if I should go with you or not."

"It was better it was just me. He opened up without you there. And speaking in Spanish."

"That's not the point. The point is, I should have known what you were doing and where you were. Next time shoot me a text, that's all."

She nodded, eyes down.

"Roger that," she said. After a pause, she asked, "So how did you know about Inglin?"

He put the stack of binders he was carrying down on his desk, pulled out his chair, and turned it so he could face her. He sat down.

"Well, I didn't talk to a potential witness about it. I got it from campaign finance records."

"On a Saturday?"

"I have a friend with access."

She looked at him suspiciously but then relented.

"Did you find out anything else?"

"Yeah, I did. In that same election year Broussard went from being all in for Inglin in January to being all in for Zeyas in May. And he stuck with Zeyas in the next election and is a primary backer of his so-called exploratory bid for the Governor's Office."

"What made him switch? The Merced shooting was right in the middle of that."

Bosch pointed at her.

"The million-dollar question."

Soto sat bolt upright.

"Oh my God, I just thought of something. One of the calls Sarah got on the tip line."

She swiveled back to her desk and grabbed up the

stack of tip reports Holcomb had brought by. Soto looked through the pages until she found what she was looking for.

"Here it is," she said. "Tip came in Friday morning, 12:09 a.m. 'Female caller said the mayor knows who shot Orlando Merced.' That's it. The call was anonymous but the register recorded the number. Do you want to call it, see who answers?"

"You really think Zeyas called in the hit on a mariachi musician?"

The question gave Soto pause. Bosch's saying it out loud indeed made it sound crazy.

"I was just going to call, see what she had to say," she finally said.

"Go ahead. But she's your crazy, then. Don't bring her around me."

"Okay, I won't."

She pulled out her cell to call.

"You have your number blocked on that?" Bosch asked quickly.

"Yes, it's blocked."

She tapped in the number on the tip sheet and made the call. Bosch watched her as she listened.

"No answer," she said. "I'll leave a message."

"Use the tip number. Don't give her your number."

Soto nodded.

"Hello, this is Detective Soto at the Los Angeles Police Department and this message is for the woman who called about the Orlando Merced shooting. Could you please call us back, because we want to follow up on your call."

Soto gave the tip line number, thanked the anonymous tipster, and disconnected.

"Don't count on hearing back," Bosch said. "Cases are made with patience and little steps, Lucy. Not lightning strikes."

"I know."

"Let's switch tracks here for a bit. There's something I want to show you."

He leaned back to his desk and pulled a newspaper clip out of the top binder from the Bonnie Brae case. He handed it to her.

"It's a profile the *Times* ran of Mrs. Gonzalez. You remember her, right?"

"Yes, of course."

Bosch could see her eyes holding on the photo of Esther Gonzalez.

"Go to the jump," he said.

She looked at him, confused.

"The continuation page. Turn it over."

She did so and he rolled his chair closer and tapped his finger on the brief about the EZBank robbery.

"Read that."

He gave her time and when she looked up at him, he began.

"I talked to Gus Braley last night and got what he could remember about the case. He—"

"We can pull the file. But what are we looking for?"

"There won't be any file. This case would have been shredded in the digital purge. Statute of limitations. They never made a case against anybody. But the old robbery journals from Major Crimes are now in the captain's office in Robbery Special. We'll look there. Usually the names of victims are in the entries. That's where we need to start."

"Start what?"

"Braley said they thought at the time that it was an inside job, but they could never prove it. That means one of the names of the victims listed in the robbery journal could be the insider. We track him down and we talk about Bonnie Brae. No statute of limitations on murder."

"Wait a minute. Bonnie Brae? How is—you're losing me."

Bosch nodded. He understood that he was moving too quickly and with information Soto didn't have.

"The robbery took place fifteen minutes after the fire was reported," he said. "It was three and a half blocks away. It was very carefully planned and involved first getting behind a bulletproof enclosure and then forcing employees to open a safe and three cash drawers. It took time. And I'm thinking they may have bought that time with something that diverted the attention of the police."

"The fire."

"Exactly. And right now I don't have a leg to stand on—Braley said they even considered it back then and discarded the idea. But that was when they first thought the fire was accidental and then later attributed it to gangs and drugs. And the robbery suspects were white and they didn't see the connection to a Pico-Union firetrap where only Hispanics lived. They dropped the idea back then, but I think we want to pick it up now."

Soto sat silently, nodding her head slightly as she apparently ran the scenario through her mind. She saw what Bosch saw and looked up at him.

"So what do we do?"

Bosch stood up.

"Well, first we go look at the journals in Robbery."

They moved through the squad room and through a door into the adjoining squad room for the Robbery Special section. It was deserted and the captain's office was locked. Bosch looked into the darkened office through the glass panel next to the door. He could see the shelves containing the robbery journals, their leather bindings cracked and worn.

"Should we call maintenance, see if they'll open the door?" Soto asked.

"They won't," Bosch said.

He looked at the doorknob. He knew it would be easy to pick. Not much emphasis was put on security inside a police headquarters.

"Go out to the hallway," he said. "If anybody gets off the elevator, let me know."

"What are you going to do?"

"Just go."

As she headed toward the door to the hallway, Bosch moved down the aisle between the detective modules, checking the desks. He saw one with a magnet holding a variety of paperclips. He took two and headed back to the captain's office, straightening one of the clips out completely and putting a slight bend at the end of the other. He did not have his lock picks with him because they were in his suit jacket and he was dressed informally for what he thought would be a Sunday morning of sifting through files.

Bosch crouched in front of the knob and went to work. It took him only a minute to open the door. He moved in, dropped the paperclips in the trash can next to the desk, and moved to the journal shelves. The bindings of the journals were marked by the years each contained.

For the past forty years or so, each year required its own book. Bosch quickly found the journal marked 1993 and pulled it. He walked out into the Robbery squad room and over to the alcove where there was a copy machine. He flipped through the journal to the date of the EZBank robbery and found its entry—just one-third of a page.

After making a copy, he retraced his steps, put the journal back in its spot, and relocked the door as he left the captain's office. He read the entry on the journal page as he walked to the hallway door. It was basic but it did include the names and DOBs of three victims, including a security guard named Rodney Burrows.

It was all Bosch needed.

Soto was standing at the glass wall, looking out into the Civic Center. It was quiet on a Sunday morning. City Hall stood in silhouette with the sun climbing the sky behind it. Monolithic, it was still the most recognizable building in the city—and the one with the most secrets.

"Got it," Bosch said.

He handed the photocopy to her as he walked past, heading back to the Open-Unsolved Unit. She followed, reading the short entry on the way.

When they got back to their module she already had an idea, but it was the wrong one.

"I'll run these names down and we can start making visits," she said. "Who do you want to start with, the security guard? Says he is Rodney Burrows."

Bosch shook his head as he sat down.

"We don't visit any of them until we know more about this and them," he said. "Burrows didn't break story when they put pressure on him in '93, so there is no reason to believe he would now. We have to find something that the Robbery guys didn't have last time. Something that gives us some leverage. We don't approach any of them until we have that."

"Okay," Soto said. "I'll start backgrounding them. What else?"

"Burrows supposedly washed out of the academy sometime before getting the job as a rent-a-cop. They might still have a file on him—if we get lucky."

"Okay, I'll check."

Bosch looked at the binders on his desk and chose one. He handed it to Soto.

"One other thing," he began. "That book has the residents list for the Bonnie Brae. Every single one of them was interviewed. You take that list and you work the names. You take those three people who were inside EZBank when the robbery went down and you find a connection to Bonnie Brae."

Soto's eyebrows showed her confusion.

"If the fire was set as a diversion, then they picked that place for a reason," Bosch explained. "Because they knew about access, they knew about the trash chute. They knew they could drop a firebomb down that chute, start the fire in the basement, and get a distraction. I don't think there was anything random about it. They knew. One of them knew. One of them had been in there. There is a connection and you need to find it or we have nothing to go at any of them with."

Now she nodded.

"Got it," she said. "Do you think they knew there was a day care down in the basement?"

"I don't know, but we'll find out."

He was about to turn back to his desk but then re-membered something else to share.

"You were still a kid, but do you remember the North Hollywood shoot-out in '97?" he asked.

"I don't really remember it from when I was a kid but we studied it in the academy," she said. "Everybody knows about it. Why?"

"Well, Gus Braley said that at one point they looked at those two guys for EZBank but couldn't make the connection."

"Wow."

"Yeah."

Bosch saw a momentary flash of what he knew was disappointment on Soto's face. The North Hollywood bank robbers were dead and she suddenly had to con-sider that her search for the Bonnie Brae arsonist could lead to such a conclusion: no trial or punishment, just the knowledge that those responsible were already de-ceased and away from the reach of law.

"Do you think you could handle it if it comes to that?" he asked.

"Well, I really wouldn't have a choice, would I?" she said.

Bosch nodded and Soto seemed to shake off the disappointment.

"Were you there that day? At the shoot-out? I heard everybody who wasn't nailed down went."

Bosch nodded.

"I went up there from Hollywood. But I got there just when the shooting was ending. I like to say I got there just in time to be sued."

"What does that mean?"

"The family of one of those guys sued the Department and a bunch of us, saying we let him bleed to death on the street. The suit claimed the detectives refused for more than an hour to allow paramedics to treat him and that he died from his wounds because of the delay."

"Did they win?"

"No, ended in a mistrial and then it just went away. It was never retried."

"So?"

"So what?"

"Did they keep the paramedics back? That part never came up at the academy."

"It was still a confused and hostile environment. We didn't know if there were other possible shooters. We held the paramedics back until we were sure it was safe for them. In the meantime, a few of us might've mentioned to the guy while he was lying there on the street that it might be best for all concerned if he went ahead and bled out. I mean, we had cops shot all over the place. I don't think anybody was too sympathetic to this guy on the ground. They were going to make sure every last cop got treated before a paramedic got near him."

She pursed her lips and nodded. She understood.

"You know nobody died on our side, but four of the cops that got shot that day never made it back to duty," Bosch said. "They were messed up pretty bad—either physically or mentally."

"I know. They told us that at the academy."

She seemed to be thinking about something and Bosch assumed it was the memory of the shooting that took her partner's life. He realized the comparison was inevitable. She had been under fire. It would call up a connection to the North Hollywood shoot-out even though it was before her time.

"Anyway," he said, "why don't you work on EZBank and I'll work on Merced. We work both at the same time. That way the captain doesn't get antsy, and nobody else knows."

Soto nodded.

"Thank you, Harry."

"Don't thank me yet. We're still working long odds— on both of these cases."

"Either way, you didn't need to do this."

"But you did. And I know what that's like."

"Someday you'll have to tell me about that."

"I will."

They turned back to their desks and went to work.

22

Bosch turned his attention back to the Merced investigation. The first thing he did was run Charles Broussard through the computer to see if by chance he had ever been jammed up before. He doubted this would be the case, or the politicians wouldn't touch him or his money, at least not publicly. The search came up dry—Broussard had a clean record, not so much as a speeding ticket.

Bosch wrote down the home address from his driver's license and now believed he had the location on Mulholland Drive where Angel Ojeda had come across Maria Broussard and their affair had begun.

He next ran a Los Angeles County property search on Broussard and found several parcels in his ownership, beginning with the address on Mulholland Drive. There were also commercially zoned sites in Pacoima and City of Industry that Bosch assumed were related to the concrete business that Virginia Skinner and Ojeda had mentioned. He found another residential address on the Pacific Coast Highway in Malibu. A beach house. All told, Broussard had his name on properties Bosch estimated were valued at more than $20 million in Los Angeles County alone.

Bosch cleared out of property records and moved his computer sleuthing to the state's corporate records. After plugging in Broussard's name, he got matches on several articles of incorporation, some long outdated but most of them current. One business that listed Broussard as president and chief operating officer was called Broussard Concrete Design. Bosch knew this to be the company that provided the concrete barriers used in road construction projects. He had seen *B-C-D* stenciled on barriers on freeways for as long as he could remember.

Broussard was listed as an officer or member of the board on various other businesses incorporated in the state. None of these drew Bosch's attention immediately but he wrote them all down along with their addresses.

One of the expired corporations caught Bosch's eye. Broussard had been listed as president of a now-defunct corporation called White Tail Hunting Ranch and Range in Riverside County, which was just across the eastern border of Los Angeles County and not far from Broussard's property in City of Industry.

Bosch copied the information even though the state records indicated the incorporation of the hunting ranch and range had lasted only four years and was dissolved in 2006, when the property was sold. What this meant to Harry was that Broussard was a hunter or at least knew hunters. Gun Chung had identified the rifle used to shoot Orlando Merced as a hunting rifle.

It was eleven o'clock and Bosch wanted to be home when his daughter woke up. He started shutting down his computer and looked over his shoulder at Soto. She was consumed with her own work on her screen.

"I'm gonna go," he said. "I want to spend some time with my kid today."

"No problem," she said. "I'm going to stay awhile."

"Getting anything?"

"Not yet. You?"

"Yeah, I think so. At the time of the Merced shooting, Broussard owned a hunting ranch and shooting range out in Riverside."

Soto looked away from her computer and directly at Bosch.

"Then he probably knew a hundred guys who could have taken that shot," she said.

"What I was thinking," he said.

"That's good. You said 'owned.' No more?"

"He sold it about eighteen months after Merced."

"And after he had jumped ship from Inglin to Zeyas."

Bosch nodded. The possibilities were expanding and darkening at the same time.

"Tomorrow," he said.

"Okay, Harry," she said. "Tomorrow."

It was clear sailing on the 101 on the way home and Bosch made good time. He got off the freeway at the Barham exit and then took Cahuenga down to the turn that would take him up the hill. There were two ways up: Mulholland Drive to the left and his street, Wood-row Wilson Drive, to the right. He turned left, deciding to use the time he'd made on the freeway to get a look at Broussard's house.

Mulholland rode the spine of the mountains that cut the city in half. The address Bosch had for Broussard was on the north side of the street with a view of the San Fernando Valley. But as Bosch drove by the address, he saw no house, just a gated driveway entrance. The drive went down and disappeared off the edge of the roadway. A block away Bosch pulled into the parking turnout for a city parks scenic overlook. He left the car and walked back along Mulholland. When he got back to Broussard's gate he looked down at a poured-concrete driveway that snaked down to a parking structure with three double-wide garage doors made of aluminum frames and shaded glass. It took Bosch a moment to realize that the six-car garage was actually the top level of a multi-tiered house that was stepped down the mountainside. The house was entirely and unabashedly constructed of unfinished concrete. The design was what Bosch knew was called industrial chic.

Bosch put his foot up on the guardrail next to Mulholland and pretended to lean over and tie his shoe. As he studied the house, he saw camera boxes at the corners of the garage and up top at the gate. The place no doubt was a fortress. Nobody got in uninvited. Nobody was unseen on approach. Bosch wondered what it was Broussard was protecting himself from.

He took his foot off the guardrail and headed back to his car.

Maddie was awake when Bosch came through the front door. She was sitting on the couch watching television and eating a bowl of cereal. It was fifteen minutes past noon.

"Hey, sweetie."

"Dad."

"I thought we were going to have lunch or breakfast."

"We are, but I couldn't wait. This is like an appetizer."

He sat down in the chair opposite the couch. She was still dressed in her pajamas—plaid workout pants and a T-shirt that said "The 1975" on it. Bosch knew it was a band she liked. The year before, he had bought her and her friends tickets to see them at the Henry Fonda.

"What do you feel like doing?" he asked.

"I don't know," she said. "Something outside."

Bosch nodded.

"When do you report tonight?"

"Five-thirty."

Bosch checked his watch. His plan would cut things close on timing. He went with it anyway.

"I was thinking, there's a range out in Riverside I want to check out. How about that? It's been a while since you've been shooting."

A few years earlier Madeline had been a competitive shooter and had ribboned in several shows. But her dedication had dropped off as more and more school and volunteer activities started crowding her schedule. Her growing interest in boys was a distraction as well.

"Yeah, cool," she said. "Where's Riverside?"

"That's the thing. It's out east of here, the next county over," he said. "We would have to go soon so you can be back in time for Meals on Wheels."

"I just have to change. All right if I do homework in the car?"

"Sure. You go get dressed and I'll get the guns out."

They were in the car in fifteen minutes. Bosch had brought her competition pistol as well as the Glock Model 30 he currently carried on the job and the Kimber Ultra he previously used as his sidearm. Since the White Tail range was part of a hunting ranch, he had a feeling it would largely be set up for long-gun shooting, but he didn't own a rifle or a shotgun. If needed, he would inquire about renting something when he got there.

The Sunday traffic was comparatively light and they made good time. Even so, it still took over an hour to get there, including a food stop in West Covina. Maddie did homework and said little, except when she used her phone to look up fast-food stops. This had become more challenging since she had stopped eating red meat earlier in the year. Fast food had almost always meant In-N-Out Burgers before that. She settled on a place called Johnny's Shrimp Boat, which was on Glendora just off the 10 freeway. Maddie ordered fried shrimp and Bosch got the chili rice. The food was excellent and Maddie put aside the schoolbooks while they ate in the parked car.

"So how was last night?" Bosch asked.

"It was good," she said. "Fun. And the movie was really good."

"Was this Jonathan Pace a gentleman?"

"Yes, Dad. He's a very nice guy."

"How many of you went?"

"Well, it ended up being just me and Jon."

"I thought you said it was a group."

"It was supposed to be, but things happen. People didn't show up. So it was me and Jon and everything was fine, okay?"

"It's okay with me if it's okay with you."

He gathered the takeout cartons and took them to a trash can in the parking lot. When he got back to the car, all discussion ceased as she went back to the books and he drove on to Riverside.

The original corporation might be defunct but the White Tail Hunting Ranch and Range still operated under the same name on the outskirts of a town called Hemet. The range was in a private reserve in the foothills of San Jacinto Mountain. It was fronted by the outdoor firing range and several outbuildings that included the office, a bunkhouse, and a skinning-and-dressing barn. Bosch entered the office with his daughter and they were greeted by a wall of photos displaying hunters and their kills. There were deer, mountain goats, and many photos of wild hogs on the ground, hunters and their rifles posed with them.

"Oh my God," Maddie whispered, as she looked at a photo of the huge crooked teeth and snout of a vanquished razorback boar.

Bosch shushed her as a man came out from a side office to the counter. He was in work clothes and wore a cap with a frayed bill and a Smith & Wesson logo on it.

"Can I help you?" he asked.

"Yes, my daughter and I were passing through and saw the place," Bosch said. "Do you need a membership to shoot on the range?"

"You do, but we sell day memberships. Twenty-five dollars."

"Do you have a short range? We have pistols."

"Sure do."

"Then sign us up for the day."

Bosch paid the money and signed a range rules agreement. They took their weapons and ammo boxes out to the range. The short range had stands that were under shelter. They chose a forty-foot range and put in earplugs. Bosch let his daughter go first, loading the weapon for her. She started off target but on the second clip she began tightening the circle and showing her old form. Bosch had brought in a pair of binoculars he kept in the glove compartment. He watched the target when she shot and called out the groupings. He no longer had to worry about her shooting form.

Maddie used all three guns and did most of the shooting. Eventually, Bosch sat back on a bench behind the stand and just watched her as he also looked around the place.

"Dad, don't you want to shoot anymore?"

"Nah, I'm good. Just watching you."

"Is there another reason why we came here?"

"Sort of. I'll tell you later."

There were only three other shooters on the range and they were all at the rifle stands, which were separated from the short range and unsheltered. Bosch studied the men. Two were definitely together and one was by himself, working with a scope. All three of them exhibited a familiarity with the surroundings that led Bosch to conclude they were not day members. They belonged.

After forty minutes Maddie had gone through all their ammo. Bosch got a broom off a tool rack and handed it to her. He told her to clean up all the empty shells so they could recycle them. He said he'd wait for her in the office, where he was going to talk to the man behind the counter.

Bosch stepped into the office and over to the trophy photo wall. He was studying the photos, looking for a hunter who might be holding a Kimber hunting rifle, when the man came out from the back room again.

"Enjoy yourselves?" he asked.

"We did," Bosch said. "Thank you. I wanted to ask you about hunting. Can you also come in on a day pass to hunt?"

"To hunt you need a two-day pass even if you just

hunt the one day. You need to bring in your hog and deer tags, too."

"Got it."

Bosch went back to the photos. He spoke without turning his eyes to man.

"My daughter's just picking up our brass and then we'll be out of here."

"You got the day pass, stay as long as you like."

"I've been here before, you know. About ten or twelve years ago. I came with Brouss back when he opened it, and I got a hog. I thought maybe the picture would be up here somewhere."

"That goes back a ways. Those photos—if there are any left—are over there on the other side of the door."

"Okay."

Bosch moved over to the area on the right side of the door and started looking.

"There's not too much from back then," the man said. "Mr. Broussard took a lot of the photos with him when he sold the place. He took every picture with Dave in it off the wall. Didn't want the reminder up, I guess."

Bosch kept his eyes on the photos and his voice casual.

"A reminder of what?"

"The accident. That's why he sold the place. He didn't want to be reminded."

Now Bosch turned from the wall of photos and looked at the man.

"What kind of accident was it?"

The man eyed him for a long moment before answering.

"No need to pick at scabs around here. Mr. Broussard

sold the place to me and we've had no problems since I took it over. Enough said right there."

"Sorry. My daughter says I shouldn't be so nosy."

"She's a smart girl, you ask me. And a hell of a shot—I was watching."

"She sure is."

23

Bosch got to the squad room at seven Monday morning and found Soto already at her desk. He noticed that she was wearing the same clothes as the day before.

"You were here all night?"

"I was working on the nexus and lost track of time. I slept a few hours downstairs. Not worth going home and back."

Bosch nodded. There was a cot room down on the garage level available on a first-come first-served basis. The room was open to male and female officers but he didn't think he had ever heard of a female officer making use of it. He was continuing to be amazed by Soto's commitment to the cases and the job.

"'Nexus'?" he asked.

"That's what I'm calling this search for a connection between the EZBank three and the Bonnie Brae apartments," she said.

"You get anything?"

"Not yet. But I'm only halfway through the tenants list. I'll hopefully finish today."

Bosch dropped his files on his desk and sat down heavily in his chair. Soto read his body language.

"What's up with you?"

Bosch shook his head and pulled a folded piece of paper out of one of the files. He handed it to her. It was a printout of a story from the *Riverside Press-Enterprise* dated March 23, 2005. It was a brief story and Soto quickly read it.

"What does this mean?" she asked.

"I think it means Broussard covered his tracks," he said. "We're not going to get him."

"I don't understand. There are no names in this. This was an accidental shooting?"

"According to that story. I'll pull the Riverside sheriff's file on it today."

"Where did this come from?"

"Yesterday I went to the range Broussard used to own out there. I did some shooting with my daughter. The guy who owns and runs the place mentioned that he got it from Broussard after the accident."

Bosch nodded at the printout in her hand.

"My kid found that in the newspaper's digital archives. No names, but the guy who ran the range for Broussard was killed in a hunting accident. The headline says 'Hunter Kills Best Friend in Accidental Shooting.' What do you want to bet that when I get the file, the hunter is Broussard?"

"There were no other stories after this one?"

"That's another thing. No other stories after that little brief. You ask me, somebody with some juice put a stopper on this."

Soto nodded as she was taking it all in.

"So why are you so sure we can't get to Broussard?"

Bosch held his hands out wide.

"Well, if we assume that whoever took the shot at Mariachi Plaza came out of that range in Riverside, then it was probably either set up by the guy who ran the place or he was the one who took the shot. Either way, he was the connection to Broussard and now that connection is gone. He's been dead for nine years."

He pointed to the printout again as if that proved his words.

"There's gotta be . . ." Soto began. "We still have Ojeda."

"He's not enough," Bosch said. "No DA would touch this with what we've got. We'd get laughed out of the CCB. We've got no evidence. No gun, no direct witness, no—"

Bosch stopped as he thought of something.

"What?" Soto asked.

"It's slim," he said. "But when I get the name of the guy who ran the range—the guy working there yesterday called him Dave—I'll run his name through the ATF computer. Maybe we'll get lucky and find out he owned a Kimber Montana. It won't be enough to get us in the door at the D.A.'s Office but it will be another piece."

He took the page back from Soto and turned to his desk. He thought about first moves. Making an inquiry at another law enforcement agency was a delicate matter, especially when it was one so close to L.A. There were invariably connections and relationships between the two—a cross-pollination of personnel that could cause difficulty for the unwitting caller. It was always better to make an entrance through a known entity—a lateral rather than direct approach.

Bosch had several contacts to choose from. Over the last few years that he worked in the Open-Unsolved Unit, there had been a number of cases with ties to

Riverside County, and he had slowly filled the space in his mental Rolodex behind the R card. He decided to try Steve Bennett, who was a missing-persons investigator with the Riverside County Sheriff's Department. Bosch wasn't calling about a missing person but he knew Bennett had been with the department a long time, had worked in several different capacities as an investigator, and would know where and how to look for what Bosch needed.

After an exchange of long-time-no-sees and other pleasantries, Bosch asked Bennett if he could find out about the fatal accident that occurred nine years before at the White Tail Hunting Ranch. Having been given the exact date of the shooting, Bennett said he didn't think it would take him long to pull up a record and check the lay of the land. He told Bosch he would call back when he had something. Bosch in turn asked him to keep his inquiries below the surface. Nobody else needed to know.

Bosch ended the call and told Soto he was going to walk over to the Starbucks a block down 1st Street. It was Monday and he was going to start the week off with something other than what came out of the machine in the PAB lobby.

"You know it all comes out of a machine, Harry," Soto responded. "A brewer. Some places are just fancier than others."

"True," Bosch said. "But every now and then I like the human touch that comes with handcrafted coffee."

It was a line he borrowed from his daughter. Soto gave no reaction.

"So you want anything or not?"

"No, I'm good. I went down there about an hour ago for the human touch."

"Right."

Bosch left the building and was halfway to the coffee shop when his cell buzzed. It was Bennett with the callback from Riverside County.

"Harry, I don't have a lot," he said. "They closed this thing up pretty quick. A real tragedy, it looks like. A guy killed his best friend when he mistook him for a deer or a hog or something in the brush out there."

Bosch walked over to a bench in a bus stop shelter so he could sit down, hold the phone in the crook of his neck, and take some notes.

"Okay," he said. "You have the names of the shooter and victim?"

"The shooter was Charles Andrew Broussard. That's bravo-romeo—"

"I got that spelling. What's the vic's name?"

"David Alexander Willman. Common spelling on all if you don't have it. Age forty-two. He was the manager of the ranch and Broussard was the owner. Says here they were best friends since high school, growing up in Hemet. They were hunting and got separated in something called the 'hog chute'—spelled C-H-U-T-E—which is described here as a narrow canyon on the ranch, and somehow Willman showed up where Broussard didn't think he was going to be. Broussard thought it was a hog they were tracking and hit him from thirty yards. Through-and-through neck wound. Willman died at the scene. Bled out."

Bosch jotted down a few words that would prompt his memory of the summary.

"What was Broussard shooting?" he asked.

"Uh, let's see here . . . an Encore Pro Hunter," Bennett said. "It was a .308."

"And what about Willman? Does it say what he was carrying?"

"Uh . . . nothing here about what he had, Harry."

"Okay, any inventory on the report?"

"Just Broussard's gun."

It had been a faint hope—that Willman's rifle would be listed or even held in evidence.

"Who was the investigator?" he asked.

"Bill Templeton," Bennett said. "He's still with the department. He's a captain now."

"You know him?"

"I know him but I don't really know him. Know what I mean?"

"Yeah."

Bosch had to think for a moment as he phrased the next question. A bus pulled up to the curb and he had to get up and walk away from the shelter to escape the noise.

"You out on the street, Harry?" Bennett asked.

"Yeah, getting coffee," Bosch said. "Listen, Steve, did you know of Templeton as an investigator? I'm wondering if he was the kind of guy that would close a case quick because he was lazy about it, or if he was the kind that could be encouraged to close a case."

There was a long silence before Bennett answered.

"Hard to tell from this report and I never worked directly with the guy. But I heard Templeton is a golfer, and before every shot, he throws a little grass up into the air to see which way the wind blows."

Bosch understood the meaning. Templeton might not have been resistant to encouragement to close the accident investigation quickly, especially if it came from above.

"Harry, you want the OSHA report number?" Bennett asked. "The report isn't here but they must have signed off on it. I have a number."

Bosch returned to the bus bench so he could take down the number. He also asked for Willman's birth date and home address along with the identifiers of his wife, Audrey. He then thanked Bennett for his quick help.

"Keep that golf thing to yourself, okay?" Bennett said. "Don't need Templeton on my ass."

"Of course," Bosch said. "I owe you one."

After disconnecting the call Bosch turned around and headed back to the PAB without completing the coffee run. He no longer needed the caffeine burst.

Back at his computer Bosch ran David Alexander Willman through the crime databases and drew a blank. Willman had a clean record as far as Bosch could determine.

He next opened up the ATF gun registration site and ran a search on Willman. Even though Willman was deceased, the database would carry any gun transactions he had legally made. This time Bosch got results. Willman was listed as a gun dealer whose federal license lapsed six years before, when it was not renewed after his death.

Bosch guessed that being a gun dealer went hand in hand with operating a hunting ranch and gun range. The ATF search also pulled up a number of transactions in the eight years before his death. Willman had bought and sold dozens of guns. Bosch combed through the list and found the purchases of two different Kimber Model 84 rifles. Willman had bought them in 2000 and 2002, long before Orlando Merced had been shot with such a weapon.

Harry then went through Willman's sales reports and found only one of the two rifles had been resold. It meant that at the time of his death Willman owned a Kimber Montana. It didn't mean he was in possession of the weapon, but it was registered in his name.

Regardless, Bosch was now encouraged. He thought he might have a line on the murder weapon. It had been nine years since Willman died. The rifle could have long disappeared. If Willman didn't dump it right after the Merced shooting, then Broussard probably got rid of it after he killed Willman. All of this was mere conjecture, Bosch knew, but he had to acknowledge that there was a chance Willman had been smart and had hung on to the rifle as leverage with his friend Broussard. He could have said he got rid of it but in reality kept it hidden somewhere just in case things went sideways.

Bosch wrote the serial number of the rifle down in his notebook and then started a new computer search, this time looking at Riverside County property records. When he got what he needed he turned to Soto.

"I'm going back out to Riverside," he said.

She turned from her computer to look at him.

"What's out there?"

"I got a callback. Broussard was the shooter out there that day. Killed his friend David Willman and it was ruled an accident. But Willman was a gun dealer and bought a Kimber Montana he never sold. It might be out there."

"Where?"

"I don't know yet. I've got the address where Willman lived but his wife sold it two years after his death and traded up. She's in Rancho Mirage. I was thinking I'd start there. Maybe I'll get lucky and she still has the gun."

Soto thought about it for a moment and then said, "I'm going with you."

"What about the nexus?"

"It can wait. You're not going out there looking for a gun without your partner."

Bosch nodded.

"You like chili rice?" he asked. "I know a good place to stop about halfway out."

24

The drive out took much longer than the Sunday drive Bosch had shared with his daughter. For one thing the freeways were more crowded and Rancho Mirage was almost an hour farther east into the Coachella Valley. He and Soto discussed both cases they were actively working and the moves they planned to make. Bosch's belief that the rifle used to shoot Orlando Merced might still be in the hands of David Willman's family was a valid investigative string to follow but it didn't approach the threshold for a search warrant for the Willman family home. He and Soto would have to knock on the door and hope for cooperation or something that would bolster probable cause.

They stopped in West Covina for an early lunch of chili rice and then conversation tapered off as they made the second half of the drive. Bosch's thoughts drifted from the case to the dinner he'd had with Virginia Skinner the night before. The conversation had been good and interesting. The door to romance even cracked open—at least from Bosch's perspective—and it was exciting to think about where it might go. It wasn't just the prospect of being with someone again. Bosch had to admit that his chances at perhaps a final romance in his life were dwindling as time went by. His hopes that Hannah Stone might be that final romance were dashed the year before.

Her son was in prison on a date-rape conviction. When Bosch refused to go to bat for him at a scheduled parole hearing, Hannah abruptly ended the relationship, leaving Bosch to wonder if her motives had been wrapped around her son's situation all along.

Thinking about Virginia Skinner, Bosch realized that there was a secret thrill in the possibility of a relationship because of her standing in the media. A romance with a reporter would be so fraught with complications that it was obviously ill-advised, and in that risk was the thrill. Whatever they did, it would have to be kept secret. In the Department it would be seen as tantamount to sleeping with the enemy. The PAB and the *Los Angeles Times* were only separated by the four lanes of Spring Street but there was an invisible wall between the two institutions that was twice as tall as City Hall. Bosch would have to be very careful if he proceeded. Virginia Skinner would as well.

"You taught your daughter to shoot?"

Soto had asked the question, pulling Bosch out of his thoughts. She had obviously been ruminating on his report of his Sunday afternoon activities.

"Uh, yeah, I did."

"That's a bit unusual, don't you think?"

"Well, you know, guns in the house and all of that. I wanted her to learn about them as a safety thing. I took her shooting a couple times and she actually was good at it. A natural. She's got a bunch of ribbons and a few trophies in her room. And now, believe it or not, she says she wants to be a cop."

Soto nodded. Bosch wondered if she was drawing some connection between his daughter learning to shoot and her own experience during the shoot-out that took her partner's life.

"I'd like to meet her," Soto said.

Bosch nodded.

"I'd like her to meet you," he said.

"Where's her mother?" she asked.

"She passed a few years back," he said. "That's when she came to live with me."

"And started shooting guns."

"Yeah."

That was all that was said until they reached Rancho Mirage.

The house Audrey Willman moved into following her husband's death was in a gated community called Desert View Estates. Bosch badged his way past the rent-a-cop at the gatehouse and found the home two minutes later. It stood three stories high and sat on a half acre of land in a neighborhood of similar-size homes and properties. There was a turnaround with a rock garden at its center surrounding a Joshua tree. Bosch and Soto approached the door and waited after pressing the bell.

"You know why they're called Joshua trees?" Soto said.

Bosch glanced back at the centerpiece tree, its multiple branches fanned out like a candelabra.

"Not really," he said.

"The Mormons named it," she said. "It reminded them of the scene in the Bible where Joshua raises his hands up to the sky to pray."

Bosch nodded thoughtfully and the large oak door was answered behind him. He turned to see a uniformed housemaid, who made them stay outside while she closed the door and inquired as to whether Mrs. Willman would speak to them. This annoyed Bosch, since he knew the rent-a-cop had certainly called ahead to the house to warn that the detectives were coming. Mrs. Willman should have already been primed to receive them.

At least they were in the shade. The dry desert heat was getting to Bosch. He felt his lips drying and starting to crack. He studied the workmanship of the front door and then his eyes traveled up to the tongue-and-groove woodwork of the interior of the porte cochere's roof. He was reminded of the major discrepancy in property values he had seen when he had looked up David Willman's address at the time of his death and the address where his widow now lived.

"Tell you one thing," he said. "Either Willman had a hell of an insurance policy or there was a payoff somewhere. This isn't the kind of place a hunting guide ends up with."

"She probably sued Broussard," Soto said. "Wrongful death or something."

Bosch nodded his agreement as the door was finally reopened, this time by a woman of about fifty who identified herself as Audrey Willman. She was tall and lean and wore a lot of gold jewelry.

"Can I help you, Detectives?" she asked.

Bosch decided on a direct approach.

"We are investigating a murder in Los Angeles that may be connected to your husband's death. Can we come in?"

"He's been dead almost ten years. How could it have anything to do with a murder in L.A.?"

"We can explain if we could come in."

She let them in and they convened in a living room, with Bosch and Soto sitting on a couch directly across from Audrey Willman, who sat in what looked like an antique leather club chair.

"So," she said. "Explain."

"When your husband died, he owned several firearms," Bosch began.

"Of course he did," Willman said. "He was a licensed dealer. He bought and sold guns."

"We understand that. What we are trying to determine is the whereabouts of one of the weapons he owned at that time."

Audrey Willman leaned forward slightly, eyebrows pulled together in suspicion.

"You're kidding me, right?" she said.

"No, ma'am," Bosch said, calling on the ghost of Joe Friday for his deadpan delivery. "We're not kidding. We need to know. What happened to the weapons your husband owned after his death?"

She held her hands out palms up as if to signal that the answer was obvious and not worth the two-and-a-half-hour drive out from L.A.

"I sold them. I sold everything—all legally. After what happened, do you think I'd want guns around anymore?"

That was the opening Bosch was looking for.

"What exactly did happen?" he asked. "I only got the shorthand from the Riverside Sheriff's Office. How did your husband end up being killed by his best friend?"

Willman made a dismissive gesture with her hand.

"The Riverside Sheriff's would be the last place I would look to find out what happened," she said.

Bosch waited but she said nothing else.

"Well, can you tell us your version of what happened?" he asked.

"I'd love to but I can't," Willman said. "There was litigation. I sued him but I can't talk about it."

She used her hands again to gesture toward the ceiling and her opulent surroundings. The indication was clear. She had taken a sizeable settlement in the matter but part of the deal was her silence.

"You're saying there was a confidentiality clause in the settlement?"

"That's correct."

"Okay, I understand. Can you tell me what it was you alleged in the lawsuit before there was a settlement and a confidentiality agreement?"

She shook her head.

"I can't say a word about anything."

She sliced a hand through the air, signifying the finality of her stand on the subject.

Bosch nodded. There didn't appear to be any way into the lawsuit with her, so he returned to the guns.

"Okay, that's understood. Let's go back to the guns you said you sold. The gun in question was never re-registered following a sale. It still is in your husband's name in the Alcohol, Tobacco, and Firearms registration computer."

"That can't be. I had everything sold perfectly legit. Ted Sampson did it. He bought the ranch and used his own dealer's license to sell everything."

Bosch assumed that Ted Sampson was the man he had spoken to the day before in the office at White Tail.

"Well, with this particular gun, there is no record of

it being sold by anyone. It was a Kimber hunting rifle. The Montana model. Does that sound familiar to you?"

"No gun sounds familiar to me. I hate guns. I have no guns in this house. When I moved here I left all of that behind. But I kept careful inventory records because before all of this—"

She waved her hand again, indicating what the lawsuit settlement had brought.

"—I thought the money from those guns might be all I'd be left with. That and a twenty-five-thousand-dollar insurance policy."

"Okay," Bosch said. "Then if Ted didn't sell this gun in particular, where would it be?"

She shook her head as if she was baffled.

"I have no idea! The garage at the old house was his gun room but we cleared it out. I'm sure of that. There was nothing left in there when Ted was finished, and I inventoried every gun we pulled out."

"Do you still have that inventory?"

She thought for a moment.

"As a matter of fact, I think I do."

"Can we see it, Mrs. Willman? It might be important."

"Wait here. It's in my tax files. I'm sure of it."

She got up and walked across the room to a set of French doors with curtains. They opened into a study, where Bosch could see a desk, bookshelves, and a stationary bike positioned in front of a flat-screen television. Willman closed the doors behind her.

She was gone five minutes. Bosch and Soto made eye contact but never spoke. They both knew that the inventory, if Willman's widow still had it, could be a solid piece of connecting evidence should the investigation ever move toward a prosecution without the murder weapon.

When Willman emerged from the study, she was carrying a yellow legal pad with several pages folded back and a rubber band around it.

"Found it."

As she approached, she pulled off the rubber band, but it had become brittle over time and snapped in her hand. She sat down and started pulling the pages back over and studying each one. Four pages into this process she stopped.

"Here are the guns."

She handed the pad to Bosch. He took out his own notebook, where he had written down the serial number of the Kimber Model 84 that David Willman had owned, according to ATF records. Soto leaned over to look at the pad and they studied the list. There were eighteen rifles and handguns listed, along with the amounts received in their sales. None were described as a Kimber make and none of the serial numbers matched the number Bosch had in his notes. Willman's Kimber had never been sold. Bosch noticed that the list also contained two ammunition bandoliers but they didn't go with any of the guns on the list.

"Can we borrow this, Mrs. Willman?" Bosch asked.

"I'd rather you not take it," she answered. "I can copy it for you. I have a copier."

"It would be better if we had the original document. We can give you a receipt for it and will return it when it's no longer needed."

"I don't understand. Why would you want it?"

"It could be an important part of the investigation. If

the gun was used in the homicide we are investigating, we need to document its origin. This inventory helps us prove that the gun went missing at least nine years ago when you documented what weapons your husband had in his possession at the time of his death."

"Okay," she said reluctantly. "You can take it but I want to make a copy and I want the original back."

"You'll get it back," Bosch said. "I promise."

"I'll write a receipt," Soto said.

While Soto went to work on the receipt Bosch asked Willman a question he had been holding back on until the end of the interview.

"What weapon was your husband carrying on the day of the accident?"

Willman made a sound of disbelief before answering. It did not seem to be directed at Bosch, but rather carried some emotion about the content of the question. It was a small confirmation of Bosch's suspicion that the lawsuit she filed and was now sworn to secrecy about had not been a routine wrongful-death claim. He guessed that Audrey Willman had alleged that David Willman's death was anything but an accident.

"He was carrying his twenty-gauge shotgun, like he always did," she said.

"A shotgun while hunting wild boar? Was that normal?"

"He wasn't hunting wild boar. The other man was. Dave was the guide. The other man had asked him to guide. So he carried a shotgun in case a boar came out of the brush and charged. He would use it to put the animal down."

She didn't say the name Broussard. Bosch wondered

257

if that was part of the lawsuit settlement or if she just couldn't bring herself to mention the name of the man who had killed her husband. He tried one more time to get behind the lock on the legal action.

"If you know something about your husband and Charles Broussard that was not in the lawsuit, we'd be happy to listen."

Audrey Willman looked at Bosch for a long moment and then shook her head.

"I can't discuss him in any regard," she said. "I can't even say his name. Would you please just give me the receipt and go? I have things to do."

Almost, Bosch thought. She had almost opened up.

25

They left the house fifteen minutes later and Bosch secured the legal pad in his briefcase. Rather than drive toward the 10 freeway, which would get them back to L.A. the fastest, Bosch pointed the car toward Hemet.

"Where are we going?" Soto asked.

"To the house Willman lived in when he was alive," Bosch said.

"The gun?"

He nodded.

"Just a hunch. It's gotta be somewhere. I want to check out the garage that Audrey said was used as her husband's gun room."

"You don't think Broussard got it? I mean, that's why he felt he was in the clear to eliminate Willman."

"Maybe. Or maybe Willman told him after the Mariachi Plaza shooting that he had gotten rid of it. Broussard may have only thought he was in the clear."

"But instead Willman hung on to it? Hid it somewhere?"

Bosch nodded.

"Maybe. Like an insurance policy. Maybe he hid it somewhere his wife didn't know to look after Broussard killed him."

Soto nodded, buying in.

"Okay. Do we need a search warrant?"

Bosch shook his head.

"Not if we're invited in."

They drove in silence for a while and then Soto asked a question.

"What did you think of Audrey? She really wanted to tell us about that lawsuit."

"She did. I think she feels guilty."

"About what?"

"She took the money and shut up. She knows the money—however much it was—was Broussard buying his way out. Over time that's got to be tough to live with. Doesn't matter how fancy your digs are. It all came from hush money. Anyway, we need to find another way into the lawsuit, maybe talk to the D.A.'s Office to see what they can do about breaking the seal on it."

"I'd sure love to read it."

They got to Hemet in a half hour. Along the way Bosch took a call from Captain Crowder, who wanted an update on where the investigation stood. Bosch told him that they were following a lead on the murder weapon and hoped to have something solid to report later in the day or by morning. This appeased the captain for the time being and he ended the call without asking further questions.

The house where the Willmans had lived before Dave's death at the hands of Broussard was a modest ranch house in a middle-class neighborhood. It was freshly painted and had a neatly trimmed yard and an attached double garage. The property records Bosch had checked said it now belonged to someone named Bernard Contreras.

A woman of about thirty answered Bosch's knock on

the door. She looked like she was at least seven months pregnant.

"Mrs. Contreras?"

"Yes?"

Bosch pulled his badge and identified himself and Soto.

"We're homicide investigators and we are out here looking for a gun that may have been involved in a case we are working," Bosch said.

The woman put her hand over her protruding stomach as if to protect her unborn child from even the word *gun*.

"I don't understand," she said. "We have no guns in this household."

"We're not talking about you or your husband," Bosch said. "We're here because the man who lived here before you had guns."

"The man who was killed?"

"Correct, the man who was killed. He was a gun dealer and we are looking for one of his guns."

"That was a long time ago. My husband and I bought this place—"

"We know that. That's why we have a favor to ask. We're hoping you'll be willing to help us with the investigation."

The woman looked suspiciously at Bosch and maintained her guarded stance.

"What is it?"

"We want to look in your garage."

"Why would you want to look in my garage?"

"Because the previous owner—the man who was killed—kept at least part of his inventory in the garage here. We want to take a look and just satisfy ourselves that the gun we are looking for is not here."

"We've lived here six years. I think we would have found a gun if one was left behind."

"I think you're probably right, Mrs. Contreras. But we're cops and we need to see for ourselves so we can rule it out. Besides, this gun—if it is here—would have been hidden."

The woman dropped her hand from her belly and seemed to relax a little bit. Bosch thought that maybe she was now curious herself.

"Do you need to have a search warrant or something like that?" she asked.

"Not if you invite us in to search," Bosch said.

She thought about it for a moment before giving the go-ahead.

"I'll open the door," she said. "But we have a lot of boxes in there. Stuff we're taking to storage and I don't want you going through it."

"Don't worry, Mrs. Contreras. We're not going to be looking through your property."

She stepped back and closed the door. Bosch and Soto walked along a flagstone path to the driveway and waited in front of the garage. The door had no windows and Bosch guessed that this was a security measure taken by Willman when he had stored guns in the garage.

The door started slowly going up. Mrs. Contreras was waiting inside, her hand back in place on top of her stomach.

Bosch stepped in and looked about. It was a standard two-car garage with a workbench taking up the space in one of the bays and storage shelves and a water heater lining the back wall. None of the walls had been finished, exposing the wood framework and insulation. It was a cost-cutting move elected by the contractor or home buyer when the house was originally built.

There was a compact car in the bay opposite the workbench and it was clear to Bosch that Mrs. Contreras got to park in the garage while her husband used the driveway or the street.

The garage had exposed rafters and a storage platform overhead. Several boxes were stacked up there. Bosch pointed up.

"Those boxes up there are yours?"

"Yes. Ours. This place was completely empty when we moved in. If there was a gun we would have seen it."

Mounted to the two-by-fours of the wall on either side of the workbench were side-by-side cabinets made of heavy steel with key locks and additional hasps for padlocks.

"Those are gun cases," Bosch said. "They were here when you moved in?"

"Yes, they were left by Mrs. Willman when we bought the place."

"Are they locked?"

"No, we don't lock them," Contreras said. "You can check them."

Bosch opened the cabinets and saw they were being used for routine storage. No guns. He used a stepladder that was next to the workbench to look over the top of the cabinets. Dust and dead bugs lay on top of each but no guns.

Bosch moved over to the workbench. A vise with a padded grip was mounted on one end and a second smaller vise was mounted at a midpoint on the six-foot-long bench. He stepped closer and could smell the faint scents of break-free oil and bore solvent, two materials every gun dealer would have in supply.

"This bench was also left here? The vises—they're set up for holding a rifle while you work on the bore or add a scope."

"Yes, the bench was also left here and we decided to use it. It takes up a lot of space, though. My husband has to park in the driveway but he doesn't mind. He likes to tinker in here on Saturdays."

Bosch just nodded. He was looking at the bench, its work surface stained with oil. It was obviously home-made, constructed of two-by-fours and plywood. It had a work surface on top and one shelf below. Both surfaces were inch-thick plywood, framed underneath by lengths of two-by-fours. It was a sturdy, heavy construction that at the moment supported a variety of power tools and other equipment.

Bosch put his hand on the bench for support and squatted down to look under the top surface. In the corner of the thick frame, he saw a gun attached to the underside with plastic ties.

"There's a gun under here," he said. "A handgun."

"Oh my gosh!" Mrs. Contreras exclaimed.

Bosch took a pair of rubber gloves out of his jacket pocket and put them on. He then pulled out his phone and squatted down to take photos of the gun in place, using the flash to illuminate the dark underside of the bench. He then grabbed a carpet cutter from the array of tools on top of the bench and used it to slash the plastic ties.

He pulled the gun free and stood up to look at it with Soto. It was a Glock P17. Mrs. Contreras leaned in to study it as well, and her face took on a look of trepidation.

After a moment, Bosch handed the weapon to Soto, who had also put on rubber gloves, and started to take off his jacket. To look under the lower shelf of the bench, he was going to have to get down on the oil-stained floor. Mrs. Contreras noticed what he was doing and pulled a tarp off one of the shelves at the back of the garage. She started unfolding it and spreading it on the floor.

"Use this so you don't ruin your clothes," she said.

Soon Bosch was down on the floor, using the glow from his phone screen to illuminate the recesses of the underside of the lower shelf. There was another firearm—this one a long gun—and he took photos again before asking for the carpet cutter to slash through the plastic ties.

He handed the heavy weapon up to Soto and then got up.

"Oh my God," Mrs. Contreras said.

She now had both her hands protecting her unborn child.

The gun was not a Kimber Model 84. Bosch recognized it as an M60 machine gun. Vietnam era, fed by ammo belts worn like bandoliers by the men who humped it through the jungle. Two bandoliers had been on the inventory list of guns and ammo sold by Willman's wife after his death. Here was the weapon the belts went with. Bosch wondered if Willman had hidden the machine gun and the Glock because they were stolen or because they were valuable memorabilia.

"Is that what you were looking for?" Mrs. Contreras asked.

"No, not it," Bosch said.

He took the weapon from Soto because he could tell she was straining from the weight of it. Those who carried the M60 through the Vietnamese jungle had a love/hate relationship with it. They called it "the pig" whenever they had to lug the heavy weapon out on patrol. But heavy or not, it was the best gun to be holding in your hands in a firefight. Bosch carefully cradled it in the jaws of the twin bench vises.

Bosch stepped back from the bench and looked around the garage one more time. He was invigorated from finding the two weapons. They weren't what he was looking for but they proved that Willman had hidden guns. It supported his hope that the Kimber Montana might still be found.

His eyes went up to the overhead rafters.

"You can go up there if you want," Mrs. Contreras said.

She was now fully supportive of the search for weapons in the home she would soon be raising a child in. There was a fiberglass extension ladder on a rack on the other side of the garage. Bosch took it off the rack and, careful not to hit the car, walked it around to the bench. He extended it and propped it against one of the crossbeams and then held it steady while Soto went up first. He followed and they found themselves ducking below a low ceiling on a makeshift floor of planks spread across the crossbeams.

Bosch looked for hiding spots, but there was really nowhere in the rafters to hide a rifle or any other weapon.

He was about to give up the search when Soto called him over to the edge of the platform. He kept his hand up on one of the roof trusses for support.

Soto pointed down through the opening between two of the crossbeams to one of the steel gun cabinets. He didn't readily see what she wanted him to see.

"What?" he said.

"Behind the cabinet," she said. "It's attached to the two-by-fours but there is room between them."

She was right. There was more than a foot between each of the two-by-fours that ran vertically along the wall frame. Each of the spaces between was crammed with strips of insulation but they could easily have been removed behind the gun cabinets to create a secret storage space big enough for a rifle. Bosch had not realized the possibility of this when he had looked over the top of the cabinets before.

"We need to take the cabinets down," he said.

It took them a half hour to remove the contents of each of the cabinets and then for Bosch—using Bernard Contreras's tools—to loosen the bolts attaching the first steel cabinet to the two-by-fours behind it. To finish the project, he then had to hand the wrench to Soto while he attempted to hold the heavy steel cabinet.

Working from the stepladder, Soto removed the four loosened bolts, and Bosch felt the weight hit him. It was too much.

"Look out!"

He let the cabinet slide down the two-by-fours to the floor, where it hit the cement with a loud bang.

"Everybody all right?"

As the two women reported that they were fine, Bosch looked at the place on the wall where the cabinet had been. There was indeed a vertical space four inches deep between two of the two-by-fours. A length of wood had been nailed into place between the verticals to create a bottom rest to the hiding place. There was no gun there but there was a sheathed sword in the space. Bosch took it down to examine it. It was caked with dust. It looked like some kind of samurai sword and had a slight bend to its long blade, which had remained shiny and clean in its sheath.

Bosch leaned the sword against the workbench and moved on to the second gun cabinet.

Having learned from the first effort, Bosch took only ten minutes to loosen bolts on the second cabinet and put Soto in position on the stepladder. This time he knew what to expect and used his weight against the cabinet to slowly slide it down the wall. He heard Soto announce that there was a gun in the second hiding spot before he even straightened up.

It was a rifle. Bosch's adrenaline kicked in. He wanted to grab it and check to see if it was a Kimber, but he waited while Soto photographed it with her phone. He then took it down from the space and held it out across his body. Soto leaned in to help examine it for brand markings.

"I need my glasses," Bosch said.

"There!" Soto said, excitedly pointing to the left side of the rifle's receiver. "'Kimber Model 84.' It has to be it."

She located the serial number to the left of the brand mark and asked Bosch if he had the number from his notes. Bosch gave her the gun and went to his jacket, which Mrs. Contreras was holding, for his reading glasses and notebook. He flipped the notebook open to the page with the serial number written on it and read it out loud to Soto.

"It's a match," she said.

Her voice had a tremble as she said it.

They had found David Willman's unaccounted-for rifle. The next step was to see if it was also the rifle used to shoot Orlando Merced.

Bosch put on his jacket and looked at the two gun cabinets on the floor of the garage. There was no way he was going to be able to put them back in place.

"Mrs. Contreras, we are going to have to take these weapons with us," he said.

"Please do," she said. "My husband's not going to believe this."

"Well, your husband may not be happy, because I'm not going to be able to lift those cabinets up and put them back."

"Don't worry. He and his friends can do that. They hang out in here enough and this will be a great story for him to tell."

"That makes me feel better. We're going to write out a receipt for you now."

They put the weapons in the trunk of the car, laying them across a blanket Bosch kept in his surveillance kit. They then thanked Mrs. Contreras and gave her the receipt.

Finally they headed back toward Los Angeles. There was an almost palpable excitement in the car. Bosch had started the day feeling that he had reached a dead end on the case because Broussard had taken the ultimate measure in protecting himself. But now things were different. He had what he believed would prove to be the murder weapon in his trunk. It had been a fast turnabout.

Bosch checked his watch and figured it would be almost five by the time they got back to the city. He pulled his phone and called the gun shop at the crime lab. He asked for Gun Chung.

"How long are you going to be there?" Bosch asked.

"I'm on the schedule till four," Chung said. "What's up?"

"We have the gun from the mariachi thing. At least we think we do. But we won't get there in time. We're coming in from Riverside."

"How far out are you?"

"I'm thinking closer to five."

"It's okay. I'll wait. Bring it right here and I'll do the comparison."

"We won't have to wait in line?"

"I'll be on my own time. I can do what I want."

"I appreciate that, man. We'll be there as soon as we can. Can you do me one other favor?"

"What is it?"

"Call up to latents and see if somebody can meet us. I'd like to see if we can pull prints off this."

"I'll see what I can do."

Bosch disconnected the call and told Soto that they were going directly to the lab where Gun Chung was willing to wait for them to do a comparison between the slug taken from Orlando Merced's spine and a bullet fired from the rifle in the trunk.

"Let's say it's a match," she said. "That we have the murder weapon."

"Okay," Bosch said.

"Let's run the scenario. I want to try to see how this works."

Bosch nodded. It was a good exercise to a certain extent. The investigator never wanted to create a scenario and then work the evidence to fit it. But starting with the assumption that they had just recovered the murder weapon led to some inalterable conclusions.

"Well, you start by going back to our original theory based on the ballistics and the video evidence," he said.

"That the bullet that hit Merced was intended for Ojeda," Soto said.

"Right. Then from there you have the confirmation that the weapon belonged to David Willman. Did he take the shot? We don't know that. Did he have the skill? Yes. Did he know someone he could have given his gun to so they could take the shot? I think that's also a yes."

He drove for a few minutes, grinding out the story in his head before continuing.

"Okay, so if you draw a line between Ojeda and Willman, who else does it intersect?"

"Broussard."

"Broussard. He grew up with Willman and was in business with him."

"And his wife was having an affair with Ojeda."

Bosch nodded.

"The way I see this from Broussard's angle is he warned Ojeda to stay away from his wife but Ojeda wouldn't move on. So Broussard goes to Willman and says, 'I need a piece of work taken care of.' Willman takes the job and sets it up with a shooter or decides to handle the job himself. I'm guessing the latter—rule of thumb, the fewer people in a conspiracy, the better."

"Agreed. I go with Willman."

"Willman takes the shot but hits Merced instead of Ojeda. Everything goes sideways. Now they know that if they hit Ojeda, it will really bring some heat because there is no way the police will continue to think the first one was a random shot or gang related. They'll know there is something going on here. So Broussard has no choice but to tell Willman to stand down—at least for now."

"Meantime, Ojeda sticks around just long enough to feed his bullshit statement to the cops and then splits town."

"So the shot actually does the job. They hit the wrong guy but the right guy goes away anyway."

"And Willman becomes a loose end for Broussard. A guy who knows the secret."

"You have to wonder why Willman agreed to go out hunting with Broussard that day. He must've told him that he had an insurance policy."

"He kept the gun."

"Broussard must've somehow thought he was in the clear, that the gun wasn't going to show up and connect up the whole thing, with him in the middle."

Soto turned completely sideways to look at Bosch as she made the next connection.

"It was the bullet! It was *inside* Merced. He must've thought when Merced survived and they weren't going to take the bullet out of him that Willman's ace in the hole wasn't as valuable as he thought. It didn't matter if he kept the rifle, since there was no slug to compare it to because it wasn't removed from Merced. There was no way to prove it had fired the shot."

Bosch nodded.

"Willman thought he was safe enough to give Broussard a gun and go off into the woods with him. Only he wasn't."

They sat with it in silence for a while. Bosch ran it all through once more and couldn't knock it down. It was only case theory but it held together. It worked, but it didn't mean that it was the way it had happened. Every case had unanswered questions and loose ends when it came to motives and actions. Bosch always thought that if you started with the assumption that murder is an unreasonable action, then how could there ever be a fully reasonable explanation for it? It was that understanding that kept him from watching and being able to enjoy films and television shows about detectives. He found them unrealistic in their delivery of what the general audience wanted: all of the answers.

He looked up at the overhead freeway signs. They were coming up on the exit for Cal State, where Gun Chung waited for them in the lab.

26

Their case theory took on a higher degree of validity after Gun Chung positively identified the Kimber rifle they brought in as the weapon that had fired the bullet that was lodged in Orlando Merced's spine for ten years.

After the weapon was processed for fingerprints, Chung fired a round from the Kimber into the bullet tank in the lab, fished it out with a net, and then compared it on the double microscope to the slug taken from Merced. The original slug was badly damaged. Still, it took Chung less than ten minutes to declare the comparison a match he would confidently testify to in court.

Bosch had Chung fire rounds from the M60 and the handgun into the tank as well. He asked Chung to run digital profiles of the bullets through the projectile database when he got a chance. The two other weapons may have had nothing to do with the Merced case, but they bore checking out. Willman had hidden the weapons for a reason. The two extra guns were loose ends that needed to be tied up.

The samurai sword should also be checked and traced if possible. But that was not Chung's domain. Bosch planned to run checks on sword thefts and crimes involving the use of such weapons as soon as he broke clear of the current investigations and had the time.

*

When Bosch and Soto got back to the PAB, there was no one in the squad to report their news to. Crowder and Samuels were long gone for the day. Almost all the other investigators had signed out as well. Bosch stored the three guns and the sword recovered in Hemet in the fire-arms vault located in the file room. He planned to run ATF traces on the M60 and the Glock the next morning.

When he got to the module, Soto was reading through the latest batch of tip sheets that Sarah Holcomb had left on her desk.

"Anybody call up and say a guy named Dave Willman took the shot?" Bosch asked. "And that Charles Broussard asked him to do it?"

"You wish," Soto said.

Bosch sat down at his desk. He was tired. Driving sapped his energy these days.

"Anything else in there?" he asked.

"Not much. Our anonymous lady who thinks the ex-mayor has all the answers returned my call, but Sarah missed it and the woman just left a message saying the same thing—talk to Zeyas. Sarah ran the number this time and it goes to an unregistered cell—a throwaway."

"Not that surprising. If she's not a citizen, she wouldn't have the proper ID and bank account to get a legit carrier. Most of the illegals in this city use throw-aways. They're cheap and available at every bodega in the city."

Soto was calling the number again, holding her desk phone to her ear while continuing the conversation.

"I have to say, her persistence makes me wonder."

"Wonder what? Whether the ex-mayor was in on the Merced shooting?"

"No, not that. That's pretty far-fetched. But who knows, maybe he knows something."

"Okay, then you're the one who gets to ask His Honor about that—based on an anonymous caller's tip. See if they'll let you keep your Medal of Valor after that."

"I know. It's crazy."

"It's not crazy. It's just reckless until something more comes up to support it, and I don't really think anything else is going to."

Soto hung up the phone.

"It went to message again."

Bosch pulled his chair over to hers and said he wanted to change the subject and discuss their next steps. It was imperative that they now gather complete profiles of both Broussard and Willman. He exercised his senior-partner status and elected to take Broussard while Soto took on Willman. He also said that he believed it was time to go to the District Attorney's Office to talk to a filing deputy about what they had and what was needed to make a prosecutable case. He would attempt to set that up for the next day, hoping to get John Lewin or another deputy he was confident would be up to the task. Lewin was a guy who always looked for ways to work with investigators to get a winnable case filed. Some of his counterparts on the seventeenth floor of the CCB seemed more interested in looking for reasons not to file cases.

"What about Bonnie Brae?" Soto asked when Bosch was finished.

"I think it's got to wait," Bosch said. "For now, at least. We have to go with the momentum we've got on Merced. On top of that, we have to assume Broussard is working against our momentum. He's got to know that Merced has died and that we now have the bullet. He might already be watching us. So our time is best spent on Merced and moving quickly."

She looked disappointed but accepted his decision.

"What if I work it on my own time?" she asked.

Bosch thought for a moment.

"I would never tell you not to work something on your own," he said. "They call them 'hobby cases' around here. But that doesn't seem like the right description for that case and what it means to you. I understand that you want to keep the momentum you have going. Completing the nexus and all of that. I just want to make sure you keep a hard focus on Merced."

"I will, Harry. I promise."

"Okay, then do what you have to do."

On his way home Bosch once again went up Mulholland instead of Woodrow Wilson so that he could cruise Charles Broussard's home. He wasn't sure what he was hoping to see. The chances of catching sight of the suspect—yes, Bosch had now reached a point where he considered him a suspect—were almost nonexistent. But still Bosch was drawn to the concrete fortress where Broussard had hidden himself from public exposure and the law for so long.

This time it was dark when Bosch reached the turnout for the northern overlook. The signs said the park was closed from dusk till dawn, but there were cars parked and people out on the promontory, checking out the vast carpet of lights in the Valley. Bosch stepped out to the view and looked to his right along the ridgeline. He could see the forward edge of the concrete house jutting farther out than the houses between it and the overlook. Bosch saw lights on behind floor-to-ceiling windows, and far down the sheer hillside at the bottom level was a lighted blue pool shaped like a kidney. He saw no human activity anywhere.

Bosch sat down on a bench and enjoyed the view like the other tourists on the promontory. But his thoughts were of murder and the kind of people who pay others to kill their competitors and enemies. The ultimate narcissists who think that the world revolves around only them. He wondered how many were out there among the billion lights that glowed up at him through the haze.

Bosch heard an authoritative voice and turned to see a city parks ranger putting the beam of a flashlight in people's faces and telling them that the park was closed and that they had to leave or be cited for trespassing. He was being an impolite jerk and was wearing a wide-brimmed Dudley Do-Right hat that undercut his authority. When he came up to roust Bosch, the only one who hadn't scurried out to the parking turnout, Harry held up his badge and said he was working.

"You still have to go," the ranger said. "Park's closed."

Bosch noticed that the nameplate on his uniform said Bender.

"First of all, get that light out of my face. Second, I'm on a case and I'm watching a house over there and this is the only place I can see it from. I'll be out of here in ten minutes."

Bender lowered the light. He looked like he was unused to people defying him.

"They really make you wear that hat?" Bosch asked.

Bender studied him for a moment and Bosch looked right back at him. In the glow from the lights below, Bosch could see his temples pulsing.

"Do you have a name to go with that badge?"

"Sure do. It's Bosch. Robbery-Homicide Division. Thanks for asking."

Bosch waited. *His move.*

"Ten minutes," Bender said. "I'll be back to check."

Bosch nodded.

"That makes me feel better."

The ranger walked off toward the stairs leading to the parking lot, and Bosch turned his attention back to the concrete fortress. He noticed that the pool light was now out. He stood up and moved farther out to the edge of the lookout. There was a thigh-high safety barrier. By propping himself against it and leaning even farther out he improved his angle of sight on the Broussard mansion. He pulled the compact binoculars out of his jacket pocket and looked through them. He could now see in through some of the lighted windows. He saw a living room with large abstract paintings on twenty-foot walls and a kitchen where a woman was moving about behind a counter. It looked like she was emptying a dishwasher. She had dark hair but he could not really see her well. He guessed it was Maria Broussard, the woman whose marital indiscretion had started it all.

Bosch's phone buzzed and startled him. He pulled himself back from the precipice and put the binoculars in his pocket. He took the call. It was Virginia Skinner.

"First of all, thank you again for dinner last night," she said. "That was really nice and I had fun."

"Me, too. We should do it again."

There was a momentary pause as that registered and then she continued.

"The other thing is, are you still interested in Charles Broussard?"

Bosch stared at the Broussard house for a few moments before answering.

"Why do you ask?"

"Well, because it was a slow Monday today, and so I was looking through all the crap that accumulates on my desk. You know, press releases and political invites and all of that. I was really looking to see what I could just throw out and move off my desk, and I came across a press release for a fund-raiser that Broussard is co-hosting tomorrow for the Zeyas exploratory committee."

"Tomorrow? At his house?"

"No, this one's actually at the Beverly Hilton. It doesn't even say that Zeyas will be there but you have to assume he'll pop in to say a few words."

"Do you need some kind of ticket or invitation to go?"

"Well, for me, no. I'm media. Otherwise it's five hundred a plate."

"Are you going?"

"Probably not ... unless ... if you were going, then I might."

Bosch thought about things. His daughter had the alcohol sting the next night. She didn't want Bosch to embarrass her by coming along, but his plan was to be there and watch over her without her knowing it. He felt the sergeant in charge wouldn't be as vigilant as he would be—even from afar.

"What time is it at?"

"Seven in the Merv Griffin Room."

"I might be in the vicinity, maybe stop and get a look at him. How about I let you know tomorrow?"

"Sure. Then you're still interested in him?"

"I can't talk about the case. We have a deal, remember?"

"Of course. I'm not writing anything until you give the go-ahead. So you can tell me anything and trust me not to use it."

Bosch started pacing back toward the steps down to the turnout. The conversation had suddenly turned awkward with Skinner's precise summary of the deal they made before having dinner the evening before. After that, they hadn't mentioned it once.

"Harry? You there?"

"Yes, here. I'm sort of in the middle of something. I'll call you tomorrow and let you know if I'll be going to that thing."

"Okay, fine. Talk to you then."

Bosch disconnected and pocketed the phone. He was about to take the steps down to his car but glanced back toward Broussard's house. He saw a figure standing out on one of the balconies now. Moving back toward the end of the promontory, he pulled out the binoculars once more.

There was a man on the balcony, wearing what looked like an open robe over shorts and a T-shirt. There was the dim glow of a cigarette in one hand. He was heavyset and had a full beard.

And it looked like he was staring back at Bosch.

Maddie was at the table in the dining room, seated at the spot where Bosch usually sat to do his work. She had her laptop open and looked like she was composing some sort of school report.

"Hey, kid, what's for dinner?" he asked.

He bent down and kissed the top of her head.

"I don't know," she said. "It's your turn."

"No, last night would have been your turn and it carries over because you did the Meals on Wheels thing."

"No, that's not how it works. Too complicated. You just gotta know which days are yours, and Monday is yours."

Bosch knew she was right because the point had been argued before. But he had been unnerved by the long-distance confrontation with the man he believed was Charles Broussard. Bosch had been the first to turn away and go back to his car.

"Well, then, I don't have anything," he said. "Who do you want to call or where do you want me to go for pickup?"

"Poquito Más?"

"Fine with me. You want the usual?"

"Yes, please."

"I'll be right back."

Poquito Más was literally right below their house at the bottom of the hill. With a good throw, Bosch could have hit the roof of the restaurant with a rock from his back deck. Sometimes from the same spot he could even smell the flavors of the Mexican restaurant down below. But getting there was another matter. Bosch had to follow Woodrow Wilson down the hill in a circuitous path and then take Cahuenga Boulevard nearly a mile up to the restaurant. It was one of the strange contradictions of the city. No matter how close something looked, it was still far away.

While he was waiting for his order to be put together, he got a call from Captain Crowder.

"You know a parks ranger named Bender?"

Bosch frowned and shook his head.

"Just met him tonight."

"Yeah, well, he didn't like the encounter."

"You're kidding me, right? I've been beefed by Dudley Do-Right?"

"Tomorrow I need you to write up a memorandum of your side of the conversation."

"Whatever."

"Did you really make fun of the guy's hat?"

"Yes, Captain, I guess I sort of did."

"Harry, Harry, Harry . . . come on, you know those guys have no sense of humor."

"Live and learn, Captain."

"What were you doing there, anyway?"

"Just taking in the view."

"Well . . . I don't think this is going anywhere but get me that memo, okay?"

"Will do."

"Anything new on Merced since we talked?"

Bosch wasn't ready to put the name Broussard out there with command staff yet. So he stayed away from that.

"We recovered the weapon," he said.

"What!" Crowder exclaimed. "Why didn't you tell me?"

"You were gone by the time we got back. I was going to update you in the morning."

"Where was it?"

"Hidden in a dead guy's house."

"You mean our shooter is dead?"

"It's looking that way."

"This is sort of great. It means no trial. We can wrap this thing up with a big pink bow this week."

"Not quite, Captain. If this guy was the shooter, someone put him up to it. That's who we want."

The woman behind the counter called out Bosch's number. His takeout dinner was ready.

"Do we know who that is?" Crowder asked.

"We're working on it," Bosch said. "I'll know more tomorrow."

Bosch had the sense that Crowder wanted additional information but Harry knew he was a direct conduit to the tenth floor of the PAB. Bosch couldn't afford to let Broussard's name start circulating on the floor that was more about politics than police. Crowder relented.

"Okay, Harry," he said. "Tomorrow. I want to know what you know."

"You got it, Captain," Bosch said.

He hung up and grabbed the bag of food off the counter.

27

On Tuesday afternoon Bosch and Soto sat in the seventeenth-floor waiting room at the District Attorney's Office for twenty minutes before being allowed in to see a filing deputy. Bosch thought the wait was because he had asked specifically for John Lewin to review their case. But they didn't get Lewin. They got a young hotshot named Jake Boland, who proudly hung his Harvard Law sheepskin on the wall of his ten-by-ten office. He was in shirtsleeves after a busy morning of filing cases, his suit jacket on a hanger on the back of his door. Bosch and Soto sat down in side-by-side chairs in front of his desk.

"We're not here in any official capacity," Bosch said.

"What do you mean?" Boland asked. "I'm a filing deputy. Let's file a case."

"We don't know if we're there yet. That's what I want to hear from you. But I don't want you to enter it on the log or treat this as a filing request, because if you reject it and we later file it, some defense attorney is going to get that out in front of a jury—that this case was originally rejected by the D.A. So let's just say we're here for advice only."

Boland leaned back as if distancing himself from the detectives and their case.

"Then I can't really give you a lot of time. I've got to

file cases. At the end of the day, that's what they look at here. If I don't file cases, I don't get that courtroom assignment I'm in line for."

"But you have to file good cases. If you file dogs, they'll never let you near a courtroom."

"Look, can you just tell me whatever it is you want to tell me so I can get on to the next one? We've got a waiting room out there with detectives who actually want to file cases. I know that might be a novel idea to you two, but believe it or not, it does happen."

At this point Bosch wanted to reach across the desk and grab Boland by his skinny purple tie, but he held his composure. Trading off with Soto, they began to tell the young prosecutor what they had, including the major developments of the morning—namely that the two other weapons found hidden in David Willman's workbench had been connected by Gun Chung to murders in Las Vegas and San Diego. One before the Merced shooting and one after. Additionally, fingerprints pulled off the Merced murder weapon the evening before were matched to David Willman.

When they were finished, Boland leaned back again and this time drummed a pen against his upturned chin as he considered the story they had just told.

"So you have a hit man out there on this hunting ranch and weapons that tie him to three killings," he said. "And no connection at all between the killings?"

Bosch shook his head.

"Other than him having possession of all the murder weapons? No. The Vegas thing was a rap DJ who was machine-gunned in his car à la Tupac Shakur. Made the police look at it like a gang thing but it was probably the end of a business deal gone sideways. The one in San Diego was probably a husband taking out his wife for the insurance. That was what was suspected at the time, but he was alibied and the cops had no leads—until we called today."

Boland paused the drumming for a moment.

"What about the sword?"

"Nothing on that yet."

"Any idea how these people knew to go to Willman for these hits? I mean, did he advertise on the Internet or what?"

"We don't know yet, but the agencies involved are on it now."

Boland nodded.

"By the way, did you get a warrant to search for those weapons?" he asked.

"Nope," Bosch said. "We were invited to search by one of the current owners of the property."

Boland frowned.

"Still should've papered it to make it clean."

"It was clean," Bosch insisted. "The lady there had nothing to do with the case. They bought the house from Willman's estate six years ago. Why would we need a judge's signature to search the garage when she said, 'Please do,' and the weapons we found were obviously abandoned by the previous owner?"

"Because when in doubt you whip it out—always bring a warrant. Come on, Detective. That's basic."

"But there wasn't any doubt. That search was clean. Are you sure you went to Harvard?"

Boland's face turned scarlet.

"Detective, you know what else is basic?" he managed

to ask. "Not insulting the prosecutor you want to file your case."

"If you were acting like a prosecutor, there wouldn't be any insult. And I didn't ask you to file the case. I asked you what we were missing, what we needed. I didn't ask you to piss on what we already have."

Soto put her hand on Bosch's arm, trying to bring him down. Boland held his hand out in a calming manner.

"Look," he said. "Let's start over. Whatever the details of the search, we live with it, and I think what you have here is a case against a dead hit man. But you don't have a case against Broussard or anybody else. Not even close."

"Broussard's wife was having an affair with the intended target," Soto said.

"Says who?" asked Boland.

"We have the witness and his story adds up," she answered. "On top of that, the guy who took the shot was Broussard's business partner. They were best friends since high school. You're saying that's not enough?"

Boland put the pen down and leaned forward.

"Guys, seriously, it's not enough," he said. "You go forward with what you've got and you can count on a number of things happening. First of all, you can count on Broussard having a drop-dead, ironclad alibi. I'm betting he was in another state with at least ten witnesses with him. That's how these guys do this. Second, you can expect his wife to deny everything—the affair, this Ojeda guy, that her husband could ever have done anything like this. She'll be a solid witness for the defense. And third, you can expect *your* witness—Ojeda—to fold before he even gets to the stand. They'll get to him first and buy him off or scare him off. One or the other."

Soto shook her head in frustration. Boland continued to dismantle the case in front of them.

"You have nothing that says Broussard asked or paid Willman to do this. Like I said, you might be able to convict Willman, but he's dead. You need a direct connection between Broussard and the crime, not just Broussard and Willman having known each other since high school. That proves nothing in a court of law."

"What about the Willman shooting?" Bosch asked.

Boland shrugged.

"It was ruled an accident by Riverside County. Fricking OSHA said it was an accident. I mean, unless you can prove otherwise, it's no help to our cause. It's probably not even admissible."

"What about the lawsuit Broussard settled with Willman's widow? Do we have any shot of breaking the seal on that?"

"Probably not. These guns you found have nothing to do with that case, do they?"

Bosch reluctantly shook his head. No one wants to be told they've come up short—especially when the telling is coming from a pompous prick. But Bosch was finally able to separate Boland's annoying personality from what he was saying. Harry understood that the young prosecutor was probably right. They didn't have a case yet. Soto was about to protest the rejection, when Bosch this time reached over to her and put his hand on her arm to stop her.

"So, then, what do we need?" he asked.

"Well, a signed confession is always nice," Boland said. "But realistically, I would want someone or something that brings us inside the conspiracy. It's too bad Willman's dead, because if he was alive we could pit the two principals against each other and play who-talks-first. But that's obviously not going to happen."

Bosch knew that Boland's take on the case was on target. It was depressing to think that Broussard might have successfully sealed himself off from prosecution for the Merced shooting.

"Okay," he said. "We'll see what we can do."

"Good luck, guys. And believe me, I don't like shooting holes in cases. I'd much rather file them. But as you said at the beginning, I need to file good, winnable cases, or I'll be stuck in this little room the rest of my career."

Bosch stood up to go. As off-putting as Boland's personality was, Bosch knew the same aspects of confidence, smarm, and ability to forecast and strategize a case would make him a solid prosecutor when he finally got that courtroom job.

Bosch and Soto walked down Spring Street back to the PAB. Their next stop would be the captain's office, where he and his lieutenant were overdue for the promised update on the case. Considering Boland's response to their efforts so far, Bosch knew that the next meeting would not go any better. Captain Crowder had told him that morning that he was getting a lot of pressure from the tenth floor and needed results. Bosch had asked for the rest of the day, and now they were at the point that Crowder would be waiting for them because the tenth floor was waiting for him.

"You want me to go in with you?" Soto asked.

"I think I can handle them," Bosch said.

"What do you say is next?"

"Not sure yet. What do you think about me telling them we're going to be putting some pressure on Broussard to see how he reacts?"

"What kind of pressure?"

"I'm still thinking. Maybe knocking on his door, maybe planting a story in the paper."

"You knock on his door and he'll probably lawyer up on the spot."

"If he does that, then that says something right there."

"What would a story in the paper say?"

"I don't know. Maybe that we have narrowed in on a suspect. Mention no names. Maybe we put it out there that we've got the murder weapon."

"That would sure let Broussard know we're close."

"And that's the risk. Do we want to show our hand like that? It's a desperate move. Are we there yet? I don't know."

Bosch hated the idea of acting desperately. A move like that put the following move in someone else's hands. It meant losing control of the investigation—bringing the media in, which was always risky, and waiting for the suspect to react, which was never guaranteed and couldn't be fully anticipated.

Bosch had seen it work beautifully before and he had seen it go horribly wrong. He had once been on a case where the lead team decided to plant a story saying the task force was closing in on a suspected serial rapist and killer. They dropped in one piece of evidence they knew would let the suspect know that they were specifically closing in on him—that the man they were looking at was a respected husband and father with a white-collar job. The 911 calls starting coming in shortly after. The man grabbed his boss and holed up in a supply closet, keeping a pair of scissors to his hostage's neck. The police moved in but were too late to stop the murder-suicide that ensued in the closet. There simply was no telling what would happen if Broussard learned that the Merced investigation was getting close to him.

Bosch thought about the fund-raiser scheduled for that night at the Beverly Hilton. They could possibly put some pressure on Broussard there—without having to resort to the media. At minimum they could get their first up-close look at the man they believed was behind the Merced shooting.

"Whatever you want to do, Harry," Soto said. "I'm with you."

"What are you doing tonight?"

"Tonight? I don't know. You want to go to Broussard's house?"

"No, but there's a fund-raiser he's hosting away from the house. I was thinking of going just to get a look at him, maybe have him get a look at us. I can try to use it to put Crowder off for another day. Tell him we'll meet tomorrow."

"That sounds like a plan. I'm in."

"Okay, then."

They walked the rest of the way in silence.

28

The Beverly Hilton was a vast hotel complex with several entrances and many different-size rooms to accommodate weddings, political fund-raisers, and other gatherings. Bosch had been there several times over the years for both professional and personal reasons. He and Soto self-parked in the garage and then walked in through the main lobby, where they moved through the crowds amassed for various events and followed signs to the escalators leading up to the banquet rooms. Along the way Bosch noticed several hotel security men in blue blazers posted throughout the lobby, radio buds in their ears, eyes scanning the crowd. He guessed that Zeyas was drawing some heavy hitters to his five-hundred-dollars-a-plate dinner.

On the second floor they walked down a long hallway with entrances to the various ballrooms. The Merv Griffin Room was actually a grand ballroom at the end of the hallway with two sets of double doors that stood open and waiting. On the wall between the doors was a ten-foot-high poster showing a black-and-white photo of Armando Zeyas shaking hands and engaged with a circle of smiling supporters. The shot had been taken with a fish-eye lens, which gave the resulting photo an exaggerated sense that Zeyas stood at the center of the people. Bosch paused in horror when he saw the slogan printed above the circle of people of every age, gender, and race:

Everybody Counts or Nobody Counts!
ZEYAS 2016

Below the poster was a long draped table behind which three women sat waiting to check people in and collect their money for the Zeyas bid for the governor's seat. Standing to the side of either entrance to the ballroom were two men with beefy physiques beneath blue blazers.

Not wanting to give away their identity right off the bat, Bosch directed Soto to the left of the welcoming table, and they walked down a short hallway to a set of glass doors leading to an outdoor promenade, which Bosch knew from times past was used as a smokers' porch.

"Where are we going?" Soto asked as they pushed through the doors.

"Strategic advantage," Bosch said. "You try to hang on to it for as long as you can."

They stepped out onto the windy promenade. It overlooked Wilshire Boulevard, which was packed with wall-to-wall traffic. The hotel was situated at the intersection of two main traffic arteries—Wilshire and Santa Monica Boulevards, a crossroads that was always a traffic knot.

Bosch leaned his elbows on the balcony edge and looked down at the traffic. In times past he would have lit a smoke.

"What's our advantage?" Soto asked.

"They don't know who we are," Bosch said. "I didn't

want to walk up first thing and badge them. Makes it a little harder to move around."

"I thought we wanted to get a look at Broussard, maybe have him get a look at us."

"Right. But we want to be subtle about it. Make him think. Make him wonder. You know what I mean?"

"I think."

Soto turned her back to the view and took in the massive facade of the building.

"So this is the place where Whitney Houston died," she said.

"Right," Bosch said. "In a bathtub."

"They played one of her songs at my high school graduation."

"Which one?"

"'Greatest Love of All.'"

Bosch nodded.

"Where'd you go? Garfield?"

"No, by then I was up in the Valley. I graduated from San Fernando High in Pacoima."

"Forgot you were up there."

"What about you?"

"I went to Hollywood High but I didn't graduate. Went into the service early and had to get a GED when I got back."

"Oh, right. Vietnam. Did you do any college?"

"Yeah, City College for a couple years. Then I joined the Department. Where'd you go after high school?"

She smiled and shook her head. She was embarrassed by the answer.

"Mills. It's a girls' school up in Oakland."

Bosch whistled.

"Nice."

Now that his daughter was a year away from college, he was familiar with most of what was out there, especially in California. Mills was a tough school to get into, even tougher to afford.

"I know, I know," she said. "How did a Pacoima girl end up at Mills?"

"More like how did a Mills girl end up in the LAPD?" he said.

She nodded. Good question.

"Well, I got a lot of scholarship money and I chose Mills because at the time I thought I wanted to be a lawyer. You know, civil rights, Legal Aid, tenant rights, things like that. But then, when I got away from L.A. and really started thinking about things, I thought about being a cop, you know, and maybe that would be the best way to help my community."

Bosch nodded but knew she was leaving something out.

"And there was the Bonnie Brae case," he said.

She nodded back.

"There was that, too," she said.

She seemed to drop the conversation at that point. Bosch went back to considering what he had hoped to accomplish by coming to the fund-raiser. There had been no real plan other than to get a look at Broussard. It was like a coach scouting the opposition. Perhaps Bosch would get a measure of the man he was zeroing in on. But now that he was here, he was trying to think of how they were going to handle getting into the Merv Griffin Room and eyeballing Broussard. Harry was beginning to realize that it was probably a faulty idea in the first place. At this level of politics, there was always a high degree of security involved. His idea of just blending in with the crowd and moving through the doors was unrealistic. He was considering bagging the whole thing and heading over to Hollywood to check on his daughter—from a distance.

"Uh, Harry?" Soto said.

"What?" he responded.

"I think we're about to lose strategic advantage."

Bosch turned away from the traffic. He saw Soto looking down the length of the promenade. He followed her eye line and saw a door sixty feet farther down. Two men in tuxedos had stepped out and were bent over against the wind as they attempted to light cigarettes. When they straightened up, Bosch saw that one was Connor Spivak, candidate Zeyas's right-hand man. The other man looked familiar to Bosch. He was big and had a full beard.

"Is that . . . ?" Soto asked.

"Broussard," Bosch said. "I think so."

Bosch had only seen photos of Broussard and glimpsed the dark figure on the balcony of his house the night before.

"We've been made," he said.

Spivak had spotted them and now he and the other man were walking toward them.

"What's our reason for being here?" Soto said under her breath.

"I'll handle it," Bosch said. "Follow my lead."

Spivak was smiling as he approached. The other man was moving a little more slowly and was a few paces behind.

"Detectives?" Spivak said. "I thought that was you two. What a surprise!"

He shook hands with both of them.

"What brings you here?" he asked.

"Well," Bosch said, "we heard about the dinner tonight and thought we'd come by, maybe see if we could talk to the candidate for a few moments. You know, keep him informed about the investigation, since he's putting his own money on the line."

"That's very thoughtful. He will be impressed. But he isn't here just yet. He had to make a stop at a synagogue in Westwood and then he's going to swing in after the dinner to say a few words here."

He checked his watch.

"That probably won't be for another hour," he said. "But I'd be happy to take the update and pass it on."

Bosch glanced at Broussard and then back to Spivak.

"Oh, of course," Spivak said. "We want to keep this on the down low. By the way, this is one of our generous hosts for the evening, Charles Broussard."

Broussard offered his hand first to Bosch. Harry shook it, holding eye contact with the man he believed had been responsible for the shooting of Orlando Merced.

"My friends call me Brouss."

Soto shook his hand next.

"You people do fine work under very difficult circumstances," Broussard said. "I wish you all the best. Stay safe."

"Thank you," Soto said.

"Brouss, maybe you can wait for me inside," Spivak suggested.

"No problem," Broussard said. "Just one last drag and then it's back in for politics as usual."

Bosch smiled at him and Spivak laughed a little too hard.

Broussard tipped his head back and blew smoke into the air. He then dropped his cigarette and stepped on it. He play-punched Spivak on the arm.

"See you inside, Sparky," he said to him. Then to Bosch and Soto, he said, "Pleasure to meet you."

Broussard started down the promenade toward the door he and Spivak had come through.

"That's sort of a backstage holding area," Spivak explained. "We snuck out."

"How much does a guy have to give to be a host at one of these things?" Bosch asked.

"A hundred K," Spivak answered without hesitation.

Bosch whistled.

"He can afford it," Spivak said. "Did you say you have an update on the Merced case, Detective?"

"Yes, for the candidate," Bosch said. "What are the chances of getting five minutes with him when he gets here?"

"I have to be honest, not good. As soon as he gets here, he's got to go to the podium. Then as soon as I get him offstage we head to the airport and I put him on a plane. He's got a prayer breakfast in the morning in San Francisco."

"What happened to 'Everybody counts or nobody counts'? We can't grab him for five minutes?"

Spivak shook his head as though he wished he had a better answer.

"I'm sorry, Detectives," he said. "It's just not a good

night. But I can take any update you want to give him. I'll keep it confidential. It will go just to him."

Bosch canted his head back and forth as though he were weighing the option of going through Spivak.

"It can wait," he finally said. "Just tell the candidate that he better get his checkbook ready."

Bosch made a move toward the door.

"Then you're getting close?" Spivak asked.

Bosch looked at him, noting the excited tone in his voice.

"That's for the candidate," he said. "Not the masses. Understand? I don't want it to end up in a speech tonight or the newspaper tomorrow."

"Of course, of course," Spivak said. "Completely confidential."

Bosch and Soto left him there and went back to the doors they had come through. Spivak headed off to his own door.

"Think he'll tell Broussard?" Soto asked, once they were inside the building again.

"I don't know," Bosch said. "Maybe."

"I wish I could be there for that."

"Let's go. I want to get over to Hollywood Station."

They walked down the short hall and saw that the table in front of the ballroom doors was now abandoned. The banquet had begun and the check-in ladies had moved inside. The security men were gone as well, probably posted inside the doors for the duration of the event.

Bosch looked around and saw that at the moment, there was no one present but him and Soto. He quickly moved behind the welcome table and pulled the poster down off the wall. He started rolling it up into a tight tube.

"Harry, what are you doing?" Soto asked in an urgent whisper.

"He stole my line," Bosch said. "I'm just stealing it back."

Bosch finished putting the poster into a tight roll and turned to head down the hallway. They were almost to the escalator alcove when Virginia Skinner came around the corner, her head down as she tried to pull something bulky from her purse.

"Ginny?"

She looked up and stopped herself from colliding with Bosch.

"Harry, you're here."

Bosch handed the rolled poster to his partner. Then he pulled out his car key.

"Take this," he said to Soto. "And go get the car. Pick me up out front."

"You got it," she said.

After Soto disappeared down the escalator, Bosch turned his attention back to Skinner.

"I thought you said you don't cover these things," he said.

"And I thought you were going to tell me if you were going," Skinner said.

"It was spur of the moment and I wasn't planning on staying, so I didn't call."

"Spur of the moment here too," Skinner said. "You're right, I don't cover these things. Not usually. But I thought I'd drop by and maybe put a paragraph or two into my column. I mean, the cat's out of the bag with

Zeyas. He's running and it's just a matter of fund-raising semantics."

"So it's nothing to do with me or what we've been talking about?"

"No, nothing. We have a deal and I'm sticking to it. I promise."

"Okay, good."

"What was that rolled-up thing that you gave her? Is that your partner? She's young."

Bosch didn't know which question to answer first.

"Yes, she's my partner. The Department always pairs the old with the new. And the rolled-up thing was just a souvenir."

"A souvenir of what?"

"Nothing. It doesn't matter."

"Did you see Broussard here?"

"Yes, I saw him. I actually met him. He was with Spivak and it sort of just happened."

"Ugh, Spivak. The only guy in the Zeyas entourage I can't stand. Too greasy. I think Zeyas would be better off without him—especially now that he's going statewide. Spivak is not a big-league guy. He's a ground-level local guy who's risen to his level of incompetence. If you ask me."

"Broussard called him Sparky."

"Yeah, that's an old one. He wrote a position paper for a candidate once. It favored replacing lethal injection with the electric chair. His thesis was that it would be a better deterrent. The idea obviously failed but people started calling him 'Sparky' Spivak after that."

Bosch nodded.

"Well," he said. "I gotta go."

"And I should go in," Skinner said.

"I'll see you."

"Yes, you will. Just remember, Harry, the deal we have is a two-way street. I better hear from you before anybody else does."

"Don't worry. When the time is right, you will."

Bosch went down the escalator two steps at a time. When he went through the automatic doors to the valet circle, Soto was waiting for him in the Ford. He jumped in and she pulled out.

"Who was that woman in the hallway?" Soto asked.

"Oh, just a friend," Bosch said. "A reporter, actually."

"She looked like she wants to be more than friends with you."

"Really? I didn't notice."

After dropping Soto off at her car at the PAB, Bosch headed back to Hollywood. He put the division's tactical channel on his car's scanner and soon learned the location of the alcohol sting involving the station's Explorers. The current target was a convenience store on La Brea south of Sunset. Bosch moved in close but not too close. His plain-wrap Ford would be easily made as a police vehicle. It would be the height of embarrassment for Bosch's daughter if he were to spoil the sting.

Bosch spent the next two hours mostly listening to the operation as the sting was carried out at several different locations in Hollywood. No arrests were made. They would be made later after the results of the operation were taken to the City Attorney's Office for filing of charges against individuals or against the license-holders of the businesses.

When he heard the field supervisor call the code that ended the operation for the night, Bosch headed home, taking Laurel Canyon up to Mulholland and then heading east. This allowed him to cruise by Broussard's house on his way home. He once more stopped at the overlook and checked on the concrete house but he saw no lights on and no figure on any of the rear balconies. Even the pool light was out.

Bosch managed to leave the overlook without encountering the park ranger Bender and got to his home before his daughter. He texted her to ask for an arrival time but she walked in the door five minutes later. He asked how the night had gone and never let on that he already knew the answer because he had ghosted the operation.

"It was great," she said. "I put in a fake nose ring. It was fun."

"How many of them sold you booze?" he asked.

"Just about all of them. It wasn't random. Each place either had a history already or there had been complaints. One skeezy guy told me he'd only sell me the six-pack if I got behind the counter and gave him oral sex. Isn't that gross?"

"Yeah."

Bosch had not heard that while monitoring the tactical channel. He decided to stop asking questions at that point. He just gave his daughter a hug.

"I'm proud of you," he said.

"Thanks, Dad. You know, I'm dead tired and I have school tomorrow," she said.

"Then go to sleep."

"I am. Good night."

"Good night."

He watched her head toward the hallway that led to their bedrooms.

"Hey, Mads."

She turned and looked back at him.

"What is 'skeezy,' anyway?"

"I don't know. Old, creepy, gross."

He nodded.

"What I thought. Good night."

"Good night."

29

Once again Soto was in the squad room ahead of Bosch. He was beginning to think she was throwing down a challenge, seeing who could be more dedicated to the job, who could arrive earliest and stay longest. No partner of his had ever been this way. He was duly impressed.

She didn't notice him until she heard the clunk of his briefcase on his desk. Then she spun around in her chair and fixed him with wide eyes and a broad smile.

"Harry! I found the nexus!"

"On Bonnie Brae?"

"Yes, Bonnie Brae. I came in early and got back to my tenants list. You were right. There is a connection between Bonnie Brae and EZBank. A big one."

Bosch pulled his chair over and sat down in front of her.

"Okay, talk me through it."

She gestured back to the open binder on her desk.

"Well, I've been going through the tenants list from '93. I started on the first floor and finally on the third floor, I found something. Apartment 3-G. A woman named Stephanie Perez lived there in a two-bedroom."

"Do you remember her from back then? Did you know her?"

"No, the place was too big and I was just a little kid. I didn't track any grown-ups beyond my parents and the ladies in day care, like Miss Esi."

Bosch nodded.

"Okay, sorry to interrupt. Keep going."

"Okay, so Stephanie Perez was interviewed. Everybody was interviewed by the fire department and the CCS, and the summaries are in binder three here. The interviewers used a number system one through five in evaluating each person as a witness as well as the value of their information—five being the highest in each category. Stephanie Perez was a one-one. So she was interviewed and quickly forgotten because she didn't know anything. She was twenty-four at the time, unmarried, and worked as a cashier at a Ralphs supermarket. No gang affiliation on record and was at work the morning of the fire."

"Okay."

"But she lived alone in a two-bedroom unit, and when she was asked about that empty room, she said her roommate had moved out a month earlier and she was in the process of trying to find a new one."

Bosch reflexively jumped her story.

"One of our EZBank people looked at the place to rent."

"No, but I thought maybe that was a possibility too. So I tracked Stephanie Perez down to see what, if anything, she remembered. They had a protocol for all these tenant interviews and it included taking down DL numbers and birth dates. It was easy to find her."

"Where is she?"

"She's still in the neighborhood but now lives in a building down on Wilshire. She's still working at the same Ralphs, too, but now she's assistant manager and she's been married, divorced, and has two kids."

"So when did you call her?"

"About a half hour ago. I waited till seven."

Bosch gave her a look. Making a call that early was risky. It could anger someone if you woke them up to talk about something that had happened more than two decades ago. Soto read his concern.

"No, she was totally cool with it," she said. "She was already awake and getting ready for work."

"You were lucky," Bosch said. "What did she tell you?"

"She moved out right after the fire, so she never rented the second bedroom. And before the fire she hadn't interviewed anybody yet. She had just put the ad in *La Opinión*."

"So the roommate who moved out is the connection?"

"Exactly. Her old roommate was Ana Acevedo, who worked at EZBank—the one who opened the door."

Bosch nodded. It was a very good lead and connection. He immediately understood that momentum had just shifted away from the Merced case and was with the Bonnie Brae investigation now. They would need to ride it and that would mean having to finesse Captain Crowder, which might not be easy.

"Is there more?" he asked. "What else did she tell you?"

"It gets better, Harry," Soto said. "Because it confirms things we already know. Stephanie Perez was the leaseholder on the apartment. She said the reason she asked Ana to move out was because she was juggling two boyfriends, and one of them was a white boy who was mean and had a habit of saying racist things even though he was dating Ana. Stephanie didn't want to be in the middle of it, especially if the white boy found out about the other boyfriend, because she thought he was the kind of guy who might be violent. She had warned Ana about the situation several times and Ana did nothing about it. So Stephanie told Ana she had to go and she moved out—a month before the fire."

Bosch remembered the name he had read off the page from the robbery journal borrowed from the captain's office in Robbery Special.

"Rodney Burrows?"

"That's what I'm guessing. She didn't remember names, but when I said Rodney she said yes, one of them was named Rodney. I said, 'Rodney Burrows?' and she couldn't remember a last name. She said she'd look at a six-pack if I brought it by the store today."

"Okay, what about the other boyfriend?"

"Same thing. I said, 'Maxim Boiko?' and she remembered Max but not the last name. She'll look at a six-pack on him, too."

"Did she talk about how long these guys were around the apartment? Were they staying over, taking out the trash, things like that?"

"I didn't get into it in detail—that question about the trash is a good one. But I did get the impression that these guys would stay over and that's where Stephanie was scared. She was afraid one might come over and surprise Ana when she was with the other."

"Right."

Bosch thought about the scenario for a few moments. It did seem to be the connection they were looking for.

"I think we're in business here, Harry," Soto said.

Bosch nodded. But his mind was still bumping over other possibilities.

"Did she ever consider that Ana might have started

the fire? You know, sort of in revenge for getting kicked out of the apartment?"

"I didn't ask. We should."

Harry nodded again.

"Okay," he said, "so let's get six-packs together for all three of them and start with Stephanie Perez at Ralphs. Let's move fast and get out of here before the captain gets in and wants an update on Merced."

"You got it."

"By the way, did you check—do any of these EZBank people have records?"

Soto nodded.

"I started address searches and backgrounds on them on Sunday after we got the names off the robbery book. Acevedo and Boiko are clean. But Burrows went to federal prison in '06 for tax evasion."

"Tax evasion?"

"Yeah. He didn't file tax returns for something like six years in the nineties and the feds caught up to him. He cut a deal to limit his time and they put him in Lompoc. He served twenty-two months."

"Nice. Anything else?"

"That's all I found."

"Where's he live now?"

"Oh, he's some kind of desert rat or something. He lives out in a place called Adelanto. I looked at his house on Street View. It looks like a shithole surrounded by fences and in the middle of nowhere."

Bosch nodded. Extreme rural address, tax evasion, washing out of the police academy on a racial insensitivity beef—Bosch was beginning to get a picture of Rodney Burrows.

"Did you request the file on the tax case?" he asked.

"No, I haven't had time," she answered defensively. "Yesterday we were going full bore on Merced."

"I know, I know," Bosch said. "I'm just asking. What about a mug shot from the feds?"

"There's one online. I just have to print it."

"Okay, for Acevedo and Boiko you'll have to use DL shots, since they've got clean records."

"Okay, but won't they be current photos? What if she can't make an ID twenty-one years later? Stephanie said she hasn't seen any of these people since back then."

Bosch thought a moment, weighing the risk. Anything they tried that came back wrong or negative could come up and hurt them in trial.

"I still want Perez to look at photos. You put that together and I'll make a call to somebody I know in the federal building, maybe see if we can get a look at the file or the presentencing report on Burrows. I want to start filling out his profile."

"You got it."

"The captain will be here by eight. Let's get moving."

"On it."

"And, Lucy, this is really good stuff."

"Thanks."

Bosch started pushing himself in his chair back to his desk but then stopped and looked at her.

"You know, I have to say I underestimated you. Two weeks ago I wasn't sure you even belonged in the unit. Now I have no doubt."

She didn't say anything. He nodded and turned back to his desk.

Bosch opened the contact list on his phone and called

the cell number he had for Rachel Walling at the bureau. It had to have been at least a couple years since he had used the number or had spoken to her. He hoped the number was still good and that she'd take his call. He also hoped she was still assigned to the Los Angeles office. With the FBI, you never knew. Here today, Miami or Dallas or Philadelphia tomorrow. He remembered that before L.A., Walling had been posted in Minot, North Dakota.

Walling answered the call.

"Well, well, well. Harry Bosch. The man who only calls when he needs something."

Bosch smiled. He deserved the rebuke.

"Rachel, how are you?"

"Things are good. How about with you?"

"Can't complain, except they're just about to pull the rug out from under me here. I'm on the DROP."

"At least you get to stay till you're, what, sixty-five?"

"Hey, hold on. I'm not that old yet!"

"I know, but what I'm saying is that around here they kick us out at fifty-seven. There is no such thing as the Deferred Retirement Option Plan here."

"That isn't fair. But, hey, you don't have to worry about that for a couple decades, right?"

He could almost hear her smile.

"Smooth, Harry. You must really, really want something from me."

"Well, I was just calling to see how you're doing, but if you really need me to ask for something, then I'll ask if you've got anybody over at the IRS who might look up an old case for me."

There was a pause but it didn't last too long.

"You know the IRS doesn't talk to anybody, not even us. What kind of case is it?"

"Tax evasion in '06. Guy went away for a couple years. Right now he lives out in the desert and it looks to me like he may be one of these 'ist' guys, you know? Extremist, separatist, survivalist, white supremacist—take your pick. Who knows, maybe he's even a polygamist. Added to that, he didn't pay taxes for six years. That isn't an oversight, you know? That's a choice."

"Well, if he is all of that, then it's most likely we had part of the case. What's your angle? You're still working cold cases, right?"

"Yeah. And I think this guy was part of a three-man takedown team that pulled off a quarter-million-dollar heist at a check-cashing store in '93. I think he was the inside man. I want to know about him but I'd also like to know who his KAs at the time were, too."

"Who died?"

"Nobody in the heist but I'm looking at a fire that started a few blocks away as a diversion. It killed nine people, most of them kids. I think it was before you were out in L.A., Rachel. You were still riding the range in North Dakota."

"Don't remind me. Give me what you've got and I'll see what I can find."

Bosch hesitated here but only for a moment. This was the point where he was vulnerable. He had just laid out his investigation to her in oblique terms. If he now gave her the name and details, there was nothing stopping her from running with the case and possibly grabbing it from the LAPD. But it was Rachel Walling. They had known each other for a long time. Bosch felt safe.

"Rodney Burrows," he said.

"You have a case number, DOB, anything else?"

"Hold on a second."

Bosch swiveled in his chair, covered his phone, and asked Soto for the information on Burrows. She held out a legal pad with the information written on it, and Bosch uncovered the phone and read it off to Walling.

"And you have no known associates?"

"No KAs. That's what I'm hoping to get from you."

He then turned back to his desk, checking the wall clock as he did so. He knew they had to get out of the squad room or be confronted by Crowder about the Merced case. He stood up.

"Okay?" he said. "You need anything else?"

"Yes," Walling said. "I need breakfast and you're going to owe me for this. How about you meet me at nine at the Dining Car?"

Bosch thought about what they were planning with Stephanie Perez at Ralphs. The store wasn't far from the Pacific Dining Car. There was also the fact that he had skipped breakfast in an unsuccessful attempt to beat Soto into the squad room that morning.

"How about ten?"

"Too late. Nine-thirty."

"I think I can do that. Is it all right if I bring—"

"Come alone, Bosch. I don't need to meet another cop."

"Uh, okay. Sure."

But he realized he was already speaking into a dead line.

*

On the way to Ralphs supermarket Bosch drove, as usual. He was quiet as he contemplated what moves they should make on the newly energized investigation. He believed they were going to get one shot, and they needed to use it well. They were heading toward a situation where they would have to put Rodney Burrows in the box and break him down. At the moment, there was little with which to do this. There were no witnesses, no physical evidence. There were just the timing and proximity of things. There was the hunch.

"Let's review for a minute before we go in and talk to her," he said.

"Okay," Soto said.

"So we can now put Ana Acevedo, an employee of EZBank, in the Bonnie Brae Arms up until a month before the fire."

"Right."

"And she's running romances with Maxim Boiko and Rodney Burrows, both also of EZBank."

"Right."

"So that's the first thing with Perez. We need to confirm these are the three people we are talking about and we have to confirm that Ana had her boyfriends over to the apartment on a regular basis. We have to put this guy Rodney Burrows in the Bonnie Brae."

"We have that. That's why she kicked Ana out. She said it was headed toward a bad end and she didn't want it to happen in the apartment."

"Okay, well, we need to hit that again with her. Hit it hard. We want him taking the trash out. We want to establish his knowledge of the apartment complex."

"Got it."

"We also need to find out about Ana and clear up the possibility that she started the fire."

"Out of revenge. Right."

"And I want you to do this interview. You already spoke and established a rapport with her. You also both lived in that place and you can use that if needed."

"Okay. We did speak in Spanish earlier."

"Okay, there you go. I'm going to hang back and if I think of something to ask I'll take you aside."

"Okay."

"Couple other things. We want to know how she knew Ana Acevedo in the first place. You know, how did they become roommates? And then we want to know if she had any continuing interaction over the past twenty years with any of these people."

"She already said no about that last part but I'll ask again."

Bosch glanced over and saw that Soto was writing his questions down in a notebook that was just like the one he carried. The notebook was new. He hadn't noticed it before.

Five minutes later they pulled into the Ralphs parking lot. It was on 3rd Street at Vermont. The parking lot was surprisingly full for the hour. Bosch guessed that a lot of midnight-shifters were hitting the market on their way home from work.

At the office at the front of the store, they asked for Stephanie Perez and were directed to the produce section, the area she was in charge of. Perez was a very small and round woman who wore an oversize white service jacket. Although she had spoken earlier to Soto, she seemed nervous about the detectives showing up at her workplace. Soto asked if there was a private place to talk and she took them to a break room in the rear of the store. It was too early for anyone to be taking breaks, so they had the space to themselves.

Perez asked if it was all right if the interview was conducted in Spanish and Bosch nodded his approval to Soto. Whatever made the witness most comfortable was the rule. Soto in return asked if it was okay to record the conversation and Perez gave her approval. Soto put her phone on the break table and turned on its recording feature. Bosch made a mental note to tell Soto after the interview that it was not necessary to ask permission to record an interview.

The women then started talking and Bosch tried to keep up. He was able to understand Spanish much better than he could speak it. But he quickly lost the thread, recognized only a few words, and then was distracted when his phone started vibrating. He pulled it from his pocket to check the screen and saw that it was Captain Crowder calling. He let it go to message and focused back on the conversation he didn't understand.

Twenty minutes in, Soto turned to Bosch.

"She would like to look at pictures now," she said.

Bosch thought for a moment. This was the big decision. If Perez couldn't identify the EZBank employees, that could be an issue down the line. It was time to make the call on it and Soto was leaving it to him.

"Okay," he finally said. "Let's do it."

Soto had carried in a stack of files. They contained three separate six-pack photo lineups. Each lineup contained one photo of one of the EZBank employees in question along with five randomly selected photos of people of similar age and race. The photos were slipped into windows cut in a piece of cardboard. They started with the easy one. Ana Acevedo. Soto had been unable to find a current driver's license for Acevedo in California or any of its neighboring states. While that was worrying in itself because it left Acevedo's present whereabouts unknown, it also meant that Soto had to use a DL photo from the time of the EZBank robbery in the six-pack. It would most likely be the easiest identification Perez had to make.

Soto opened a file containing photos of six women of Latin ethnicity. Within two seconds Perez put her finger on Acevedo's photo.

"That's Ana," she said.

"Okay," Soto said.

She popped the photo out of its cardboard frame and asked Perez to sign the back of it as a confirmation of her choice. She then returned it to the file and put it to the side of the table. Soto opened the next file, which contained shots of six men of Eastern European heritage. Perez leaned over and studied all six photos before tapping the photo of Maxim Boiko.

"This one is Max," she said.

Soto went through the same process of having Perez sign the photo she had selected.

Now came the big one. Soto opened the last six-pack and put it down in front of Perez. Soto didn't say a word. She knew it was important not to speak or communicate anything through body language that was encouraging or confirming to the witness. That could result in a tainted identification in the eyes of a judge and jury.

Perez once again leaned forward and studied the

photos—this time of six white men in their mid-forties. All homegrown Americans. Bosch knew there were all kinds of theories on inter-ethnic identification and that the process they were engaged in was fraught with issues relating to accuracy. The best they could do was present the photos, say nothing that might direct an identification, and simply wait. If she made an ID, the lawyers could fight about it later.

Perez studied the photos for nearly a minute and then slowly put her finger down below one of the photos.

"Him," she said. "This is Rodney."

Bosch and Soto exchanged eye contact and then Soto had Perez sign the photo she had chosen. It was the photo of Rodney Burrows.

"I have to return a call to the captain," Bosch said to Soto. "You finish up and I'll be in the car."

Bosch thanked Perez for her time and cooperation and made his way back through the store and then out to the car. On the way, he listened to the message left on his phone by Crowder.

"Harry, this is Captain Crowder speaking. I want my update and I'm not fucking around. Call me. Now."

Bosch got behind the wheel and turned on the engine. It was a cool morning and he wanted heat. He called the captain's direct line.

"Where are you, Harry?" Crowder said by way of greeting.

"In the field," Bosch said. "Something's come up."

"I don't want to hear that. I want to hear the update on Merced. What've you got for me? It better be good."

30

They traded updates once Soto made it back to the car, and Bosch headed toward the PAB. She summarized the interview with Stephanie Perez and then he recounted his conversation with Crowder, reporting that the captain was at first upset to hear that the Merced investigation had temporarily stalled but then was placated when informed that Bosch and Soto were closing in on something regarding the much bigger Bonnie Brae case—a break that happened to come out of an anonymous call to the Merced tip line.

"Speaking of Crowder," he said, "I need to drop you back at the PAB while I go to breakfast. Crowder said media relations approved an interview with you and a reporter from *La Opinión*. It's been over a week since Orlando Merced passed and they want to run an update. I told him to set it up now so we have the rest of the day. You do that while I meet my federal friend."

"Okay," Soto said. "How much do I tell the reporter?"

Bosch took the car across the 110 freeway overpass and glanced down as he considered Soto's question. All ten lanes looked as though they were frozen.

"Well, you don't mention Broussard by name."

"Right. What about the rifle?"

Bosch wasn't sure.

"Ask Crowder," he said. "Let him decide. We put it

out and we might stir things up. Put some pressure on Broussard."

"Okay, I'll ask. Does Crowder know about Broussard?"

"I've left that out of my updates."

"Does he know we're looking at someone?"

"I left that out, too."

"Got it."

"Good. In the meantime, if I don't get back by the time you're finished, try to confirm locations on Ana Acevedo. We might be most interested in Burrows but we need to talk to Acevedo to tie in the story. Boiko, too."

"Okay."

"By the way, did you ask Perez if she ever thought Ana had started the fire?"

"I did and she said no. She said Ana wasn't a good roommate but she was a good person. She said she would never have done something like that."

Bosch thought about this answer. They were looking into the possibility that, good person or not, Ana Acevedo had direct involvement with the fire or at least the men who started it—as well as the robbery connected to it.

"Harry," Soto said. "Do you want me to reschedule my shrink session?"

Bosch came out of his thoughts and looked over at her. He had forgotten. It was Wednesday and Soto had her regular afternoon session with Dr. Hinojos at Behavioral Sciences.

"Yeah," Bosch said. "See if she'll let you skip this week. We have things moving on this. Let's not break momentum."

"I'll call her."

"And I'll be back in an hour. Maybe we'll know more about Burrows by then."

"Who is this agent you're meeting?"

"She works in an intelligence unit. They throw out the net, you know. Then they analyze."

"I thought it was a she. Your voice completely changed when you were talking to her on the phone today. It was like when you talk to your daughter. You get all nice."

Bosch glanced over at her. He didn't know whether to compliment her perception or tell her to mind her own business.

"Yeah, well. There's a history."

"And she wants to meet you by yourself."

"That's just the way she is. She'll say more if it's just me."

"Whatever works, Harry."

Bosch nodded. He was happy to move on from a discussion about Rachel Walling.

"Okay, let's go back to Stephanie Perez for a minute before you jump out. Through her we have all three of these EZBank people in the Bonnie Brae."

"That's absolutely solid. We have her six-pack IDs and her take on Burrows, which confirms the racist attitudes."

"Okay, what about Ana? How did she and Perez hook up? How long did they share the apartment before Perez made her move out?"

"Stephanie said they lived together for a year and she got her after putting a roommate-needed notice on the bulletin board in the complex's laundry room."

"Ana was already living there?"

"No, but she had lived there when she was a kid. She was back visiting friends, saw the notice, and made contact with Perez. She said she wanted to live there because she knew the place and could walk to work. She didn't have a car."

Bosch nodded. This was all good. In her earlier summary of the Perez interview Soto had also said that Burrows spent at least two nights a week in the apartment with Acevedo over a three-month period leading up to the point where Acevedo was asked to leave. Boiko was a less frequent visitor but was still an occasional overnight guest as well. But when Perez started complaining about the situation, Acevedo reacted by making both men get involved in the upkeep of the apartment. This included chores such as taking out the trash.

All of this was based on Stephanie Perez's twenty-one-year-old memories but it was positive in terms of case momentum. What Bosch and Soto needed now was further confirmation through Acevedo, Burrows, and Boiko themselves.

"We really need to find Ana Acevedo," Bosch said.

"I told you," Soto said. "I'm on it."

They were stopped at a light at 1st and Hill, a few blocks from the PAB.

"Gus Braley said the video showed her pulling the alarm before the robbers came in," he said. "Based on that, they decided back then that she wasn't part of the robbery."

"You're thinking otherwise?"

"Not yet. But I'm looking at the video from the opposite side of things now."

"Meaning what?"

"Meaning, if you knew there was a camera on you, then you probably knew that if you didn't pull the alarm, you were guaranteeing you would be considered a suspect."

Soto thought about that for a bit and then nodded.

"I get it," she said.

"That's why we need to find her and talk to her," Bosch said. "You said she's disappeared. No DL, no record, whereabouts unknown. I don't like that."

"Neither do I. Do you think she's dead? Maybe they used her and buried her in the desert."

Bosch nodded. It was a possibility.

"The other thing is, we don't have any idea about the two gunmen," he said. "All three of these people we're talking about were inside EZBank. They didn't commit the actual robbery."

"Or start the fire."

"If one of these people is the insider, they lead us to the other two."

"Can we back up and just talk about how the whole thing went down?"

The light changed and Bosch proceeded.

"You have the two guys in the car," he said. "Their first stop is the Bonnie Brae. One of them goes in and drops the Molotov down the trash chute."

"They start the fire, then head to the cash box," Soto said.

"Right. They've got a scanner in the car and pull up close to the target and wait to hear the response on the fire. When they hear 'all units,' they go to the cash box. Or maybe they're not that sophisticated. They just pull over and wait for sirens. When they hear the big response, they go in, hit the target, and have time to get away before police can respond."

Bosch pulled the car up to the courtyard that fronted the PAB. Soto hopped out and looked back in at him.

"I think it works," she said.

Bosch nodded.

"See you in an hour," he said.

Rachel Walling was waiting for Bosch in a booth in a back room of the restaurant on 6th Street. It was the room reserved for heavy hitters and regulars. With three round tables for big parties and three booths for smaller parties, the room was at capacity, and Bosch recognized half the faces from City Hall. He wasn't sure who they all were but they were at least mid-level important or they wouldn't be eating breakfast at 9 a.m. on a workday.

Rachel Walling didn't look like she had aged a day since he had last seen her. Her jawline was cut sharply, her neck taut, her brown hair with hints of raven in it. Her eyes were always the thing with Bosch. Dark, piercing, unreadable. A vibration went through him as he approached, a reminder of what could have been. There was a time when he had this woman, and then things went wrong. When it came to the women in his life, there were only a few regrets. She would always be one of them.

She smiled and put aside the folded newspaper she had been reading as he slid into the booth.

"Harry."

"Sorry I'm late."

"You're not that late. Are things happening?"

"Beginning to."

Walling indicated the newspaper she had put to the side.

"You were in the paper last week about that mariachi musician dying. Can I ask, were you asking about Rodney Burrows in regard to that?"

"Not really, no. I have other cases. You know how it is."

"Sure. I was just curious about the fit on this."

"No, like I told you on the phone, I'm interested in the fire that killed all those kids. Were you able to get me something? I see the newspaper but I don't see a file or anything."

She smiled as if parrying an insult.

"You know we don't give files out. We're not really the sharing kind."

The waiter came up with a coffeepot and Bosch signaled that he'd take a cup. The waiter asked if they knew what they wanted to order or needed a menu. Bosch hadn't needed a menu in the Pacific Dining Car in twenty-five years. He looked at Rachel.

"Are we going to eat or is this going to be short and sweet?" he asked.

"We're going to eat," she said. "I told you, I'm hungry."

They ordered without the menu and the waiter went away. Bosch took a draw of hot coffee and then fixed Walling with a look that said it was time to give.

"So," he said. "Rodney Burrows . . ."

She nodded.

"Okay, this is the deal," she said. "You had Rodney Burrows pegged correctly and he was on our radar for a long time, but then he went away on the tax conviction and he's been quiet ever since. At least we think so. So I need to know if the bureau is going to be embarrassed by anything you are doing."

Bosch shook his head emphatically.

"Not unless the bureau dropped the ball in '93. This is strictly a cold case investigation. This guy lives out in Adelanto now and as far as I know he's been quiet as a mouse."

"Okay, I'll trust you on that."

"So tell me what you've got. When did he hit the FBI radar?"

"Well, by the mid-nineties we started watching a lot of these types. You know, militia sympathizers, Posse Comitatus, Christian Identity—all those 'Don't Tread on Me' anti-government hate groups. In the space of two years we had Waco and Ruby Ridge and you couple that with the riots in '92 right here in L.A. and you sort of have this call to arms that speaks to a lot of these fringe dwellers. Some of them, like your guy, believed the riots constituted the first warning of a coming race war. Mix in your standard anti-government views, stand-your-ground arms accumulation, and a lot of those other 'ist' allegiances you mentioned earlier, and you have yourself a loose-form movement. We picked up on this happening in many places across the country. Obviously there were many that didn't get our notice—the Oklahoma City bombing happened in '95."

"So what about Burrows?"

"He and some of his fellow numbskulls formed something they called the WAVE. It was a benign-sounding acronym standing for White American Voices Everywhere. They became part of this national association of groups that wanted to close borders and get ready to defend white America when the race war began."

"Didn't Charlie Manson preach the same thing back in the day?"

"He did. But just like somebody should have been watching Manson back in the day, we *did* start watching Burrows and his group."

"When?"

"We didn't get onto them until about '94, when they started putting leaflets on windshields from L.A. to San Diego—which, by the way, they called *Ban* Diego."

"Cute. My case was a year before that."

"I know. I can't directly help you there. You asked me what we had on Burrows and it's all '94 and on."

"What were they doing besides printing up leaflets?"

"Nothing much. They had a compound out near Castaic and they shot their guns off and trained recruits and listened to a lot of speed metal on the stereo. Your basic hate group—long on rhetoric but not much else. The boldest thing they ever did was print up a racist manifesto and put out leaflets inviting people to an open house at the training camp. We kept a loose watch on them, had a plant inside the clubhouse, and the determination was that these guys were all talk and no walk. They would not start the war, they would just be cheerleaders when it came."

"A plant? Did you bug the place?"

"No, we had a CI. One of the members of WAVE got jammed up on something else and agreed to inform."

"Where'd the money come from for this compound? Did these guys have jobs? What?"

"The summaries I read before coming here described them as very well funded, but the source of that funding was not determined. These guys were security guards and long-range truckers. It didn't account for their funding."

"The robbery I'm talking about netted two hundred sixty thousand. There was another one a few months before that that could have been connected."

"Well, that could explain it, but I saw nothing about that in the summaries."

"Was Burrows the top man?"

"No, he was just a worker bee. WAVE was started by a guy named Garret Henley, who was a long-haul trucker. He was the initial recruiter."

Bosch got out his notebook to write the name down.

"You won't be able to talk to him," Walling said. "He died twelve years ago. Killed himself after being indicted for tax evasion. He knew he was going to go away. That's how we got most of these guys—they stopped paying taxes."

"Then, who else?" Bosch asked. "Who were Burrows's known associates? My case involved him and two gunmen."

Walling reached over and unfolded the newspaper she had put to the side. For the first time Bosch could see she had written notes on the edges of the columns. Walling read her own notes and then flipped the paper closed again.

"The summaries said there were two brothers who were tight with Burrows. Matt and Mike Pollard. Also, if you are looking for a getaway driver, there was a wannabe stock car driver named Stanley Nance in the group. His nickname was 'Nascar Nance.' Maybe he was your driver."

Bosch liked all of this. It seemed to fit. Walling read his excitement.

"Now, before you jump up and start doing an Irish jig, I ran a quick check on these three guys and you're not going to like what I found," she said.

"What?" Bosch asked.

"Well, Nascar Nance is driving the big oval in the sky. He killed himself in '96 when he hit a bridge abutment at ninety-five miles an hour on the five. And both the Pollards were sent to federal prison for tax evasion but only one came out alive. Mike Pollard was sent to Coleman, which is in Florida, where he was stabbed to death in the prison library in '06. Case was never solved and is suspected of being racially motivated."

"And the other one?"

"Matt Pollard served his time in Lewisburg and paroled out in '09. He had a five-year tail and reported to the federal parole office in Philadelphia. But he cleared parole two months ago and his whereabouts are currently unknown. These diehard anti-government types like to stay below the radar. They avoid driver's licenses, Social Security, paying taxes, and so on."

Bosch frowned and was reminded that Ana Acevedo had likewise dropped off the grid. But then he thought of something that seemed like a discrepancy regarding the men of WAVE.

"Burrows didn't go to prison until '06," he said. "And he was out in twenty-two months."

"What can I tell you? The process is slow," Walling said. "I don't know the details of each case but they went after these guys one at a time, and Burrows came up last, I guess."

That didn't sound right to Bosch.

"Okay, but Burrows went up to the country club at Lompoc," he said. "How does he get Lompoc, and the Pollards get Lewisburg and Coleman? Those are hard places. It sounds like Burrows caught a break."

Walling nodded.

"You'd have to pull all three cases and see how they lined up differently. You didn't ask me to do that. You asked about Burrows. Who knows, maybe his offenses were not as extensive. Plus he took a deal, and maybe the other two went to trial. A lot of things can explain the discrepancy."

"I know, I know. I'm just wondering if he got a payoff for being the confidential informant all those years before."

Walling shook her head.

"There was nothing in the file I looked at that said anything about substantial assistance being given by the defendant," she said.

"That doesn't mean it didn't happen," Bosch said.

"Either way, you're now asking things above my pay grade. I don't have access to CI lists. For obvious reasons, those are under lock and key."

"Did you write down any of the case numbers? I could talk to the prosecutor."

"I did."

"What about the case agent who handled WAVE? Who was that?"

"Nick Yardley. And he's still in the L.A. office."

"Think he'd talk to me?"

"He might, but you have to remember, Burrows went to prison on an IRS case. Technically we would only have been assisting. Nick might shine you onto them, and if that happens you can forget it. IRS agents don't talk to locals."

"I know."

"If you talk to Nick, don't tell him you've talked to me. Tell him your information comes from the court file."

"Of course."

The waiter came with the food then. Bosch wanted to leave and keep moving with the case but he knew if he was rude to Rachel she might never help him again. He didn't want to risk that.

They started to eat and he tried some small talk.

"So what's Jack doing these days?" he asked.

Jack was Jack McEvoy, the former *Times* reporter that Rachel had been with for the past few years. Bosch knew McEvoy as well.

"He's doing well," she said. "He's happy—and lucky, considering today's journalism market."

"He's still working on that investigative website?"

"He recently jumped to a different one. It's called Fair Warning. It's consumer protection investigations and reporting. You should check it out. The government, the newspapers—nobody's really watching out for Joe Citizen anymore. They do some interesting stuff on the site. And he loves the work again."

"That's great. I will check it out. Fair Warning dot com?"

"Dot org. It's a nonprofit."

"Okay, I'll take a look at it."

Bosch thought about asking her about the tightrope she walked at the bureau by being in a relationship with a reporter, but before he said anything, he felt his phone vibrate in his pocket. He put his fork down and checked it. It was a text from Soto.

Ready to go

A not-so-gentle reminder that the case was waiting. He looked at Walling, who was taking her time spreading cream cheese on a bagel.

"You gotta go, right?" she said without looking up from her work.

"Sort of," Bosch said.

"Then don't worry about me. Go."

"Thanks, Rachel. For everything. I'll grab the check on the way out."

"Thank you, Harry."

Bosch took the English muffin off his plate and started to slide out of the booth.

"Don't forget this," Rachel said.

She handed the newspaper across the table. Bosch took it from her and stood up.

"Tell Jack he *is* lucky."

"What? You mean about the job?"

"No, Rachel, I mean about you."

31

Bosch didn't want to go into the squad room and get caught up in anything with Crowder or Samuels. So he texted Soto and waited in the same spot where he had dropped her off an hour earlier. It took her less than ten minutes to get out of the PAB and across the front plaza. She was carrying her iPad.

She got in the car but Bosch did not pull out. They needed to set a plan for the rest of the day and he also wanted to know what she had told Crowder with regard to both of their current cases.

"Okay, so where are we at?" he asked.

"I did the interview and that was easy," she said. "The reporter didn't ask anything too tough and the only thing I gave him was the gun. He was really happy with that and the captain and lieutenant were happy and now we're good to go on Bonnie Brae."

"What did you tell Crowder about that?"

"Just that we're looking at it as a diversion from the EZBank robbery and that it was an angle the first-run investigators didn't explore. I told him we had a solid connection between the two locations and needed to hit the road today to nail it down."

"Perfect. Now, we have Burrows and Boiko padded down. Still no location on Ana Acevedo, right?"

Soto shook her head with disappointment.

"I can't find her. I've tried all the software and data banks. AutoTrack, DMV, Lexis/Nexis, utilities, voter registration, auto loans—you name it."

"Think she's dead?"

"If she is, it wasn't recorded anywhere I can find."

"Maybe she just changed her name."

He said it hopefully even though he was increasingly starting to believe Ana Acevedo had been killed and buried where she would never be found. If she had been used by Burrows and the two other robbers, she became a liability as soon as the robbery was over. Adding the Bonnie Brae deaths to the tally probably made her too risky a liability.

"Nothing comes up in the usual places," Soto said. "Marriage licenses, petitions to change names. If she switched her name, she didn't do it legally or she went somewhere far away to do it."

"Maybe Mexico."

"Well, if she did, she never came back across and got a driver's license or a bank account or cable TV. She just disappeared, and as far as I can tell, nobody ever reported her missing. At least not in this state."

Considering her work in just the past week, Bosch had no cause to doubt the thoroughness of Soto's search for Ana Acevedo.

"All right, then," he said. "Maybe we use that to our advantage. We go to Burrows and Boiko and say she's the one we're looking for. That'll be our angle in with them."

Soto nodded.

"I like it," she said. "Which one do we go to first?"

"I like Burrows," Bosch said. "With what I just heard

at breakfast, he's the one. The EZBank job could've been all about getting money to start the white supremacist outfit he was part of back then."

"What a guy. I can't wait to hear this."

"Yeah. He's a quite a citizen."

Bosch pulled onto 1st and headed down to Los Angeles Street so he could get over to the freeway. Adelanto was going to be an easy two-hour drive out into the Mojave. There was more than enough time to tell Soto everything Walling had told him about Rodney Burrows.

Adelanto was off the 15 freeway almost halfway to Las Vegas. As he drove, Bosch was quiet and contemplative while Soto used her electronic tablet to continue her search for Ana Acevedo. The past decade had seen an explosion in the availability of digital search sites that could be used for finding people. While almost all of them used the basic identifiers such as name, birth date, and Social Security number, there was still a wide range of ways in which those identifiers were applied. Some sites were more real-estate based, others more reliant on banking or legal data. Still others specialized in auto purchasing and financial data. The bottom line was that the prudent investigator didn't rely on only one or two search engines for conclusive results. There was always another data bank to check.

As Soto occasionally cursed or muttered things like "That's not her!" and "Would you give me a break?" Bosch was slowly realizing the gravity of the situation he had put himself in. Before that morning, the Bonnie Brae case had seemed like an abstract long shot, and by encouraging Soto and helping her he was solidifying their bond as partners. Now, because of Soto's good work, they were on the verge of confronting the man who could very well be responsible for the deaths of nine people, including Soto's childhood friends. He realized that there was no way he should let Soto anywhere near this man, but the circumstances he had set in motion made it inevitable. He was going to have to be as careful about Soto as he was about Burrows—should the two meet.

"How are you doing, Lucy?" he asked.

Soto was looking down at her tablet screen. She glanced over at him and he put his eyes back on the road.

"You've been with me just about all morning," she said. "Why do you ask that?"

"It's just that, you know, Burrows—this could be the guy. You're going to be cool, right?"

"I'll be cool, Harry. Don't worry."

Bosch took his eyes off the road again to look at her for a long moment.

"What?" she said.

"I just want to be sure I don't have to worry about you," he said.

"Harry, I'm a cop and I'll act like a cop. Totally professional. I'm not going to go all apeshit on the guy, okay? This is about justice, not revenge."

"There's a thin line between those two things. I'm just saying that if you start to pull anything, I'll be all over you in a second. Understand?"

"Yes, I understand. Can I go back to work now?"

She held up her tablet as part of the question.

"Sure. But you follow my lead if we talk to this guy. I

want to run the missing-person play on him, see if I can get him to talk to us about Ana. Then we go from there."

"Sounds like a plan."

"Okay, then."

Rodney Burrows's address corresponded to a neighborhood of small houses on narrow but deep lots. There were no trees or bushes or even a lawn that Bosch could see anywhere in the neighborhood. It was all burned out and left dusty and barren by the desert sun.

The Burrows homestead was surrounded by a chain-link fence that was topped with razor wire and that probably wasn't all that different from the fence that surrounded the federal prison where Burrows had done his time. Bosch wondered if the similarity was lost on Burrows.

As Bosch studied the man's fenced compound, the irony was not lost on him. Burrows, like many others with his beliefs and practices, had most likely moved eighty miles away from the city and into the desert town because he wanted to get away from all that he felt was wrong with society and its large urban centers. In his estimation the problems came down to things like immigration and crowding from growing populations of minorities who sapped the infrastructure and lived off the government dole. So he lit out, as they say in white-power circles, for open spaces and white faces. He found Adelanto and established his homestead, only to find that the small town was no different from the big town. It was a microcosm—a ladle dipped into the melting pot and coming out with the same mixture of ingredients. Adelanto was a town with minorities in the majority, and so it was no wonder to Bosch that Burrows had

338

surrounded himself with a six-foot chain-link fence, his last-ditch effort to keep the world out. And the capper to the irony was that Adelanto was the Spanish word for "progress."

Burrows's fence formed a chute that Bosch angled the Ford into so he could reach out the window to a call box at the entry gate. The box featured a keypad, a camera lens, and a call button. It was attached to a pole below one sign that said "Beware of Dog" and another that showed the black silhouette of a handgun above the words "We Don't Call 911."

Bosch was uncomfortable the moment he saw the setup because it would allow Burrows to control the situation in terms of the initial contact and confrontation. Soto was uneasy as well.

"What do we do?" she asked.

"Nothing much we can do," Bosch said. "We see if we can get him to open up."

Bosch reached out the car window and pushed the call button to make contact. He had to push it a second time before getting a response. The voice on the box was male and gruff.

"What is it?"

Bosch held his badge out to the camera but intentionally held it in a way that one of his fingers covered the embossed letters that said Los Angeles.

"Police, sir. We need you to come out to the gate, please."

"Why would you need me to do that?"

"We have an investigation and we need you to help us, sir."

"What sort of investigation?"

"Sir, would you please come out?"

"Not until I know what's going on."

"It's a missing-persons case, sir. It will only take a few minutes."

"Who's missing? I don't know anyone in this neighborhood. They could all go missing as far as I'm concerned."

This was not going the right way. Bosch decided to go strong.

"Sir, you need to come to the gate. If you refuse, then we are going to have a problem."

There was a long pause before the voice came back over the box.

"Just hold your horses. It's going to take me a few minutes."

"Thank you, sir."

Bosch backed up from the box enough to be able to open the door and exit the car. He put it in park and looked at Soto. He still was unsure of how she was going to react to seeing the man who might be responsible for the tragedy of her childhood, if not her life.

"Okay, I'm going to get out, act casual, and wait for him," Bosch said. "You stay in the car. I'll signal you if I need you."

"Okay," Soto said. "What are you going to do?"

"Not sure yet. Play it as it lays."

"Sounds good."

Bosch unbuckled his seatbelt and got out of the car. He walked to the front and leaned against the grille in a very casual pose, hands back on the hood for balance. The house was about fifty yards up the driveway. Soon he saw the garage door open and a pickup truck that had been backed into it start down the driveway to the gate. As it got closer, the automatic gate in front of Bosch began to slide open. He could see a man behind the wheel and a dog on the seat beside him. He then saw a rifle in the rack behind the driver's head. Bosch started to get concerned but tried not to show it. The truck stopped twenty feet short of the gate and the man left it idling as he climbed out. Bosch heard him tell the dog to be good.

The first thing Bosch saw when the man closed the truck door was that he had a western-style holster on his belt and strapped around his right thigh. There was a pistol in it. This escalated things quickly and Bosch dropped the casual pose and stood up off the front of his car. He pointed at the man and issued a command.

"Stop right there, sir!"

The man stopped in his tracks and looked around as if confused by the circumstances. He was shorter than Bosch expected. For some reason his adversaries always loomed large in his imagination, and then, more often than not, they didn't measure up to what he expected. Burrows had a beefy physique beneath his plaid shirt and jeans. He had a bushy red beard and wore an old John Deere hat.

"What is it?" he asked.

"Sir, why are you wearing a holstered weapon?" Bosch called back.

"Because I always do and because I have a right to bear arms on my own goddamn property."

"What is your name, sir?"

"Rodney Burrows and would you stop with the 'sir' all the time?"

"Okay, Mr. Burrows, I want you to reach across your

body with your left hand, take the gun out of the holster, and put it on the hood of your truck."

Perhaps sensing something in the tone of Bosch's voice, the dog started barking and had moved over to the driver's seat to be closer to its master.

"Why would I do that?" Burrows asked. "I'm on my own property."

"For my safety, sir—Mr. Burrows," Bosch responded. "I want the gun on the hood of the truck."

By pointing at the truck, Bosch set off another paroxysm of barking from the dog. It started moving back and forth in the truck cab, jumping from seat to seat. Bosch heard the passenger door of the Ford open behind him and knew Soto was getting out. But he did not want to turn his eyes away from the armed man in front of him.

When he saw Burrows start to raise his hands, palms out, he knew Soto had drawn her weapon.

"Sir!" Soto yelled, her voice high and tense. "Put the weapon on the hood!"

"Soto, I have this," Bosch said. "Stand down."

"Sir!" she called again, ignoring Bosch. "The weapon!"

"Okay, okay," Burrows said. "I'm doing it."

He started moving his right hand toward the holster.

"Left hand!" Bosch yelled. "Left hand!"

"Sorry," Burrows said casually. "Left hand. Jesus!"

He removed the gun from the holster with his left hand and casually tossed it onto the pickup's hood. It banged hard on the steel and caused the dog to increase its volume and animation.

"Lola, shut up!" Burrows yelled.

The dog did not oblige. With the gun on the hood of the truck Bosch felt safe enough to glance back at

Soto. She was behind the open passenger door of the plain-wrap in a two-handed combat stance, arms braced on the windowsill, her weapon still aimed at Burrows's center mass.

"Soto, cool it," Bosch said. "I've got this."

"I've got you covered, partner," she said.

"Stand down," Bosch said evenly. "Holster your weapon."

He waited for Soto to comply, then turned back to Burrows and stepped forward, putting his body in the line between Burrows and Soto.

Bosch pulled Burrows away from the truck and over to the plain-wrap. He proned him over the hood and started checking him for other weapons. He looked over him at Soto, giving her a hard stare.

"Here's a tip," he said to Burrows. "When the cops knock on your door, don't answer it with a gun on your belt and a rifle in your truck."

"I don't know what you're doing, man," Burrows protested. "I am on my own land. I have every right to—"

"You are a convicted felon in possession of a firearm," Bosch said. "That trumps any of your bullshit."

"I don't recognize your law."

"Yeah, well good for you. The law recognizes you. Do you have any other weapons?"

"I got a knife," Burrows said. "Back pocket. This is bullshit. This is government harassment. And this hood is fucking hot!"

Bosch didn't respond. He didn't care how hot the hood was. He dug the knife out. It was a switchblade. He pushed the spring lock and a four-inch blade popped out. He held it up high so Soto could see it and would be able to deflect any claim that Bosch had planted it. He closed it and put it on the car's hood, sliding it out of reach.

Bosch leaned his weight on Burrows, pushing his chest down on the hood. He could feel the heat Burrows had complained about. Then in a long-practiced maneuver, he kept a forearm on the man's spine to hold him in place while he pulled the handcuffs off his belt and hooked one onto Burrows's left wrist.

"Hey, what are you doing?" Burrows asked.

Bosch brought Burrows's left arm up behind his back and shifted his weight to the other forearm so he could bring the right wrist back to complete the cuffing. He then stood Burrows back up and turned him around.

"You can't do this," Burrows said. "Arrest me on my own property."

"Wrong," Bosch said. "I own you now, Burrows. Is there anyone else in your house?"

"What? No, no one."

"Any other dogs besides the one in the truck?"

"No. What is this? What do you want?"

"I told you. We want to talk about a missing person."

"Who?"

"Ana Acevedo."

Bosch watched his reaction, seeing how long it took Burrows to recognize and remember the name. It took a few seconds and then it hit.

"I haven't seen her in, like, years."

"Good. We'll talk about that. You now have a big decision, Rodney. You want to go inside and talk here? Or do you want to drive back to L.A. with us and do it at the station?"

"You're from L.A.?"

"That's right. I guess I forgot to mention that. You want to answer questions here or there?"

"How about I just ask for my lawyer and you don't ask me a fucking thing?"

"That would be a choice. We'll take you down to L.A. and get you a phone as soon as we get there. I promise."

"No, right now. Here. My lawyer's up here. L.A. is a shithole. I don't want to ever go there again."

"Then make a choice. Talk to us here or call your lawyer from L.A. I'm sure he'll be able to get you out by morning—after a night in the zoo."

Burrows shook his head and said nothing. Bosch knew they were skirting very closely around an interpretation of whether or not he had just asked for an attorney.

"Okay," Bosch said.

He pulled Burrows back from the hood and started walking him toward the rear door of the car.

"We'll get animal control out here for the dog," he said.

Immediately Burrows tensed and tried to stop moving.

"Okay, okay," he said. "We can go inside but I don't know anything about Ana Acevedo."

"We'll see," Bosch said.

"What about my dog? And my truck?"

Bosch looked back at the truck. It was still running. The dog had its front paws up on the dashboard and was looking intently back at Bosch.

"They'll be fine," he said.

He turned Burrows toward the house, keeping one hand on his upper arm. With the other he signaled to Soto to get the gun and the knife.

"You have to close the gate," Burrows protested. "Otherwise, they'll come in."

"Who will?" Bosch asked.

"The people out there. The kids on the street."

"How do we close it?"

"There's a clicker in the truck."

"We're not opening the truck."

"The dog is harmless. She likes to bark."

"Okay, I'll open the truck. But just so you know, if the dog comes at me, I'm going to shoot it."

"She won't."

Bosch signaled Soto over so she could take control of Burrows while he walked over to the pickup. He drew his weapon and then lowered it to his side. He opened the door and was greeted with a paroxysm of barking. But the dog backed up against the passenger door. Bosch reached in and pushed the button on a remote clipped to the windshield visor. The gate to the Burrows compound started to close.

"Lola, down," Burrows shouted.

The dog leaped out of the truck and past Bosch in a gray blur. By the time he had raised his gun, the dog was already on the ground and by Burrows's side.

"Good girl," Burrows said. "Can you kill the engine? Gas ain't cheap around here."

"It ain't cheap anywhere," Bosch said.

He reached in and turned off the engine, then grabbed the rifle off the rack.

32

Bosch kept Burrows in the cuffs until they were inside the house and he had made a complete walk-through to confirm there was no one else inside. He found a table and chairs in the kitchen and sat Burrows down against a wall adorned with a Nazi flag. He put the two weapons on a counter, then returned to Burrows, uncuffed him, and took the seat across the table from him. Soto stood to the right, next to the counter by the guns. The nearby sink was overflowing with dirty plates and glasses. She took out her phone, turned on its recording app, and placed it down on the counter while Burrows exaggeratedly rubbed his wrists to restore feeling in them.

The dog went to the bowl by the back door and started loudly lapping up water. They waited until the noise subsided.

"What is she?" Bosch asked.

"Part pit, part Rotter," Burrows said.

Bosch nodded toward the flag.

"Goes with the flag, huh?" he said.

Burrows didn't respond. The dog found a spot by the door, circled around twice, and then lay down.

"Do you live here alone?" Bosch asked.

"Yes, I do," Burrows said. "Can we skip the small talk now? I just want to get this over with."

"Sure. Where did you get the guns?"

"A gun show in Tucson. All legal. I was living there at the time."

"Except you forgot to mention you were a convicted felon."

"I bought from a private citizen and he didn't have to ask. Besides, my attorney is petitioning the court to have that conviction expunged from my record. I served the time and completed the probation."

"Yeah, good luck with that. Do you have any other firearms in the house?"

Burrows didn't answer right away.

"Don't lie," Bosch said. "We'll tear this place apart."

"I have a shotgun next to my bed," Burrows said. "I'm surprised you didn't see it when you tromped all through my home. I only hesitated just now because you asked about firearms in the house. I also have a Colt .45 in the glove box of the truck, but you didn't ask about the truck."

Bosch nodded to Soto and she left the kitchen to collect the weapons. Harry checked to see that she had left her phone still recording on the counter and then turned back to Burrows.

"Okay, I'm going to read you your rights now."

"What do you mean? I thought we were just going to talk?"

"We are. But I haven't decided what to do about the firearms yet. The switchblade is illegal, too. Let's just see how we get along here and let's do everything right."

Without taking his eyes off the man in front of him, Bosch pulled his badge wallet. He then glanced down and read Burrows his rights off a card he kept in it.

"Do you understand these rights as I have read them?" he asked.

"I don't recognize these rights," Burrows said.

"I don't care if you recognize them. Do you understand what I just read to you?"

"Yes, but I don't—"

"I bet you're paying your taxes now, right?"

"Under protest."

"Okay, same thing. These are your rights under the government of this land. You can protest that government but those are the rules. Do you want to proceed with the interview or do you want to get in the back of the car and head on down to L.A.?"

"I understand the rights. I will talk to you without my attorney present."

"Good, we're making progress here. Where's Ana Acevedo?"

Burrows physically moved back in his seat as if Bosch's bluntness was a solid object he had been struck with.

"Look, that's what I've been trying to tell you from the start," he protested. "I have no idea where she is. I haven't seen that girl in twenty years."

"When and under what circumstances did you see her last?"

Before he could answer, Soto came back into the kitchen. She put the two new weapons she had collected with the others, then reclaimed her position by the counter.

Bosch turned back to Burrows and repeated his question.

"Tell us about the last time you saw Ana Acevedo."

"I don't—we're talking about the nineties here. How can I remember the exact—"

"But you lived with her. You ought to be able to remember when you—"

"No, I did not. Who said that? I would never . . ."

His voice trailed off.

"Never what?" Soto asked. "Never live with a brown person?"

Bosch threw Soto a back-off look. He wanted to keep Burrows off guard and the best way to do that was to have one person in control of the interview.

"If you didn't live with her, then you at least visited her at the Bonnie Brae," he said. "We have witnesses."

"Yes, yes, that's exactly right," Burrows said. "I *visited* her there. I didn't live there. I never lived there and I never lived with her."

The plan was to use Ana Acevedo to get Burrows to admit things that could be useful and used against him in a case involving the Bonnie Brae fire. Bosch had just checked the first and most important box. Burrows had just admitted that he had been in the Bonnie Brae Arms to visit Acevedo. This started them down the road toward establishing familiarity with the place. That road ended with Burrows knowing where the trash chute was located.

"Then, what exactly was your relationship with her?"

"She and me worked together and it was her who came on to me. It was against the rules but she came on to me, and so we had a thing. It was all less than six months long."

Soto made a derisive sound with her mouth. Bosch ignored it.

"You're talking about the check-cashing business?" he asked. "It was against the rules there?"

"Yes, we both worked there," Burrows said. "For a year. I did the security. Then she quit the job and she quit me and I never saw her again. I swear, that's it."

"Why did she quit?"

"There had been a robbery. And I got assaulted and she got roughed up. They held a gun to her head. An AR-15. She got spooked and didn't want to work there anymore—like PTS syndrome or something, but they never called it that back then. I never saw her again after that. She visited me one time in the hospital after the robbery and that was it."

"Where did she go?"

"I just told you, I don't know."

"And you never tried to find her."

"No. I wasn't . . . look, it was just sex. We weren't in love. I let it go."

"Did your buddies in WAVE know about her?"

A glimmer of surprise showed in Burrows's eyes. Bosch knew about WAVE. Burrows didn't answer, but Bosch pushed it.

"Did you tell them?" he asked. "Did you brag to the guys at the clubhouse about banging a Mexican? What is it you people would have called her, a 'border monkey'?"

"No, I didn't tell them," Burrows said. "I didn't tell any of them and I didn't call her that."

Bosch stared at him for a long moment, assessing him, thinking about where to go next.

"How many nights did you stay at the Bonnie Brae?" he asked.

"I don't know," Burrows said. "Thirty, forty, I was there a lot. We were . . ."

"You were what? In love?"

"No, no way. It wasn't love."

"Did you leave clothes there?"

"Yeah, I left some work uniforms there so I would have them."

"Did you do laundry, take out the trash?"

"I helped out, yeah. It doesn't mean we—"

"You took out the trash for a woman you didn't love?"

"Look, man, you're totally twisting this."

"How? Did you take out the trash or not?"

"I took out the trash but it didn't mean shit and it doesn't matter, because I still haven't heard from her in twenty years and I don't know where the fuck she's at."

Bosch paused. He let things calm down even though inside he was roaring because he had everything he needed from Burrows.

"What do you do for a living now, Rodney?" he asked.

"I drive a parts truck," Burrows said.

"What parts?"

"American auto parts."

"Where is Ana Acevedo? What did you do with her?"

"*What?* I did nothing! I don't know where she is!"

He yelled it and the dog picked her head up off the floor.

"You know what?" Burrows said. "I don't care anymore. Just take me to L.A. I want to see a lawyer."

He started to stand up but Bosch was waiting for the move. He jumped up, reached across the table, and drove Burrows back down into his seat with one hand on his shoulder.

"Sit down. And don't get up until I tell you to."

Bosch heard the low rumble of the dog's growl from the doorway.

"You're violating my civil rights," Burrows protested. "You can't come in here to my home on my own property and tell me what to do."

Bosch looked over at Soto and nodded toward the phone. Burrows had asked for a lawyer so the interview was technically over. She switched off the recording app.

Bosch turned back to Burrows.

"Funny how you guys always say the same thing," he said. "You want nothing to do with this country and its laws and then all of a sudden you want us to play by the very rules you deny."

"I want my lawyer."

"You invited us into your home, Mr. Burrows. You had a choice and you invited us in. If you're saying you want a lawyer, then we'll stop all of this right now, take you to L.A., and book you."

Burrows put his elbows on the table and drew his hands over his face.

"Or," Bosch said, "you could just tell us about that robbery at EZBank."

Burrows shook his head like he had no choice.

"Two guys," he said. "They came in, shot up the place, and gave me the butt end of one of the guns. I got a cracked skull and a concussion and couldn't really remember anything after that. But what I was told was they had me on the ground and they put the gun against my head to shoot unless someone opened the security door."

"What happened?" Bosch said.

"Ana opened the door. She'd already pulled the silent alarm. She knew the police were coming, so she opened

353

the door. Then the robbers came in and made them open the vault and the cash drawers."

"Made who open the vault?"

"The manager of the place was back there with her. It was him."

"Who was that?"

"Uh, his name was . . . I can't remember. It was like a Russian name."

"You mean Ukrainian?"

"Whatever."

"Was it Maxim?"

"Yeah, that was it. We called him Max."

"He was fucking Ana on the side, too, right?"

Again the surprise showed.

"No, that's bullshit," Burrows said. "That's not what happened."

"You sure?"

"I woulda known."

"Really? You said you weren't living with her. You weren't there every night. You just told me."

"But I woulda known."

"How many days a week were you there?"

"Three or four times. It woulda been more but her roommate didn't like me. But there was nobody else."

"So what you're saying is that after this robbery Ana Acevedo quit her job and quit you at the same time?"

"That's what happened. She had PTS."

"I get that about the job. But what about you?"

"She said I was a reminder of what happened at the store."

"What store?"

"The place we worked. EZBank. We called it the store."

"When was the next time you saw Ana after she quit?"

"How many times I gotta tell you? She came to the hospital to say good-bye. I never saw her again."

"So she bagged you. How'd the police treat you after the robbery?"

"Yeah, that's who you should be investigating. Those bastards, they tried to put the whole thing on me. They said I set it up. Like, yeah, part of the master plan was to have my skull cracked open like an egg."

"They arrest you?"

"I was never charged. You know why? Because I had nothing to do with it. I had a fucking concussion and these guys were telling me while I was in the hospital bed that I set the whole thing up. What bullshit!"

Bosch didn't respond. He was assessing things. He had checked all the boxes he'd come to check. They had Burrows, by his own words, solidly inside the Bonnie Brae and aware of the trash chute—he had taken out the trash. It was time to sharpen the blade, time to get on point with Burrows. He glanced back at Soto and she nodded slightly. The recording was back on. It's legal viability would be questionable but Bosch wanted this part recorded just the same.

"Tell me about the fire," he said.

Burrows looked confused.

"What fire?" he asked.

"At the Bonnie Brae."

"That fire that same day? I don't know anything about it. Ana didn't live there anymore. Her roommate

355

had kicked her out. That fire was set by the gangbangers who owned that street. Like the year before with the riots, these people burning down their own neighborhoods, killing their own children. How fucked is that? I mean, this was our whole point."

In his peripheral vision Bosch saw Soto come off her relaxed lean against the counter. He turned and gave her another look that pushed her back down. Now was not the time to air personal emotions and clash with the racist. They had a purpose here, and the more they kept Burrows talking, the closer they got to it.

"Explain that," he said to Burrows. "Who are you talking about? What was the point?"

"The WAVE, man," Burrows responded. "We saw this coming. It's only a matter of time."

"Before the race war?"

"You could call it that. But it doesn't matter what you call it, it's coming."

"Which one of the Pollard brothers made the firebomb?"

"What firebomb?"

"The one they dropped down the trash chute at the Bonnie Brae."

Burrows seemed stunned speechless.

"Before they robbed the EZBank," Bosch said.

"You're crazy," Burrows said. "We were completely nonviolent. We never hurt anyone. You can't pin that on us. In fact, I didn't even know those guys back then. That came after."

Bosch leaned across the table.

"Bullshit. You don't just say, 'I think I'll sign up for a race war now.' You knew them and you all knew what you wanted. And you needed money to build your little clubhouse out in Castaic."

"No! You're crazy and that's it, I'm done talking. Either take me in and book me or get the hell out of my house and off my property. Now!"

Bosch stood up and signaled Burrows to get up.

"Then, stand up."

"Why? What are you doing?"

"We're going to L.A."

"Oh, come on, you're not going to do this, are you?"

"Stand up, please."

"We talked! I helped! What do you want? I don't know anything about Ana Acevedo! I had nothing to do with that fire and you have zero evidence that I did. I met the Pollards a year later in Castaic."

Bosch walked around the table, coming toward Burrows. Soto joined him and the physical message was clear.

"Okay, okay," Burrows said, raising his hands. "I get it, I get it. You people don't give a shit about the truth. You just need a scapegoat and I'm it. I'm always the easy fucking target."

"That's right," Bosch said. "You've got it."

Burrows stood and Soto moved in behind him to cuff his wrists.

Bosch walked him out of the house while Soto carried the weapons. They closed the door with the dog inside and moved down the driveway. At the truck, Bosch opened the door and used the remote to open the gate.

Burrows was placed in the back of the Ford and the guns went onto the blanket in the trunk. Bosch then waved Soto back toward the pickup so they could talk without Burrows's being able to hear.

"So what do you think?" he asked.

"I think he's a racist dirtbag like we knew all along," she said. "What do you think?"

"He's that, for sure. But I don't think he's our inside man."

"Why? He puts himself in the Bonnie Brae. He admits he knew where the trash chute was. He had access. He had motive. And he couldn't have cared less about who might've been hurt in that place."

Bosch paused for a long moment and looked over her head at the Ford. It appeared that Burrows had his head down. Bosch could not see him.

"It's not so much what I heard," he finally said. "It's what I saw. The reads I got. The tells. He didn't know about Boiko and Ana. He didn't know a lot."

"And what, you believe him?"

"Lucy, I've been reading people for almost forty years. You reach a point where you trust your instincts. My read on this one is that he's not the guy."

She folded her arms tightly across her chest.

"I wish I was that good at reading people. Have you ever been wrong?"

"Sure, I've been wrong. Nobody bats a thousand. But that doesn't change what I'm feeling here right now."

"Then, what do you want to do, just kick him loose? He was wearing a gun on his hip like he's some kind of cowboy."

"No, I don't want to kick him loose. I want to turn him over to the San Berdoo sheriff on the gun charges and let them sort that out. Then we get out of here and go on to the next one."

"Boiko."

"Yeah. And then Ana. We still need to find her. And look, I'm not saying we close the book on Burrows. We've still got our nets in the water. Maybe we come up with something that changes how we look at him. But for now . . ."

He looked back at the Ford again. Burrows had now straightened up and Bosch could see him staring out through the windshield at them.

"You want me to call the sheriff?"

"Yeah, go ahead. Tell them they'll probably want to bring animal control out too."

Soto nodded glumly.

"You got it, Harry."

33

They waited almost an hour for a cruiser from the San Bernardino County Sheriff's Department. It then took another half hour to explain the situation and transfer custody of Burrows to the reluctant deputy. By the time they got back on the freeway, most of the afternoon was shot and Bosch felt the edginess that comes with having wasted time on a dead end. Soto, on the other hand, was silent. She kept her eyes on the screen of her tablet and said nothing.

"You hungry?" Bosch asked. "We can stop somewhere."

"No, not after that," Soto said. "Let's just go talk to Boiko."

"Okay, where to? North Hollywood?"

"Yes, but not his house. He'll likely be at work. He's now general manager of EZBank, and they're centrally headquartered in North Hollywood at Lankershim and Oxnard."

"Got it."

The headquarters for the chain of check-cashing stores turned out to be an unmarked building in a block of small industrial businesses on Oxnard. It took almost two hours to get there, and once again Bosch had to pull the car up to a gate and show his badge to a camera.

This time the gate was opened without issue and

Bosch pulled in and parked. Before getting out of the car, he instructed Soto to turn on her phone's recording application and make sure that everything was recorded if they got the chance to talk with Boiko. The two detectives then got out and entered through a door marked only with the word *Entrance*, stepping into the operational center of the business, which essentially sold cash through an array of distribution centers. There was a small waiting room with generic landscapes on the walls, a receptionist seated behind a desk, and a uniformed security man standing next to a door that Bosch noted had no handle or knob.

"We're here to see Maxim Boiko," Bosch said.

The receptionist looked down at a calendar book on her desk and frowned.

"Do you have an appointment?" she asked.

Bosch detected a slight accent. Eastern European. He pulled out his badge again and showed it to her.

"This is my appointment," he said. "Tell Max it's about the robbery."

She kept her frown as she picked up a phone and made a call. She then spoke briefly in a language Bosch assumed was Ukrainian. After she received instructions, she hung up and looked at the security guard.

"Take them back to Mr. Boiko's office," she said.

The guard turned and looked up at a camera lens mounted over the door. He nodded and there was an electronic snap and the door opened. He held it for Soto and Bosch and they moved into a mantrap where they waited for the first door to close before the next one was opened. From there, the guard led them down a hallway past several closed doors until they reached the end of the hall and an office that contained two side-by-side desks facing a wall of video screens depicting the interiors of check-cashing stores as well as the operations inside the headquarters. Bosch noted that one of the screens was tuned to CNN International. Above the bank of monitors was a red-and-white poster that said "HANDS OFF UKRAINE!" and a collage of photos that showed street fighting between Russian troops and masked Ukrainian insurgents. Bosch saw one photo of a man using a slingshot to fire a projectile toward heavily armed troops.

One desk was empty and behind the other sat a man of about fifty with thinning, jet-black hair that was waxed back over his skull. He nodded at the security guard, a signal that he was no longer needed.

"Maxim Boiko?" Bosch asked.

"Yes, this is me," the man said. "Are you here about Van Nuys or Whittier?"

Boiko still had a heavy accent despite his decades in Los Angeles. Bosch assumed Van Nuys and Whittier were the locations of the most recent robberies of EZBank stores. On the drive down from the desert Soto had shared some of her research on Boiko and the business. EZBank now had thirty-eight money stores in the tri-county area, more than two-thirds of them concentrated in the Los Angeles urban sprawl.

"Neither," Bosch said. "We want to talk about Westlake. Nineteen ninety-three. You remember?"

"Holy smokes," Boiko said. "Yes, I remember. I was there. You have found the bastards who rob me?"

Bosch didn't answer. In an exaggerated way, he looked around the small room as if looking for a place to sit down. There were no other chairs besides the two behind the desks and Boiko was in one of them.

"Is there a place we can sit down and talk?" Bosch asked.

"Yes," Boiko said. "Of course. You follow me."

Boiko led them out of the office and back down the hallway. They went through a door into a loading-dock area where Bosch saw three white-panel vans that advertised a twenty-four-hour plumbing service on the sides.

"We disguise our delivery vans," Boiko said. "So nobody knows we coming with the cash, you see. And the plumber, he pay us too for free ads on vans."

Bosch nodded. He thought it was a good idea. He never understood why armored trucks were so obvious, practically announcing *here is the money* wherever they went. He didn't mention that if the plumber paid for the ads, then they weren't free.

They crossed the dock and Boiko opened the door to another office, which contained a lunch table with four chairs.

"Please sit at table," he said. "Would you like a coffee?"

Bosch and Soto declined. They sat down and Bosch formally introduced them. Bosch had decided to use more or less the same tack with Boiko as he had with Burrows: use Ana Acevedo as the tool for digging out information about the Bonnie Brae fire. But Boiko had a clean record and that gave Bosch less leverage. He had to use more finesse this time around. There was that one piece of intelligence Bosch had received from Gus Braley about Boiko's being more concerned at the time of the robbery that his affair with his employee would be exposed than he was about the robbery itself. That gave Bosch an edge. It wasn't a hammer but it was something.

"We are taking a look at the robbery in '93 and hope you can help us," he began.

"Of course," Boiko replied. "We lost very much money. But twenty-one years? Why do you come now?"

"Because it came up in another investigation. Something current that I can't tell you about."

"Okay, I guess. But will I get the money?"

Bosch didn't recall there being any sort of reward offered in the case.

"What money is that?" he asked.

"That was taken by the robbers," Boiko said.

"Oh, well, like you just said, it has been twenty-one years. I would not count on there being any money. But you never know."

"Okay."

"You guys recovered the losses through insurance anyway, didn't you?"

"Not all. We took the bath. We learn, though, on insurance. Never have more than what is insurance, you see? We never have that problem again."

"Good to hear. And you, you've come far, too. You had a couple stores then, now you're everywhere."

"Yes, I am very successful with the company."

"Congratulations. Your wife and children are very proud, I bet."

"Wife, yes. No children. Too busy. Work, work, work."

"Right. Well, we don't want to keep you from it for too long. The reason we are here is that we're looking for someone and we were told you might be able to help us."

"Okay. Who is this?"

"Ana Acevedo."

Boiko frowned and then made a very bad effort to look confused by the name.

"Who is this person?" he asked.

"You remember Ana," Bosch said. "She worked in the store with you. She was there the day of the robbery. You opened the safe when the robbers put the gun to her head."

Boiko nodded vigorously.

"Oh, Ana, sure, yes. I could not remember, being very long time. She's not working here anymore. Not since then."

"Right, we heard she quit."

"Yes, quit. She said too much stress, things like that. She thought the robbers would come back again."

"We were also told that she was your girlfriend, so we were hoping—"

"No, no, no, no. She's not my girlfriend."

Boiko put his hands up as if to ward off an attack.

"Well, maybe not now," Bosch said. "But back then. You used to visit her at the Bonnie Brae apartments where she lived. You remember that."

Boiko went back into his mouth-open, eyes-on-the-ceiling pose of amnesia.

"No, her boyfriend was the security man who guarded us," he said. "They were together, yes."

Bosch leaned across the table as if to speak confidentially man to man. He lowered his voice.

"Look, Maxim, it's in the file," he said. "You and Ana. That's why you opened the safe."

"No, please," Boiko responded. "Take out of the file.

This is not a true thing. I am married man. My wife I love."

He signaled toward the door as if his wife were standing on the other side of it. It made Bosch wonder if the woman who had received them and spoke in another language on the phone was his wife.

"Look, Max," Bosch said. "We're not here to embarrass you or cause you any problems. So calm down a beat. But we do have the file and there are witnesses in there who say you visited Ana at the Bonnie Brae on a regular basis and you even admitted this to Detective Braley way back then."

"Okay," Boiko said, his voice a whisper. "Back then, but not now."

"Okay, back then," Bosch said, making the concession. "That wasn't so hard. It was a long time ago so, so what? It happens. You said you knew about the other guy, the security guard?"

Boiko shook his head as he realized that his admitting to the affair now opened a door to what might be a cascade of questions.

"I did not know and then I did," he said. "And so I stopped."

"You stopped going to the Bonnie Brae to see Ana?" Bosch asked.

"Yes, this is true."

"Why didn't you tell her to stop seeing the security guard? I mean, you were the boss at the store, right? Why were you the one who stopped?"

"No, I had my wife, you see. I wanted very much to stop. She—Ana—had started the whole thing and it was very big mistake for me."

"You mean she came on to you first?"

"Yes, exactly as you say."

Bosch nodded like he completely understood how Max had been taken advantage of.

"Okay, how often were you at her apartment before that?"

"Not too many."

"Where is Ana Acevedo right now, Maxim?"

Boiko held his hands out in an almost pleading manner.

"This I don't know. I tell you. Not since her quitting time."

"You haven't seen her since then? We have witnesses who—"

"No! That is a lie. What witness? This is security guard tell this? Burrow?"

Bosch thought it was curious that Boiko could still remember the partial name of the security guard he worked with twenty-one years before.

"I can't tell you who the witness is," Bosch said. "But you're saying you haven't seen her since back then, correct?"

"This is correct," Boiko said.

"What about talking to her on the phone? Any contact with her at all since then?"

"Only for her taxes."

"What do you mean, for taxes?"

"When she wanted to file for IRS refund, she had new address and ask me to send to her the taxes."

"You mean like a W-2 or a 1099 form?"

"Yes, exactly."

"So she had moved away after the robbery and wanted you to have her new mailing address?"

"This is what happened, yes."

Bosch tried to keep a calm tone in his voice. But it was difficult. Boiko's answer gave him renewed hope of finding Ana Acevedo.

"You have employee records here, right?" he asked.

"Of course," Boiko said.

"Okay, is there still a file on Ana Acevedo? A file with that address in it?"

"But it is twenty years ago."

"I know, but she was an employee and there might still be a file."

"Okay, sure."

"Where? Are the files in this building?"

"Yes. I could check if you—"

"Yes, I want you to check. Right now I want you to check. We can wait."

Boiko got up and left the room. Bosch looked at his watch. It was almost five. He had a feeling that these last few minutes were going to lead to something that would salvage the whole day.

"What are you thinking?" he asked Soto.

She pursed her lips for a moment and considered her response before giving it.

"Probably the same thing you're thinking," she finally said. "Both these guys today said Ana pursued them. Seems a little out of the ordinary. Like she was a nympho or she maybe had a plan."

Bosch pointed a finger at her. Exactly what he had been thinking.

"Couple that with her disappearance and what do you get?" he asked. "And I'm not talking about her just leaving town. I mean, she disappeared."

"You get somebody who moves to the top of the list," Soto said.

Bosch nodded toward the door.

"When he comes back we have to ask him about that day," he said. "About the suspects and the identification of them as being white. If that still holds up we have to look into her life and find the intersections. The nexus, as you call it."

Before Soto responded, the door opened and Boiko returned. He was holding a sheet of paper.

"I have an address for you," he proudly announced.

He put the sheet of paper down on the table between Bosch and Soto and then returned to his seat. Bosch leaned over the table to look at the paper. It was a photocopy of an Internal Revenue Service W-2 form for 1993 earnings and deductions. It was made out in the name of Ana Maria Acevedo and carried an address in Calexico, California, on it.

"Calexico?" Soto asked. "What's in Calexico?"

"She moved there," Boiko said, helpfully stating the obvious.

Soto pulled her bag up from the floor and dug out her digital tablet. Bosch looked at Boiko.

"Do you remember her mentioning Calexico?" he asked.

"No, I don't remember," Boiko said.

"What about family? Did she have family there?"

"No, she was born here. She told me. And she had family in Mexico."

"Do you remember where in Mexico?"

"No, I don't think—"

"Harry," Soto interrupted. "Take a look."

She passed the tablet to him and he looked at the screen. Soto had plugged the address from the W-2 into Google Street View. Bosch was looking at a photo of the street address to which the IRS form had been sent in early 1994. It was a large building of Spanish Mission–style that looked like a school. But closer reading of a sign posted near the tiled walk out front told Bosch otherwise.

SISTERS OF THE SACRED PROMISE
Convent established 1909
Archdiocese of San Diego

The facts tumbled together for Bosch. The EZBank robbery and Bonnie Brae fire occurred in October 1993. By the time Ana Acevedo filed a 1993 tax return six months later, she was apparently living in a convent in a town on the California-Mexico border.

It was becoming obvious to Bosch why she had gone there. Redemption, salvation, and refuge were the first things that came to mind.

34

They now had too much momentum to stop. They made the two-hundred-mile drive that night after filling the gas tank and grabbing convenience-store food to go. Bosch took the 10 freeway east and then at Indio turned south on State Road 86. The route took them down past Borrego Springs and skirting along the Salton Sea. It was open and desolate country with the Chocolate Mountains in the far distance to the east.

"You ever been down this way before?" Soto asked.

"A long time ago," Bosch said.

"On a case?"

He happened to have been thinking about it when she asked the question.

"Sort of," he answered. "I was looking for my partner."

"Your partner? What happened?"

"It's a long story. In fact, it would probably fill a book. He went off the reservation and he . . . well, he never came back."

"You mean he disappeared?"

"No, he got killed."

Bosch glanced over at her.

"You knew about me when we got assigned to each other, right?" he asked.

"Not really," she said. "I was just told I was with you."

"Well, just so you know, I've lost two partners.

Another one got shot but survived and then I had one who ended up killing himself, but that was a long time after we were no longer partners."

That filled the car with silence for a few miles. Soto eventually went back to looking at the screen on her tablet instead of taking in the pink hue of the desert air.

"It's a strange place down here," Bosch said after a while. "These two towns on either side of the border. Calexico on our side, Mexicali on theirs. Hard to figure out what's going on. I remember when I went down here—it would have been even before the case with my partner, I think. And I checked in like you're supposed to do and I got no help from the locals. But then I go across the border and there was a guy . . . an investigator . . . and it was like he was the only guy who wasn't corrupt and wanted to get something done . . . on either side of the border."

Soto didn't respond. He figured she was probably still working out the math on all the partners he'd had who died.

"Anyway, strange place," he said. "Watch yourself down here."

"Copy that," she finally said. "Are we going to check in with the locals?"

Bosch shook his head.

"I don't see the need to," he said.

"Okay by me," she said.

"What have you found out on that thing?"

"Well, not a lot. Out here I'm not getting any kind of signal—Wi-Fi or cell. But back when we were still close to the city, I started a search on the Sisters of the Sacred Promise and downloaded some stuff. They have convents in California, Arizona, and Texas. There're five of them on the border and then they have a couple more in Mexico. Oaxaca, and Guerrero."

"What are they about, catechism and stuff like that? Baptisms?"

"There's that but it's a little more hard-core. They take the vows, you know? All of them. Poverty, chastity, obedience, and everything else. The sacred promise is life everlasting in heaven in exchange for all the suffering and sacrifice on earth. They go on missions, taking the word of the Lord into some pretty bad areas. I'm talking about cartel areas, the poppy fields of the Montana region in Guerrero. Some of them don't come back, Harry. Each convent has a memorial wall that lists the ones they've lost. Reminds me of the station memorials we have."

"You'd think they'd leave the nuns alone."

"Apparently not. Nobody's safe down there."

Bosch thought about things for a few moments. His one memory involving a nun was of the one who told him that his mother was dead. He was eleven years old at the time and she was the volunteer house mother in the county youth hall where he had been placed after the state removed him from his mother's custody. It was supposed to be a temporary stay, but everything changed in his life that day. Somehow, in all the years since, he had connected the idea and image of nuns with death.

"What will we say to Ana?" Soto said. "I mean, if she's there all these years later."

"It doesn't matter if she's a sister or even the mother superior," Bosch said. "She's a suspect and that's how we need to treat her. Remember, there's two people out there directly responsible for dropping that firebomb down the chute. One of them could be the pope for all I care, and we're still going to take him down. Ana Acevedo is our link to those two. She might not have known what they were going to do—my guess is that she didn't. Maybe that's why she ended up in a convent."

"Right."

They drove in silence after that and Bosch kept coming back to the memory of the nun and the indoor pool they had at MacLaren Hall. After he got the news, he broke away from the nun and dove down to the bottom of the pool. He screamed his lungs out, but not a sound broke the surface.

They got into Calexico shortly after nine. Soto had plugged the address into her phone's GPS app and she directed Bosch into the western segment of town. The convent was located on Nosotros Street in a largely residential tract. Bosch parked at the curb right in front and opened his door.

"Bring the photo of Ana," he said. "Just in case."

"Got it," Soto said.

The darkness of the evening was pierced by the shrill pitch of a cicada perched somewhere in one of the trees that lined the front lawn of the convent.

"I hate those things," Soto said.

"Why?" Bosch asked.

"I don't know. They always mean bad news in the Bible and in movies."

"You're talking about locusts. That's a cicada."

"Same difference. It still means bad news. You wait and see."

The gate surrounding the convent was unlocked. They passed through and went to the door. Through a side window it appeared all was dark inside. There was a glowing doorbell button and Bosch gave it a good ride.

"What if she's taken a vow of silence and can't answer our questions?" he asked while they waited.

"I didn't see the vow of silence in anything I read," Soto said.

"I was just kidding. Somebody's coming."

He could see a shadow behind the glass, coming closer. The door was opened and a startlingly young woman in a full nun's habit opened the door. She had a pretty face and dark eyes. She opened the door only a foot.

"Yes, can I help you?" she said.

"Sister, we're sorry to bother you so late at night," Bosch began. "We are from Los Angeles and are with the police up there."

He showed her his badge and Soto did the same.

"We are looking for a woman who may be here at the convent," Bosch said. "We need to talk to her."

The woman seemed confused.

"You mean today?" she asked. "We've had no one come—"

"Actually, she came about twenty years ago," Bosch said.

The nun studied him for a long moment. Bosch guessed that she was about three years old when Ana Acevedo came to the convent—if she actually did end up there.

"I'm not sure I understand," the nun said.

Bosch nodded and tried a comforting smile on her.

"I'm sorry," he said. "It is a bit confusing. We need to speak to a woman about something that happened in

Los Angeles a long time ago. It's a cold case. We are cold case detectives and the last known address we have for this woman is this convent. She forwarded mail to this location in 1994. Her name is Ana Maria Acevedo. Do you know that name? Is she here?"

Bosch could clearly see by her reaction that the name meant nothing to the nun.

"I know this was long before you got here but maybe there is someone else here who—"

"This is Ana," Soto said.

She proffered the photo from Ana Acevedo's last driver's license. The nun leaned forward to look at it in the dim glow from an overhead light.

"That looks like Sister Esi," she said. "But she's not here."

Bosch and Soto couldn't help but break pose and look at each other. Ana Acevedo had taken the name of the beloved woman who had died trying to save the children in the Bonnie Brae fire.

"Are you sure?" Bosch asked.

"Well, no, but it looks like her," the nun said.

"Is that her full name?" Soto asked. "Sister Esi?"

"No, it's Esther," the nun confirmed. "Sister Esther Gonzalez, but we're not always that formal around here."

"What is your name?" Bosch asked.

"I'm Sister Theresa."

Bosch asked her to look at the photo again and confirm the ID. She did so and nodded.

"She's obviously older now," she said. "Sister Geraldine is here and she's been here the longest. She would know for sure."

"Can we talk to Sister Geraldine? It could be very important."

"Could you please wait here? I'll see if she is still awake."

"That's fine. But before you go, can you tell me where Sister Esther went? You said she's not here."

"Let me just see if Sister Geraldine is awake. I really shouldn't be the one speaking for the convent. May I take the photo?"

Soto gave her the photo and Sister Theresa closed the door. Bosch and Soto looked at each other. Things were falling together.

"She took Esi's name," Soto said. "If that's not a guilty conscience, I don't know what is."

Bosch just nodded and tried to reserve his excitement. Sister Esther was not in the convent. Even if she was Ana Maria Acevedo, they still had to find her and hope she'd be able to lead them to the men who started the fire.

Five minutes went by before the door was reopened. The young nun handed the photo back to Soto and announced that Sister Geraldine was waiting to speak with them.

They were led into the building and down a hallway. On one side was the memorial to the nuns who were lost. There were nine names and photos, all of them of the women in habits. They all looked the same.

They arrived at a sparely furnished sitting room with an old box television in the corner. Another nun was waiting for them. She was in her sixties and wore rimless glasses in front of sharp eyes that Bosch guessed had seen things that rivaled what his own had seen.

"Detectives, please be seated," she said. "I am Sister

Geraldine Turner but around here people call me Sister G. I believe the woman in the photograph you gave Sister Theresa is our Sister Esther. Is she all right? What is this about?"

Bosch lowered himself onto a padded bench across a coffee table from the nun. Soto sat next to him.

"Sister G, we have no news about Sister Esther," Bosch said. "We are looking for her because we need her help on a case we're working on."

Sister G put her hand on her chest as if to calm her beating heart.

"Thanks be to God," she said. "I thought perhaps the worst had happened."

"Where exactly is Sister Esther?" Bosch asked.

"She is on a mission to Estado de Guerrero, Mexico. She went to the village of Ayutla and we have heard reports that vigilantes and narcos are fighting there. We have not heard from her in over a week now."

"Why did she go there?"

"We all have missions, Detective. We bring books and medical supplies and we bring the word of God to children. It is our calling."

"When was Sister Esther supposed to check in or be back? Is she overdue?"

"No, she is not overdue. She doesn't return for another two weeks, in fact. But we make weekly contact with home base when we can. This is home base, Detective. It has been ten days since we heard from her."

Bosch nodded. Sister G made the sign of the cross as she sent a quick prayer up for Sister Esther.

"Were you here when Sister Esther came to the convent twenty years ago?" Soto asked.

"Yes," Sister G said. "I believe I am the only one of us here now who was in the convent then. Many of us have gone to the Lord."

"Do you remember the circumstances of her coming here?" Soto asked.

"It was a long time ago," the nun responded. "I do remember she was from Los Angeles—I remember because it was as though we had received an angel from the City of Angels."

"How so?" Bosch asked.

"Well, we were in dire need at the time," Sister G said. "We had a mortgage then and it was well overdue. We were faced with losing this wonderful place we call home base, and then she arrived. She paid off the whole mortgage. And she said she wanted to join us. We took her under our wing and led her to the vows."

Bosch nodded.

"Would you like to see Sister Esther's work?" Sister G asked.

"How do you mean?" Bosch asked.

She pointed to the old television to her right.

"We keep video records of our missions," she said. "It helps with fund-raising. I believe we have Sister Esther's last mission in the DVD player. She went to a school in Chiapas. Have you heard of the *cinturones de miseria*?"

Bosch looked at Soto for a translation.

"The barrio," she said. "The slums."

"Chiapas has the most extreme poverty in all of Mexico," Sister G said.

The nun took a remote control off the table next to her chair and turned on the television and DVD player.

Soon the screen was depicting a scene in a school where two nuns in all-white habits were serving food to children in a threadbare classroom. The children had dirty clothes and many had swollen bellies. Bosch didn't have to ask which nun was Sister Esther. He recognized her from photographs of Ana Acevedo.

Sister G fast-forwarded the DVD and stopped it at a point where the nuns were conducting a class. Sister Esther was reading from a Bible with an ornate gold design on its leather cover. The children, who ranged in age from about six to early teens, listened with rapt attention.

Sister G jumped the video again and stopped it at a scene in which the two nuns were leaving the village where there appeared to be no paved roads and no power poles. They were about to board a colorful but old bus. Over the windshield of the bus the destination read "Cristobal de las Casas." Bosch had never heard of the place.

A young boy of about eight didn't want Sister Esther to leave. He was clinging to her white habit and crying. She was softly caressing the back of his head, trying to calm him.

Sister G turned the television off.

"That is Sister Esther," she said.

"Thank you for showing us," Bosch said.

He wondered if Sister G had a sense of why they had really come to see Sister Esther and had shown them the video to earn sympathy for her. Soto was about to say or ask something but Bosch put his hand on her arm to stop her. They had what they needed for now. He was concerned that too many more questions would create

380

suspicion—if they hadn't already—and word might get back to Sister Esther. He didn't want to spook her before he got the chance to talk to her himself.

"Well, Sister," he said, "if you don't mind, we're going to check with you at a later point after Sister Esther makes it back okay. When she does, we'll come back to speak to her. We're sorry for this intrusion and thank you for your time."

He started to get up.

"Can you tell me what this is all about?" Sister G asked.

"Sure," Bosch said pleasantly. "I don't know if Sister Theresa mentioned it, but we work on a cold case squad and try to solve old cases, old crimes. Sister Esther— back when she was Ana Acevedo—was a witness to a crime and we are taking another look at it. We would like to talk to her and see if she remembers anything she might not have shared with police back then. You would be surprised by how much is imprinted on the memory and has the tendency to bubble up to the surface over time."

The nun checked her watch and looked at Bosch suspiciously.

"I'm sure I would be," she finally said. "If you want to leave a business card I will have Sister Esther call you as soon as she returns, the Lord willing."

"You don't have to bother, Sister," Bosch said. "I'm sure we'll be in touch."

It was after 2 a.m. by the time Bosch came in the front door of his home. The lights were on but all was quiet. His daughter's bedroom door was closed. She had gone to sleep long ago. He had spoken to her from the car during the drive up from Calexico.

Bosch was keyed up despite the long day, most of it spent in the car. He went out onto the back deck and stood against the railing, taking in the city and thinking about the strides made on the Bonnie Brae case. In the morning he would bring Captain Crowder up to date and then they would need to decide whether to go to Mexico in an attempt to find Ana Acevedo, aka Sister Esther Gonzalez, in the cartel-controlled mountains of Guerrero, or be content to await her return to American soil. Either way had its risks and Bosch would leave it to the captain to make the call.

He made a note to himself to attempt to find out in the morning if Ana Acevedo had legally changed her name to Sister Esther Gonzalez, and if so, why the transaction had not come up during Soto's efforts to locate her. He assumed she traveled to Mexico on a valid passport. There should have been a record somewhere of the change.

His thoughts of Soto's efforts seemed to conjure her. Bosch's phone buzzed and he pulled it out of his pocket. Her name was on the screen.

"Lucy?"

"Harry, were you asleep?"

"No, not yet. Where are you?"

Bosch had dropped her off at her car inside the garage beneath the PAB.

"At the squad. I'd left my keys up here."

He wasn't sure she was telling the truth.

"And?"

"And I just checked on things before I was going to

go home. I pulled up the story on the Merced case in *La Opinión* to see how it came out, you know?"

"Okay."

"Everything was fine with the story. It got good play and I wasn't misquoted. It said we recovered the murder weapon. So then I scrolled down to the comments. You know what I'm talking about?"

"Not really—I don't really read newspapers, online or not. But go ahead."

"Well, online, readers can make comments about any story on the website. So there were some comments, including one I am sure is from our anonymous caller. The woman. She won't give up and I'm thinking we need to talk to her."

"What did she say?"

"It was in Spanish but it basically says the police are liars. They know who did this because they've been told but it's a big cover-up to protect the mayor and the real man in charge behind him."

Bosch thought about it for a few moments.

"We still think she's talking about Zeyas, right?"

"Right."

"Who would be the man in charge? Broussard?"

"I guess."

"And she didn't put her name on there, right?"

"No, you can type in any name or words you want. She typed in '*Lo sé*.' I know."

"Is that sort of thing traceable?"

"Probably with a court order. I doubt the paper will help us without it. I was just going to keep trying to call her, get her to answer. Then we set up a meet."

"No, let's not keep calling her. We spook her and she

383

throws away the cell. She wants to be anonymous for a reason."

"Then what?"

"We ping her."

"Okay."

"Go home now, Lucy. Get some sleep. We'll set it up in the morning. I know a judge who will sign the order."

"Okay, Harry."

"And good work. It's getting hard to keep up with you."

"Thank you, Harry."

Bosch clicked off the call. He wasn't so sure he had said it as a compliment.

35

On Thursday morning Bosch finally beat Soto into the office, arriving before dawn with a coffee in hand from a twenty-four-hour Starbucks. He found the call-in tip sheets on her desk and immediately went to work preparing a search warrant application that would allow them to locate the cell phone used by the anonymous caller who had repeatedly complained of a cover-up in regard to the shooting of Orlando Merced.

The advent of the cellular phone had brought a sea change in law enforcement in the prior two decades. The Communications Assistance for Law Enforcement Act of 1994 had been updated and expanded almost annually to accommodate the rapidly changing electronic landscape and the many ways it was exploited by criminals. The law required manufacturers and service carriers of telecommunication devices to include surveillance capabilities in all designs and systems. That was where pinging came into play. An unregistered or throwaway cell phone might appear to be the perfect tool for anonymous communications, whether legal or not, but the device could be traced and located by its constant connection with cell towers and the cellular network. With a court-approved search warrant, the LAPD's tech unit would be able to send an electronic pulse to the phone—a process called "pinging"—and pinpoint its location to within fifty yards by longitude and latitude coordinates. The tech unit worked quickly. Once a ping order was in hand, the process would begin within two hours.

That was why Bosch had come in early. The plan was to have a warrant on Judge Sherma Barthlett's desk before she got the chance to convene court for the day.

Bosch was not new to the process of pinging cell phones. It had become a useful tool in running down suspects in cold case murders. Often, finding the suspects was more difficult than identifying them after many years. The process started with a database where all cellular numbers were listed, along with the service provider behind them. Under the CALEA law, even the service providers on throwaway phones had to be listed. It took Bosch less than five minutes to ascertain the service provider on the number belonging to the anonymous caller. He then used a search warrant template to begin writing the warrant on his computer.

Once he had printed out the warrant, he was good to go. He first called the tech unit to alert the sergeant in charge that he would be coming in with a priority-level ping order later in the morning. Murder investigations always jumped to the front of the line, which was primarily stacked with orders relating to drug cases. The throwaway cell was the favored tool of drug dealers around the world.

The plan now was to swing by the nearby Starbucks for a cup of coffee and a pastry that he would take to the judge along with the warrant. Bosch wrote a note for Soto and put it on her desk, but he almost walked into her when he was going through the squad room door.

"Harry, you're in early."

"Yeah, I wanted to get the ping going. I left you a note. I'm going to see my judge and hopefully we'll be in business before lunch."

"Great."

"We should think about what we're going to tell the captain about Acevedo and Bonnie Brae. I figure we'll go talk to him while the tech unit's doing their thing with this."

He held up the file containing the warrant he had just authored.

"Okay, sounds good."

"You okay, Lucy?"

She looked tired and out of it, as if all the long hours of the past week and a half had finally caught up with her.

"Yeah, fine. I just need coffee."

"I'm heading to Starbucks to get something to smooth my way in with the judge. You want to go?"

"No, I'm good. I'm just going to drop off my stuff and go downstairs."

"The machine. You sure?"

"Yes, you go. Get that warrant."

"Okay, I'll be back."

Bosch carried a latte and a straight coffee on a cardboard tray that locked the cups into place and guarded against spilling in the crowded courthouse elevator. He wasn't sure how the judge took her coffee. He also had a slice of banana nut bread and a blueberry muffin in a bag. It would be judge's choice.

Judge Barthlett was in Department 111, the courthouse adhering to its long tradition of referring to courtrooms as departments. The room was empty save for the judge's clerk, who was in her pod to the right of the bench. She had her head down as she worked on the morning's schedule and didn't notice Bosch's approach.

"Meme?" he said.

She almost jumped out of her chair.

"I'm sorry," Bosch said quickly. "I didn't mean to scare you. I was wondering if I could get in to see the judge real quick. I brought her a coffee or a latte."

"Um, the judge drinks tea and brews her own," Meme said.

"Oh."

"But I'd take a latte."

"Sure."

Bosch pulled the cup out of its mooring and put it down on her desk.

"Think she'll want a muffin or some banana nut bread?" he asked.

"She's on a diet," Meme said.

Bosch wordlessly put the bag down on the desk.

"Let me go ask if she can see you now," Meme said.

"Thanks," Bosch said.

An officer in the tech unit named Marshall Flowers was assigned to Bosch's ping order. His job was to make contact with the service carrier for the phone in question and initiate the pinging. The Department was charged for this service and the tech unit had a budget. Subsequently the pinging of the cell phone was intermittent, usually twice an hour until it was determined if the phone was in motion and would have to be tracked on a shorter interval.

Flowers told Bosch that results could start coming in within a couple hours and that he should go back to his squad room and wait. When coordinates for the phone were determined, they would be e-mailed to him with a link to the location on Google Maps. Bosch had given his partner's e-mail address as the contact since Soto was more adept at maneuvering on Google Maps than he. Besides, Bosch planned on being the wheelman when they started tracking the phone.

Bosch returned to the squad room, where Soto was at her desk. She told him that Captain Crowder wanted to see them as soon as he returned. When they got to the office, they found Lieutenant Samuels waiting with the captain.

"Okay, let's hear it," Samuels said. "You two have been all over the state the past couple days. What do you have to show for it?"

Samuels was Crowder's dog and he had obviously been allowed off the leash. The fact that he opened the meeting made it clear that Crowder had deferred supervision of the Bosch/Soto team to the dog because he was tired of waiting on results.

On the way over to the office, Bosch and Soto had split responsibilities for the report. Soto would take Bonnie Brae and Bosch would handle the update on Merced.

Captain Crowder said he wanted to start with Bonnie Brae; it was, after all, the bigger case.

"I'll take that," Soto said. "Yesterday we think we identified an individual who was an accomplice on the EZBank robbery that occurred almost simultaneously to the fire. As you know from our last update, we are working on a theory that the fire was started by the robbers as a diversion. We now just need to find her."

"That's what you were doing yesterday?" Samuels said. "Looking for her all over hell and back?"

"Part of the day, Lieutenant. But we determined she is out of the country and we'll await her return."

Neither Samuels nor Crowder responded and Bosch quickly jumped in.

"Unless, Captain, you want to authorize a trip to Acapulco. We think she's down there somewhere in the state of Guerrero. Up in the mountains. We could fly into Acapulco and hire a guide and a Jeep."

Bosch could tell by the captain's face he wasn't interested in flying a team of detectives to Acapulco, even if their final destination was the treacherous mountain region of Guerrero. Just the thought of putting it into a budget report that would be reviewed on the tenth floor was enough to make the sweat pop on his forehead.

"Is she scheduled to return soon?" Samuels asked.

"Within two weeks," Soto said.

"Then I think we can wait," Crowder said. "You two have plenty to do in the meantime. In fact, let's move on to the Merced case. Where do we stand?"

Bosch took it from there.

"We've got a thing working today," he said. "There's somebody out there who we think has some information. She's repeatedly called the tip line anonymously—or so she thought—and she left a blind comment on the story that ran yesterday in *La Opinión*. We got a ping order about an hour ago and we're hopefully going to run that down today and talk to her face to face."

"What do you think she knows?" Crowder asked.

"Well, she seems to think that the ex-mayor knows who's behind the shooting and that there's a cover-up," Bosch said.

"You're talking about Armando Zeyas?" Crowder asked. "She sounds like a loon. Don't tell me this is coming down to you two chasing crazies."

"She's adamant about it," Bosch said. "There's enough there that we need to find this woman and talk to her. It's probably a long shot but sometimes long shots pay off."

"Probably a long shot?" Samuels said. "You're telling us after more than a week on this case, all you've got is a long shot? Some crazy who's probably just making a beef to try and collect some reward money? Who do you think you're kidding, Bosch?"

"We have other leads and are closing in on a suspect," Bosch said calmly. "But the investigation dictates we identify and talk to this woman. That's what we're—"

"You're wasting resources, is what you're doing," Samuels interjected. "Who's this suspect you're telling us about for the first time?"

"Willman, the man who owned the murder weapon," Bosch said. "It's in the reports."

"Your report said he's dead," Samuels said.

"He is, but we still think he took the shot," Bosch countered.

"Why did he take the shot? For who?"

"We're working on that," Bosch said. "The other firearms we collected from his house have come back tied to other killings in San Diego and Las Vegas. It's looking like this guy was a killer for hire."

"So who hired him to take the shot at Mariachi Plaza?" Crowder asked.

"That's what we're working on," Bosch said. "We're tying up loose ends and this anonymous caller is one of them."

Samuels wasn't mollified. He shook his head disdainfully.

"You two have till end of watch Friday," he said. "You put something together on this case or I'll put a team on it that gets results."

"Fine," Bosch said. "That's your call."

"Damn right it's my call," Samuels said. "You two can go now."

Bosch and Soto walked silently back to their cubicle. Bosch realized his teeth were clenched so tightly that his jaw was beginning to ache. He tried to relax but couldn't. He wanted to turn around, go back to the captain's office, and throw Samuels through the glass window next to the door. The guy wasn't a detective. He had never worked cases. He was an administrator who believed the best way to motivate people was to belittle their efforts and show zero patience with difficult cases. He would be just the type of bureaucrat Bosch wouldn't miss for a minute once he left the job.

When they got back to their desks, Bosch sat down and put his hands flat on the blotter and drummed his fingers on the surface, hoping it would somehow dissipate some of the bad energy he was carrying.

"I thought you didn't want to tell them about the firearms yet," Soto said to his back.

Bosch answered without turning to her.

"I had to give them something," he said. "Just to get out of there."

Bosch looked over toward the captain's office. Samuels was still in there, talking to Crowder, gesturing with both hands.

"Hey, Harry!" Soto said. "We got our first ping from the tech unit."

Bosch turned and pushed himself in his chair over to her desk. Soto had clicked on the link provided in the e-mail from Marshall Flowers. It went to a Google Maps page, and Bosch saw that the address in question was on Mulholland Drive between Laurel Canyon Boulevard and the Cahuenga Pass.

"Go to Street View," he instructed.

Soto clicked her wireless mouse on the appropriate tab and soon her screen showed a street-angle photograph of the address from which the first ping on the anonymous caller's cell phone had emanated. The image was of a roadway with a guardrail and beyond it a wide-angle view of the city sprawled below.

"There's nothing here," Soto said.

She was about to manipulate the image with her mouse when Bosch put his hand on her arm.

"Wait," he said. "That's Broussard's house."

"What? There's no house. How do you know?"

"Because I've been there. I've driven by. That's his house. You go down the drive from Mulholland. The house is below and you can't see it from the street."

"Oh, man. That means the phone's in his house. The anonymous calls came from ... it's his wife! All this time, she's been trying to rat him out."

36

They decided it was too risky to go directly to the house. There was no telling if Broussard would be home, and even if he wasn't, the exterior camera surveillance of the house suggested that there might also be interior monitoring of the premises as well as of his wife. Instead, Bosch and Soto put the house under surveillance, taking a position at the public overlook a block away. The plan was to wait for Maria Broussard to leave the home and then move in at the appropriate moment to confront her about the anonymous calls and ask her what she knew about the Merced shooting.

They split the surveillance, with one of them remaining in the car and the other sitting on one of the benches out on the overlook. It gave them front and back angles on the Broussard property fifty yards away. To help avoid boredom, they switched posts every thirty minutes, stopping long enough during the change to discuss the case or whatever else had come to mind.

During one of the transitions, Bosch told Soto about a previous surveillance he had been involved in on Mulholland Drive. It was a case from almost twenty years before when he had been assigned to the Hollywood Division detective squad and was partnered with Jerry Edgar. Edgar was a stylish dresser who liked custom-tailored suits and tasseled shoes. They were watching a house and were not even sure the subject—a suspect in a series of rapes and murders—was inside. It was winter cold but in the car it was stuffy because the windows were up. Both detectives had stripped off their suit jackets. The sun went down and no lights were visible from the house under surveillance. An hour went by and took them into full darkness. Still no light behind any of the windows of the house. Frustrated, Bosch finally said he was going to climb down the hillside and try to get a look at the back of the house for signs of life. Edgar urged him not to go. He warned that in the darkness he might easily slip and fall, possibly hurting himself, not to mention dirtying his clothes. Bosch told him not to worry as he reached over the seat to grab his jacket.

Sure enough, Bosch fell down the hillside. He didn't hurt himself except for a few minor scrapes and bruises. But he muddied his clothes and ripped the seam between his suit jacket's sleeve and shoulder. He also determined that the house in question was empty.

The surveillance a bust, Bosch and Edgar drove back to Hollywood Station, where it was revealed in the harsh fluorescent light of the squad room that the torn and muddied jacket Bosch wore was Edgar's.

Soto laughed so heartily at the story that she didn't hear Bosch when he announced "Car!"

He had to grab her arm and tell her again.

"There's a car pulling out," he said, directing her back toward their Ford. "Let's go."

"Can you tell, is it her?" Soto asked.

"I can't see the driver. But that's a woman's car."

"Oh, really? What makes it a woman's car?"

"I don't know. I just don't see a guy driving that."

They jumped in the Ford and Bosch started the engine. The car that had left the Broussard residence was coming their way. Bosch waited for it to pass the parking turnout and then pulled onto Mulholland behind it. The car was a two-seat silver Mercedes. Its windows were tinted and there was no way to confirm who the driver was, let alone if it was a woman. He realized that his comment about the car was probably sexist but his gut told him there was a woman driving that car. Whether it was because of the model of the car or not, he had to go with it.

"It's gotta be her," he said.

"Better hope so," she said.

They got no help with a confirmation when Soto called the com center and asked an operator to run the Mercedes's plate. The car was registered to Broussard Concrete Design, which meant it could easily have been driven by either one of the Broussards.

Bosch gave the Mercedes some distance and followed it west on Mulholland. At the light at Laurel Canyon it went straight and Harry began to entertain all manner of paranoid ideas about them being led astray. Perhaps they had been spotted on the overlook and someone left the house in the Mercedes on a leisurely cruise along the mountain ridge in an effort to pull them far off the surveillance.

But finally the car turned right and started down the northern slope of the mountain on Coldwater Canyon Boulevard. The car now appeared headed into Sherman Oaks or Van Nuys, but then it turned sharply just before Ventura Boulevard into the parking lot of a Gelson's supermarket. Bosch quickly made up the ground between them and pulled in as well. He got eyes on the Mercedes and parked one lane away from it.

When the driver's door of the Mercedes opened, it was indeed a woman who emerged from the vehicle. She was small and dressed in silver pants and a knee-length coat worn open over a pale blouse. She had blond hair, which threw Bosch because he expected a brunette.

"Is that her?" he asked. "She's blond? Didn't she have dark hair in the photo from the mayor's election?"

"She did," Soto said. "She also has dark hair on the DL issued three years ago."

Bosch opened his door.

"Let's go in," he said.

They followed the woman in and watched as she pulled a shopping cart out of the stack and proceeded down the store's first aisle. Gelson's was an upscale chain that attracted customers who were interested in quality over price. As the woman began filling her cart, Bosch didn't see her check a single price tag. It gave him confidence that they were following Maria Broussard. Still, the blond hair threw him and he wasn't sure why.

"It's a dye job," Soto whispered when they casually moved in closer to the woman in the produce section.

"How do you know?" Bosch whispered back.

She held up her phone to him. On the screen was a photograph Soto had Googled of Charles and Maria Broussard. It showed them embracing for the camera. Maria had dark brown hair.

Soto then thumbed to the next image, and the screen displayed the same woman with blond hair.

"She's dyed it," she said. "Judging by dates here, I'd say sometime in the past year."

"Okay," Bosch said. "Let's talk to her."

They moved in on her from either side of an end display of bananas.

"Mrs. Broussard?" Bosch asked.

The woman looked up from the banana bunch she was considering with an easy smile. It froze when she saw a stranger's face. It then dropped off her face like an avalanche when she saw the badge he was holding.

"Yes?" she said. "What is it? What's wrong?"

"We want to talk to you about your husband and the phone calls you've been making."

"I don't know what you mean. My husband's fine. I was just with him at our home fifteen minutes ago."

"We're talking about the anonymous calls to the police tip line from your house," Soto said.

Maria Broussard spun around, not realizing that Soto was behind her.

"That is crazy," she said, her voice tight with panic. "I have *never* made a call to the police, anonymous or otherwise. Calls about what?"

Bosch studied her for a moment, trying to read her. Something wasn't tracking here.

"About the shooting of Orlando Merced," he said.

He saw something flare in her eyes. Some sort of recognition, but he wasn't sure if it was of the name or something else.

"Stay away from me," she said.

She grabbed her purse out of the shopping cart and moved between Bosch and Soto and away. She walked as quickly as her high heels allowed her.

Soto started after her.

"Mrs. Broussard—"

Bosch grabbed her arm.

"Wait," he said. "Something's wrong. She . . ."

He didn't finish. He pulled his phone and went to the recent calls list. He hit the number he had used that morning to make contact with the tech unit. He asked for Marshall Flowers and started moving toward the market's exit.

"Let's go," he said to Soto.

"Where?" she said. "What are we doing?"

Flowers picked up the call.

"Marshall," Bosch said urgently, "I need you to ping the phone again."

Flowers seemed confused.

"What do you mean?" he asked.

"Ping the phone. Do it now."

"We hit it twenty minutes ago. It hasn't moved all morning, Detective."

"Ping it again and call me back. Now."

He disconnected before Flowers could protest. They exited the store and Bosch saw Maria Broussard striding toward her car. She was on her phone.

"We have fucked up," Bosch said.

He started walking and then broke into a run toward the Ford. Soto gave chase, calling across the roof of the car when she got there.

"Harry, what are you talking about?"

"The woman I saw had brown hair. Get in."

Bosch pulled out onto Ventura Boulevard and pinned the accelerator. He wasn't going back to the Broussard house the way he had come. It was too slow and he didn't think Mulholland was the way to approach it. He flipped down the red flashers on the windshield but reserved the siren for when he needed it at intersections.

"Harry, what woman?" Soto demanded. "Tell me what's going on."

"Hold on," Bosch barked back.

He had his phone out and had called Flowers again. He waited as the line buzzed repeatedly and the call was finally picked up.

"Flowers, talk to me."

"We just got it. No change, Detective. The coordinates are still the same."

Bosch disconnected and dropped the phone into the center console. He was angry with himself. He glanced over at Soto but only for a moment. He was now going sixty on crowded Ventura Boulevard and needed his eyes on the road.

"I should've said, '*I* fucked up,' back there. It wasn't you, Lucy. It was me."

"Harry, what the hell is it? What are you talking about?"

"The other night I was at that overlook on Mulholland. I was watching Broussard's house."

"Why?"

"I don't know. I wanted to get a measure of him, I guess. I thought maybe I'd get a look at him or something."

"Okay. What happened?"

"Nothing happened. But the lights were on and I could see into the house. I had my binoculars. I saw a woman in the kitchen. She was emptying the dishwasher. And she had brown hair, not blond. I didn't . . . I didn't remember that till back there at the store."

"I don't—who was it?"

"It was the maid. Our caller is the maid, not the wife, and now Broussard knows. His wife just called him."

Soto didn't respond at first as she followed the trail and came to the end with the same conclusion as Bosch.

"Shit," she said.

"Yeah," Bosch said. "Hold on and check to the right up here."

He hit the siren as they approached a red light at the intersection with Laurel Canyon Boulevard. Bosch looked left and Soto looked right.

"Clear!" she yelled.

Bosch never looked, trusting his partner. He saw the left was clear and blew through the intersection unscathed.

"Okay, you have your iPad?" he asked.

"Yes, in my bag," Soto said. "What do you need?"

"Pull up a map that shows Broussard's house."

She pulled the tablet out of her bag.

"What am I looking for?"

"Up top on Mulholland the place is a fortress, a concrete vault. But down at the bottom there's a pool."

"Right, I saw it today."

"There's got to be access to it from down below. Find the pool man's way in. What street is down there?"

"Got it."

She went to work on it and Bosch concentrated on driving. Ventura Boulevard was a four-lane road. He had room to maneuver and keep his speed.

"Okay," Soto called out. "Right on Vineland. That'll take us up."

Thirty seconds later Vineland came up. Bosch took the right and they were on a steep two-lane street through a residential neighborhood. Winding curves and curbside parking made it narrow and treacherous at speed and Bosch throttled back. Luckily, there were few other moving vehicles to contend with.

"Okay, what's the next turn?" he asked.

"Wrightwood Drive, you go right," Soto said. "Then left on Wrightwood Lane. That puts us right below the house. The access has to be there."

Bosch made the first turn and then almost immediately came to the second.

"Here," Soto said.

"Got it."

They were now running parallel to and below Mulholland. Bosch leaned forward to look up through the windshield. The angle was bad.

"Look up there," he instructed. "Do you see the house?"

Soto lowered her window and leaned out to look up.

"No, not—wait, yes, we're coming up on it," Soto said. "Right up here!"

There was a panicked urgency in her voice. She didn't want to be wrong about the path she had put them on. Bosch pulled up to a large concrete passageway recessed into the slope between two residences. It was closed with an iron gate, behind which Bosch could see three city-issued trash containers against the right wall. Blue for recyclables, green for garden cuttings, and black for trash—the L.A. way. Beyond them the space retreated into darkness. The gate was locked with a chain. Anchored above it on the concrete wall was a camera housing that matched those Bosch had seen on Broussard's house from up on Mulholland Drive.

"This is it," he said. "The chain is padlocked on the inside. There's got to be a back entrance to the house."

"What do we do?" Soto asked.

"I can break that chain with the tire iron," Bosch said.

"There's a camera."

"We've got to hope he's not watching. Let's go."

After retrieving the tire iron from the trunk of the car, Bosch quickly moved to the gate and slipped the long tool into one of the chain's links. He was about to start winding it to leverage pressure on the chain when he looked at Soto. This was new territory for her.

"I consider this exigent circumstances," he said. "We have to go in."

He was laying down the legal groundwork for breaking into the premises of a suspect in a murder investigation. The threat of imminent danger to an individual created the exigent circumstances that allowed them to act and enter without court order.

"Right," Soto said. "Of course. Imminent threat to life. Our witness is in there and we have strong reason to believe the suspect knows."

Bosch nodded.

"Okay, be ready."

"For what?"

"Anything."

37

The chain was no obstacle. Bosch easily opened one of the links and they were in. He and Soto moved around the trash containers and through the storage space to a steel door at the rear. Bosch grasped the handle and found it unlocked. He looked back at Soto and whispered.

"Ready?"

"Ready."

Bosch pulled his weapon from its holster and held it down against his thigh. Soto followed suit with hers. Bosch opened the door and they stepped out onto the deck surrounding the kidney-shaped pool Bosch had seen from the nearby overlook. There was no one present but he saw a glass containing a drink with ice in it on a table next to a chaise longue. There was an ashtray along with a pack of cigarettes and a disposable lighter as well.

There was no entry to the house on this level. A set of concrete stairs led to the first of three stepped balconies going up the sheer hillside. Bosch looked up and saw no one on any of the balconies. With his gun he pointed toward the stairs and they moved in that direction.

There was a table with an umbrella on the first balcony, as well as a row of French doors and another exterior staircase to the next level. Curtains were open behind the doors and Bosch could see a large bedroom that appeared empty. He moved down the line of doors, checking the handles until he found one that was unlocked. He opened the door, half expecting an alarm to sound.

But there was no alarm. Only the sound of voices from inside the house.

Bosch stepped in, followed by Soto. As they moved across the room, the voices grew louder, one of them angry in tone. But the words were not clear. The unfinished concrete design of the house's exterior carried into the interior design, leaving the home with concrete walls that created a crosscurrent of echoes and left the words indistinguishable. All Bosch could tell was that a man was yelling at a woman and the woman was barely able to say anything in her defense.

They moved quickly through the bedroom and into a hallway that led to another bedroom, an elevator, and a stairway. The voices were coming from above, so Bosch continued up, Soto following behind him on the stairs.

The stairway led to the middle level of the house, where there was a hallway with three doors. The voices were coming from a room with an open door and now the words were clearer.

"WHAT DID YOU TELL THEM?" the man's voice boomed.

"I didn't," the woman replied. "I don't—"

There was the sound of flesh striking flesh. More of a slap than a punch. Bosch picked up speed and moved into the room, his gun now up and leading the way.

A dark-haired woman was holding one hand to her face while using the other to gain purchase on a desk as she climbed up from the floor. She wore no uniform but had an apron tied around her waist. A man with his back to the door stood over her, menacing her. He was at least twice her size. Suspender straps crossed his broad back. It was Broussard. As the woman stood up, he raised his right hand to strike her again. Bosch saw his hand wrapped around a black object.

"Please," she begged.

"TELL ME!" he barked.

"Police!" Bosch yelled. "Stop!"

Suddenly two shots echoed loudly off the concrete walls and in all directions. The bullets hit Broussard center mass, just above the Y formed by his suspenders. He momentarily arched his back at the impact. But then his arm dropped like it was dead weight and he collapsed into an awkward heap on the floor. Bosch knew his spine had been shattered, all the body's infrastructure crashing in an instant. The object he had been holding had dropped to the floor next to him. It was a stapler he'd grabbed off the desk in his rage.

Bosch looked down at his weapon, unsure if he had fired. Then he turned to Soto, who held her weapon out in a two-handed firing position, her finger on the trigger. She had fired.

His attention was then drawn back to the desk by the shriek from the woman pressed up against it. Looking down at Broussard, she'd brought her hands to her face and released a sound that started low and deep in the throat and then rose into a shrill scream.

"Lucy!" Bosch yelled. "Holster and then get her out of here."

Soto moved past him as she holstered her weapon and then stepped around Broussard. She gently gripped the woman by the arm and shoulder and ushered her back past Bosch and then out of the room. Bosch didn't take his eyes off Broussard.

"Secure her and then be ready for the wife," he said. "She'll get here any minute."

"Got it," Soto said.

Bosch moved forward and crouched next to Broussard. His eyes were open and moving.

Bosch holstered his own weapon and leaned down.

"Broussard, listen to me," he said. "There isn't a lot of time. You're not going to make it. You want to make a dying declaration? You have anything you want to say to me?"

Broussard opened his mouth but said nothing. He only blinked. Bosch waited a moment and then tried again.

"You had Willman shoot Merced, didn't you? And then you killed Willman. Admit it, Broussard. This is the end. Clear your conscience and go in peace."

Broussard's mouth started to move and Bosch heard the air coming out of his lungs. They were shutting down. Bosch leaned in close and heard a whisper.

"Fuck you."

Bosch pulled back and looked at him and tried one more time.

"Zeyas knew, didn't he? Your maid told him. She thought she'd get the reward. Only Zeyas used the information to blackmail you. Just nod if I have it right."

Broussard's face looked as though he was forming a smile. He then started to whisper again. Bosch leaned down close and turned his ear toward the dying man's mouth.

"You don't have shit. You . . ."

Bosch waited and didn't move, but nothing else came. He finally turned his head to look at Broussard and saw that his eyes were fixed. Broussard was dead.

Bosch started to get up. He looked around the room and realized by the photos on the walls of Broussard with various politicians and celebrities that this was the man's home office. He stepped over to the desk to look at its contents. He saw an iPhone on top of some paperwork. He pulled a rubber glove from one of the pockets of his jacket and snapped it on.

The phone was not password protected. He went to the recent call list and saw that Broussard had received a call from a contact that simply said Maria just fifteen minutes earlier. As Bosch had guessed, Broussard's wife had called him after the encounter with Bosch and Soto at the supermarket. Their mistake had put things in motion. Broussard had confronted the maid in an attempt to find out what she knew and whom she had talked to.

Bosch and Soto had done the rest. Their mistaken focus on the wife instead of the maid had cost them the chance to arrest Broussard and possibly leverage a confession from him that revealed the involvement of Zeyas.

Bosch put the phone down on the desk, backed out of the room, and closed the door. He knew he needed to call in the shooting but he wanted to wait.

"Lucy?"

"Here."

Her voice came from one of the other rooms on the middle level. Bosch opened a door to a bathroom first and then one that led to a home theater with two rows of plush seating. Soto was standing in front of the maid, who was sitting in the first row. Soto stepped away and signaled Bosch into the hallway.

"Alicia, just stay there," she said. "I'll be right out in the hall."

Soto pulled the door closed so they could talk privately. Soto looked at him anxiously.

"Is he dead?" she asked.

Bosch nodded. Soto's face blanched.

"Don't worry," he said. "It was a good shoot. He was about to hit her. You did what you had to do, Lucia. Are you all right?"

"What was it? What was he holding?"

"A stapler."

"A stapler? Oh my—"

"It doesn't matter what it was. He was going to hit her and he could have killed her with it. Are you going to be okay?"

"I think so," she said. "It was just so fast. Not like last time."

"Well, you'll be fine. What about the maid? How is she?"

"Her name is Alicia Navarro. She admits she's our anonymous caller. She said Broussard got a call—which we know most likely came from his wife—and went ballistic, pushing and slapping her, demanding to know who she had talked to."

"Did she say she felt scared for her life?"

"Definitely."

"Okay. Did you ask her about the mayor, about Zeyas?"

"I was just getting into it. But she said she never spoke to or met the mayor. She said it was Spivak. Ten years ago she talked to Spivak about the reward. She said she was in the house and overheard Broussard and his friend Willman talking about the shooting at Mariachi Plaza. That's how she knew it was him. She got confused when Zeyas put up the reward, and she tried to call him instead of the police. The call somehow went to Spivak. She said he took the information, but there was never a reward. Spivak then threatened her. Told her she was in danger if she spoke up. That if she said a word, he would have every one of her family members deported."

"That prick," Bosch said. "He held it back because it didn't pay for the police to solve the case. They needed Merced to be the perfect victim. Crippled by a shot in a part of town the police didn't care about. It wouldn't have worked if we had solved the case."

"Not only that, but there was the money. Spivak knew he could milk Broussard forever."

"Every election, probably every year."

"So what do we do about it?"

"You get her statement on record. We—"

"I already have it. I've recorded everything on my phone. Since we got here."

She reached into the front pocket of her purse and pulled her phone up over the edge.

"You have the shooting?" Bosch asked.

"Yes."

Bosch didn't know if that was a good or bad thing. He would have to think about it. But there were more pressing problems to consider right now. He had just heard a door close upstairs. Someone in high heels was crossing the floor on the level above them. Soto's eyes turned up toward the ceiling. Bosch whispered.

"Go back in and stay with Alicia. I'll go up for Maria. Once she is secured we need to call out the shooting team."

"Okay."

"You will have to stay with them. As soon as I can, I'm going to leave."

"Where are you going?"

Before he could answer, there was a call from upstairs.

"Brouss? Are you here? Alicia?"

Bosch turned from Soto and headed up the stairs. Before he got to the top, Maria Broussard appeared on the landing, saw him, and screamed.

"What are you doing here? Where's my husband?"

Bosch rushed up the remaining stairs, raising his hands in a calming gesture. He then put his hands on her shoulders and tried to turn her from the stairs. She struggled to break free.

"Don't touch me! Where is Charles? Brouss, what did they do?"

Bosch managed to control her by angling her against the wall when she tried to go past him to the stairs. He leaned against her and considered cuffing her if only to control her, but then passed on the idea.

"Mrs. Broussard, you need to calm down."

"No, I won't calm down. Not until I see my husband. Brouss!"

She tried once more to get past him but he had her pinned tight against the wall. He gulped down air and then whispered into her ear.

"I am sorry, Mrs. Broussard, but your husband is dead."

For the second time in ten minutes an earsplitting scream echoed through the house.

Bosch felt Maria Broussard's body go limp. He pulled away from the wall and partly supported her weight as he walked her toward a couch in the living room. Once she was secured and seated, he pulled his phone so he could start making the calls.

38

The Zeyas for Governor exploratory committee was in the process of opening new offices on Olvera Street near the Avila Adobe, the oldest standing residence in Los Angeles. They were going for the easy metaphor of starting the campaign at the very spot where the city was founded. Another new beginning—not only for Los Angeles but for all of California—was afoot. The storefront headquarters was a beehive of activity as desks were being positioned and phone banks installed. Volunteers working for the man who would be governor moved about the three-room suite at the direction of a team leader with a pencil behind her ear. Bosch walked into the main room and asked the lady with the pencil if Connor Spivak was around. She studied Bosch and the two men he was with for a moment, then decided not to ask them to state their business.

"Connor," she called out. "Visitors."

"I'm back here" came the chief of staff's reply.

The team leader removed the pencil and pointed it at one of the side-by-side doors at the rear of the main room. Bosch headed that way and entered a smaller room with a desk already in place and Spivak sitting comfortably behind it. On the wall to his rear was a duplicate of the "Everybody Counts" poster Bosch had removed from the Beverly Hilton earlier in the week. The last man in after Bosch closed the door.

"Detective Bosch, what a surprise," Spivak said.

"Is it?" Bosch said.

"Yes, but a pleasant one. Who have you brought with you? Two of L.A.'s finest?"

Bosch turned to his left and right to introduce Detectives Rodriguez and Rojas.

"You might remember them," he said. "The original investigators on the Merced case."

"Oh yes, I think I do," Spivak said. "Do you gentlemen have an update on the case I can share with the mayor?"

Bosch nodded.

"The update is that he's going to need to find some alternate funding for the campaign."

Spivak looked confused.

"Really?" he said. "Why is that?"

"Because Charles Broussard has written his last check," Bosch said.

The confusion turned to skepticism.

"I'm not sure what you mean by that but—"

"I mean he's dead."

Bosch paused for the reaction but Spivak was able to keep a blank face. Bosch then delivered the next bit of news that was guaranteed to change that.

"And besides alternate funding, the mayor's going to need to find a new chief of staff. You're under arrest, Spivak. Accessory to murder."

Spivak burst out laughing and then abruptly stopped.

"That's a good one, Detective," he said.

Bosch wasn't laughing.

"Stand up, please," he said.

"What the fuck?" Spivak said. "Are you serious?"

"Deadly. Stand up."

"I can't be. You're arresting me based on what?"

"Based on the fact that you were told ten years ago by an employee of Charles Broussard that she had overheard Broussard and a man named David Willman discussing the shooting of Orlando Merced, which Willman had carried out at Broussard's request."

Bosch gestured to the men standing on either side of him.

"Rather than pass this information on to the detectives investigating the Merced shooting, you kept this information to yourself and used it to coerce Broussard into donating heavily and repeatedly to Armando Zeyas's campaigns."

Spivak laughed out loud again, but this time there was a nervous twinge underlying it.

"That is fucking nuts," he said. "It's crazy. But even if it's true, there is no accessory charge in there. I'm not a lawyer and even I know that. This will get laughed out of court."

"Maybe," Bosch said. "If I was referring to the Merced case. But I'm not. You had information that could have led to the arrest of Broussard and Willman. If that had occurred then, Willman would not have been free to kill a thirty-eight-year-old housewife in San Diego seven months after the Merced shooting. You helped facilitate that murder for hire, and for that you are under arrest for accessory to murder. Now, stand up. I'm not asking again."

Bosch started moving around the desk from one direction while Rodriguez came from the other. Spivak quickly stood up and held his hands up as if he could push this problem away. Each detective grabbed an arm and roughly moved it down behind Spivak's back. Bosch nodded to Rodriguez and he put his cuffs on the man's wrists while Rojas pulled a rights card from his coat pocket and started reading Spivak the Miranda warning.

"Do you understand these rights as I have read them?" Rojas asked in conclusion.

Spivak didn't answer. He seemed to have dropped into some sort of internal reverie as he considered his situation.

"Do you understand them?" Rojas barked.

"Yes, I understand them," Spivak said. "Look, Bosch, come on. We can work something out here, can't we?"

"I don't know," Bosch said. "Can we?"

"I mean, I'm not who you really want, right?"

"I don't know. You look pretty good to me. Broussard's dead. Willman's dead. That leaves you."

Spivak walked the room with his eyes, going from Bosch to Rodriguez to Rojas and then back to Bosch.

"I can give you Zeyas," he said desperately. "He knew. He knew everything and he approved it."

"You've got evidence of that or just talk?" Rojas asked.

"I have e-mails and memorandums," Spivak said quickly. "I wrote everything down just in case."

"What about recordings?" Rodriguez asked. "Do you have him on tape?"

"No, but I could get that. I could wear a wire. You send me in and I tell him Broussard's dead and we have an exposure problem. I'll get him on tape, camera, you name it. He's home right now in Hancock Park—I just talked to him. We can get this done before it all hits the news. What do you say? He's the one you want, not me."

Bosch nodded to Rodriguez and he stepped in to remove the handcuffs from Spivak's wrists. Things were going the way he'd hoped and expected them to go. The arrest had been a bluff. Spivak had certainly committed moral crimes, but prosecuting him as an accessory to murder was a huge legal stretch. Instead, Bosch's goal had been to gain his cooperation.

Once Spivak was uncuffed, Bosch put his hand on his shoulder and gently pushed him back down into his desk chair. Bosch casually sat on the edge of the desk and looked down at him.

"We are going to give you one chance at this," he said.

"I won't fuck up," Spivak said. "I promise."

"You do and we're back to hanging it all on you. You understand?"

"I promise. I can deliver him."

"What we're going to do is walk on out of here like we had a good visit and everything's cool. Nobody out there needs to be suspicious about anything. We're going to walk over to the parking lot in front of Union Station and wait for you there. You've got fifteen minutes to tell your minions out there that you're taking off to go see the candidate and then you come meet us. If you don't show up, you better have a Learjet standing by with the fuel tanks topped off. Because we'll come looking for you."

"I know. I'll be there, I'll be there. I promise."

"Good. We're going to take you over to the D.A.'s office, where we've got a guy standing by to structure the deal and give you the parameters of what we expect and what you'll get for delivering."

"You mean you knew? You knew I'd make a deal?"

"Let's just say we had a plan. You start with the little fish if you want the big fish. You still in, Spivak?"

"I'm in. Let's do this."

"Fifteen minutes, then. Don't be late."

Bosch stood up from the desk and looked over Spivak's head. He stepped around him and yanked the poster down off the wall. He left it torn on the floor.

39

Bosch waited until noon on the Friday two weeks after the Broussard shooting to approach Lucy Soto at her new desk. On Fridays the squad room was half empty because of the four-tens workweek option. The rest of the detectives were at lunch. Soto was "riding the pine"—on desk duty—pending the outcome of the officer-involved shooting investigation and psych evaluation. She was assigned the desk outside the captain's office until she got Return to Duty orders. Her job was to answer the tip line. Holcomb was back working with her partner.

"So," he said. "What do you hear?"

"Dr. Hinojos gave me the RTD stamp on the psych eval yesterday," she said. "Nothing yet from OIS but the captain said I can move back to my desk Monday. I don't think he likes me sitting so close to his office and hearing stuff."

Bosch nodded. He liked that she had referred to the Officer Involved Shooting team instead of what the unit was called now—FID, as in Force Investigation Division. It showed her old-school allegiance.

"Good," he said. "You shouldn't have any trouble with the OIS. They just take forever because of the paperwork."

"I don't know," Soto said. "Two incidents in less than a year . . . they might think there's some kind of pattern."

Bosch frowned.

"Twenty-five years ago they would have given you a medal and a raise for a pattern like that," he said.

"Different times, Harry," she said.

He nodded and decided it was time to move off the subject, even if the next part of the conversation was going to be uncomfortable.

"So . . . I have some news on Sister Esther," he said.

"What is it?" Soto said, not hiding her excitement. "Is she back at the convent?"

Bosch shook his head.

"Uh, no. And she's not coming back. I talked to Sister Geraldine yesterday. She said they killed her down there."

"What? Oh my God!"

"She said the narcos came into the village where she was and dragged her out, said she was an informant for the Judicial Policia. They did things to her and then they killed her, left her on the side of a road to be found."

Soto rolled back in her chair and stared into oblivion as she considered the fate of Ana Acevedo aka Sister Esther Gonzalez.

"I can't believe it," she finally said.

"Well, I'm not sure I do either," Bosch said. "Not yet, at least. That's why I'm going down there. To Calexico. The body is supposedly coming across the border today for burial in a cemetery behind the convent. I'm going to check things to make sure, and Sister Geraldine said she'd let me look through Sister Esther's room and her belongings. I wanted to see if you're interested in going down with me."

"Harry, I'm riding this desk. That captain's not going to let me—"

"That's why I'm going tomorrow. I figure Saturdays you're on your own time. The captain can't tell you what to do. They're putting her in the ground Sunday. So it's tomorrow or never."

Soto was nodding before he was finished.

"I'm in," she said.

"Good," Bosch said. "I want to get an early start."

"I'm okay with early."

Bosch smiled and nodded.

"I know. Let's meet here at seven."

Soto got that faraway look in her eyes again.

"What?" Bosch asked.

"I was just thinking," she said. "Do you think Sister Geraldine told her that we had been at the convent asking about her?"

"Yes," Bosch said. "I asked her that and she said she did tell Sister Esther we were there and we wanted to talk to her. She finally heard from her a few days later and that's when Sister Geraldine told her."

"Okay," Soto said. "So do you think she . . ."

Soto didn't finish but Bosch knew what she was thinking and what she was about to ask. Could Sister Esther have informed on someone because she knew the word would get back to the narcos and there would be swift and sure consequences, no matter that she was a nun on a mission in the region?

"Yes," Bosch said. "That's exactly what I think."

They got to the Sisters of the Sacred Promise convent at noon Saturday. They came directly from the funeral home in downtown Calexico, where they had first stopped to view Sister Esther's body and confirm both her death and identification. Bosch had borrowed a mobile fingerprint reader from Flowers in the tech unit. He used it to take the right thumbprint off the body and then sent it to the state Department of Motor Vehicles database, where it was matched to the print taken from Ana Maria Acevedo when she had applied for a driver's license in 1992—the last license she had before disappearing.

Young Sister Theresa greeted them at the convent door and invited them in. She had been told by Sister Geraldine to expect the detectives from Los Angeles and to allow them access to Sister Esther's room. She led the way up a flight of stairs and then down a long hallway that looked like a college dormitory except for all the religious iconography and Bible quotes on the bulletin boards between doors.

"Will you be staying for the funeral mass tomorrow?" Sister Theresa asked.

"No, we're just here today," Bosch said.

"Oh, that's too bad. It's going to be very special. Sister Esi is going home to the Lord."

Bosch just nodded. He didn't know what to say to that.

Sister Theresa stopped at the last door on the right side of the hall. There were a variety of holy cards stuck into the edge of the door and she removed them before opening the door. It had not been locked.

"It's small," she said. "So I am sure you don't need me in there taking up space."

"I think we'll be fine," Bosch said. "This shouldn't take long."

She glanced down the hall as if to confirm that they

were alone and Sister Geraldine wasn't watching.

"Can I ask you something?" she said. "What are you looking for? What is it you think Sister Esi did? I don't think I've ever met someone as kind as she was."

Bosch thought a moment. He didn't think there was any need to taint anyone's vision and feelings about another human being—especially if that human being was dead. Besides, she would probably find out soon enough when the story hit the media.

"We're just trying to confirm if she happened to be a woman who disappeared a long time ago in L.A.," he said.

"Oh, okay," Sister Theresa said. "I thought it was something really bad and we would be unable to celebrate her union with Jesus tomorrow. Did you see what we're putting on the stone?"

"No, what's that?"

"Well, *she's* actually putting it on the stone. She wrote it in her funeral instructions. It's going to say, 'Sister Esther Gonzalez, She Found Redemption for the Children with the Children.' Isn't that beautiful?"

Bosch nodded.

"'Redemption for the Children with the Children,'" he repeated.

"Yes," Sister Theresa said. "She wrote it a long time ago. Her final instructions were found in that old box on her bed."

She pointed through the open doorway into the room.

"Okay, well, thank you, Sister," Bosch said. "Like I said, we won't be too long."

"My room is last on the left at the other end of the hall," she said. "That's because I'm the newest."

She proudly bounced on her heels.

"Okay, we'll find you."

Bosch turned and entered the room, followed by Soto. As expected, it was sparely furnished. There was a single bed with a crucifix on the wall over the wooden headboard. It was accompanied by a side table, bureau, and a desk with a shelf of books mounted on the wall above it. There was a closet with no door that was no bigger than one of the old phone booths at Union Station. But that was all the room that was needed for the few things hanging in it.

Bosch and Soto separated and started opening drawers. Most were empty or contained the meager clothing and belongings of a person who had held true to the vow of poverty. Bosch checked the box that Sister Theresa had pointed at. It contained mostly loose pages of notes. There were handwritten sermons and prayers and Bible verses, many of them with the word *redemption* underlined. Ephesians, Galatians, Romans . . . the quotes were written on half pages, envelopes, and other scraps.

Bosch chose two of the inscribed envelopes and slid them into the inside pocket of his jacket.

Let the redeemed of the Lord say so, whom He has redeemed from trouble.

—Psalm 107:2

Who gave Himself for us to redeem us from all lawlessness and to purify for Himself a people for His own possession who are zealous for good works.

—Titus 2:14

Bosch dug further into the box of papers and brought out a folded document that was revealed to be a birth certificate for Esther Maria Gonzalez. It was issued in 1972 in Hyde County, North Carolina. It was printed on heavy-stock paper and appeared legitimate but Bosch had no doubt that it was phony. He knew that the easiest way to build a new and false identity was to start with what appeared to be a birth certificate from a small rural county in a state far from the state where the fraud would be perpetrated. A birth certificate was the only requirement to apply for a California driver's license. The problem was, there was no national template for birth certificates. Thousands of counties across the country issued them, each with its own design. A DMV clerk in California would be hard-pressed to declare as false a certificate from Hyde County, North Carolina, if the document presented appeared official and legitimate.

A driver's license would be only one stop on the way to a full identity package, with Social Security number and passport to follow. The document Bosch held in his hand explained a lot.

Harry sat down on the bed as he slipped the birth certificate into his jacket pocket with the other papers. He put the top back on the box and looked at Soto, who was still going through the closet.

"Does this bother you?" he asked.

She turned around and looked at him.

"Does what bother me?" she asked.

"I don't know," he said. "I guess that she chose her own penance. She came here and went on missions and took care of children and all of that. Vow of poverty, paid off the mortgage, whatever. But she didn't turn herself in and say, 'I'm responsible.' She didn't tell all those parents how come their kids died."

He gestured to the box.

"She talks about redemption. But she chose all of this. Nothing was taken from her. You know what I mean?"

Soto nodded.

"I understand," she said. "It's going to take a while for me to process everything about this. I'll tell you how I feel when I know. Okay?"

"Yeah," he said. "Okay."

Soto went back to work in the closet, and Bosch moved on to the desk. The top surface was devoid of anything of a personal nature and the single drawer contained more of the same—pencil writings with themes of redemption and multiple references to children.

Bosch closed the drawer and looked up at the shelf. There were four different versions of the Bible as well as a Spanish dictionary and books on the sacraments, catechism, and teaching methods.

He grabbed the first Bible off the shelf and fanned the pages, hoping a nicely folded, handwritten confession would drop out of the book into his lap.

Instead, he found a holy card that depicted Christ ascending to heaven. The card marked a page in Acts where words had been underlined intermittently and formed a sentence if read consecutively. *Repent . . . and . . . your sins may be blotted out.*

"Harry."

Bosch turned to Soto. She was crouched on the floor, a photo album open in front of her. From its pages she had raised what looked like a photo cut from a newspaper.

"This was loose in this photo album," she said. "It's them, isn't it?"

Bosch took the clip and studied it. It was faded newsprint depicting side-by-side photos of two men. Bosch had no trouble recognizing the two North Hollywood bank robbers. There wasn't a cop in L.A. who wouldn't recognize them.

He nodded.

"It's them."

"So Gus Braley was right?"

Bosch kept staring at the photo. Remembering that day.

"I guess so," he finally said. "But he couldn't connect the dots back then."

Soto came over and sat on the bed next to his chair so she could see the clip as well.

"It's not a picture of her with them," she said. "It doesn't prove anything."

"Maybe not in court," Bosch said. "But it pretty much closes things for me."

"But where did they all cross paths?"

"Good question. I remember something about the two guys meeting in a gym somewhere. I think Venice."

"Ana was about as far from Venice as you could get. They must've crisscrossed someplace else."

"Well, we may need to find that place if we ever want the D.A. to sign off on our closing it."

"What if we put it out to the media? Maybe somebody comes forward with the connection."

Bosch thought about that. Twenty-one years had gone by. It was a long shot but he didn't want to be pessimistic with Soto.

She seemed to read him anyway.

"All those families who lost kids," she said. "They should know. The family of Esi Gonzalez, too. The real one."

She took the clip out of Bosch's hand and studied it.

Bosch remembered something and snapped his fingers. It was the thing that had bothered him before, after he had spoken to Gus Braley.

"Varsol," he said.

"What?" Soto said.

"I just remembered something. That day of the shoot-out . . . I got there at the end and I was put on the evidence team. I had their car, actually."

He pointed at the men in the clip she held.

"I basically had to babysit it until an evidence team could get to it. And that took a couple hours because they were needed all over the place that day for, like, a five-block stretch. Anyway, while I'm waiting, I put the gloves on and poke around the car, and there is this army blanket in the backseat covering up something. So I pull it, and there are a few more guns laid across the seat and there's a Molotov cocktail held under the seat-belt so it wouldn't move."

"Was it made with Varsol?"

"I don't know. I don't know if it was ever even analyzed that way but we could find out. Either way, the use of Molotov cocktails is another link between these guys and the Bonnie Brae."

Soto nodded.

"So what do you think? Was Ana a planner or just a gofer?"

Bosch thought a moment and then shook his head.

"Hard to say. It looks like she played Burrows and Boiko like a pro. Got close to them and knew they would open up at the shop when she was threatened. But she could have been directed by one of those guys. I don't think we'll ever know."

They sat in silence for a little bit. Bosch knew Soto had something she wanted to say. Finally, she spoke.

"I sure thought it would be different," she said.

"What would?" Bosch asked.

"Ever since I wanted to be a cop I thought about solving the case. It was my motivation. It burned inside of me, you know?"

"Yes."

He thought about what he had said before about opening the door on a burning room.

"And now, here I am," she said.

"You solved it," he said.

"But there's no . . . it's just not what I thought when I had all those fantasies."

Bosch nodded. There was nothing he could say. After a few moments, Soto seemed to put her angst aside for the time being and spoke in a positive tone.

"So," she said, "I think we're done here. I want to go home, Harry."

Bosch nodded once more.

"Okay," he said. "Let's go."

40

Bosch arrived in the squad room to find Soto already in place at her desk. In fact, she revealed, she had been in place since Sunday. She had come in to write the Bonnie Brae investigative summary that would be submitted to Captain Crowder for approval and then to the District Attorney's Office, which also had to sign off on the official closing of a case by means other than arrest and conviction. Bosch had given her the summary assignment, since it was her case in more ways than one.

The report was twelve pages long. It was thorough and complete and Bosch found himself unconsciously nodding as he read. She had ordered the facts they had gathered in such a way that the report was conclusive, and yet they still didn't have the exact nexus where Ana Acevedo crossed paths with the two men who started the Bonnie Brae fire and then committed the EZBank robbery.

He thought that there would be no pushback from Crowder because there was no downside for him. He could announce that he had cleared a major case, and there would be no trial to possibly prove him wrong. That was a perfect world for him. But the next step would be the tough one. The D.A.'s Office would not so readily sign off because of the lack of a confession, hard evidence, or a direct connection between all of the players involved.

There would be ways to handle the D.A.'s Office, Bosch knew. The closing of the case would be a huge story in the media, not only because of the number of victims and who the dead suspects were, but because of the investigator who pursued it. Soto's summary revealed her personal ties to the fire. All of that could be used and marshaled in support of the official closing of the case.

When he was finished reading it for the second time, Bosch had only one question for Soto.

"Lucy, are you sure you want to reveal your connection to this?"

"Yes. It's my story. Even if it gets me in trouble, it's time."

Bosch nodded. He wasn't going to talk her out of it. She was right. It was her story and it was time to tell it. It would, however, reveal that when she had applied to the Department, she had left out any mention of the Bonnie Brae fire as a motivating factor in her decision to become a police officer.

The phone on his desk buzzed and Bosch picked it up. It was Crowder.

"Harry, I need you to come in here," he said.

"Good," Bosch said. "We were just going to head over to see you."

"No, just you. Come over now."

"But Soto has—"

"Just you."

Crowder hung up before he could argue further. Bosch put the phone down and told Soto they would submit the report to Crowder later. He walked the perimeter of the squad room and entered the open door of the captain's office. Lieutenant Samuels was sitting in one of the chairs in front of the desk.

"Harry, take a seat," Crowder said.

"That's okay, I'll stand," Bosch said.

"Well, I don't want you going all ballistic when you hear this."

"Hear what?"

"Just got a call from the D.A.'s Office. They're not going to proceed against Zeyas."

It took Bosch a moment to process the news and come up with a response.

"What cowards," he said. "What bullshit."

"Look," Crowder said. "The guy who called me—Boland—said the evidence isn't there for conviction. There's no independent corroborating evidence. Zeyas didn't say anything remotely incriminating on the tape—he totally played Spivak—and all of Spivak's so-called evidence is self-serving bullshit any defense lawyer in the land could knock flat. So if it comes down to that, Zeyas wins, especially if he gets an Eastside jury."

Bosch shrugged as if the news was a minor irritant.

"I'll refile it with somebody else over there," he said. "Boland's a kid afraid of the dark. Either that or he was bought off."

"No, Harry, you won't refile with anybody," Crowder said. "The decision wasn't Boland's. It came from on high. It's over. Lucky Lucy put Broussard down and that's where it ends. Case closed. You can take comfort in knowing that Zeyas has no shot at the governor's mansion and no other candidate out there will ever hire Spivak again. Not after the way the *Times* has been blowing this thing up the past two weeks."

Virginia Skinner was leading the charge for the *Times*—thanks to Bosch making good on his promise. But none of that mattered at the moment. Bosch was suddenly sick to death of everything.

"Is that it?" he asked. "Are we done?"

"No, we're not done," Crowder said. "Lieutenant?"

Samuels got up and stood in front of Bosch. It looked as though whatever he was about to say, he was going to be happy to say it. And that didn't bode well for Bosch.

"Detective, I need you to put your weapon and your badge on the captain's desk," he instructed.

"What are you talking about?" Bosch asked.

"Gun and badge on the desk. Now. You are suspended, Detective, pending the outcome of an internal investigation."

Bosch glanced at Crowder and saw the captain watching impassively. He'd get no help from him. Samuels remained pointing at the desk, his posture stiff, like he was about to get physical if necessary. He was much bigger, wider, and younger than Bosch. It would be no match.

Bosch slowly pulled his gun from his holster and placed it on the desk. He followed that with his badge. Crowder immediately took them and put them into a desk drawer.

"I don't know what you're talking about or what I supposedly did," Bosch said. "But Soto and I are about to close the biggest case cleared around here in twenty years and you are going to look like—"

"You want to know what I'm talking about?" Samuels interrupted. "I'll show you what I'm talking about. I just played it for the captain."

Samuels walked over to the TV monitor that was on top of a four-drawer file cabinet. He picked up the remote that was beneath it and hit play. A darkened room appeared on camera. In the background there was a rectangular, floor-to-ceiling window next to a closed door. The window allowed for some light to enter from the outside room.

"Captain Gandle over in Robbery Special collects pens, did you know that?" Samuels asked.

"No, I didn't," Bosch said. "Who gives a shit?"

"Well, Captain Gandle does, and the problem is that people have been coming in his office and stealing his pens and, hell, some of them were worth a lot of money. So the captain got himself a nanny cam and set it up on the shelf in his office. And look what he got."

On-screen the door opened and an overhead light was flicked on. There was Bosch entering the room. He tossed something into the trash can and proceeded to the shelves holding the robbery journals.

"That's breaking and entering right there, Bosch," Samuels said. "You should contact your union rep, because you're going to need one."

"This is bullshit," Bosch said. "I needed to look at the robbery journals. I didn't take a goddamn thing out of that office."

"The rules are the rules," Samuels said. "The door was locked and you picked the lock. Captain Gandle found your bent paperclips in the trash basket. It's still an illegal entry whether you took something or not. You're

434

lucky you're not under arrest right now, but the good captain here determined that wasn't necessary."

Bosch looked at Crowder one more time.

"You're okay with this?" he asked.

"Harry, what the fuck?" Crowder said. "You broke into a captain's office. Was that really necessary? Does any case make that necessary?"

"Go home, Bosch," Samuels said. "You are suspended pending further investigation. You will be advised as to when the investigation is concluded and if you must appear at a Board of Rights hearing."

Bosch was so stunned, he seemed to have lost the ability to move.

"Go home," Samuels said again. "And I sure hope you did not involve your partner in your actions. I'd hate to lose a young gun like that."

Bosch found the will to move his feet. He turned and headed to the door. Samuels stopped him.

"You know, Bosch, a short-timer like you, you really ought to think about just pulling the pin and not dealing with all this bullshit," he said. "You've put in your time. Why hassle with this?"

Bosch looked back at Samuels, and the lieutenant pantomimed pulling a badge off the left breast of a uniform blouse.

"This is weak, Samuels," he said. "Just like you."

He slowly stepped out of the office and started toward his cubicle. He felt several eyes on him. People had seen through the glass as he had turned over his badge and gun. The word was spreading. Something like this could never be contained in a room full of detectives.

Soto was at her desk in the cubicle and she turned in

her chair as he entered and went to his own desk.

"Harry, what is going on?" she said. "People said they just took your gun and badge."

Bosch pulled his chair over to hers. He sat down and leaned in close.

"I'm suspended," he said.

"*What?*" she exclaimed. "For what?"

"Listen to me. When they come and ask you about the day I broke into the captain's office in Robbery, you tell them you weren't there. You say you stayed back here and I went alone. Got that?"

"No, Harry, I'm not going—"

"You have to do this, Lucia. I am going to say the same thing. You weren't there. And guess what? You weren't. You were out in the hall. You just tell whoever comes from Professional Standards that you just stayed at your desk. Okay?"

"Okay."

Bosch glanced over at the captain's office. Samuels was standing in the doorway watching him. Harry figured he had another five minutes max before Samuels called for a couple of patrol officers to escort him from the building.

"I've been down this road a few times," he told Soto. "Protect yourself and you'll be fine. I will be, too. I can beat this."

Then, almost under his breath, he added, "If I want to."

He pushed his chair back to his desk and gathered up a few belongings. The photos of his daughter were the priority. He had no idea if he would ever get back to this desk again.

Tim Marcia peeked over the half-wall from his cubicle.

"Hey, Harry, can I have your parking spot till you get back?"

It brought a smile.

"Fuck you," Bosch said to him.

When he had everything packed in his briefcase and was ready to go, he looked back at Soto, who was sitting in her chair, staring at him.

"This isn't right," she said.

Bosch stepped over, leaned down, and put a hand on her shoulder.

"It's not about what is right," he said. "I'll be fine. The thing you have to remember is that you are one hell of an investigator. You know the secret. So don't let the fools around here drag you down. You have things to do, Lucy."

She nodded.

"Okay," she said. "I feel like crying."

"Don't," Bosch said. "Instead, take your summary report in there and close that case. Take about a day or two to savor it and then get back to work. There's only ten thousand more cases waiting for you."

She nodded again and tried unsuccessfully to smile. Talking was going to be a problem for her.

Bosch squeezed her shoulder and left her there. He grabbed his briefcase off his chair and walked toward the exit door. Before he got there, he heard someone clapping behind him. He turned back and saw it was Soto, standing by her desk.

Soon Tim Marcia rose up from his cubicle and started to clap. Then Mitzi Roberts did the same and then the other detectives. Bosch put his back against the door, ready to push through. He nodded his thanks and held his fist up at chest level and shook it. He then went through the door and was gone.

Acknowledgments

The author wishes to thank several people who contributed to this novel in many, many ways.

The detectives: Rick Jackson, Tim Marcia, Mitzi Roberts.

The editors: Asya Muchnick, Bill Massey, Pamela Marshall.

The researcher: Dennis "Cisco" Wojciechowski.

The family: Linda Connelly, McCaleb Connelly, all the Connellys.

The readers: Terrill Lee Lankford, Henrik Bastin, John Houghton.

The support team: Heather Rizzo, Jane Davis, Mary Mercer, Sue Lillich.

The publisher: the many people at Hachette Book Group who worked so hard on this and the many other books before it.

The author couldn't do it without you.

Cheers to all.